Blank Mastermind

By

Rosey Mucklestone

#

Dedicated to all those lovely people who stand, literally or metaphorically, over my head with whips while I write. I appreciate it.

Table of Contents

Chapter 1: Waking Up

I lay still, feeling nothing.

It felt almost like I didn't exist.

There was no sound… I was totally numb.

A slight twinge of pain leaked in through the numbness and I winced. Then headache ripped across the base of my skull and feeling rushed back into the rest of my body.

It felt like I'd been through a food processor — or a rock tumbler. Maybe both.

I tried to reach my hand up to put on the back of my head to try and lessen the pain, but only the ends of my fingers twitched.

Where was I? What had happened? Why did I hurt so much?

Focusing my teaspoon full of energy, I opened my eyes. One was slightly harder to open and I felt a bruise over it.

Ropes, cloth and darkness blurred in and out of focus above me. I blinked a couple of times and my vision cleared a little.

There was… also a pagoda, apparently. I frowned.

So this was backstage of something, probably.

My feet dangled off the ground… what was I lying on?

My muddled mind stubbornly held back from giving answers to the hundreds of questions I had.

A bit of energy was coming back, and even though I didn't want to move, that seemed like the best way to figure out what the heck was going on. I bit my lip, steeling myself.

Somehow, that made my nose hurt too.

Taking a breath, I gripped the edge of the container I was in and pushed myself up.

Holy smoke, did *everything* hurt?

I closed my eyes again, clenching my teeth against the pain. When I opened them again, I was able to collect a few more facts about my situation.

The container I'd been lying in was full of paper fans, keeping with the pagoda theme. I was wearing a tuxedo covered in blood. There were a few guns on the ground. And…

A dead man, lying facedown in a puddle of blood. Only a few feet from where I was.

I gagged, putting a hand up to my mouth. My head pounded and my vision blurred again.

Something inside me prodded to get up. Get out and leave. I needed to get away from here. I pushed the rest of the way out of the fan container and my feet landed on the ground. My knees almost gave out, but I managed to keep myself in a standing position.

What happened? Who killed that guy? Well, there was only one other person around…

Did… I kill him? I didn't remember killing him.

But what did I remember?

How I got here? Nope, that was a blank.

How the guy died? Nothing there either.

Start with something basic. What's your name?

My name.

What was my name?

I had to know that. *Come on, think...* I closed my eyes and concentrated, trying to pull out a simple answer from my stubborn brain. The feeling of it danced around the edges of my mind, just out of reach. I couldn't think. Couldn't remember anything.

Panic started to rise inside me. The back of my head pounded like it was telling me to stop bugging it by trying to think. I reflexively put my hand up to hold it.

What did I know? I had to know something...

Gritting my teeth and trying hard, I managed to grasp one solid feeling.

Something was missing. There was something of mine that I needed and didn't have.

I swiveled around, squinting into the shadows and trying to find my... whatever it was. My gaze rested on a crumpled, dark heap by the curtain. A leather jacket.

That. That's it.

I let go of the edge of the container and stumbled over to the jacket. Steadying myself by holding onto the curtain, I picked it up and fumbled it on. The jacket slipped on perfectly over my shoulders, feeling like home. One solid thing that felt right in this whole confusing mess.

So I knew I was a guy with a leather jacket now. Great. Now if I could just find a phone or a wallet or something useful...

I stuck a hand in one of the pockets. A dog-eared piece of notebook paper, its edges soft from age, met my fingers. I pulled it out and unfolded it slowly, smudging the corner with the blood that was smeared on my fingers.

For Mom, it read, in a slanted scrawl of handwriting, *for Dad, for Peter, for Eloisa. That which killed, shall be killed. Die by the sword.* My thumb brushed over another spot in the paper that felt puckered. Like it had been wet. *A tear?* I felt goosebumps prickle my arms, but I didn't remember any of those names.

I checked the other pocket. My finger poked out through a singed hole. A bullet hole. I sucked in my breath.

So I'd been shot? Or... the jacket, at least. But who would shoot an empty jacket? Of course it had to be on me... but who...?

Wincing, I put my hand to the back of my head. I felt a gash there and when I pulled my hand away it was covered in even more blood. My head started to throb again and I quickly put my hand back where it was.

The floor tilted. I clung to the curtain, trying to get my balance back.

Okay, okay... I just needed to put together what I knew... figure stuff out from there...

Before I could get all my mental ducks in a row, there was a sound of someone whistling outside the door. I jumped, my heart pounding.

The brief thought that I could ask him for help flashed across my mind, but I quickly dismissed it.

I was no crime scene investigator... or at least I didn't think I was... but if this guy put half a thought into the scene in front of him, it would look like I'd murdered that other tuxedo guy. And amnesia was a pretty flimsy story if anything went to court.

I took advantage of the curtain I was next to and slipped behind it just as the door thumped open. A janitor came in, pushing a squeaky old cleaning cart in front of him and whistling something. *Row, Row, Row, Your Boat.*

Of course I remembered a stupid nursery rhyme song, but not my own name.

The whistling ended in a strangled gasp at the sight of the body. And man, he got out of there fast after that. The wheel squeaking went up to double-time as he barreled back out the door.

Well. Couldn't blame him for the reaction. But now I probably had cops to worry about. Time to get out.

There was another exit on the other side of the curtain. I took a deep breath and zipped up my jacket to cover the blood all over my front before starting towards the door, trying not to sound like some wounded animal whilst doing so.

I got to the door and groped at the handle a couple of times before managing to pull it open. It squeaked as it swung open and I flinched. Hope no one heard that.

My hands reflexively went to straighten my jacket collar before I stepped out into the hall. The posh, golden carpet muffled my unsteady footsteps. All people noises were absent. There was only the calm whir of the heater, accompanied by a faint propane smell.

Only a back hall, but I could still almost smell the fanciness permeating this place. The reason why I decided to have a life-and-death brawl backstage an opera continued to elude me.

I looked both ways down the hall. There. A door with a sign proclaiming "EXIT" was to my right.

I took a few steps towards it, but my knees buckled under me and I crumpled to the floor. Well, it was going to happen sometime with the shape I was in. I had more appreciation for the lovely, soft carpet now. I was almost sorry I got so much blood on it.

I gritted my teeth at the pain and rolled on my side, trying to gather the strength to get back up.

The heater sound cut out all of a sudden and I heard another noise from far away.

Sirens.

Get up, idiot. Get out of here.

I groaned and started to push myself up, but I heard another sound. Way closer than the sirens. It was down the hall in back of me. And it was a person.

I jumped and scooted myself up against the edge of the wall before stopping and listening. The adrenaline started to subside. Only soft moaning. And the movements sounded even more pathetic than mine.

No one who could stop me if they tried. Not my problem.

I went to start towards the door again, but was stopped by the next sound. A soft word.

"Help."

Something about it tickled a memory at the back of my mind. Was it the voice? Or the word it spoke?

Whichever it was, it did a pretty good job of changing my mind. I needed to help whoever that was.

I leaned forward, but couldn't see anyone. Behind one of the doors, maybe? My guess was pretty well affirmed with the next un-soft moan, clearly coming from a door labeled "Employees Only".

Locking in on my target, I made use of the wall to pull myself up. I'd saved up enough energy to stagger my way over to the door without falling over again. Though I did kind of run face-first into the door... which didn't do wonders for my headache.

I adjusted my position a little so I had my ear to the door and listened. The moaning had stopped. Only a faint whimpering came from the room now. Whatever had happened, the guy didn't sound in too good of shape.

I gripped the door handle and turned it, the shiny surface slipping a little from the blood on my hand. The door swung open into the room, squeaking and catching so it didn't open all the way.

Security monitors glowed blue, illuminating the rest of the trashed area around. Knots of cords tangled on the floor and I saw what looked like a bullet holes in the wall behind.

And there on the floor was a man. He was smaller than me and smaller than the other man I had seen. Maybe "boy" was a better term. Or... just a small man.

Anyway, I was certainly right about his being in worse shape.

At least one, if not two, of the bullets someone had generously sprayed around the room had made it into his midsection. Even in the dark I could see the blood that was all over his suit front and staining the ground. He lay on his back, his pale face showing in the blue light. His eyes were closed.

My stomach flipped.

Oh please no. Not two dead people... please don't be dead...

10

After a second of groping by the door, I found the light switch and flicked it on. The boy winced at the sudden light, moaned again and rolled sideways, clutching his stomach.

Still alive.

I stepped over the wires and dropped down next to him. "It's okay. I'm here to help." My voice cracked a little as I said it. Wasn't sure quite how much help I was able to give, really... but I'd give what I could.

The kid's eyes opened out of his pained squint and focused on me. Green eyes. He blinked. I swallowed my own pain and managed to give him a grin.

His eyes popped wide open and he sprang up like a coiled spring. He got his back slammed up against the wall farthest away from me before sliding to the ground again. Still, his green eyes stayed as open as windows with the shutters broken.

"Whoa... calm down," I stood with effort and took a couple steps toward him, "I heard you and came back to help. It's okay..."

The boy shook his head slowly, his eyes fixed on my face with a mix of terror and confusion. "Nobody comes back to help the person they just shot."

Suddenly, I didn't want to know who I was.

Chapter 2: Dallas

I swallowed and my head pounded again, harder. "I shot you?"

Not usually the million-dollar question.

The kid looked even more confused than before. He blinked at me and his mouth fell slightly open.

Probably how I'd look if someone who just shot me asked if he'd shot me.

What kind of trigger-happy jerk was I, shooting random security kids?

My mouth felt dry and I licked my lips, tasting blood. "Right." Well, no changing the past. We had to move forward from this point.

I managed a few more steps forward, holding up one hand in a hopefully peaceful gesture. Only it was covered in blood, so that probably didn't help.

The kid's eyes went wide again and he scrambled to stand, trying to get as far away from me as possible. He clamped his arms over his middle, his whole body clenched tight in pain. His face blanched white, standing out in stark contrast in the dark corner he was in.

His effort didn't get far. More red came from his middle onto his white collared shirt and he doubled over, sliding back down the wall.

I got over next to him and sat down on a crate before my legs gave out again. Getting better, though. I'd stayed on my feet longer than I had before. Being the one who could somewhat walk gave me a slight upper hand. I started calculating exactly what acrobatics I'd have to pull to be able to carry this kid.

He opened his squinted shut eyes and looked sideways at me, quivering like a scared rabbit. I could almost see the suspicion puddling around him.

I let out my breath, meeting his gaze. "Look, kid… we both need a hospital pretty bad. Common goal here. Putting aside what's happened… before… don't you think we could work out some sort of truce?"

His expression didn't change.

My head gave another stabbing pain and I flinched. I hauled myself to my feet again, propped one arm on the wall and held out a hand to him. "C'mon. I came to help you out."

He looked at it like I had claws. His voice rasped and cracked as he spoke. "You're lying."

"And you're dying."

He met my eyes for a second and then looked back down at his bloody midsection. He closed his eyes for a second, looking close to tears.

So trusting me or dying was a toss-up. Man, my self-confidence was just soaring at this point.

"Kid, do I look like I could pull anything right now?" I asked.

The kid looked back up at me. He seemed to only glance at my injuries before locking in on my eyes. His green-eyed gaze felt like it was digging deep inside of me. Searching for something. Trying to figure me out.

Finally, his lips tightened in a line, he let out his breath and then took my hand. I just about fell over as he pulled himself up. He paled even more upon being upright and blinked hard a couple of times. His legs nearly collapsed under him.

I caught him, partly steadying myself. "So we're good?"

He swallowed, looking sick, but nodded slightly.

"Well," I slung one of his arms over my shoulders, wincing as I discovered yet another bruise. "To the land of Parking-Lot we go."

And we were off like a herd of turtles. Wounded turtles.

With me doing most of the actual footwork, we got to the door and out into the hall. But having another person leaning on me took more effort than I figured in before and we got just a few steps beyond the door before collapsing in a heap on top of each other.

If there was any hope of my previous bloodstains on the posh carpet going unnoticed, the one the two of us left in that spot was only going unnoticed if the janitor was blind.

Lying on the floor wasn't helping much, so with a lot of bumping around and probable worsening of injuries, we got back on our feet.

Well, on my feet at least. The kid was fading fast. He slumped against me, his eyes barely open.

"Hey, stay with me…" I pulled him up as I straightened. I felt more blood from my head wound trickling down my neck. I fought against a wave of dizziness threatening to knock me down again. I bit my tongue and sucked in a breath.

Keep both of us going. Talk to him. Start a conversation.

"So…" I began, shifting his weight against my shoulder and looking for conversation starters that might clue me in. "What's your name?" He might be too out of it to notice anything wrong with me saying that. If I already knew him, that was.

He gave me a tiredly confused look. I gave him a grin, though I'm not sure what I thought that would help. He blinked, "Dallas... Knight." His voice was a weak whisper.

I was losing him.

"Knight, huh?" my leg clanged up against a vent on the wall as I stopped to catch my breath, "Got any shining armor?" I kept my eyes on the exit sign at the end of the hall. We just needed to get out that.

Dallas moaned and doubled partway over, pressing his arm against his stomach. His other arm started to slide off my shoulders.

I struggled to hold him up, "Hey, hey... we're almost there, bud. Hold on. Just to the exit sign, kid. It's not that far, look..."

"Y-you..." Dallas choked out, trying to reply, but he didn't get past the first word. His muscles went slack and his head hung forward.

I didn't realize how much of his own weight he'd been holding up to that point. Until I was suddenly trying to keep my balance while holding all of it at an awkward angle.

I staggered sideways, trying to keep my balance and grunting with the effort of holding him up. My head pounded like I had an angry drummer stuck up in there.

Falling partly against the wall, I got him readjusted into more of a piggyback position with both his arms around my neck. I recalculated the distance to the door with this new change in plans.

Might take a while. It wasn't like I had a ton else on my schedule.

I pulled Dallas's arms up more and started stumbling forwards.

It felt like there was something else... some time crunch...

Oh right. Weren't there...?

A door slammed distantly behind me and I froze.

Cops.

"Which way?" came a deep, commanding voice.

"Th-this way officer... to the backstage."

Footsteps getting closer.

No way no how was I getting to the door before they got here. And the position I was in right now looked like I was trying to hide a body.

I reflexively swore under my breath. Even if I wasn't usually the cussing type, this situation would probably get an obscenity out of the most devout priest.

There had to be something... I looked around the hall as I limped along, skimming the labels on all the doors and trying to find something that would work.

All of them were shut and locked. Employees only. Danger. Electric. But then one door was cracked open just a tiny bit. The cleaning supplies closet.

I guess there's an upside to scaring the crap out of the janitor.

The voices and footsteps were getting closer. They'd be in sight of me within the minute, if not sooner.

Make an effort, come on... I clenched my teeth and summoned all my strength, staggering towards the closet with all the furious speed of a snail.

My vision was starting to cloud over when I got there. I blinked it away, pulling the door open the rest of the way. Brooms and mops and bottles of cleaner left barely any room next to the thin shelves. I made room.

I'd just pulled the door closed when the footsteps rounded the corner. I would have probably fallen over, except there wasn't room for that. Dallas's limp form pressed against my back and my forehead rested on the door. At least I was in an excellent position to hear what they were saying.

"... nothing that I know of, officer. Here I was, just coming in as usual to do the morning cleaning and I thought I might take a quick peek backstage and... and there's this guy lying there and there's blood just... everywhere..."

"Calm down, Mr. Gip, we'll figure it out. Now, was there any sort of... disturbance at the performance last night?"

"I don't think so, sir."

The voices were getting closer.

"Was that blood there before?"

I held my breath. The footsteps stopped.

"Y-yes, officer... there's just... blood everywhere..."

"Calm down, Mr. Gip."

There was silence for a few seconds, then the officer spoke again, starting to walk. "I doubt it's a coincidence that this sort of thing happens so soon after you-know-who got let out of prison..."

I strained to hear. *No, I don't know who. Please, tell me.*

The janitor's voice again. "Y-you think it might be?"

"An SPI agent was reported missing this morning. Around this area, too. This has the Wolf's fingerprints all over it."

Somehow I doubted they were blaming the incident on the local wildlife. *The wolf, though? How would you earn that sort of nickname?*

"Right over through this door..." the footsteps were muffled as the door thumped shut behind them.

Silence in the hall. About time. Air was running a little low in that closet.

I got a grip on Dallas with one hand and twisted the doorknob with the other. I nearly faceplanted as the door swung open, but managed to just use my momentum as a head start in my stumbling towards the exit.

Thankfully, the exit was a push door, so I was able to charge through it easier. And before the cop and the janitor came back out. It swung shut behind me with a satisfying click.

I leaned up against the brick wall and let myself slide down, dropping Dallas next to me and gulping in long breaths of the outside air. Every part of me ached and my head pounded with every beat of my heart.

Even with no memories, I was pretty sure that was the most pathetic race for life I'd ever had.

After I'd sufficiently caught my breath, I looked up across the parking lot. Five cars sat in various spots, a couple looking like they'd been here for a while, and all of them looking like trash. This was probably a back lot. Even on an off day, I'd guess an opera house would have a few more employees hanging around.

I hadn't thought this escape through very well. What were Dallas and I getting to the hospital in? We certainly weren't walking…

I patted down my jean pockets for a key. My fingers closed around a keychain in my right pocket and I pulled it out.

A car key, a house key and a key fob dangled from a large ring, along with a kind of knot of paracord and some little robot thing with a whisk and a plunger attached. It shone a dirty bronze. I tapped on the robot, watching it swing and spin on its ring for a second before shifting my fingers over to hold the key fob.

Anything to drive would be absolutely fantastic at this point, but I still found myself hoping for a cool car. I might be a jerk, but hopefully I was a jerk with a ride that wasn't a ratty old minivan.

Here's hoping for a hot-rod.

I stuck my hand up in the air and hit the lock button. None of the five in this lot lit up, but I heard a "beep-beep" from somewhere distant.

Pushing off the wall, I made my way to the corner by the other parking lot and pressed the button again. The ones around front were definitely better cars, but I didn't see any of them light up either. Still, a "beep-beep" sounded, less distant than before.

I frowned and hit the key fob again, looking around. I saw headlights flash from behind the trees on the other side of the road. Definitely not minivan headlights, but I couldn't quite make out the type of car. It looked quite intentionally hidden. And it also looked very far away from where I was standing.

I groaned, adding yet another item to the list of my complaints against myself, and limped back to where I'd left Dallas. He still lay in a crumpled heap by the wall, not having moved. I hauled him up on my back again, took a few shaky breaths and started towards the dim outline of the car.

It took longer to get there than I'd care to admit, but I did it before any cops came out of the opera building. And it was worth the trek for the convertible, black Mustang behind the trees.

One good fact about myself: I'm a man of excellent taste.

The top was down and I got Dallas settled in the backseat, then myself in the driver's seat.

If I'd been running low on energy before, I was basically in the negative numbers for it now.

I dropped my head back on the seat and closed my eyes as I caught my breath. Well, the next step in the plan had been to find a hospital. But was I really driving us there? What were the alternatives?

Both of us bleeding out in the parked car? Waiting until the cops found us?

Taking a nap? This seat is really soft... I barely caught myself from drifting off. I blinked my eyes open and shook my head. My hand came up to run over my hair almost by itself. My hair stuck up horribly in the front and was matted with blood at the back. I needed some sort of bandage to tie over it. I had to have something around that would fit the bill...

I looked around the front seat area and discovered that I kept an unfortunately clean car. Nothing in sight.

Darn me.

I bent over and felt under the seat. My fingers touched on a solid case of something. I pulled it out, flicking the latch open. Inside was a rather large gun and a kerchief tucked in next to it, probably for cleaning purposes.

Hey, it worked for bandaging purposes too.

I pulled out the handkerchief and pushed the case back under my seat. My hands trembled as I folded the red cloth and wrapped it lopsidedly around the back of my head. Pain stabbed through my skull as I tied it, but after that, the pressure seemed to help a bit.

I let out my breath and stuck the keys in the ignition, giving them a turn. *Here goes crazy...*

The engine purred to life and I steered the car out onto the road. The motion of the car and the wind in my hair steadied my shaking hands a little as I got further away from the opera. There was also classical music on the radio. Weird, but I kind of liked it so I didn't turn it off.

The freeway entrance came up and I merged on. Hospitals usually had signs on the freeway, right? I'd find one eventually.

Turns out "eventually" isn't the best timing for medical care.

Forcing myself to focus on driving became a constant task. I had to continually remind myself what I was looking for and where I was going. The road signs got too fuzzy to read, so even if I'd passed a hospital, I might not have noticed. I lost track of how long I'd been driving.

I rubbed a hand over my face and blinked hard. The bowtie on my tux was starting to get annoying, so I brought my hand down to loosen it. There was movement in my rearview mirror. I glanced back.

A pitch-black, giant pickup truck was right on my tail. The driver had sunglasses and a scowl on and looked like the living embodiment of bad news. Bad news was the last thing I needed.

I looked back at the road. *Well, he's not necessarily following me. Maybe I'm just on his commute route or something. He just happened to get behind me. He feels a bond because we both have black cars.* My eyes went back to the mirror.

The driver caught my eye and made a few gestures, shaking his head and looking ticked off.

I quickly looked away, flicking the turn signal to take the next exit to some middle-of-nowhere town. The car almost veered off the road as I came to the intersection. My breath was coming shorter now and my head felt like a helium balloon that might float away at any second.

Keep it together... I was barely able to register when the light turned green. The car seemed to steer itself down the empty road away from town.

I wasn't even sure where I thought I was going. I was able to hold myself together for another few minutes. Until the only things around were me, these wacky looking, red rocks… and the black pickup, still following me.

Who cared if he caught me at this point? I was too tired to care.

My grip loosened on the steering wheel and my foot slid off the gas pedal. The car coasted along, veering slowly off the road and grinding to a stop in the gravel.

Out of energy, my eyes drooped shut and I wilted against the steering wheel. The pickup door slammed shut behind me, but I didn't have the energy to turn my head.

The sound of footsteps approaching the car faded away.

Chapter 3: Bad News

Uncomfortable, sharp awareness worked its way into my mind and feeling trickled back into my limbs. One of my arms was numb from hanging at an awkward angle.

I took in a breath and moved my arm a little, but my eyes were too heavy to open. My nose was smashed up against the rough fabric of a couch arm and warm puffs of my own breath deflected back into my face.

I needed a mint.

Swallowing, I squinched my eyes for a second before forcing them open. Deep purple fabric was about two inches away from my face. I turned my head away and squinted at the rest of my bedding.

It felt almost like I'd been chucked onto the couch by someone at the other end of the room. One leg hung off the side and the other propped up on the opposite couch arm. A blanket was wrinkled up diagonally over my body with a corner tickling my nose. Nothing was over my feet, though my shoes were still on.

It was hard to decide whether this was a friendly kidnapping or a clumsy rescue.

I untangled myself somewhat, twisted onto my back and braced myself on the couch. I pushed into a sitting position, wincing as the steady, dull pounding started again at the base of my skull. Blinking, I waited until my eyes adjusted to the dim light and cleared away the spots, looking around the room.

Dallas was sprawled across another couch with his hair in disarray. Probably similar to the position I'd just been in. A blanket was bundled at his feet and an ace bandage wrapped crookedly around his midsection, pinning his bloodstained tie to his chest. Red showed through the cloth and his face was pale, but he was still breathing at least so, hey, some success there.

Light filtered into the room through grubby curtains that looked like they'd been stolen from a bad hotel. From the pinkish hue of the light and the distant chattering of birds, it looked to be around sunrise.

Dust covered the rough wood floor in uneven streaks and dead bugs garnished the corners. A few framed comic strips hung on the wall. Something colorful with a boy and a tiger.

I turned to look at the opposite wall and jumped upon seeing a reflection turn to look at me.

By the way the reflection jumped — and the interesting clothes — I guessed it was mine. No one else had my quaint charm of a bloody tuxedo-leather jacket combination with the worst case of bed-head to ever see the light of day. My bowtie hung limp around my neck from where I'd loosened it before. The bandana was gone and I could see blood streaking through my hair.

The reflection blinked, looking shocked and stupid. But I couldn't stop staring.

This was… me.

To say I didn't like how I looked… wouldn't be quite accurate. My reflection… my face… scared me. I looked like someone I'd intentionally avoid on the street. Someone who'd shoot you if you took one extra crumb of cake.

I could see the person in the mirror killing that guy backstage and shooting Dallas, easy. It was a face of someone who'd killed before.

I didn't blame Dallas now for his underwhelming desire for my help.

The pain in my head and the sick feeling in my stomach were ganging up on me to stop the reflection psychoanalyzing, so I moved on to the shallower things about my appearance.

After almost a full minute of squinting, I gave up trying to figure out what color my eyes were and moved on in my inspection. I guess I'm just Mr. Color-ambiguous, because my hair couldn't seem to decide whether it wanted to be brown or blond. And then there was the cowlick at the front of my head, spiking my hair up wildly.

No, scratch that. That wasn't a cowlick. That was like a whole-herd-of-cows-lick.

I ran my hand over it and tried to pat it down to no avail. It sprung right back up at a weirder angle. I gave up and looked away, focusing on the fuzzy comic strip on the other wall.

I had plenty of other problems to address. For instance, Mr. monster truck and sunglasses. I still wasn't sure whether he was our rescuer or kidnapper.

He was probably a friend of either mine or of Dallas's. It seemed those two would be mutually exclusive, judging by Dallas's opinion of me. Either way, he probably knew who I was.

But after all the stuff I'd put together so far… my stomach twisted uncomfortably at the thought of finding out who I actually was. Did I really want to know? Maybe I was different now. Maybe I'd run away… away from all these people who knew past-me… to the jungle or something. I'd be a wilderness man and survive.

All that great stuff that my brain decides is a good idea at five in the morning after almost dying. I shook my head and leaned back, just wanting to go back to sleep and forget about all this.

My elbow bumped against something behind the couch arm and I twisted around to look. A smiley cup of grape Kool-Aid with a green straw, still sloshing a little from my bumping it. Sunlight shone through it, lighting up the eyes in a creepy way.

An old leather wallet sat next to it, with a little P.O. box address tucked in the front pocket. The handwriting was a familiar, sideways scrawl, just like the note I'd found in my jacket. Probably mine.

Oh boy. More information about myself that I'd probably hate.

I grabbed the Kool-Aid, flicked out the straw and drained the stuff in one swig. I would have preferred alcohol of some sort... and in larger quantity. But whatever.

A click from the other side of the room behind the mirror made me jump. There was a squeaking noise and a door swung in. And who should come lumbering in but the scary-sunglasses-man himself. Only he was in a big pickup truck before. The fact that he was almost seven feet tall had escaped me up until that very moment.

My eyes widened and I felt the blood drain from my face. I didn't realize I'd dropped the Kool-Aid cup until I heard the plastic clatter on the floor.

The giant looked over at me and I saw his eyebrows go up to touch the edge of his black fedora. "Hey! Morning, sunshine." It was shocking how friendly that deep of a voice could sound. He grinned at me and touched his hat brim.

I kept my jaw from dropping and forced a wobbly smile back.

Though I doubted I was much of a sunshine, it was reassuring. He liked me, at least. Maybe he didn't bring me back to his shack to eat me.

He crossed the room in a couple of strides and tipped his head down at me, "I slapped a Band-Aid over top that whack on your head. Does it feel any better?"

I put my hand to the back of my head and found a big adhesive patch stuck on top of my hair. I tugged at the edge a little and winced. "Um... sure." For now. Taking it off would be a study in the art of torture.

I craned my neck up at the mountain next to me and dug frantically in my nearly empty memory bank for some recollection of him. Some connecting memory. He knew me. I had to know something about him.

But looking at that face... the suit and tie... those sunglasses... that fedora on top of that towering head... my mind seemed unable to think anything but "bad news".

And that wasn't reassuring.

He tugged at his tie and his crooked grin shifted slowly into a frown. That wasn't good.

Just then, Dallas sucked in his breath and stiffened, his eyes popping wide open to stare at the ceiling. Back in the land of the living at last. The transformation from rag doll to rigid board in less than two seconds was quite remarkable.

Giganto looked over at him, put one hand on his hip and pushed his fedora back a little on his head. He glanced back over at me and nodded towards Dallas. His mouth twisted sideways in confusion.

"I was gonna ask, is he with us now or something?"

Dallas's eyes rested on the resident giant and I swear he just about passed out again just then. I felt like I should say something to reassure him, but I honestly wasn't too far below Dallas on level of fright.

"'Cuz I mean, I assumed you were gonna kill him," the big guy continued. "But you had him in the back of your car so there's something I'm missing here."

Dallas swallowed and I saw his breath coming faster. He closed his eyes and moved his mouth silently.

I just stared. How long had I wanted to kill Dallas? *Why* did I want to kill Dallas?

The giant looked between the two of us, shrugged and sat himself down on the floor, leaning his back up against the coffee table. His head was still above mine, even though I was on the couch and he was on the floor.

"Well, I guess the other night went kinda sideways, huh?"

I blinked at him.

"I got kinda worried when you didn't come back, so I headed out to pick you up and patch you up. Make sure you were doing okay. All that. And, if you needed me to, hand out some" he coughed into his elbow, then grinned his great chasm of a mouth at me, "bad luck."

Dallas made a strangled sound.

I didn't like the picture that was emerging from the precious few jigsaw pieces of my life at the moment. It looked like a perfectly decent, polite kid like Dallas was my enemy, I had a hit man at my command and the blood of at least one person on my hands, not to mention a mysterious note about my apparently murdered family.

"So, what ended up happening anyway?" My giant shifted his position like he was settling down for a story.

I let out my breath and ran my hand over my hair again, mentally scrambling for what details I knew. "Well…"

I couldn't tell him anything other than what was pretty much obvious already. He knew me. And he could probably kill me with about as much effort as blinking if he wanted to.

Lying wasn't worth the risk.

I glanced over at Dallas and licked my lips, "I… don't remember."

Dallas blinked at me and stared. A look of realization spread across his face, followed by a hint of relief.

The giant tipped his head and his brow furrowed. "Don't remember the other night?" He scratched at the side of his head by his hat. "Well, I suppose that lines up," he muttered. "The conk on the head you took and all…"

"No, I mean… everything about my life," I looked between them, "I know that's probably a lot. Guessing I'm about twenty-something. So," I gestured a little. "Could I maybe get like a short summary of… who you guys are, exactly? I'm a little lost."

The giant looked surprisingly sympathetic. "Seriously? Man, that's rough." He stood, "Hey, I have ice cream in the freezer. You love ice cream. Do you want some?"

Well, ice cream sounded tempting, I'm not denying that. But it wasn't quite my top priority at the moment.

I held up a hand, "Not... at the moment. Hold on, just tell me your name real quick, okay?"

He straightened up and adjusted his tie as though giving a school recitation, "Baden News," he rumbled out "Though no one really calls me Baden. So, Bad News."

This guy was literally named Bad News.

Well, first impressions aren't always correct. But it looked like mine was spot on.

If ever a name fit a face... I swallowed hard.

Mr. News pointed over to the kitchen, "I'm going to get the ice cream now."

I nodded. Ice cream certainly wasn't the worst thing this guy could want to give me.

As soon as he was gone, I looked over at Dallas. He'd regained a little of his color and gotten in a more upright position on the couch. Also he was looking at me. With less terror than before, thankfully.

I forced a smile to my lips, "So... what sort of terms are we on?"

"The terms where you would shoot me for annoying you... the last time I checked, at least." There was still a slight nervous quaver in his matter-of-fact tone.

I winced, "Sorry... "

"It's more from relation than anything else," Dallas shrugged, looking down to his hands, twisted in his lap. "I'm the sidekick of... your arch-enemy."

Something held me back from asking who my sworn enemy was. I guess I was nervous it would turn out to be Mother Theresa or something. Instead, I just nodded and reached for the wallet on the table next to the couch. I turned it over in my hands a couple of times, then held it up to Dallas.

"Is this mine?"

Dallas shrugged. He's such a chatterbox.

My hands trembling slightly, I opened it.

It flipped open in my lap, revealing a small wad of bills and, in a clear pocket, a driver's license with my smirking face on it.

Well, I could actually learn some solid facts about myself now.

I looked at myself with a furrowed brow for a second, then moved on to the part where it said my name.

And, printed in all its ridiculously long glory, there it was.

My name was Wolfgang Dankworth.

Cue the creepy organ music… dim the lights… good glory. It sounded like an overkill fairy tale villain name. A crook who murdered for a living and spent his free time cackling evilly in corners and stroking his evil pet… something.

I swallowed against the bile rising in the back of my throat.

I looked up at Dallas again, "Wolfgang Dankworth? Is that seriously my birth name?"

Dallas blinked, like I was asking something that had never occurred to him. "Yes, as far as I know."

I rubbed my thumb over the letters, feeling goosebumps on my arms. "Sounds quite villainous."

"Well… yes." He rubbed his hand on the back of his neck and gave me another confused frown.

As if that was a given. Jeez, my predisposal to evil was nonnegotiable with this kid.

Examining more of my license, I found I was licensed to drive in the state of Utah. Random. I thought criminal types as myself would stick to the slums of New York. But the red rocks made sense now…

I skimmed over the rest of the details and was suddenly annoyed with myself that I wasn't able to grow another measly inch and get to six feet tall. At twenty-three, I guessed I was probably done growing.

On to the other pockets of the wallet. Some thank-you note from a pawnshop. An old ticket to a Seattle Mariners game. A Target membership card. A piece of paper with the letters "DM" and a scribbled phone number. An opera ticket made sense, at least.

My fingers hit one last thing that felt like photo paper. I pulled it out. A snapshot of a little kid grinned back at me with eyes that I couldn't decide the color of. Dimples showed in his cheeks and cowlicked, light brown hair poked up in all directions.

Indistinct memories prodded at the back of my mind. Was that me? No... my face was too angular for that. A brother? I blinked. Was this the "Peter" I'd written about in my note? He wasn't very old. Four, at the most. But the photo paper felt kind of old...

A loud thud sounded on the table next to me. I jumped, sticking the picture back in my wallet.

Bad News grinned down at me. "Got some strawberry." He dropped a spoon down on the table next to the open, pink ice cream. The frozen top sparkled in the light from the windows.

"Um... thanks." I gave him a casual salute with my shaking hand and picked up the spoon.

"I think someone broke in here," News pushed his fedora back on his head. "All the spoons are gone. That's just my backup one." He patted his coat pocket and looked over at Dallas. "So if you wanna share with Knight, you two gotta share the spoon too. Unless you want to eat with your fingers..."

"I'm alright," Dallas assured.

The phone rang just then and Bad News dashed out to get it, his tie whipping over his shoulder. His pounding footsteps stopped after a few seconds and the ringing stopped. I strained to hear what he was saying.

"... got him... bit banged up... Wendover... bomb... see ya."

The phone clicked and he was back.

"The gang's on their way."

Oh, I had a gang now too? Fantastic.

Any color Dallas had regained was immediately gone. And I could imagine why.

If he'd been as scared as he was just within proximity of Bad News and myself… a whole gang?

I set the ice cream spoon down and stood up, ignoring my head's sharp protest to the movement. "Leave a note, News. I'm going for a drive."

While I had a head start, at least. And an alive Dallas.

Bad News grabbed his coat off a hook on the wall and shot me a grin. "Awesome. I'm coming too. Nothing like a morning drive, huh?"

He had to live up to his name.

Chapter 4: Going For a Drive

I didn't realize until I'd already pulled out of the driveway that I had no idea where in the world I was. Yeah, that might hang the escape up a little.

"Hey, News…" I turned to the fedora-d grizzly bear in the passenger seat.

He looked up from pawing through the CDs in the glove compartment. "Hmm?"

"What's this place called?" I waved a hand to the city around us in general.

Bad News pulled his sunglasses up and squinted into the sun for a second before dropping them back down and giving his hat a tug. "Utah."

Oh gee, thanks. Specifics. What kind of navigation expert did he take me for?

"Whereabouts? Like do I turn left or right?"

Bad News picked up a particularly colorful CD with a cartoon drawing on the front and set it on the dashboard. He gave me a weird look. "You really got your head emptied, huh?"

I opened my mouth and closed it again. "Um… yeah." *Make this more awkward than it already is, why don't you…*

He watched me for another few seconds, then shrugged, tugging his tie. "Well, to go towards your hideout, you'd just keep going straight out of town, then head North at Salt Lake City." He shoved his chosen CD in the player and leaned back in his seat. "Guessing that's where you're headed?"

Well, that would probably involve running into the gang. My gang. That would probably kill my backseat passenger. And avoiding that was sort of the whole reason I was driving away in the first place.

Explaining that whole thought process to News didn't seem like a good idea, but I still pulled off and got myself turned around. Hopefully my gang–leader status would give me a bit of an edge for doing what I wanted.

Thankfully, all I got from him was another odd look.

Dallas shifted forward from the back. "You'll be in Nevada in a few minutes. I think this is Wendover." His voice was quiet.

I nodded, "Thanks."

Sure enough, in just a few minutes, a sign welcoming us to Nevada came up on the right. Still as rocky and desert-looking as ever. And hopefully out of suspicion area for my gang.

It was strange to be running away from my own gang. How scary were they, really? What sort of gang was it?

A biker gang was the first thing that came to mind. But the fact that News drove a truck and I drove a Mustang sort of pulled the rug out from under that idea. Maybe going with the black theme, they were a bunch of Goths. Everyone with eyeliner and spikes and all, glaring at each other.

Maybe it was just a bunch more thugs like Bad News. I'd have my own mountain range.

Or a rag-tag band sort of thing. Grab bag of goons. In any

case, they were probably as bad of criminals as I was. If not worse.

Bad News's music choice finally burst my thought bubble and I actually listened to the words for a second.

"... *elementary my dear, two times six is twelve...*"

News's mouth moved in perfect synchronization to the words and he nodded his head in time. He hit his knee with his palm occasionally, adding to the percussion.

Because... hit men need to know their multiplication tables...?

I blinked at the radio.

Seriously, would it be the end of the world if something within ten feet of me even remotely made sense?

Far be it from me to criticize Giganto's music choices, but curiosity got the better of me. "Hey, what's this called?" I carefully kept all scorn out of my voice.

"Schoolhouse Rock."

I nodded slowly. "Ah."

Like that was any less confusing. News didn't really strike me as a "schoolhouse" type of guy. I avoided looking at him, keeping my eyes on the dry mountains on the horizon as I drove.

My head was a lot clearer for this drive, thankfully. Bad News must have done a bit more than the Band-aid. It still ached and occasional stabs of pain came, usually triggered by my thinking too hard. Keeping thinking down wasn't easy though, with all the questions I had about... well... everything.

Also I was still at a loss for a plan and that wasn't a good place to stay in. I was driving away from the gang. I was keeping Dallas alive. I was hopefully not getting eaten by gorilla in my passenger seat. Good start. Where was I going from there?

I looked up in the rearview mirror so I could see Dallas.

His face had a bit more color than before and he didn't look three-quarters dead anymore. More like... a third, if I was being optimistic. The wind ruffled his brown hair off his forehead as he looked out the window. His expression rested in a slightly uneasy poker face.

I cleared my throat. "Hey, Dall."

He looked up to meet my eyes in the mirror.

"How're you doin'?"

Dallas blinked and glanced to the side, "Fine… thank you." He said it like I'd asked him a trick question.

I waited for a second, then nodded, "Good." I swallowed and shifted my gaze back down to the road.

Well, he wasn't very talkative to begin with, but at least he wasn't unconscious any more. And that was one of the more normal sounding of our interactions.

Out of the two passengers in my car, he was obviously the one that represented the law-and-order side of things. If I had previously aligned myself with the opposition to that, I really didn't need to drag Dallas into enemy territory. I could figure out my life without putting him in danger too.

Even if I'd tried to kill him at the opera, I had no intention of finishing that job.

I needed to get him out of this.

I formulated a bit more of a plan in my mind and leaned over to News, dropping my voice low. "So, at the next town…" I looked over at him. "I'm thinking we drop Dallas off at the police station or something so he can get to some medical attention and head back to wherever he came from. We can meet up with the gang afterwards."

"Police station?" Even through the sunglasses, I could tell Bad News really thought I'd gone insane. "Man, we'd be in a cell sooner than you could put the parking brake on. No police. That's one thing you need to know straight off. You and police…" he spread his arms, "… stay faaar apart."

A jolt of cold went through me at that statement. I shivered a little. "Okay…" I licked my lips, "Well, what can we do with him?"

News shrugged and looked out the window. "There's a nice empty stretch of road out there. Give him some trail mix and he can hitchhike his way to town."

I looked back at Dallas, who was attempting to wrap his lopsided, bloody ace bandage tighter around his middle and wincing.

I looked outside at the landscape. Dry, rocky and empty. A dead body would be an unsurprising addition to the scenery.

Drop him by the side of the road? In the shape he was in? It would be kinder to shoot him now.

"News, he'd die." I shook my head and kept my eyes on the road.

News scratched the side of his head. "And you'd mind that?" He sounded honestly confused with me. Like I was doing something out of character by not killing someone at the drop of a hat.

Was I really that heartless of a killer?

I swallowed and dropped my gaze to my hands on the steering wheel. They were shaking. I could see the white bone in my knuckles. A sharp jab of pain slashed through my head and I sucked in my breath. The car swerved.

Dallas's eyes widened and he held onto the door handle.

"Whoa, there…" News leaned over, putting a ham-sized hand out to steady me. "You okay?"

I gritted my teeth and waited for the throbbing to subside. "Just… my head."

Nodding, Bad News pulled back and dug in his coat pockets for a few seconds, then pulled out a tiny bottle. He tapped out two pills. "Aspirin?"

One moment, advising me to kill a polite young gentleman… the next, offering me Aspirin.

It was approximately that moment that I decided to stop trying to figure out Baden News.

"Sure." I took the pills with one shaky hand and swallowed them down. That would help my headache, but not the dilemma of my backseat passenger.

I obviously couldn't keep him around and alive if I was trying to play the part of Wolfgang Dankworth. But what other options were there?

I looked down at my steering wheel again.

The little plunger-whisk robot on my keychain jangled against the key fob and there was a click.

36

"Exterminate!" said a tiny, metallic voice.

I don't take advice from keychain robots.

"Hey, Dallas?" I looked at him in the rearview mirror. He raised his head. "So, are you good sticking with us for a bit? I'm not really... liking the other options at the moment. Unless you have any other ideas...?" I cleared my throat and straightened myself up a bit in my seat.

Dallas held my gaze for a long time, his green eyes seeming to search mine deeply. Kind of like he'd done at the opera, only about three times more intense. I hoped News was watching the road while I had my soul searched.

In a few seconds, I found that he was

"Gang at six o'clock, Wolf," he rumbled.

We were out of whatever grace time my drive had bought.

Dallas's look tightened, but he kept my gaze for a few more seconds, mouthing something very clearly.

I trust you.

I tightened my jaw and gave him a firm nod. My eyes went back to the road for approximately five seconds before I looked back over at Bad News. I'm a horribly attentive driver.

"Introduce me to the gang." I adjusted the mirror so it focused on the car behind us. It was still a ways back, but I could make out general outlines if I squinted.

"Ho boy." News took a quick look over his shoulder, then looked forward and rubbed his hands together. "Roy's the kid driving with the toothpick in his teeth. Spiky hair and sunglasses. You see 'im?"

I nodded.

"He's usually sort of the assigned getaway driver, since he's the best at ignoring speed limits. Been driving since his foot could reach the pedal without breaking the moisture seal on his diaper." Bad News pushed his hat back a little. "Correct me if I'm wrong, but I think you've known him the longest?"

I wasn't really in the position to correct anything, so I kept quiet, filing away the information on the person in the driver's seat behind us. The car started to veer a little and I looked back down, correcting course. I pressed down a little harder. *Give us a little more time.*

"Liza's the one with turquoise hair in the passenger seat," News continued. "She's the main mechanic. I mean... you do quite a bit too. She works out the plans and stuff though."

I moved my gaze to the head of turquoise hair. Quick to make judgments, but it didn't seem like that brightly colored of hair would usually top a brilliant mind. "Mechanic for...?"

The giant didn't seem to hear me. He glanced over his shoulder again. "Chris is the older guy with the cowboy hat. He... talks to you and shoots stuff and swears a lot, I guess."

Oh yippee. Sounded like a productive role.

"And Cardboard is the little girl with the orange shirt and the big hair."

It took effort not to veer the car off the road while I stared at the dark-skinned, tiny child in the rearview mirror. The oldest she could possibly be was seven.

Cardboard?

"Is there... a reason she's named Cardboard?"

Bad News shrugged. "She's Roy's kid. Roy likes naming things weird. And he found her in a dumpster marked 'Cardboard Only', so he thought it would be pretty funny to name her that."

I looked over the faces again as the car got closer. The hotshot getaway car driver... the turquoise haired mechanic... the sour-faced cowboy... and the little girl named after a packaging material.

That wasn't counting the elephant-sized enigma named Bad News in my passenger seat.

And I was supposed to be their leader. Only I had amnesia and would kind of... rather not be a criminal. Which left me the task of trying to convince them not to kill an innocent teenage boy I'd already shot once.

Look up "predicament" in the dictionary. I'm pretty sure you'll see some reference to this situation.

Holy. Freaking. Smoke. I'll have a mutiny on my hands. I'll get Dallas killed. I'll get me killed. What am I doing…?

My head pounded and I tried not to hyperventilate. *Think… there's got to be something to do…*

Roy pushed his sunglasses up on his forehead and waved, pointing to the side of the road.

Out of time.

I let out my breath and slowed down, pulling the car to the side of the road. The red car behind us closed in fast, pulling up right behind us.

"Okay. News, Dallas… game plan time." I put the car into park and ran a shaking hand over my hair. "You two…" I pointed to both of them in turn, "… are going to be the only ones who know I've lost my memory."

Chapter 5: The Gang's All Here

There was a crunch of gravel and a car door slammed behind us.

I gave News and Dallas each a look that hopefully communicated both "don't worry" and "shut up" at the same time, then looked back to see who was getting out.

More car doors slammed.

Okay, apparently everyone was getting out.

I'd better get this act right the first time, because I wasn't getting another chance.

They think you're an evil gang-leader guy... play the part.

I felt like it would be better to meet them standing up, so I popped my door open and stepped out, straightening my jacket. Hopefully my stance looked commanding enough for my position.

There was a sliding of fabric on leather in the back seat and the top of Dallas's head disappeared from my view. I wasn't sure if he was trying to hide or if he'd passed out again. I didn't blame him either way.

Roy was the first one who'd gotten out so he was the first one who got to my side of the car. The tiny bit of fluff named Cardboard skipped along at his heels.

Roy stopped and plucked the toothpick out from in between his teeth, giving me a slightly confused frown. "Man, where were you going?"

"Just…" I shrugged. "… for a drive."

He glanced behind me and down the road. "Pretty slow drive."

Because fifteen miles over the speed limit was pathetic, apparently. I had to recall what News had said about Roy and speed limits.

Cardboard peeked over into the car, standing on her tiptoes. She grinned at Bad News. "I like this song."

Bad News grinned. Roy frowned. I took note that Schoolhouse Rock was a point of contention.

The other footsteps crunching on the gravel came closer and in a few seconds, Liza and Chris had joined us.

Chris gave me a withering look out from under the brim of his hat. "This is cutting it a bit close for what we're doing tomorrow, don't you think?"

Oh fantastic, we had something going on tomorrow? I glanced over at News. He was turning up the music, which was pretty much the opposite of helping at the moment.

Just stay vague… stay vague…

My hand unconsciously went up to tug at my hair as I opened my mouth to respond. Liza cut my response off.

"Give him a break, Chris," she soothed. "News said the other night went sideways. He couldn't have predicted that." Her voice was an even, medium-pitched tone. And she had an accent that it took me a few seconds to categorize. British, maybe? Slightly different tone. It could be Australian.

She turned to me, tipping her head like a curious, turquoise-headed bird. "What happened to your head, Wolfy?" She took a few steps closer, trying to get a look at it.

I took a step back. "Ah… not much. Just… there was a scuffle and that other guy… knocked me out."

Liza didn't seem deterred by my step back and came to my side. Reaching up a hand, she put it on my hair and turned my head to get a better look. Her fingers were small, thin and cold.

She winced and sucked in a breath. "Oh, that's nasty…" I felt her fingers brush against the side of the gash not covered by News's band-aid.

My muscles all clenched tight as I waited for her to finish her inspection.

Stop touching me… please, stop touching me…

Liza stepped back, finally. "No wonder Bad didn't bring you back right away."

Chris had his arms folded across his chest. He raised an eyebrow. "You've had worse, Wolfgang."

I resisted the urge to shudder at my name and nodded. "Yeah, I know." *At least now.*

That fact was both reassuring and frightening at the same time. So I'd be fine… but how many other deadly shootouts had I been involved in?

"So," Chris brushed a hand over his close-shaven beard. "Did you kill him?"

The image of the dead man backstage vividly reappeared in my mind. My stomach twisted and I swallowed back the urge to gag. My headache pounded worse for a couple of seconds, making my vision swim.

"Mm-hmm." I nodded, gripping the edge of the car door to steady myself.

"Then what's he doing in the backseat?" asked Roy.

Chris and Liza stiffened at the same time.

"What?"

And suddenly all attention was on the slouched form in the back of my car.

So Chris had meant Dallas. That was the whole point of what I'd gone to do. Kill Dallas.

"I... I meant..." I stammered for a second, then clamped my mouth shut again and focused on not losing my breakfast.

"You... brought him along with you?" Liza tore her gaze off Dallas and stared at me.

Chris narrowed his eyes. "Wolfgang, what's going on?"

I'm doomed.

"He knows what he's doing. Chill out," News's voice came from the front. He turned around, pushing his hat back. "It's for tomorrow, isn't it, Wolf?"

Bad News was the only one here who knew both sides of this conversation. And he was helping me.

I took a second before I noticed that I was just staring at him.

"Oh... um... yeah. He's here for... tomorrow." I nodded, swallowing. "For a... hostage. We need a hostage."

Dallas's eyes widened.

Blank, disbelieving stares from the gang met my statement.

Oh please let it not be an unrelated gang rumble...

Bad News cleared his throat, nudging Chris's arm. "You'll have to give him some slack, guys." His voice was low and he cupped one giant hand on the side of his mouth like he expected me to not hear. "Conk on the head, y'know? He's still a little..." he spun a finger at the side of his head. "... out of it. A few marbles loose at the moment. Just go along. It'll be fine."

I suppressed the knee-jerk reaction to tell News to shut up and defend my sanity. He was saving my skin. If saying I was a bit out of it kept a mutiny at bay and kept

Dallas alive... so be it.

All eyes went to me again.

I forced a wobbly grin, unsure of what else to do.

For some reason, that seemed to cement News's statement as true.

Liza relaxed and smiled back at me, amusement dancing in her blue eyes. "Well, probably best to get going back, then?"

Roy needed no further prompting. He sprang up and started back for the car, stopping only a second to pat my shoulder.

"A *hostage* though?" Chris hissed back to News. "We don't need a hostage, News. This is…" his voice dropped lower and I heard a few muttered obscenities.

Dallas shrunk back down in his seat.

Bad News waved a hand dismissively. "It's fine, man. Trust me. Wolf knows what he's doing. Just a little mixed up about explaining things at the moment."

Chris shot another look over in my direction.

"Just head back to the car." News gave him a small shove in that direction.

"Fine," Chris pushed off the car, with one final look at Dallas and an eyebrow raise at me, and headed back to take his seat in the red car. Roy had already started the engine.

I let out my breath in a whoosh as I pulled my door back open. My legs gave out as I sat down behind the wheel.

Wow. How many near-death experiences was this in the space of twenty-four hours now?

News buckled up again, turning down the radio so it was singing slightly quieter about the number eleven. "We need to pop back by Wendover to get my truck before heading up to the Den. So if you'll just swing around…"

I frowned at him. "The… Den?"

"Your base of operations," supplied Dallas quietly.

News nodded. He held up his hands, gesturing a little. "You know… 'cause you're the Wolf. We're your Pack. Where we hang out is the Den. Get it?" He grinned and chuckled.

I nodded slowly as I turned the keys in the ignition. "Clever." And creepy.

You're the Wolf.

That dangerous criminal who'd just gotten out of prison… the one that policeman was talking about at the opera… that was me. All the blood and gore… my signature, apparently.

I pulled the Mustang out onto the empty road and got it

turned around back facing towards Utah, pushing back that sick feeling in my stomach again. The other car was already speeding off down the highway like a red bullet.

The song on the radio changed and Bad News reached over with his enormous hand to turn up the volume again. "This one's good."

"Now, if man had been born with six fingers on each hand... he'd also have twelve toes, or so the theory goes..."

He looked over at me with an expression that seemed to demand my admitting the awesomeness of this particular multiplication song.

"... well he would have added two more digits when he invented his number system..."

This counted as... music?

Well... counted.

Of course it counts. *It's math.*

I fought the crazy urge to burst into hysterical laughter. It came out as more of a half snicker, half snort. The lingering panic from a few minutes before only served to make it funnier. I turned away from News, leaning partly over the steering wheel and hoping he couldn't see me laughing.

Get it together, idiot. You're acting drunk.

Bad News didn't say anything. The song played on.

I finally got myself under control and went back to focusing on driving.

"Hey, little Twelvetoes, I hope you're well... must be some far-flung planet where you dwell..."

Well, getting myself back under control was relative. I hoped News didn't find anything wrong with my sudden coughing fit.

Bad News just watched me with a crooked smile on his face. He reached over, patted my shoulder and leaned back in his seat.

"Everything happens for a reason, you know," he observed philosophically. "And with you?" giving me another grin, he nodded. "Amnesia's an improvement. I'm cool with this."

An improvement... from what?

I nodded back cautiously. "Um… thanks."

"… little Twelvetoes… please come back soon…"

I pulled my mind away from Schoolhouse Rock and focused it on how to stay alive through whatever was coming next.

#

The Den actually didn't have heads on spikes all around it. No paintings of my hideous name in blood. No crocodiles in the moat. In fact, no moat at all. All it ended up being was just an old grocery store with graffiti on the walls and faded shadows of sign letters torn off the front.

I don't think it even counted as being in town. It was backed up against a patch of woods by the mountains along a torn up old strip of road. Vines crawled up the sides of the building and the paint over the parking spots was barely visible anymore. A lone lamppost bent sideways stood to the side of the parking lot. Long abandoned. By everyone but us criminals, of course.

I'd followed News's truck for the drive back, since I obviously didn't know where we were going, despite his directions. He left me in the dust near the end of the drive, but I could tell I was in the right place by the big truck and red car poking out from the other side of the building.

I slowed down and turned

It really wasn't all that creepy of a place. I could call it lots of things, but creepy wasn't at the top of my mind.

Didn't make much difference to Dallas, though. He shivered like we'd driven into an arctic fortress.

The conversation on the drive had been very sparse. I got a sense that Dallas wasn't the most talkative kid to begin with. The fact that up to this point I'd been trying to kill him and had just pinned him as a hostage probably didn't help matters.

"So…" I coasted up in front of the store and put the car into park, "We're here, I guess. Everyone else looks like they're inside already." I turned my head to look back at him, "Ever been here before?"

Dallas swallowed, "Yes sir." He looked down at his shoes, like he was trying to unsee something bad. "And in the same car, too."

I'd pretty much gotten used to the ice-water bursts through my veins by now, but I still flinched a little. "Well…" I coughed in the back of my throat and tried to think of something to say, since I was sure WolfMart probably wasn't renowned for its five-star accommodations.

I'm sorry? Did the car run smoother back then? Should I take my shoes off inside my lair?

I settled on just opening my door and getting out.

Dallas followed suit, clicking open his own door a few seconds behind me. He swung his feet out and shot up into a standing position.

Not the best idea with a hole through your middle.

He wavered on his feet for a couple seconds, his face going white, then toppled back over into the backseat. That was just what I needed. We couldn't even walk to a building that was a stupid twenty feet away without me hauling him.

Extra chance for me to redeem myself. Fantastic.

Mustering up my pathetic lack of strength, I bent over and pulled him up with me, throwing one of his arms across my shoulders. Nope, that wasn't working.

Like it wasn't taking enough of my strength to just keep me upright at this point…

I glared at the top of Dallas's head, "You did this on purpose, didn't you?" Biting my lip, I pulled him around so I could get my arms under his legs and back.

His head flopped back against my arm as I stood.

Nursemaid Dankworth, at your service.

I limped us both towards the door, lecturing Dallas under my breath on how passing out was no way to face life's problems.

"It would have been easier for me to just conk myself on the head back there instead of talking to the gang and sounding knowledgeable about my own stupid life," I propped his legs up on one of mine as I pushed open the door. "but did I cop out like that? No, I bucked up and stayed conscious…"

My voice trailed off into a low growl as I pushed inside to the noises of people talking. I just about fell over as I tried to get my arm back under my protégé's legs.

The air around us was only slightly warmer than the air outside. I took in a breath, trying to place the smell. Cigarette smoke, definitely. Something like beer or some other sort of alcohol. And then something homey and sweet smelling… vanilla?

Evil smells like vanilla? I frowned in confusion, adjusting my grip on Dallas again.

"You knock him out?" Roy's voice came from somewhere nearby.

Yeah, like I'd put myself through this on purpose. "No," I grunted, "He just stood up a little too fast."

"Well at least he's not zapping all over the place this time," the disembodied Roy-voice observed. "That was a pain to deal with. Teleportation junk…"

Now I was starting to doubt my hearing. *Dallas… teleporting? What in the name of…?*

I swiveled around, trying to locate Roy. He was sitting on top of a stack of shipping pallets, swinging his legs and chewing on his toothpick. Pushing off with his hands, he vaulted to the ground, his red sneakers landing with a loud smack on the cement floor next to me.

He nodded to Dallas. "Want me to put 'im somewhere?"

"Th-that would be great, yeah," I handed Dallas off to him and resisted my own urge to collapse right there.

"Your head any better?" Roy effortlessly pulled Dallas into a piggyback position as he spoke.

I shrugged. "A little… I guess."

He shrugged back and turned, giving a little whistle. Cardboard came popping out from around the corner of one of the old grocery aisles and saluted both of us with a grin.

"Wolf's here so you can head back now," Roy informed her. Then, to me: "They're just hanging out back there right now. News was hungry."

And that probably doomed any pantry store we had…

Roy started back towards a corner with a few doors. Cardboard glanced briefly at me, then skipped off down the aisle without bothering to wait up.

I took a couple of deep breaths to try and clear my head and walked slowly down the same aisle, following the sound of voices. Sound bounced off the bare, metal shelves and echoed through the dimly lit building. It was a lot more sinister inside the store than outside. What a way to make creepy work on a budget.

My eyes adjusted to the dark and I saw a few bits of machinery and wire sitting at the back of the shelves at intervals. News had said Liza and I were mechanics on something…

I peeked around the end of the row and saw Bad News, Liza and Chris all sitting in different chairs by a shabby old lamp. Liza and News were passing a tub of chocolate ice cream back and forth while they talked.

I was getting the impression that News had a thing for ice cream.

Chris sat frowning from under his hat and drumming his fingers on his chair arm. I wasn't sure if he disapproved of the ice cream's presence or the fact that he wasn't getting any.

Cardboard jumped into an old, flower patterned camp chair next to him, her wide smile providing a huge contrast for Chris and making me once again marvel at how both of them could be in the same gang.

I stepped out and walked towards the small circle. Bad News somehow spotted me in the dark with sunglasses on and waved with his spoon, gesturing towards the biggest chair.

I took the directed seat: a giant, leather, wing-backed chair. Very mastermind-esque. Went with my leather jacket, too. News handed me a spoon and I got myself a scoop of ice cream out of the tub.

"Despite all distractions…" Chris cuffed up one sleeve of his flannel shirt and shot me a look, "Are we still on for tomorrow?"

Clearly my hostage decision still wasn't a hit with him.

I swallowed my bite with effort, "We should be…" I stopped and thought of something ambiguous, "… that is, if everything else is ready." Liza and News's conversation stopped and I hoped desperately they'd say something that would clue me in to my evil schemes, since News seemed to forget how much I didn't know.

Liza licked daintily at the ice cream on her enormous spoon, "So, I *did* get the bomb finished earlier…" Her tone of voice was what any other girl would have used to say she got her hair cut. She smiled over at me like I should be proud.

That was the kind of mechanic she was?

I choked on my ice cream but coughed into my elbow and managed to avert most of the attention.

"Finally got that one circuit worked out?" asked Roy as he walked up and boosted onto an old barstool.

Liza sucked the rest of the chocolate off the spoon and then spun it around her small fingers. "Yep. Finally. It's a big old thing now that everything's hooked up, but Bad's truck should get it there alright."

News nodded and smiled.

"That thing takes forever to get moving." Roy groaned, "What about my ride?"

Liza snorted, "If 'your ride' had more than a square foot of trunk space, I'd consider it."

She dug out another spoonful of chocolate ice cream and resumed her dainty licking, "After all, no pillbox is gonna blow up a baseball stadium."

Chapter 6: All The Good Villain Bits

Quick tally.

I now have a gang, a bomb, a hostage, an evil hideout and a plan to blow up a baseball stadium killing who-knows-how-many people.

And to stay in character as myself right now, I should be calmly eating ice cream.

Add "no conscience" to the list.

It was true. I was a horrible human being. A murderer. I had yet to see anything hinting at the alternative.

Probably manifest destiny, if my name was Wolfgang Dankworth...

I resent manifest destiny.

"Also, the magnet on the back was a good addition, Wolfy," Liza's voice brought me back to the uncomfortable present. "I installed that yesterday."

I cleared my throat around the ice cream I was having trouble swallowing. "Great. Yeah."

"Should play through smooth as silk after all these bugs we had to work through." Liza resumed her mesmerizing spoon spinning. "One would hope."

Roy sat on his barstool, tossing a ping-pong ball to himself. "Hey, News — you might want to take a look at Dallas, back there," he nodded towards back where he'd just come from. "I mean, normally I wouldn't mind, but much more blood loss and he won't be mobile at all. It's always a pain to bring hostages along anyway. Having to *drag* them…"

Bad News frowned thoughtfully, twisting his mouth to one side. "Yeeeah, but I gotta make lunch, man." He looked over at Liza. "Think you could check him out? I mean, you know a bit of that first aid stuff."

Liza shrugged and stuck her spoon back in the ice cream container. "Sure."

"I'll… um…" I stuttered as I stood up, "I'll go with you. Just… in case you need help. Or intimidation… or something." The voice of pure evil, I'm sure. They all cower in fear of me.

She gave me an odd look and a half hidden smile. "If you want to." She started walking towards the doors at the back.

I caught a thumbs-up from Bad News as he ducked into the kitchen and a confused frown from Chris. Not much I could do in reply to both of them at once, so I just turned back and took a couple of longer steps to catch back up with Liza.

She looked over at me and smirked, "I'm sure Lucius has been keeping a good eye on Knight for us."

Lucius? I had more gang members? Probably a hooded executioner or something lovely like that.

I nodded, forcing a chuckle back, "Just as long as he understood we were keeping the prisoner alive…"

"There is that." Liza laughed.

There were footsteps following Liza's and mine and I glanced over my shoulder. Chris was walking along behind us. He nodded to me.

Just what I needed. Someone else to try and keep up the pathetic act with. Like he wasn't suspicious enough already.

Liza glanced back too, but seemed unperturbed by the addition to our group. She reached one of the doors with the scratchy words: "Employees Only" painted on it and turned the knob, pushing it open. Dim yellow light came from the inside.

"Yeah, he'd prolly eat Knight's gizzard or something if Roy wasn't clear with him." Her face was straight and her tone earnest. As matter-of-fact as you could get.

Holy smoke, did I run a tribe of cannibals? I mean, I knew this was a dangerous place for Dallas to be, but I hadn't counted having his organs eaten into the danger tally.

And he had a nice, gaping wound to get the process started...

I turned my head aside for a couple of seconds while I got my gag reflex under control. Throwing up would be a bit hard to explain, if gizzard eating was so commonplace here.

Chris stopped next to me and raised an eyebrow.

"Coming or what, Wolfy?" Liza's voice came from inside the room.

I swallowed hard and put a hand on my stomach, "Yep." I slipped through the door after Liza, Chris following close behind.

Dallas lay sideways on a little floor cot, his face pale, his brown hair even messier and his white shirt more bloodstained. But it didn't look like anyone had been trying to eat his gizzard.

My muscles un-tensed a little, and I glanced around the rest of the room. Nothing horribly unusual decorated the area. No rotting bones, thank heaven. Just a few wooden chairs... a cupboard... a lamp.

Hold on, though.

I squinted at the lamp. The lampshade had a huge claw mark across it. Three huge claw marks were torn through the cloth and fabric scraps dangled from the edges.

It looked like some ominous horror movie clue to the monster hiding in the basement. I felt goosebumps on my arms.

I swallowed and opened my mouth to say something, but an

inhuman screech cut me off. A lightning fast shadow and the flash of something sharp descended towards me with a ghostly whoosh. I barely had time to take a step back before something dug into my shoulder and pushed with an unexpected weight.

I yelped, stumbling back and reaching to whack it off. What on earth...?

"Wolfgang, really." Chris stepped closer. His tone tinged with skepticism and annoyance.

The something on my shoulder stared at me with wide eyes set in a dark face, calm as anything.

It was a dark brown, almost black falcon. Tilting its head to one side, it blinked those wide eyes at me like it was asking what it had done wrong. Besides give me a heart attack, of course.

"You rascal," Liza pinched the end of the big bird's beak, scrunching her nose, "Always scaring the socks off everyone, aren't you, Lucius? Even got Wolfy that time."

The bird made chirruping noise in the back of his throat.

Lucius.

The gizzard-eating conversation was only slightly less disturbing now.

Chris raised an eyebrow at me and I swallowed.

"You should really train him out of doing that to everyone," Liza advised, letting go of the bird's beak. "He'll claw someone's face off one of these days."

I tried to stop my hand from shaking as much as I petted down the feathers on the side of the Lucius's head. He closed his eyes contentedly and rubbed against my hand.

Man, I didn't leave out any of the good villain bits, did I? I just couldn't hold my head high if I didn't have a creepy pet.

"So, you shot a hole in him or what?"

I looked down to see Liza kneeling next to the cot and rolling Dallas over roughly. She hadn't really seemed that rough until then. Dallas's face scrunched and he gave a barely audible moan.

I winced for Dallas and nodded, dropping my hand down to stick in my coat pocket. Having a big bird sitting on my shoulder was really awkward for my balance. I adjusted my stance. Did I usually just walk around like this? Or did I keep Lucius in a cage and bring him out for only especially sinister occasions?

Liza pulled up Dallas's shirt a bit and unwrapped News's Ace bandage. She examined the wound for a minute, prodding with her small fingers, then pushed to her feet. "Well, he'll live, looks like," she commented as she walked over to the cupboard. A small box sat inside and she pulled it out.

"It'll be a bit of a stretch, bringing him for tomorrow…"

Chris coughed, "If that's still your plan, that is."

In case he hadn't blatantly stated his opinion enough already.

"… but we should be able to manage." Liza sat back down next to Dallas with her legs crossed. She pulled the lid off the top of the box and got out a bundle of bandages, a rag and a bottle that looked suspiciously like whiskey.

After tilting her head to look at the wound a bit more, she wiped off a good amount of the blood with the rag. "I'll just disinfect it and wrap it up really quick. Get some water down his skinny throat and he should be okay for tomorrow."

Liza grabbed the bottle and gave the cork a quick twist, popping it out. She sniffed it, took a quick swig and then doused a generous amount onto Dallas's middle.

That woke him up.

Dallas let out a yell and curled in on himself to hold his stomach. He opened one of his eyes to squint up at Liza.

Liza propped a hand on one hip and raised an eyebrow, unimpressed with his pain. "C'mon," she tucked her teal hair behind one ear. "Straighten back up so I can get you patched."

Dallas's gaze scanned the room for a few seconds, coming to rest on me. His eyes widened, the fright only growing.

I raised my eyebrows and tilted my head a little, shrugging. Remembrance seemed to come back then and he relaxed slightly. Holding his breath, he pulled his arms away and lay flat and tense on the cot.

Nice to know I was somewhat of a reassuring sight — even

with the evil bird on my shoulder.

Liza grabbed some white cloth and a fresh bandage and, with a few quick wraps and pins, Dallas had a bandage around his middle that looked like it might actually help his health.

Dallas opened his scrunched-shut eyes and peered down at the new bandage, then looked back up at his turquoise-haired nurse. "Thank you." His voice was dry and cracked.

"It's just so we don't have to drag you like a sack of potatoes tomorrow," Liza informed him, not making eye contact as she whisked her things back into the shoebox. She grabbed a bottle of water off the nightstand and shoved it at him. "Drink up, boy wonder."

Dallas closed his hand around the bottle and pushed himself into a stiff sitting position. He looked over at me, "Tomorrow?"

I cleared my throat and put my hands on my hips, which was a little awkward for Lucius to keep his balance. "We... blowing up a baseball stadium." Lucius flapped a bit, whapping my face. I winced.

Chris's eyebrows went up and he gave me a sideways look, which I ignored. Did this guy have any other moods than "ticked off" and "aloof disapproval"?

I was the gang leader. I could make decisions without consulting Sheriff Grumpy. Or at least, I hoped I could.

"Alright," Dallas said, ducking his head before any of us could see his expression, and taking a hesitant drink from his water bottle.

It was quiet for a couple of seconds, though I could feel tension starting to simmer under the surface.

"Justice, Mr. Knight," Chris's voice broke in. "Long overdue justice." His tone made my skin crawl. Even, but brimming with venom. His jaw was tight.

Liza stood to put her things back and I could see a similar look coming onto her face. She shoved the box into the cupboard, then looked back at Dallas. "You're such a *hero*. You know a bit about that, don't you?"

Dallas kept his voice quiet and didn't look up. "Enough to know the right and wrong ways to get it. And the wrong people to blame."

Liza gave him a tight smile, but her eyes narrowed angrily. "I'm sure you do. Though I have a feeling you're a bit biased, Knight."

I had a feeling I should have been the one leading this dispute, not the one standing cluelessly off to the side. Clearing my throat a little, I attempted to add to the conversation.

"Well, too bad we didn't run my plan past you, then, Dallas." I kept my voice a tone that was hard to distinguish between sarcastic and serious.

"Too late for that now," Chris growled, keeping his gaze smoldering into Dallas. "Your chance to do something about it was gone a long time ago."

Liza chewed her lip and leaned down again. "You're lucky to be even breathing right now. And there's no zapping away from us this time."

Zapping. Teleporting. There it was again. What were they talking about?

Chris shook his head. "You could never seem to get to the right places with that, anyway. Always late." He muttered something that sounded like "one time, in particular," under his breath.

Dallas didn't shoot any more comments back, but just nursed on his water bottle.

I scrambled to grab some loose end of the conversation to tie in. "So you'd better not try anything tomorrow. No… zapping." *Whatever that meant…*

That comment seemed to pop the tension bubble in the room.

Liza turned her head and gave me a strange look. "Are you feeling okay, Wolfy?"

Okay, so I tied that end in wrong. Time to return to News's temporary insanity plea.

I blinked a couple of times and put a hand to my head, which protested painfully at my touch. My knees felt close to returning to

Jello state. I winced, crossing my eyes slightly to add to the effect. "I… think I should go lie down."

Which was no lie.

Much more and I felt like I could drop dead from all the mental and physical exhaustion. I literally couldn't remember the last time I'd had a good sleep. And passing out a couple of times didn't count as restful.

"Well, your room's right down the hall," Chris folded his arms over his chest and nodded to the door.

I could see it in his eyes that he was testing me. He knew something else was up.

I swallowed. "Um… yeah, right. I'll go." I started for the door, barely catching myself on the hinge as one of my knees started to give out. Lucius flapped off my shoulder, hopping to the ground and looking at me.

Liza's doubtful voice came from behind me as I stumbled into the hall. "Chris, why don't you go with him?"

There was a second of silence, then a grunt of assent. One of Chris's rough hands grabbed over the leather of my jacket sleeve and pulled me up straighter as we walked. Lucius hopped up onto my other shoulder for the ride. We passed a few other scratchy "employees only" doors in the short hall before turning a corner and stopping.

A door to the outside and one more door that looked like it used to read "storage".

Only the "sto" was mostly rusted off. So a door that read "rage".

Classy.

Chris nodded. "Think you can limp the last few feet to your bed without me?"

"Ah, yeah. I'll be good." I forced a grin and nodded back at him. "Thanks." I pushed the door open and looked in, trying not to look like it was the first time I remembered seeing the place.

I'd gotten the impression from my car that I was a tidy sort of person. My room canceled that out. Junk of all sorts — papers, bits of machinery and tools — littered the floor and piled in the corners. There was a beat-up desk sort of thing with a chair against one wall. The curtains seemed to be from a matching set of the one at News's shack.

Lucius jumped off my shoulder and flapped in towards a bird perch by the window. I rubbed at my shoulder, getting used to the shift in weight.

Across from the desk, a small mattress on a grungy boxspring was pushed up against the wall with a few blankets tossed over it. By far the most beautiful thing in the room. I felt like I was looking at paradise... the only thing I wanted... the softest bed in the world...

I'd probably been looking for too long, so I glanced back.

Chris didn't move, still giving me a strange look. His eyes narrowed slightly, showing the wrinkles at the corners.

I felt weird going in while he was still standing there like he was going to say something, so I just kept my hand on the knob and waited.

Chris finally spoke, his gravelly voice low. "We haven't found your phone yet, but... there was an alarm on it earlier this morning. Rang for a minute or so. We looked around, but couldn't figure out where it was coming from." He stuck his thumbs through his belt loops again. "You know what the alarm was for?"

I opened and closed my mouth, shrugging helplessly. "N-no... well... for tomorrow, I guess. Just a reminder... thing."

He stuck his tongue in his cheek and his brown eyes met mine. "Big step we're taking tomorrow."

"Justice," I agreed, simply parroting him from earlier.

"Make him pay," Chris nodded, still locked on my gaze. "Eye for an eye. For your mom... your dad... your brother... and your sister..."

I'd only looked at the note in my pocket that one time, but one of the names popped back into my head and came out my mouth.

"Eloisa."

The name came out in a different tone for some reason.

The doubt I saw in his gaze evaporated. "Yes. Eloisa." Another second and he put a hand on my shoulder, squeezing. "It's about time Utah's *superhero* got a taste of his own medicine, Wolfgang. I'm glad to be part of the team serving it to him."

I nearly choked.

A superhero?

All the good villain bits. My arch-nemesis couldn't just be a normal guy; I have to get a superhero.

Chapter 7: Explosives

I can't begin to describe how good it was to get out of that tuxedo. My wardrobe was actually that of a normal human's, which was a relief. I was able to get myself into something not covered in blood and ice cream splatters.

I had under a minute to appreciate my clean jeans and t-shirt before finally passing out on that heavenly, unmade bed. Ah, sleep… that wonderful thing I couldn't even remember having.

I slept like a dead brick.

Cardboard came bouncing in and woke me up at eleven, though. Early bird.

"Time to get up! Breakfast!" Her chirping voice shrilled through the room. Pattering footsteps receded down the hall.

I lay in bed, blinking at the ceiling for a good ten seconds before remembering what that knot in my stomach was about.

I'm a villain. And today I'm going to plant a bomb.

Right.

Big day.

I pushed myself up on my elbow and rubbed my face, trying to keep my eyes from closing again. They closed anyway. Groaning, I forced myself to get my feet planted on the floor. I fumbled around to grab my jacket off the end of the bed and pulled it on as I staggered out through the door.

I was vaguely aware of a whooshing flap overhead as the door swung shut. The hall seemed to tilt under my feet and the light coming in through the few windows seemed way too bright.

How had I gotten into that room in the first place? How was I going I get to... wherever I was supposed to get to?

I stood there, blinking hard for a few seconds and trying to get my bearings. Where was Cardboard, anyway? She'd just woken me up a few minutes ago...

My head pounded and I ached all over. Going back to bed and sleeping the rest of the day sounded like a much better plan than going out and blowing stuff up. I was just about to follow through with my new and improved plan when Mr. Bad News himself showed up.

"Good morning," he gave a little wave and grinned at me. His sunglasses and tie were off, though his hat was still in place. A wet dishtowel hung over his shoulder. That last bit seemed more of a scullery maid thing than a hit man thing.

Does a giant... do my dishes?

My brain wasn't at the capacity to register where exactly he'd come from, so I was just as lost as before.

"G'morning." I rubbed my hand over my eyes again and through my hair, giving a yawn that nearly split my face. I blinked hard, trying to get rid of the gritty feeling, and squinted up at News. "So... is there food?" My voice sounded croaky with exhaustion.

He nodded. "Yep. I made cake. There's some left over from breakfast."

Life was just one big birthday party for this guy. Did we eat anything other than cake and ice cream here?

"Feeling any better?" News lowered his voice and leaned a

little closer, "and you still got that whole amnesia thing going on?"

I shook my head, then nodded. I ran both my hands over my face and muttered under my breath. Man, I felt like I could just keel over.

One more fact to take note of, for future reference: I'm very much not a morning person. Probably from bad habits of staying up past midnight and murdering people.

Bad News rumpled my hair, even though it really didn't need the extra help. "Do you want some coffee?"

I gave a short, humorless laugh, "Does a heart attack victim want a defibrillator?"

News snickered and tipped his head to one side, "Food's over here." He started walking.

Forcing my legs to move, I followed him towards the back, over to a bar counter and kitchen. New addition into my map of this place. It looked like it used to be a grocery store bakery, when this place was still in business. And now it was a gang bakery, so we could come gorge on sugar when we weren't committing acts of atrocity. How charming.

A couple of spinning stools sat nearby and Lucius was perched on the edge of the counter. I waved to him, even though that probably means nothing to birds, got up on one of the stools and laid my head down on the counter.

I never thought a countertop could feel so soft.

Lucius came over and started pulling on my hair with his beak. Team effort to make sure my hair kept up the rebellion against gravity.

"Our fearless leader awakens," a British accented voice came from behind me. There were footsteps and a soft thump of someone sitting down on the stool next to me.

"Barely," I mumbled into the counter, waving a hand at Lucius to try and get him away. "How's… the hostage?"

"I can carry my own weight," said a quiet voice that was distinctly not Liza's. I lifted my head to see Dallas, sitting unsteadily on the stool next to Liza in a fresh, green shirt. Probably my green shirt, since it looked way too big for him. He held the sides of the stool cautiously as he sat.

Liza gave him a look, "Not technically. He at least needs to lean on one of us, if he's to stay up for any extended amount of time. Still…" she nodded to me, "He's on the mend. And won't be a total deadweight as a hostage."

There was a scooch noise on the counter and a plate bumped into my knuckles. I looked down to see a hefty piece of chocolate cake on it. News pushed a mug of black coffee up next to it, grinned, then stabbed a fork into the cake like he was murdering it.

I jumped at the "clank" of the fork hitting the plate. Lucius gave the cake a weird look and flapped off.

"Th-thanks," I grabbed the coffee and took a long gulp, letting the strong, cigarette-smoky taste burn down my throat. The bitterness filled my mouth and spread down, almost making my eyes water. I finished my swallow and coughed into my elbow.

Holy smoke, Bad News must double duty this stuff as fuel for his monster truck…

"Keep an eye on Knight for a second," Liza slid off her stool, her bare feet hitting the floor. "I'm gonna go load the disguises."

Disguises? I almost asked, but my vocal cords were still recovering from the coffee assault.

"So," I managed, after I'd recovered my voice and Liza was around the corner, "what time are we taking off?" *On our lovely errand of killing civilians?*

"The bomb's already in the truck, so as soon as you're finished." News swiped a rag over the counter, barely missing my breakfast, "Eat up, Champ." He nodded and shot me a grin.

Dallas and I exchanged a look.

I ate my cake very slowly.

#

I was especially thankful for two things on the drive to Salt Lake City: one, Schoolhouse Rock is a pretty good conversation killer on long car drives; and two, gang leaders always get shotgun, despite all protestations from members.

Diesel trucks aren't really smooth riding, so leaning my head on the window and conking back out didn't really work. And I wasn't tired enough to willingly give myself more head trauma.

I sat sideways in my seat and watched out the window as we came into town. My hands were starting to shake again, so I stuck them in my jacket pockets. I felt my fingertips again brush the worn paper in my pocket. The secret revenge note or something.

I pulled it out, unfolded it with one hand and looked over the scrawled words again. One side was torn and blue guiding lines striped the page. Not that I seemed to have paid any attention to the lines.

The tiny wet spot still puckered the paper and there was a dark smear from the blood on my hand when I'd taken it out before.

Blood, tears… and by how sticky my palms were, I'd say I now had sweat on the note, too. A completed collection of total dedication to that paper scrap.

I rubbed a finger over it, feeling how hard the pen had pressed on the paper.

That which killed shall be killed. Die by the sword.

So I was killing someone who was a killer themselves? Pot call the kettle black, but it made me feel better for a half second before I remembered we were using a big bomb, not a sniper. Plenty of innocent people would die, along with whomever I was trying to get.

Who did I think was worth that many other lives? How was I justifying this?

"I'd think…" Roy's voice came from right next to my shoulder and I jumped, "that you'd have that thing drilled into your head by now. Reading it before *every* strike…"

I folded the note in half in my hand and pulled away from him reflexively.

"What's even on that thing that's so important, anyway?" he made a lazy swipe at the paper.

I quickly stuffed it back in my pocket and redirected my gaze out the window without responding.

"I saw a little bit over his shoulder," Cardboard piped, "I think it said… die by the sword?" She looked over at Liza, who raised an eyebrow.

"Ohh, so that's where you got all those pep-talks?" Roy leaned forward interestedly.

"Drop it, guys." Bad News snapped from the front.

The car went quiet. I telepathically thanked News.

We pulled up across the street from a full parking lot and the engine sputtered to a stop as Bad News put the truck into park. He straightened his tie. "We're here."

Yippee.

I unbuckled and hopped out of the truck onto the blacktop. The tires, tar and a faint whiff of popcorn scented the air. The sun's heat soaked into my black jacket, but the air was still chilly.

Roy hopped out right after me, and Cardboard followed, tugging Chris out of the back seat.

Liza gave Dallas a pat on the back and hopped out to go to the truck bed, leaving her patient to get out of the tall truck by himself.

I rolled my eyes when I was sure she wasn't looking and helped Dallas down myself. He stumbled a bit upon hitting the pavement, but he quickly shifted to leaning his weight on the side of the truck.

He nodded to me, only wincing a little. "Thank you."

"C'mon," Bad News slammed his door shut on the car and came around to our side, swinging his arms. "Let's get the disguises and bomb bits handed out."

I raised my eyebrows in mock enthusiasm. "Yes, let's." And let's announce it to the whole neighborhood, while we're at it.

We came around the back, News unceremoniously dragging Dallas behind him.

I stopped in my tracks and blinked a couple of times to make sure of what I was seeing. Bad News wasn't kidding about disguises… this was a practiced drill.

Roy was busy slicking his spiked hair down into a side-part. Round glasses perched on the end of his nose and a neat polo shirt took the place of his normal ratty t-shirt, though a toothpick still poked out from in between his teeth. Liza wore a blonde wig and a flowy skirt. Chris's hat and flannel shirt had disappeared, replaced by a baseball hat and t-shirt.

Cardboard seemed to be the only one who hadn't totally transformed her appearance. Well, with the exception of Dallas and Bad News…

Liza adjusted her wig, looked back over my shoulder and grinned. "That's a good look for you, News."

I turned around and bit down on my tongue hard to keep from cursing.

"Well?" Bad News grinned at me from under the brim of his red, white and blue top hat. The stick-on goatee stuck to his chin moved in a disturbing way as he spoke. "They got all the mascots here. See? I'm Uncle Sam."

If he were really Uncle Sam, it would be enough to make any sane person want to leave the country.

I had no idea how he'd produced the blue-silk coat and red and white striped trousers so quickly, but he looked even bigger with them slipped over his other clothes.

I opened and closed my mouth a couple of times before getting my voice back. "H-how did you…? Where…?"

News shrugged, slipping his sunglasses back on and giving his fake goatee a thoughtful stroke. "I went out last night and got a drink with the actual guy who's supposed to be Uncle Sam. I let things get a little competitive." He chuckled. "Don't worry, Wolf. He won't be showing up today."

I hoped that only meant the guy was hungover and not… dead.

Liza laughed from behind me. "Enough gawking. You're the only one left, Wolfy." I turned to see her reaching up into the truck bed.

Oh no. What was I going to dress as now? Dracula?

She pulled a bundle out and unrolled it. Revealed were an awful, red-haired wig and a green argyle sweater

I saw Dallas's eyebrows go up as he glanced over at me.

Nope. This was more horrifying than dressing as Dracula.

Liza just smirked at me and stood on tiptoe to slap the wig on top of my head. It fell partway down over my eyes. I pushed it up so I could see and held up my hands to defend from that sweater.

"Come on," Liza swung the sweater in one hand, holding it out to me.

Chris checked his watch and stationed himself by Dallas. "We don't have all day, Wolfgang. Put it on."

Putting that on would require taking off my jacket — the one thing that had stayed with me from the moment I first woke up. Pretty much my armor... my one security in this whole craziness.

And I was supposed to take it off for... that green argyle monstrosity?

All those thoughts flashed through my head in a split second and came out my mouth in one word.

"No."

I straightened my leather jacket defensively.

Roy blinked at me through his fake glasses. "Dude, it's just... for a little bit."

Chris cursed at me under his breath. Bad News seemed not to notice, busy adjusting his costume.

I tensely stepped backwards from the second part of my disguise. Stiff, reddish-brown hair flopped down almost into my eyes from the wig.

Liza frowned at me for a few seconds before looking over at Chris. "Well... y'know the cowlick and that gash on the back of his head are the most obvious things." She looked back at me, tipping her head. "You could pass, I suppose. If you keep your head down. It's not a big deal."

She looked to News for approval and he nodded consent.

I relaxed a little.

Liza and Chris exchanged a look and Liza shrugged before hopping up into the truck bed. She shoved the sweater aside, pulling the tarp off the thing in the corner instead.

But it wasn't a bomb... it was just a pile of baggage underneath.

She turned with a grin. "Well... come get your crackers, lads." We all came closer and Liza pushed a briefcase towards News, a backpack towards Chris and a messenger bag over to Roy.

Cardboard bounced up and down, gripping the edge of the truck bed. "What do I carry? What about me?"

"You, Cardy..." Liza handed her a smaller, pink and orange striped backpack, "get to carry the giant magnet. Careful with that, now."

Cardboard reached her hands up for the backpack and almost dropped it from the sudden weight, but managed to haul it up and onto her back.

Roy came up from behind and tugged one of her curls. His smile looked a bit nervous. "First strike you're here for, kiddo. Excited to be helping out?"

The question was met with a solemn nod.

Yeah, start the mad bombers young. They'll be even more likely to spend their days in prison cells.

I stuck my hands in my pockets and tried to ignore my churning stomach.

"Wolfy, c'mere" Liza waved me over as the rest of the gang moved away.

I came closer and hopped up into the truck bed, nearly falling on my face as my temperamental muscles decided to take a break again. The wig fell sideways over my eyes. I pushed it back up and scooted over to Liza, some of my dignity still intact, "What is it?"

"So, this bit's going in your bag," she held up a plate-sized piece of machinery with a nest of wires on top.

"This right here was the bugger that hung us up last time." She gently twanged on a strand of yellow-coated wire as she ran her fingers over the piece. "See, if this spot disconnected, all we'd get would be an impressive short-circuit. That's hardly what we're looking for. And it's somewhat fragile. So…" Liza slid the bomb piece into a blanket-padded backpack and gave it a pat. "You're carrying this one."

I felt a sort of reluctance in her grip as she handed it to me. Almost like she was handing me her child to hold. I took it gently and swung it onto my shoulder. "Got it."

She winced at the thump of the bag hitting my back. I got a feeling I wasn't a very reassuring babysitter.

We both slid off the end of the truck and joined the rest of the gang. They were standing seriously. Quite the contrast with their ridiculous disguises. The gang held their bags close and their stances almost looked like soldiers about to head out into battle. Dallas, with Chris's death grip on his arm, looked like exactly what he was: a hostage.

They all turned as I approached.

I stopped. *Oh, please don't let me be in the habit of giving speeches to rally my thugs…*

Still, they waited. Everyone's eyes were on me.

News made a small gesture with his hand and tipped his head briefly, which was meant to be a helpful hint, I'm sure. Only, I didn't understand it in the slightest.

Though by the looks on everyone's faces, I was pretty sure by now that they expected some kind of speech. I cleared my throat.

"Well…" I took in a breath, "We've all been waiting for this for a long time… and… so have I." I bit my tongue as the words came out.

Charisma. That's me.

Say something deep-sounding, you idiot.

"But, it will be worth the wait, I'm sure. That which killed shall be killed. We'll just go in there…" I faltered again. Holy smoke, I was bad at this.

" And show Amazing Man that the classic hero's way is not always the right way." Bad News finished for me. The gang nodded in agreement, seeming satisfied with the speech.

I made a small thank-you motion to Bad News.

He gave a nod, adjusted his top hat, then swept an arm out towards the entrance to the stadium. I caught the hint.

"Onwards, then!" I imitated News's motion, "To... plant the explosives!"

Poetry.

Chapter 8: Short circuit

As we came into the stadium, I was really glad ticket sellers can't read minds. My thoughts were pretty much just a loop of *"we're carrying a bomb... we're carrying a bomb... we're carrying a bomb..."* I kept my hands deep in my jacket pockets, where they shook like I'd stuck them in a freezer. My head pounded even worse than when I'd first woken up and I felt sick to my stomach.

We came through the gate in shifts. Roy, Cardboard and Chris had gone ahead of us with Dallas. I followed with Liza and Bad News a minute or so later.

Liza paid for the tickets, casually flirting with the kid at the counter as she did. He distractedly asked about our bags, but just nodded and waved us through when Liza said they were snacks and jackets.

I guess Bad News' look-at-me-I'm-on-stilts act worked, since he only got a smile and wave from the ticket seller. I'll reluctantly admit it was a smart disguise. With his usual outfit, that guy is practically a caricature of what all security guys are supposed to keep out.

I felt like I could breathe again, once we got through the gate, but the nauseous feeling in my stomach still sat there as we met back up with the others and walked through the crowd. Great, so we hadn't gotten arrested. But I knew we should have been… so was it a victory or not?

I looked over at Dallas involuntarily. It was almost like he'd become my compass of sorts. My tiny candle in the dark cave that was my life.

My candle/compass had his eyes closed. Chris kept hauling him along without looking.

"Wait, stop." I kept looking at Dallas and held up my hand. The gang came to a halt and looked at me. Dallas opened his eyes. I let out my breath.

"What?" Dallas and Bad News said at the same time.

I made a motion that everyone could keep walking, trying to bring my heart rate back down to normal. I went to run a hand over my hair and ended up just nearly knocking off that awful wig. I straightened it and put my hand back down.

Chris came up next to me as we kept walking, his eyes narrowed. "Seriously, what?"

"I just…" I shook my head and gestured to Dallas, "He had his eyes closed so I was… concerned."

Chris frowned slightly as we started walking again. "Ah."

Dallas poked his disheveled head around Bad News's red-striped pantaloons so he could see me, "Sorry. I was praying." He bit his lip right after saying it.

Oh.

My stomach twisted strangely at the word. I bit my tongue to keep from asking whether it was for me.

The crowd started filing into the stadium, filling the bleachers. We started to follow. I thought desperately of how we thought this was going to work. What were we going to do? Just sit there and pass all the bomb pieces around until we had it put together, then toss it out onto the field with an evil laugh?

Oh yeah. Inconspicuous.

But the upside was that the stupider we were about it, the fewer people would die.

Liza stepped ahead of the group and nodded to a corner near the bathrooms with no one nearby. We all veered off from the main crowd, following her, and grouped together there.

Liza pulled her fake blonde hair over her shoulder and unshouldered her backpack. "Wolfy, News, unzip your packs. Roy, give yours to Knight."

Everyone did as they were told and there was a small, confusing shuffle-around of the backpack contents as everyone gave their pieces to Dallas, News and me.

The last piece went into News's bag. Liza smiled and gave it a reassuring pat as someone glanced our direction.

Great. Giving higher death risks to only her favorite people.

Liza stood upright, pulling her backpack back on. "Right. The seat numbers are…" she looked down at something written on her wrist, "25b through 28b. Roy and I will find them. Cardy can drop her pack in through the bleachers and you guys can go underneath and find it to plant the crackers."

Bad News chuckled. Probably at the "crackers".

Dallas looked sick.

I frowned. Seats. Why was there more than one person?

"Split, then." Roy took Cardboard's hand and started towards the stadium entrance with Chris close behind.

Bad News grabbed Dallas and his bag and began dragging them both off.

I started to follow, but Liza's hand slipped into mine and I stopped. She squeezed my hand and nodded, her mouth set in a firm line.

"Die by the sword, right?"

"Um…" I made a determined face and nodded back. "Yeah. Die by the sword." Like that was supposed to be reassuring. Before she could give me any more disturbing catchphrases, I pulled my hand away and scrambled after my star-spangled Goliath with sunglasses. It took me a few seconds to catch up with his long strides.

"So… where exactly are we heading?" I said out of the side of my mouth.

"Somewhere dark and smelly," he stated bluntly, giving a tug on Dallas's shirt to bring him back up in stride with us.

I suppressed my excitement for our destination. "How are we planning to get there?"

Bad News stopped at a door that we were quite obviously not supposed to go in and tipped his head towards it as he let go of Dallas's arm. "Through this door."

He dug around in his pockets for a couple seconds and fished out a screwdriver that looked microscopic in his huge hands. A few quick spins on the screws around the doorknob, and it was off. After whacking out any working lock mechanism, a few hard kicks against the door and it was practically off its hinges.

News pulled a flashlight out of his jacket and pushed his sunglasses up onto the brim of his top hat. He shot me a grin and nodded to the door, making his fake goatee move strangely. "C'mon." Ducking his head, he disappeared inside the dark, pulling the unwilling Dallas along.

I swallowed, practiced mouth breathing for a second or two, then stepped in after them.

Shafts of dusty light filtered in through the gloom, illuminating various candy wrappers and bits of abandoned food. Footsteps clanged on the metal above us. Dust drifted in front of News's flashlight beam as he shone it around and up. News dropped the bags he was carrying at his feet.

"Now, we wait," he declared.

Waiting in the stinky dark until you can assemble a bomb isn't the nicest way to spend your time, but I didn't have much choice.

Dallas's eyes were closed again, his brow was furrowed and in the dim light I could barely see that his mouth was moving.

I opened my mouth to tell him to knock it off, but then closed it again. He was probably praying for whoever was the intended recipient of our bombing. And they needed as much help as they could get.

There was a fabric scooching noise from a little ways away, then a loud thump as something was pushed in between the bleachers and dropped. News shined his flashlight in that direction and the beam rested on a little pink and orange backpack.

We walked over to it, pulling the other bags along. Bad News set his flashlight to dim and handed it to me while he unzipped Cardboard's pack.

"There's our magnet," he pulled it out with both hands and squinted up at the underside of the bleacher seats above us. "Shine the light up there, will ya?"

I flashed the light upwards and News gave a nod. With a loud clank, the magnet was set in place underneath the bench. The sound echoed and went deeper down into my ears than any sound should. I winced.

"Now, the fun part." News grinned. He rolled up his sleeve and squinted at some marker writing on his arm. "Okay, it's my bag's piece that goes on first…"

It felt like we spent the next year working on assembling the bomb, based on the smudged instructions on Mr. News's arm. Lots of plugs and wires inserting into particular places. Thank heaven Liza color coded them.

Finally, we'd reached the last step at the top of News's arm. I stood on my tiptoes and craned my neck around to read.

"Wolfy's part goes on last," the writing instructed. After a few wire-plugging specifications and switches we needed to flip, there was another note. I tilted my head sideways and squinted at the smudged ink on News's arm.

"DON'T TOUCH THE YELLOW"

That's when I got a great idea. What if I touched the yellow? Augh, I'm brilliant.

Only, there was a gorilla with a flashlight to club me down if

I did, so I was a little concerned. *Well, I can be discreet...*

"Okay, got it." I dropped down onto my flat feet and nodded, nearly shaking my wig loose again. "My piece is the last one."

Dallas, who had been deemed the custodian of the bags, since he couldn't reach the magnet, pulled out my piece and dropped the blanket onto the ground. He held it out to me.

"I suppose you would like to do the honors?" He said it in the tone of someone asking if I wanted sugar with my tea, but I saw the disgust in his eyes.

I tipped my chin up a little, "I would, in fact." I held his gaze as I took it. *You little goody gumdrop... I'm sabotaging my own project right in front of you, isn't that enough?*

I don't think he got all that from my look. Let's add "horrible telepathic communicator" to the extensive list of my faults.

I stood on a couple of empty bags to give me a few inches' more height up to the magnet. My hand trembled slightly as I brushed over the wires, fastening the piece in place.

The very tip of my pinky finger hooked ever-so-lightly on the yellow wire and I felt a tiny pop as one end came loose.

Gotcha.

"Hey, Liza said to not touch the yellow wire."

Bad News's sudden voice just about made me jump into the next state. I shifted my movements to make it look like I was getting a different angle, not having a heart-attack. "Y-yep, I know. Just getting the other wires in place."

I methodically stuck the other wires in place...even though now they'd do absolutely nothing... and flipped two switches. A tiny red light bulb blinked on at half power over on the corner of the bomb. It glared at me like an accusing eye.

"Isn't that supposed to be brighter?" my hit man and anti-conscience mused.

I hopped down, wiping my sweaty palms on my jeans. "Nope." I kept a nervous waver out of my voice and stuck my hands in my pockets to hide their shaking. "I think we're good. Let's head up to the other guys."

We found the gang in seats directly across the stadium from where we'd planted our gift.

Total accident, I'm sure.

Dallas and I slipped into the seats left for us across the aisle. Bad News practically steamrolled everyone to get to his seat.

And there we all sat, waiting for a totally different show than everyone else was.

I went to run one hand over my hair as we stood for the national anthem and almost knocked my wig off again. That thing was annoying. The hand over my heart trembled, despite my strongest willing of it to stay still.

As the last notes were fading away and everyone was starting to sit down, a hand brushed my arm. I jumped at the touch. It was Liza, reaching across the aisle. She grabbed a phone out of a pocket in her ruffled skirt and handed it to me, reaching up to tuck her blonde-wig-hair behind one ear with the other hand.

"Here. Find the app labeled 'Project Eloisa'. I connected it into the wireless network thing I had set up." She kept her voice and expression purely casual.

Eloisa.

Memories pressed forward from the back of my mind. A brief image of a young girl's face, dimpled in a smile, flashed in my vision.

I blinked and it was gone.

My head hurt.

"Thanks," I took the phone from her small, cool hand and clicked it on.

Liza tapped my arm one more time before I pulled back. "The seats to watch are right over there." She pointed to a smaller clump of seats that seemed to be cordoned off for some special group.

"Okay, got it." My voice trembled. How the heck did she

manage to sound so nonchalant about this?

She nodded, "It's your call for when to go."

Wonderful.

I gave her a tight look that was originally supposed to be a grin and sat back in my seat. The phone had turned off again. I slid the bar to unlock it and found the app. It had a little firework symbol on it.

Liza has quite a dark sense of humor.

I decided I'd wait a bit and set the phone in my lap.

It was a good baseball game. The home team was winning, so that was a big hit with all the home fans. I didn't really love the frenzied cheering, which only grated on my already fried nerves and had me nearly jumping out of my wig every time someone made a home run.

Dallas sat ramrod straight in his seat the whole time, clapping mechanically every now and then. But he always kept an eye on the phone in my lap. I didn't blame him. I was doing the same.

He started to move his hand towards it once, but Chris cleared his throat loudly, shifting something at his hip.

A gun.

Dallas stiffened. I winced. He didn't make any more moves towards the phone.

I watched the seats on the other side more than the actual game. For about the first ten minutes, they stayed empty.

I'd started to relax a little. Well, that would solve my problem if the intended bombing recipients just decided not to show up. No use in blowing up empty seats. We could just go back and I would just… not kill anyone.

As if some evil force had heard my wish and decided to grind it into the mud just then, the seat occupants walked up the steps and filed in.

It was a pretty young mom and three little kids, giggling with their hot dogs and cotton candy. The two little boys had brought baseball mitts and the smaller one had decided to wear his as a hat. The little girl wore a team t-shirt that hung down past her knees like a dress.

I felt sick in more ways than one.

I wanted to kill an innocent family. I couldn't have any justification for this. There's nothing anyone can do to make killing little kids right.

But there I sat, detonation button in hand.

I took a deep breath and stuck my hands in my pockets. It was okay. It was just going to short circuit and maybe spew a little smoke. The worst that would happen would be a few bruises.

It was okay. Now, at least.

But what if I hadn't pulled that wire? What if the plan had continued? What if... I hadn't lost my memories? Those poor kids and their mom would probably already be blown sky high. Just the thought seemed to push any memory further back into the shadows of my mind.

I clenched my jaw and concentrated hard on the game going on below. The teams were just switching positions on the field. A voice crackled over the speaker.

"We'd like to welcome some special guests to the game tonight," the voice echoed over the stadium speakers. "Tonight we have joining us the wife and children of our city's own *Amazing Man!*"

The camera screen above the field flicked over to show a mom and three kids, one wearing a baseball glove as a hat, one with a too-big t-shirt and one with his hair spiked in all directions and a sideways grin on his face. Smiling a small smile, the mom stood up, motioning for her kids to do the same. They all stood and waved.

Dallas made a noise in the seat next to me.

I stared.

The kid without the baseball glove on his head. I'd seen his face before. The dimples. The round face. The cowlick.

"Let's give them a hand!" cheering and clapping echoed through the stadium. Even the baseball teams joined in.

Call it a bad sense of timing. Call it dramatic flair. But I decided that moment was a good time to "set off" the bomb.

The instant my finger touched the screen, there was a loud "POP" and a good section of the seats around the bomb visibly jumped. The people around the area wobbled and fell like pieces on a gameboard. The cheering instantly turned to screams as smoke started pouring out from under the bleachers.

My stomach dropped for a second. *Oh jeez, did it work after all?*

But the smoke seemed to be the only damage done beyond some pretty effective frightening.

Pretty much all of my gang's jaws dropped. Dallas looked pretty surprised too, but in a much better way than Liza.

Liza's shocked and disappointed look quickly turned into a furious scowl. She knew what went wrong. And she was going to find out who made it go wrong.

And, oh look, she was turning towards me.

Time to put some theatrical skills to work.

I stood on my seat, ripped off the wig and spiked the phone on the ground with a roar. "That was supposed to WORK! What the…" I tugged at my hair angrily and swore, throwing the wig for extra effect. It hit some bewildered spectator below me in the face.

That got quite a bit of attention. Also absolutely no suspicion from the gang. They were too busy running away. Dallas stayed, petrified, next to me.

"It's the Wolf!" someone screamed. Other people started running in terror.

Yet more proof of my wonderful reputation.

I let out another curse and pointed dramatically towards where the family was, all the kids huddled around their mom, crying, as they moved away from the smoke.

"Just you wait!" I yelled, racking my mind for some villain cliché to make use of. "You haven't seen the last of me! I'll get you yet!"

The lingering screams unexplainably subsided for a second, then there was the start of another cheer. Something told me that it wasn't for my dazzling performance.

Three things happened at once.

I heard an almost bird-like whoosh behind me.

Dallas, who was looking that way to begin with, called out: "Sir!"

And the cheer changed to words. *"Amazing Man!"*

Amazing Man…?

I started to turn, but something from behind cracked against the back of my head, right on the already existing gash.

Then everything exploded into pain and whiteness.

Chapter 9: Hospitality

My very existence on this planet was defined by headache.

For a few minutes, it was the only thing I could feel. Then feeling started tingling back into the other parts of my body.

My fingers twitched and I felt a blanket. Why was there a blanket? It wasn't cold. And who would give me a blanket?

My head throbbed again and I closed my eyes tighter. Soft music drifted in from somewhere in the distance and I heard voices talking seriously a little nearer by.

Swallowing, I forced my eyes open and found myself looking at a cheery yellow ceiling. For some reason, I'd thought it would be grey. Metal or cinderblock... something like that.

Why did my head hurt so much? I tried to pull one of my hands up to put on it, but there was a clank and my hand was held back by something. I frowned and my fingers touched a thin chain, shackling me to a bar along the side of the bed. Handcuffs? I'd think I would remember being handcuffed.

Not this again.

Again?

I closed my eyes, pulling at memories in my muddled mind. Slowly, things began to surface.

There had been a bomb. Something had gone wrong. There was a family. A gang. A boy with green eyes. Why couldn't I remember their names?

One name emerged.

I was Wolfgang Dankworth. The man with the worst luck in the world and about enough memories to fill a teacup.

I groaned. *But how'd I get here?*

The talking voices grew a little louder and I lay still, trying to make out the conversation.

It took effort to focus on the individual words being spoken and work out what they meant. But I felt like I needed to figure it out. It was probably important. Or I'm just a pathological eavesdropper.

"… but turning it back on would really be the best thing for you. I mean, look what almost happened with it off! That had the potential to end much worse than last time. You could have died. As it is, you got shot…"

"Sir, it's really an unnecessary measure. And I'm here now. Everything worked out fine. Turning them back on would just create more… incidents like last time. I can manage without. It won't happen again."

I knew the second voice. That way it said "sir". I shifted slightly under the blankets, careful not to rattle the handcuffs.

What are they talking about? My head pounded rebelliously at the nudge to think.

They dropped in volume again.

"Dallas, we can't take that risk… you'll learn. I'll help you…"

Dallas. Right. That was the green-eyed boy's name.

It was quiet for a minute, then the first voice said something I couldn't hear. There was a sigh.

I shifted again and the chain rattled. I winced for a number of reasons.

Silence.

"I think I'll go check on him," said the second voice.

I had a feeling I was "him."

Footsteps came steadily closer and the noise of a door opening and closing sounded just across the room. More footsteps, then the light thud of someone sitting down.

I kept my eyes closed. My head swam and it felt like the bed tipped. The someone who'd come in shifted in the chair. I took in a slow breath through my nose, though I'm not sure what I thought that would help.

Maybe I could smell who it was through some incredible piece of detective work. I smelled antiseptic and a faint piney smell. The antiseptic was probably me. Pine, though... maybe a lumberjack. A tiny one, because those footsteps were very quiet.

I took a chance and cracked one eye open.

Dallas sat in a folding chair, wearing a dark green jacket over a shirt with a red, white and blue shield on it. His hands were clasped between his knees and he looked out the window with his brow furrowed in thought.

I had my eye open for a couple of seconds before he glanced back over at me. I quickly closed my eye again, hoping he hadn't noticed.

Silence for a couple seconds.

"How's your head?"

Dangit.

I squinted my eyes shut tighter. "About to explode."

"It'll feel a little better in a bit. The painkillers should kick in."

Oh, that's nice. I'm not muddled enough.

That would also explain the needle and tube I'd just noticed going into my arm. Not only had he knocked me out, he had to go pumping things into me without permission. Rude.

I heard Dallas shift in his seat.

Well, as much as I didn't want to put forth the mental effort of making conversation, that did seem like the only way to get any answers.

"So," I began, opening one of my eyes again, "how did I end up... here?" *Wherever "here" is...*

Dallas glanced around the room and rubbed at the back of his head, "Mr. Fernsby brought you. I... talked to him a bit."

I opened my other eye in a pained squint. "Fernsby..." I sorted through the few, fuzzy faces in my memory bank, "Is that the guy with the sunglasses? And the ice cream?" The words slurred together strangely, not sounding like mine.

"No, that's Mr. News. Are you sure you're feeling okay?"

Didn't I just say I felt like mud just two minutes ago? I gave Dallas a look.

He sighed and stood up, pulling something out of his pocket. "Mr. Fernsby is Utah's Hero. Also known as Amazing Man. I'm his sidekick. You're his arch-nemesis. This is his house and he wants to talk to you."

Dallas stepped forward and took a hold on the handcuffs. A quick jab and twist from the thing in his hand, now obviously a key, and the handcuffs clattered limply to the side of the bed.

Oh perfect. Yes, let's chat. We're on such good terms right now. I tried to kill his family... he belted me across the back of the head and nearly cleared my memory again...

Dallas moved around and the cuff fell off my other hand, "Mrs. Fernsby has breakfast and coffee all made."

Well, if you put it *that* way... Any differences can be put aside for the sake of a decent meal.

I sat up a little faster than I probably should have and my head objected piercingly. I put my hand up and felt a bandage wrapped around my head in a thick band.

This Fernsby guy was very illogically hospitable.

Shaking my head, I swung my feet down to the floor, peeled back the tape and pulled out the IV tube. I gritted my teeth and rubbed at the sting on my arm, then stood up.

My vision lost color and started to darken and I felt my knees go wobbly. I'm telling you, headrush is much worse when you have a gaping head wound.

"Easy, now." Dallas held out his hands as if to catch me.

"Hey, you're not the picture of health yourself," I pointed out, my voice hoarse. One of my knees buckled and I barely caught myself on the windowsill.

Dallas came up next to me and pulled my arm over his small shoulders. "It's just a little ways down the hall. I'll let you walk the last stretch yourself if you let me help you for just a bit."

I got my legs under me again pretty well, but Dallas stayed under my arm. I gave him an eyebrow raise. "Not the usual positioning for the two of us going anywhere."

"Let's call it even," he grunted.

I rested just enough weight on him to make him feel helpful, but held myself up the rest of the way.

After a polite disagreement over who would open the door, we made it out into the hall. Fingerprints smudged the yellow walls and generous wads of tape held up crayon doodles.

Higher up, happy family portraits and nature pictures hung in pretty little frames. There was one picture of Dallas and another, taller man being given some sort of trophy thing. Amazing Man, I guessed. He was the one with the wacky outfit and the good hair.

Another one looked like a newspaper action shot, by the blurry, faded printing. One of him flying down and punching a guy in a leather jacket square on the jaw.

Gee, wonder who that could be... I rubbed at my jaw a little.

We moved on past before I got a good look.

I'd get a better look soon, anyway. Just hopefully not at his knuckles.

I swallowed.

"Just around that corner." Dallas nodded down the hall and slipped out from underneath my arm. He stood next to me, steadier on his feet by a microscopic amount.

"Thanks." I stood up tall and squinted at the corner, readying myself. I straightened my leather jacket collar, adjusted my bandage, tried to look cool and walked into the room.

The young mom I'd seen at the stadium stood over the stove, cooking something in a frying pan. A little blond boy sat on the counter watching her.

And on the couch in front of me, a man sat with a little girl in his lap. They were both bent over a book and he was reading softly to her with a smile in his voice.

Any entrance drama I'd concocted melted away. I felt dirty in front of all this. The family. The love.

I wished I could disappear and not ruin the picture in front of me. A hood in a grubby leather jacket kind of wrecked the whole family scene.

Just then, the little girl looked up. Her blue eyes went wide at seeing me.

I raised my hand to wave and started to smile.

The girl screamed and threw a tiny, stuffed pig at me before burying her face in her dad's shoulder.

I flinched as the beanie butt of the pig hit my chest and dropped into my hand awkwardly.

Mr. Fernsby looked up from the book. His blue eyes showed a tiny glint of something akin to apprehension, but he gave me an open, friendly smile that accentuated his square jaw. It almost didn't look forced.

"Hey, you're up! Is your head feeling any better?" He stood, propping his little girl up on his hip with one arm, and held out his other hand to me.

It took me a second to realize he wanted to shake hands.

"Um... yeah. Thanks." I shook his hand. Man, this whole arch-nemesis thing wasn't as bad as I thought it would be.

He stepped back and looked me over for a second, a question in his eyes. He started to open his mouth and tipped his head a little like he was preparing to ask a possibly rude question.

My mind went into overdrive, preparing for the ultimate test of whether or not I could hide my memory loss. I swallowed hard.

I could do it. It worked with the gang. And he didn't know me as well.

Yeah, well there's no Bad News to plead insanity for me this time... I'm supposed to be being antagonistic towards this guy and I don't even know what for...

Mr. Fernsby nodded slowly and licked his lips. "So you don't remember anything?"

Well, I get a big, fat F on that test.

I just blinked at him. Dallas came up beside me and nudged my arm.

"I told him."

The first thing I felt was a gush of relief. It was shortly followed by a slight annoyance at Dallas.

I mean, in hindsight, I probably could have pulled it off. He didn't *need* to tell. I probably could have bluffed my way through. Improvised and all that. I totally could have done it.

Dangit, Dallas.

Oh well. Having something in my life be easy wasn't the end of the world.

I swallowed and nodded to Mr. Fernsby. "Yeah."

He slowly set down his little girl, who let go for a brief second, then latched back onto his pant leg.

A slightly amused smile quirked his mouth. "In that case, we have a lot to talk about."

"You can do it over breakfast," a voice came from the kitchen. "It's ready." Mrs. Fernsby walked to the table with a dish of scrambled eggs and veggies and set it on a little wood holder, then walked over next to us. The little blond boy still trailed behind her.

I felt like someone was missing here, but my head hurt trying to remember who it was.

"Smells great, hon." Mr. Fernsby leaned down and kissed his wife's head.

She frowned slightly as she saw me and set down her dish on the counter. She looked back over at her husband, her expression softening. "With an extra person here, I think we might need to move the table more to the center of the room. You know, so another chair will fit…"

"Absolutely." Charles turned, pushed the chairs aside and gripped the edge of the solid, dark wood table with one hand. He looked over at us and jerked his head a little. "If you folks will step back for a second…"

I just frowned in confusion. What was he going to do?

Dallas grabbed my arm and pulled me backwards just as Mr. Fernsby flexed, pulling on the table.

The table lifted up like it was made out of papier-mâché and Charles effortlessly swung it into a different position. He set it down and patted the top. "That good?"

Mrs. Fernsby twisted her mouth to the side. "Maybe a little bit that way…?" she nodded to one side with her head.

Charles picked it up and moved it again, barely even straining. "How's that?"

"Perfect." She smiled at him and set the dish down on the middle of the table.

I mean, I'd heard he could fly and all that… he *was* a superhero. But *seeing* it…

I realized my mouth was hanging open and quickly closed it, wondering again why I'd chosen to be arch-enemies with a man who could throw my car like a Frisbee if he wanted to.

Charles dusted his hands off like he'd finished as normal a task as drying the dishes, then started moving the chairs back around the table. "Okay, kids. Take a seat."

The little boy and girl jumped up into their seats at the furthest end of the table from me. I sat at a corner and tried to look unintimidating. The effort only got me another "one-wrong-move-and-you're-dead" look from Mrs. Fernsby.

Dallas sat next to me without hesitation, and Mr. Fernsby sat across from me with only a little hesitation. The seat to my left stayed empty.

"I mean *all* of the kids." Mr. Fernsby said, a little louder than his first command.

There was a noise behind the couch, a flash of dirty hoodie and the empty seat next to me held a little boy with a big cowlick, staring at me with bright hazel eyes.

I stared back at him and my stomach did a flip. This was the kid from my picture I had in my wallet. But why did I have a picture of Amazing Man's son? I thought for sure he was my brother…

But the family resemblance to the Fernsbys didn't go very far. What if…?

What, would they steal my brother?

I blinked.

"I win," said the kid, like we'd been in a staring contest. He immediately dove into scooping eggs onto his plate, accompanied by a grand total of two veggies.

After a quick grace-before-meals, just to make me feel more like a godless heathen, everyone started eating.

Mr. Fernsby finished first. He looked around the table and gave me another smile that seemed to almost hold a sort of request for forgiveness. He kept looking at me like that.

After another second, he cleared his throat to break the silence and shifted forward in his seat. "Well… since, with memory loss and all, you don't know us, I suppose some introductions are in order." He gestured between himself and his wife. "So, I'm Charles. This is my beautiful bride, Angela." He put an arm around her before continuing.

He pointed to the little peanuts at the end of the table. "Down there are Jilly and Beckett." His easy tone faltered a little as he moved his gaze to the kid next to me. Charles swallowed a little. "And that's… Leif."

Leif's hand shot up into the air like he was asking for permission to speak, then quickly came back down again as he fixed his gaze on me. He kicked his feet, fidgeting with his hands in his lap. "Hey, did you know that I…"

"… need to eat more vegetables," Angela cut in, rather forcefully. She raised her eyebrows at him. "That's what you were going to say, isn't it?"

Leif wilted in his seat, giving the vegetable dish a baleful look.

I was pretty sure that hadn't been what Leif was going to say, but didn't want to get more on Angela's bad side than I already was.

I swallowed the last of my eggs, "Well... nice to meet you all." Again. You all probably met me as a cold-blooded murderer, before now. But hey, let's enjoy breakfast.

It was pretty quiet for the next few minutes, while the kids finished their food. Leif only whimpered occasionally at the forced veggie eating. I kept thinking I should say something, but at this point I wasn't sure if breaking the silence or keeping it would be more awkward.

Charles ended up doing it for me.

"Okay, kids. We're going to talk for a bit. Can you guys go play Legos?"

"*Yeah!*" Jilly and Beckett ran, tripping over each other, into the other room.

Leif started out of his chair, hesitating at a look from Angela. He tugged at his hair a little. "I can go... right?"

Angela sighed and nodded, and he was gone in a flash. I followed the vanishing cowlick with my gaze, squinting in thought. Yet another thing that made absolutely no sense in my life...

Charles cleared his throat and I straightened in my seat, looking back at him. He held my gaze and his brow furrowed slightly. His blue eyes felt like they were boring holes through my skull.

I remembered when Dallas had done this same thing. At least I wasn't driving this time. I swallowed.

Finally, he blinked and the staredown was over. Mr. Fernsby opened his mouth for a second, then clamped it tightly closed like there was something he didn't want to say. He sighed and looked down at his hands, where they were clasped on the table.

"I've tried many times before... to talk with you like this. Reasonably. Civilly."

The picture I'd seen in the hall of him nearly breaking my

jaw came to mind. I coughed politely.

Charles closed his eyes. "I know it won't mean much to you now. But I just want to tell you again while I have the chance that… I'm sorry. I really am *very* sorry." He dropped his head down almost to the tabletop, guilt twisting his face.

Angela reached over and rubbed a hand on his back. "Honey, it's okay."

Like things could get more confusing. Did he think he had to apologize for having me over for breakfast? If anything, I'd think I should have been apologizing for trying to blow his family up.

I opened my mouth cautiously. "Sorry for what, exactly…?"

"I believe we had something else to address, sir," Dallas broke in. "The note, remember?"

"Right." Charles took a breath and straightened up, pulling his composure back into place. He drummed his fingers on the tabletop for a second. "We need your help, Wolfgang. There are… many things we could discuss here. But to get right to the urgent point…" he reached down, pulled a paper out of his pocket and unfolded it on the table. "We need to know if you heard or remember any details on this."

I leaned forward, pulling the paper towards me and scanning the words. It was a printed note, informing the Fernsby household of a plan to kidnap Leif and daring them to try and stop it.

Signed by me.

I squinted at the writing for a second, taking slight issue with the odd way I wrote the W. My gaze moved down to the kindly included date on which the kidnapping would take place. April 16.

I leaned back and ran a hand through my hair, "Sorry, I'm a little turned around. When is that date?"

Dallas rubbed at his nose, "It's today."

Ah. Now I saw the urgency.

"Well, no one mentioned anything on it when I was around. We were all tied up with the whole baseball stadium bombing thing. And if I'm captured here…" I shrugged, "I would guess the kidnapping would be called off."

Just then, a scream shrilled from the other room. Charles shot to his feet.

"That's Leif."

Chapter 10: Kidnapper

The scream was cut off suddenly, and two other screams took its place.

Everyone around the table shot up out of their seats. Charles took the lead, almost seeming to lift off the ground, he zipped into the other room so fast. His wife and Dallas were right on his heels.

I was the only one plugging my ears as we ran. Seriously, just one of those kids' screams would have made my hair stand on end. Two of them made me concerned for the safety of my eardrums.

Well actually, they ran. I limped along behind and tried to keep myself from passing out again.

Angela tried to kick the door shut behind her and just about smashed my face in, but I stuck my foot in the door and slipped in behind her. Charles was already down comforting the kids.

The two that were in sight, that is.

"Shh... shh... it's okay." He spoke quietly, smoothing back their hair and holding them. I could still see from his face that it was far from okay.

Lego creations lay smashed and forgotten on the carpet, and the curtains from the window were snagged on the closed corner. I squinted, scouring every corner of the room with my gaze.

No one.

I frowned. "Where's Leif?"

"He's *gone!*" Angela snapped, clenching her fists by her sides. Her dark hair whipped around her face as she turned to face me, eyes flashing and jaw tight.

I took a step back and my hand came up defensively.

"I can't believe..." she took in a shuddery breath and put her hands to her face. Her voice dropped to a whisper. "I can't believe Charles trusted you. Of course you'd..." she trailed off.

A Gordian knot settled in the pit of my stomach. I swallowed.

Jilly started whimpering again. Her dad brought her close. "Shhhh... what happened, sweetie?"

She gulped and pointed to the window, "There was... there was a noise. Out there. A-and Leif was near the window and he opened it to look out and... and there was..."

"There was a guy and he had a really scary face," Beckett finished, rubbing at his eyes. He glanced over at me. I wondered what his definition of a scary face was.

"Did he come in?" Charles asked, struggling to keep his voice calm.

"No." Jilly shook her head, "He just grabbed Leif. And Leif screamed and kicked and smashed his Lego castle and then the guy pulled him out and closed the window. I threw Pinky at him, but..." Her face crumpled and she started crying again.

Dallas strode over, pushed aside the stuffed pig with his foot and opened the window. I walked up behind him, looking over his shoulder.

Unless the neighbor's dog was the kidnapper, we'd missed him.

"Anything?" Mr. Fernsby asked.

"He's gone," I stepped back from the window. Dallas kept staring stubbornly out over the neighborhood.

Charles bit his lip and looked up at the ceiling. He shook his head with a shaky sigh.

"I warned you," Angela said through clenched teeth. "After all this time, I'd think that you would know even better than me, Charles…"

Charles shook his head again, rubbing a hand over his face. "I really thought… I believed Dallas. I thought Wolfgang would never…"

"*Me?*" I spread my arms wide, "Look, I was having breakfast in the other room and trying to recover from a head wound. You saw me. How could I have kidnapped someone from the other room when I didn't even…"

"It's not like you don't have a *gang* who could do it for you. Who else could it be?" Angela's fierce gaze was redirected at me and she took a few steps towards me, her thin hands in fists by her sides again.

Beckett folded his arms, imitating his mother's scowl.

Everyone but Dallas was looking at me like they expected me to have Leif in some hidden pocket of my leather jacket.

I shrugged, gesturing helplessly with my hands as I tried to find the words to defend myself, "How should *I* know? Less than a week of spotty memories and I'm supposed to know everyone *else's* enemies? I don't even know my own! I barely even know who I am!"

My voice bounced violently off the walls, echoing back into my ears. I winced and slowly let my hands back down by my sides.

"Oh, I know who you are," Angela said coolly, her dark, angry eyes freezing me in place, "and you're not fooling me for one second, Wolfgang Dankworth."

I opened my mouth, but the words stuck in my throat. I swallowed.

Dallas opened his mouth hesitantly for a second, then closed it again. Jilly hid behind her dad's leg. Charles trained his look of suspicion on the floor, but Angela's venomous gaze stayed fixed on my face. A feeling of distrust hung in the air like cigarette smoke.

"Wolfgang's right, you know." Dallas's quiet voice came. Everyone looked over at him. He looked at the floor, but continued. "It's not him. He really does have amnesia, sir." His gaze went to Mr. Fernsby, then to Mrs Fernsby. "It's not him, I know."

The room went quiet again. With an extra dollop of awkward this time. But at least Angela wasn't silently scathing me anymore.

A buzzing noise broke the silence. I jumped.

Charles patted his pocket, "That's mine." He pulled out his phone and frowned at the screen. "Unknown name, unknown number…" he forced out a slight laugh, glancing over at me. "Either this is a telemarketer with awful timing or a ransom call."

I wasn't sure which one he wanted it to be.

He took a deep breath and hit two buttons, then held the phone out so the rest of us could hear. "Hello?"

"Is this the Fernsby residence?" A garbled voice came over the speakerphone.

It was the opening line of a telemarketer, but that voice didn't sound human. I'm not even sure how I was able to make out the words. It sounded like a broken robot trying to talk while blowing bubbles in milk.

"Yes… Who is this, please?"

Something that sounded halfway between a chuckle and a choke made goosebumps tickle my arms. "That's for me to know, Amazing Man."

Charles stiffened, his expression hardening. Jilly whimpered and covered her head.

It was pretty safe to assume it wasn't a salesman, at this point.

"Exactly how much are you willing to give to get your boy back?" the tone was conversational and was almost more disturbing that way.

Charles's jaw tightened and his hand clenched around the phone. "Whatever it takes."

"Ah, that's good. Let's make it..." the connection crackled a bit and there were popping noises I couldn't quite identify. "How about... two hundred dollars..."

"Done." Charles, Angela and Dallas said all at the same time.

Even knowing barely anything about the villain business, two hundred bucks sounded like a pretty pathetic ransom. You could rob a gas station if you needed that kind of cash. This guy wasn't done negotiating.

I held up a hand and made a shushing noise, keeping my eyes on the phone.

"Hold on now, Mighty Mouse... I'm not done. There's one other thing..." the voice trailed off for a second and static crackled again.

Drag it out. Start up a drumroll, why don't you...

Dallas tugged at his sleeves and Charles stuck his tongue into his cheek. If laser vision was one of his superpowers, I'd be concerned about the safety of the phone, with how hard he was staring at it.

Finally, the creepy voice spoke again. "Bring your houseguest."

It took me a moment to register who he was talking about.

Holy smoke, I'm just Mr. Popular, aren't I?

Charles looked confused, "My... houseguest?"

"A certain Mr. Dankworth. I know he's there. And by the extra noise, I'm probably on speakerphone. Hello, Wolfgang."

I stared at the phone.

This wasn't anyone from the gang. I couldn't tell the actual voice, but none of them talked like that. This was someone else.

All eyes in the room again turned to me, though this time it was with more bewilderment than accusation. Even through the weirdest forms of reverse psychology, this plan made no sense for me to have pulled off.

Besides... even with the note as evidence, wasn't I planning to blow Leif to bits before the kidnapping threat would even take effect?

So I'd fail at blowing him up, get captured, have a henchman kidnap Leif and then plan *myself* to be the ransom to get him back? That was like a bank robber stealing just enough money to bail himself out of jail.

In other words. Stupid. Stupid with two Os.

"Are you still there?" came the garbled voice again, stuttering with static.

Charles looked over at me with a question in his eyes. It was my freedom we were bargaining with here, after all.

Angela gave him an incredulous look and shook her head, gesturing silently. Clearly not concerned with my well being.

Well. It was my choice.

Sort of.

I took a deep breath, raising my voice so it would come through clearly on the speaker. "Where do you want to meet?"

The voice made that disturbing choke-laugh again. "Ah, I knew you were there. As to the question… " More of that unidentifiable popping noise. "Let's make it just south of Logan at ten tonight. Sound good?"

As good as a meeting with a kidnapper can sound.

No one answered.

"Good. And of course, the technicalities…" a sigh came over the line. "No calling the police or the child dies… the dynamic duo comes alone with the ransom…"

Oxymoron. Or I don't qualify as human now.

"… and, you're to leave as soon as we make the switch. Got it?"

"Yeah." I couldn't quite work out what the expression on Amazing Man's face was.

"Well, see you tonight, then. *Ciao!*" The line went dead.

Probably the most perky kidnapper ever. It grated on my nerves, hearing him talk like he loved his job.

The room was quiet. No one was looking at me now.

I was getting lightheaded again, and my legs were shaky, so I sat down on the floor. Which I should have realized was a bad idea, if I were a tad more mentally present at the time.

As it was, I sat down on someone's Lego rhinoceros and swore.

Jilly plugged her ears.

Beckett tugged on his mom's shirt and whispered loudly, "Mommy, is Mister Dankworth going to die?"

She shushed him, though I was wondering the same thing.

I guessed I'd find out.

#

It was obvious that wasn't the first Fernsby family crisis.

They continued on with the planning and the comforting of children like a well-oiled machine. While I awkwardly stood off to the side like a rusty old bucket.

Clearly, there wasn't much I could do, so I took my leave to go lie down again and get some rest.

I walked down the hall with my hands in my pockets, retracing the route that Dallas and I had taken before. My headache was letting up slightly, by that point. Probably thanks to the painkillers Dallas had told me about.

I glanced up at the pictures hanging in the hall again, on my way past. Leif's face seemed to burn into my vision in every picture I saw.

But I didn't *do* anything. It wasn't my fault.

Was it?

I mean, I'd signed the note... did I set something in motion? Was it another ally I had yet to be informed of?

Fantastic, yeah. I need more guilt right now.

I stopped by the door to the room I'd been in before, and reached for the knob, then stopped, glancing towards the door to the outside.

There could be something outside. Some clue that they'd missed by not going out there. Maybe I could redeem myself somewhat by being helpful.

My head throbbed as if to say "bad idea," but I ignored it and continued towards the door. The painkillers would shut it up soon enough anyway.

A minute later, I made it out onto the sidewalk next to the house. A couple of cars puttered past in the street and the neighbor's dog barked at me.

I gave him a look. *You're the prime suspect at the moment, buddy. Shut your mouth.*

I went to run my hand over my hair as I looked around, but ended up just knocking my head bandage sideways. Examining the outside of the house, I managed to find the window through which the abduction had taken place and went over to check it out.

I stood cluelessly by the garage bay for a minute or so, scuffing my shoes on the pavement and squinting at the surroundings. Nothing but a few bystanding crickets.

My career as a crime scene investigator wasn't looking promising.

For one, I didn't know what was normal for this area; for two, the pain drugs in my system weren't helping my train of thought at this point. Hard to spot clues when my vision kept going fuzzy and/or sideways.

Well, this was a stupid idea. I muttered under my breath and kicked at a clump of grass sprouting from a crack in the pavement. Who did I think I was, Sherlock Holmes?

I heard a clacking noise and a tiny blue Lego brick skittered out from the grass clump and onto the pavement.

Hey...

I looked up at the angle of the roof from the window down to where I was standing. Leif could have easily been holding the Lego and dropped it after the guy got him down here and made off. This was right about where they would have landed...

Going down on my heels, I picked up the little brick and held it between my fingers for a few seconds before rolling it into my palm. It was something. Not something I could really do anything with, but it was something.

What did they usually do with evidence stuff anyway? Check for fingerprints?

Well, I'd probably just smudged up any chance of that with my own fingerprints now, so never mind that.

I sighed and rubbed a hand over my face. I really should have just gone to lie down when I said I was.

Better late than never. And I'd rather they didn't find me passed out on the ground out here. I started to stand up.

A hand grabbed my jacket collar from behind, speeding my process considerably. The next thing I knew, I was forced nose-to-nose with a scowling face and backed up against the brick wall of the house.

Definitely not Charles or Dallas. This guy was way beefier than either of them. And definitely angrier. My heartbeat pounded in my ears. I was partially glad he was holding my jacket collar at the moment, since I didn't trust my legs to hold me up.

Was this guy mugging me? Seriously, all I had at the moment was a Lego brick and a head bandage.

I held up my hands defensively. "Listen…"

"No, Dankworth. *You* listen." The man's dark eyebrows furrowed further and he cursed at me in a thick, nasal, Brooklyn accent. "If it was my choice, we'd have cut you loose long ago. *This,* though? New breed of stupid, kid. I have to clean up after enough of your antics as it is, ya moron. Can you give it a rest and just do what the boss says for once?"

I blinked at him. My mouth hung open, failing to begin voicing the questions pounding in my mind.

The boss? I had a boss?

The man rolled his eyes at me, then moved in closer, his scowl intensifying to match his awful garlic breath as he hissed into my face. "Listen, Dank. One more move like this… one more mess up… and if you even *think* about spilling the beans to anyone… I don't care what the boss says. You're getting stiffer punishment than just being some kid's ransom, and that punishment's gonna come from me." He tapped his chest with a thick finger and raised his eyebrows. "Got it?"

I still couldn't get my voice to work, so I just nodded.

Distant footsteps sounded and he looked up. After one more threatening look, he let go of my collar and ran back off faster than I thought anyone his size was capable of.

The leather of my jacket rubbed against the rough bricks as my legs collapsed under me and I slid down the wall, sitting on the pavement.

I had a boss. I was getting punished for doing heaven knows what and going against orders. And I now had yet another potential death threat hanging over my head.

I took in a deep breath. *Man, if I needed to lie down before…*

As the thug's footsteps receded, the other ones got closer, coming around the corner. A tall, heroic form appeared and was by my side in a flash.

"There you are, Wolfgang." He let out his breath as he got down to help me up. "What were you doing? I thought you said you were going to lie down. Did something happen?"

I opened my mouth, all the words to explain coming to mind. They were stopped short as one phrase echoed back in my mind.

And if you even think about spilling the beans to anyone…

I closed my mouth and shook my head. "No, I'm fine. Just got distracted."

I needed to get my rest, anyway. I had a big date with a kidnapper tonight.

Chapter 11: The Ransom

The rest of the day was spent either being watched while I slept or carefully keeping my metaphorical beans un-spilled. I didn't fancy Mr. Garlic Breath coming back to exact whatever punishment he had in mind for me. It felt like I was complying with something my past self had set up, and I hated it. But I liked my face intact, so I didn't say anything about whatever more seemed to be going on behind the scenes.

This was a punishment of some sort... I had a boss...

Endless questions and multiple debilitating head wounds. Why life had dealt me this hand, I had no idea.

At least I could take naps.

#

The seating arrangements were a bit different on this car trip with Dallas.

This time, I was the wounded bargaining chip twiddling my thumbs in the back, while he sat shotgun, casting occasional worried glances back at me.

Charles did a good job of hiding it and acting really concerned and sorry for me, but I could tell he was relieved about the ransom. I didn't really blame him. I mean, "give me the jerk that you probably don't want in your house anyway and enough money for a semi-large shopping trip and I'll give you back your adorable son."

Barely a decision.

Dallas was more concerned about it than I'd have expected. I mean, giving me a gun would have been better, but he managed to slip my pocketknife back to me while Angela wasn't looking. Nice. Hopefully I'd remember whatever mad knife-skills Dallas had so much faith in before we had to meet the kidnapper.

I was honestly surprised Angela didn't throw confetti or something when I finally got in the car to leave. She treated me like an evil alien she'd been forced to welcome into her house.

I brushed my fingers over the knife clip on my pocket as I watched different shades of black and grey speed past as we drove along. Quiet, acoustic-sounding music came from the radio up front and I appreciated it simply for not being Schoolhouse Rock.

I shifted my legs up and swung them onto the seat next to me, stifling a yawn. Nothing moved in the front seats. I tipped my head to see if Dallas was still awake. He was, and just staring straight out at the road. Man, these guys were quiet.

Not like I could blame them that much. Just my presence was probably squelching any conversation they might have had anyway.

I listened to the music, moving my foot to the beat for a few seconds. It sounded... sort of familiar, actually. I knew the lyrics.

I frowned, tracing it back in my mind. Where had I heard it... ?

The memories of any music I'd listened to over the past few days scrolled through my mind. Maybe Roy had played it or something. It seemed like his type of thing.

The chorus repeated and I kept tapping my foot. Hey, singing kept spirits up, right? Bad News seemed pretty upbeat with all that Schoolhouse Rock singing he did.

It came back to a part I knew, and I started to sing along softly.

But whatever noise came out of my mouth just then, I'm quite positive it *wasn't* music. The sounds coming out of the radio actually sounded nice. My voice was just… flat and awful. I clamped my mouth shut.

Neither Charles nor Dallas seemed to notice my musical atrocity, as the car remained silent. Maybe I'd just hit it badly on the first try. I quietly cleared my throat and tried again.

Nope, that was worse.

The song ended just then, and a song I didn't know came on, stopping any further attempts.

Dallas looked back at me, a frown creasing his brows. "Are you… okay?"

Well, I certainly didn't feel as bad as my singing was. I shifted in my seat, feeling my face get red. "Y-yeah, I'm fine." *Not a dying walrus, though it might sound like it.*

So much for singing away problems. That just made everything worse.

Dallas watched me in concern for another few seconds, then turned back to the front. He nudged Fernsby's arm and whispered something.

The silence descended again, the awkward so thick in the air I could almost stir it with a spoon.

I mean, there was plenty I wanted to know, but… asking about anything seemed like it would be even more awkward.

I let the quiet be until it started to get suffocating, then cleared my throat a little. "Sooo… Charles." The upright, respectable name stuck on my tongue, tasting too clean and soapy in comparison to my own. I wondered briefly if he'd be okay with me calling him Charlie or Chuck.

I sat up straighter in my seat. "You… have super strength."

He looked over at Dallas. I got the impression he was exchanging some silent message regarding the state of my sanity. Clearly, this was an established fact between us.

"Yes I do, Wolfgang." He spoke slowly.

I ran a hand through my hair. "I mean… can you do anything else? Laser eyes… flight… any of that stuff?"

Charles looked at me in the mirror with his brows furrowed. "You really… don't remember anything, do you?"

If I could only start getting a dollar for every person that asked me that…

"Well, there's always the Alamo."

Everyone remembers that. God knows why.

I might have seen a slight bit of amusement come into his eyes, but he looked back at the road before I could be sure. "I can fly. Laser eyes… are too much of a physical impossibility." His voice was tired.

Well yeah. He did fly up and knock me out at the baseball stadium. My memory was just especially fuzzy right around that part.

I nodded, "Cool." He sounded reluctant to explain, so I didn't push for more info. And besides, another nap was sounding nice since I had very little idea of what the rest of the night would look like.

I let my head fall back against the car window. The rattling of the bumpy road on the glass jackhammered my head for about ten seconds before I'd had enough. I wanted to sleep, not knock myself out. Again. I sighed and put my head against the side of the seat instead, folding my arms across my chest.

Just when things were starting to get fuzzy and fade away, the car slowed down and I slid forward in my seat. The tires crunched against the gravel and the motor rumbled to a stop.

There was a click as Charles put the parking brake on. "We're here."

Figures.

I swung my feet down off the seat and stretched my arms

behind my head. My fingers brushed against the bandage and I pulled on it a little.

I mean, sure it might be decent cushioning… and that thug had already seen me with it on. But facing my fate while looking like a lobotomy patient didn't do much for my confidence.

I gave the bandage another tug and it unrolled, landing in white, bloodstained loops around my neck. I untangled it from that position and dropped it on the floor of the car.

Hopefully that would look less stupid. Except… there was my hair. I patted at the spikes shooting up all over my head from my cowlick plus the day's many spontaneous naps.

No, it was punk. It worked with the leather jacket. I was fine.

"Are you feeling okay?" Charles looked back at me. Good attempt at friendly concern, but it fell a little flat, seeing as he was about to hand me over to a kidnapper.

I shrugged and nodded just to be polite. "Could be worse."

Could be a lot better, too. But it's not like anyone actually cares about my well being besides Bad News.

Charles took a deep breath, "Well then… dear Lord, keep us all safe tonight." He clicked the handle on his door and it swung open letting in a gush of cold. Dallas zipped his hoodie up higher and followed suit.

I fiddled with my unobliging door lock and stumbled out gracefully, a few seconds after them.

The doors slammed shut and I blinked to try and adjust my eyes from headlight-light to moonlight.

Road dust still hung in the air and I muffled a sneeze in the crook of my elbow.

Charles stuck his hands in his coat pockets and nodded ahead of us, a slight breeze ruffling his light hair up on one side. "Looks like our man is already here."

I wiped at my nose and looked up.

Bad News's truck.

My mouth fell open.

I regained control of my jaw and swallowed as we walked

forward. I'd thought for sure… no, I was still sure that phone call wasn't made by any of the gang. And there was that other guy who'd threatened me and was definitely involved. I knew he wasn't part of the gang… But then, what was Bad News doing here?

Was *he* my supposed "boss"? But then shouldn't I be the one serving him endless cake and ice cream, not the other way around?

Well, this was our haunt… maybe he just happened to be around? In the exact spot we were. At ten at night.

Yeah, no. Something was up.

Our shoes made scuffing noises against the dirt in an uneven beat as we walked toward the black truck. The moon reflecting silver off the dark paint was pretty much the only reason I could see it.

It glowed with ghostly light in the dark, looking almost holy. Which was extremely doubtful because if there was one thing Bad News and his truck were not, it was holy.

Something moved around the side of the truck. I squinted at it. It was probably a person. Though he didn't look big enough to be Bad News…

He walked around to the front of the truck and leaned on it, the moon glinting off the hood behind him and silhouetting spiked up hair and a toothpick dangling from his mouth.

I knew that outline, even from my few memories of seeing it.

Lovely. More gang members in on the kidnapping.

Charles stopped. "Hello?"

No answer. Only literal crickets in the background.

I kept walking forward, keeping my pace slow. If anyone would talk to him… I guessed I'd have the best track record to do so.

"Roy?" The shadow didn't move and I wondered if he'd heard me.

I took a few more steps, making the distance between us even smaller. It seemed like he'd turned into a statue. I stood still, watching him for a few seconds.

I blinked, going against an odd feeling that I shouldn't.

The spiky-haired shadow shot forward and a fist just about pulverized the left side of my jaw.

The ground swooped up from in back of me, hitting the spot on my head that seemed particularly attracted to pain at this point.

The stars above got suddenly brighter for a second and bounced around crazily as I blinked up at them. The shadow, which was now quite obviously Roy stood over me and swore.

"I thought I *knew* you, man! We were *friends!*" his tone was an angry hiss. "And then you go and do… *this?*"

I blinked again. *Do what? Be a ransom for a kidnapped little boy? Right there with ya, Roy.*

I opened my mouth to incoherently defend myself, but my train of thought was cut off as his fist hit my nose. Pain warmed my face and I smelled blood, but my hand refused to move up to shield my face.

"Of all the low-down, dirty…" Roy pulled me up by the collar of my coat and reared back for another blow. I closed my eyes hard, bracing for the probable knockout punch.

"Get off," said a voice that sounded far away and quiet.

There was no noise for a bit, but I didn't open my eyes. The ground tilted sideways under me and my head swam.

"Mr. Tucker, get off of him." A stronger voice, but it still sounded far off.

I felt Roy shift a little. "You're kidding me, Wolf. You're in with *them?*" His tone was half betrayal and half pure shock. His fist unclenched from my jacket and I fell to the ground again. Pain spiked through my head. A few more things were said, but I didn't make them out.

After a few seconds they got a little clearer and I opened my eyes. The stars had finally decided to stop whatever crazy dance party they'd been having. More footsteps crunched on gravel near my head. Not eager to get my skull crushed in the deal, I pushed up onto my elbow and put my hand to my nose. It came away wet.

I held my jacket cuff to it and turned my head to see an enormous shoe next to my hand. Bad News's voice came from somewhere up in the atmosphere,

"Bloody nose?"

I looked up at his dim outline. Again with the sunglasses. Gotta block out that blinding moonlight. "Um… y-yeah."

He nodded and looked back up. "Keep pressing up on it and it should stop."

Thanks. I'm not an idiot, Dr. News.

I pulled myself to my feet, trying not to fall against him as I did. A bit of blood dripped off my sleeve onto my shirt. So much for not looking pathetic for my kidnapping.

Roy was right next to me with his fists clenched and his jaw jutting out… still looking very much like he wanted to clean my clock.

I swallowed down the sick feeling in the back of my throat, along with a bit of blood.

Dallas stepped closer, scowling at Roy, "Is this how you treat your ransom?"

"Ransom, my foot." Roy smacked my arm away from my nose and grabbed the collar of my coat again. I coughed. "Where's Cardboard, you double-crossing scumbag?"

Cardboard?

"How should I know?" I shot back, trying to pull away. "Catching cockroaches in her dumpster, probably. Or maybe she's taken up boxing."

That awful pun earned me a hit to the stomach. I curled in as much as I could with the iron grip on my jacket and moaned.

"But…" Charles sounded confused as to why we were all talking about packaging instead of the reason we came in the first place. "Where's Leif?"

Roy's grip loosened a bit, but it didn't seem like it was on purpose. "Leif? You mean Wolf's…"

"I mean my son," Charles cut in, his voice turning hard. "Where is he? We agreed to meet the kidnapper here with the ransom." He nodded to me. I felt so important.

"What about Cardboard?" Roy let go of my jacket in favor of advancing threateningly on Fernsby and I went to my knees, coughing.

Dallas shook his head. "We didn't take her."

Bad News gave his tie a tug. "We were supposed to meet the kidnapper here, too…" He patted his coat pocket, "Got the ransom right here."

I wasn't in the best mental state, but even I could spot the pattern here. This kidnapper had organized an unwilling reunion and I was caught in the painful middle.

A smile pulled at the side of News's mouth as he looked down at me. "Never heard of a person being the ransom before."

"Yeah, yeah. Chuckle it up, News." I wiped the blood off my face with my sleeve as I stood. If I kept this up, my coat would be brown, not black.

Roy pulled the toothpick from his lips and snapped it between his fingers. "What a joke," he spat and swore some more. Dallas looked close to plugging his ears.

I hadn't pegged Roy as someone with that much of a temper. Maybe he had only brought News's truck to carry the body of whoever had taken his little girl.

"Jeez, the bickering, guys…" a familiar, New York-accented voice came from surprisingly close by. Everyone jumped.

A man in a black baseball hat, ski mask and jacket stepped forward onto the gravel. I recognized the big nose even under the cloth. He pulled Cardboard with one hand and Leif with the other. Both looked grubby and scared.

Charles and Roy tensed like coiled springs. Dallas's fists clenched. News's eyebrows went up. I'd already had this surprise somewhat spoiled for me, so I just held my bloody nose.

A glint of white teeth showed through the ski mask's mouth hole. "Ya got the ransom?"

Chapter 12: Good little captive

At the word "ransom," everyone looked at me.

I appreciated the valiant effort to keep the scary, ski-mask man guessing, but I was probably obvious enough already.

"Here," I raised the shaky hand that wasn't holding my bloody nose.

The man's head turned and his gaze flicked over me like he was examining some beat up car he'd already agreed to buy. Probably wondering why he didn't give Roy a head start on destroying my face earlier.

He nodded. "Right. And the two hundred?"

Charles dug in his pockets distractedly, worry wrinkling his forehead. Leif shivered and whimpered out something that sounded like "daddy."

"It's okay, buddy." Charles's voice cracked slightly. His hand emerged from the pocket with two crisply folded bills. He raised his eyebrows at the masked man and held it out.

The man edged forward slightly, releasing Leif's arm for a second and holding out his gloved hand. "Give it here."

Charles moved forward and slapped it into the man's hand, probably harder than necessary.

He stepped back, looked over the money briefly, then gave Leif a shove towards Dallas and his dad.

Leif stood there, frozen for a second. His hazel eyes were wide and his chin trembled, wrinkling like a tiny walnut.

Dallas stepped towards him, leaning down a little. "Are you hurt?"

Leif shook his head, then barreled into Charles, burying his face in his rough coat material. The two were wrapped up in an indistinguishable lump of hug and I heard a coughing sort of crying.

The masked man finished his one-handed examination of the bills and stuffed them in his pocket. Cardboard jumped up and made a weird little "nya" noise. There was a clicking noise as her little teeth chomped together next to his ear.

"I hate you," she chirped.

"Shut it." The man gave her arm a downward jerk.

I reflected briefly on the differences between kids under stress. One cries and looks scared while the other bounces around and tries to bite her kidnapper.

Couldn't guess which one had spent her whole life with a gang of criminals.

"Alright," the kidnapper sighed, "the ransom for this one, please?" No drama there. Just wanting to get this little piranha off his hands.

A flicker of a grin flashed across Roy's face, but quickly iced over again with protective fierceness as he looked back at the kidnapper.

News stuck his large hand inside his coat, "Right here."

I expected him to bring out an envelope full of money or something valuable, but instead it was just a simple, turquoise notebook with grease and ink stains all over the cover.

This kidnapper was a total idiot. Kidnap two kids and only

ask for two hundred bucks, a ratty notebook and a wounded criminal.

I could do better than that, even with a gaping head wound, all my memories gone and an impressive collection of smaller injuries.

Bad News stepped forward at the kidnapper's gesture and handed over the book, ruffling the pages open a little, almost like an affectionate goodbye. I caught a glimpse of familiar, loopy cursive curling across the paper and frowned. Just where I'd seen it before didn't come to mind, but I knew that writing.

The masked man nodded and released Cardboard, who gave a parting precision kick to his shin before running back over to Roy. Sweet little thing.

The man grunted, but said nothing. After another quick flip through the pages, he tucked the notebook in his bag, along with the money.

"Nice doing business with you all," he nodded, then turned to me. "Come on, Dankworth."

Like I was his stupid dog or something. I couldn't read any facial expressions through the ski-mask, but his stance was obviously impatient.

Swallowing, I started to walk towards him. I brought my hand down from my nose and rested it on the clip of my knife in my pocket. The moment my fingertips touched it, he had a gun out and aimed right at my head.

I froze and my fingers clamped over the knife.

"Don't do that," the man sighed, like I'd already put him through enough by just breathing. His nasal voice grated on my nerves. He made a motion with his gun. "Take it out of your pocket. Drop it on the ground."

I did as he said. Throwing it at his face and spreading the joy of bloody noses sounded a lot better, though.

The knife made a clacking noise as it hit on the gravel. I winced at the empty feeling on my hip.

"That's better. Come on nicely this time."

As much as it grieved me, I did. I stuck my hands deep in my pockets to hide their shaking and swallowed back the rising feeling of nausea in the back of my throat.

He nodded and I saw another glint of teeth through the mask's mouth hole. "Thank you, fellas. And no following us, please."

I glanced back at Dallas right before following the man to devil-knows-where. I wondered if he ever got tired of my constant glances in his direction.

Dallas brought his hands up and I squinted for a second at the strange way he held them.

Karate? Was I supposed to know karate?

Oh. Praying.

Something I probably had even less practice with.

I clung to the thin hope that Dallas's prayers would help as we left the group behind, slipping into the dark beyond the road.

#

After I tripped about a hundred times in the dark, we finally reached what I thought was a jeep parked on a gravel side road. I was settled comfortably in the back with tied hands, the doors locked and my head in a bag that smelled like barf and we were off.

In my memory, I'd never had any experience being a ransom, but by Zorro's previous threatening I guessed I should probably just sit there and shut up.

I hated doing both.

We bounced over a few potholes in the road and I felt a small drip of blood trickling out of my nose. Great. And no hands to hold it with, either.

I twisted my neck into a position it should never be in and got my nose pressed against my shoulder, which helped the bleeding a bit. I'd probably look like I got murdered once the bloody sack came off, though.

Well, giving my captor a heart attack would be a bit of

justice. Not to mention it would be hilarious.

I pressed my nose into my shoulder again and turned my head from side to side, smearing the blood around the widest area I could.

But despite my violent treatment of my nose, it eventually stopped bleeding, cutting off the material for my art project.

And with nothing left to do but rattle around and get carsick, I conked out fairly quickly. Probably the one good thing about being head-wounded.

#

There was the click of a car door opening and a sudden light on the back of my eyelids. I groaned and shifted my position. My neck felt like it had a knife in it and my throat felt as scratchy and dry as the bag over my head.

"We're here." The New York accented voice came from somewhere above me.

Yippee.

"You up?"

My mouth was to dry for me to voice any response, but I moved my head a little in an attempted nod, sending yet another stabbing feeling down my neck.

Hands grabbed the bag along with a good fistful of my hair and yanked.

"I said I'm *up*," I croaked irritably.

The grip was readjusted and the bag slipped off my head. I blinked up at the man's now unmasked face as my eyes adjusted to the light. He looked only slightly less ticked off than the last time I'd seen his face.

He wrinkled his nose a little at the sight of all the dried blood smeared across my face, but didn't remark on it as he went to untie my hands. Probably to spite me. All that work for nothing.

The rope fell down, hitting the car floor with a soft thump. My hands tingled as circulation fully came back.

I guessed it was probably time for whatever "punishment" he'd so ominously hinted at earlier.

Groaning again, I sat up. All the bruises from Roy's beating decided to wake up right then as well, and spots danced in my vision. I rubbed at my eyes and looked out the windows.

Lower level parking garage. Spot D-13.

Exotic.

Not many other cars were down here and the corner we were in was pretty much abandoned. It didn't seem like a place you could brutally murder someone and get away with it, though, so that gave me a little hope.

I looked back over at the New Yorker, who was pulling a few things out of the glove compartment. He straightened up and closed the car door, then handed me a wet wipe. "For the blood," he clarified, gesturing to my face.

I rolled my eyes as I took it. I rubbed at my face with it as much as I could without making it hurt, then handed it back to him.

He didn't look terribly impressed with my cleaning job, but I guess it was good enough. Exhaling, he handed me a small paper bag.

"Put this on."

"Haven't I had enough bag for the day?"

"It's *inside* the bag, genius."

I reached my hand inside and touched something that felt almost like... skin? Grimacing, I pulled it out. It looked like an older man's face, flattened and folded in half. Rough, plastic-feeling hair poked up in tufts. My fingers poked through what seemed to be an eyehole.

A mask?

I wasn't an attractive enough prisoner to exhibit my own face, apparently. He'd rather have the company of an old man.

I looked up at the resident thug. He watched me impatiently.

Well, he was the one with the gun... I ran a hand over my hair to try and smooth the cowlick down and pulled the sticky-feeling rubber down over my head. After quite a bit of blind struggling and head pain, I got my eyes to actually line up with the eyeholes. I thought that was pretty good, considering. But the New Yorker had to come straighten it for me, adjusting the rubber in random places around my face. I think we were both glad when that was over.

"There," he finally stepped back. I wondered if he always looked this disgusted or if I just naturally brought out the sneer in everyone. "Now get this on, and we'll be set." He pulled a twill jacket off the back of his seat and held it up, nodding to my leather jacket, "You'll need to take that one off, of course."

Yeah, right.

I zipped it defensively. What was wrong with an old man in a leather jacket?

The New Yorker scowled at me, "Stop acting like a two-year-old, Dank. You'll get your dumb jacket back afterwards."

By the look on his face, it was probably either take off the jacket, or get a hole blown through the jacket with me still inside it.

I scowled back at him and reluctantly unzipped it. The jacket slid back onto the seat, with one sleeve refusing to flop down because of all the dried blood. I felt like I'd just agreed to leave part of my body behind.

I slipped into the twill jacket and buttoned up the buttons about halfway. I spread my arms, "Happy?" The rubber felt strange around my mouth as I formed the word.

He didn't answer, gesturing for me to follow him towards the stairwell. "Come on." He set off at the brisk pace of someone who hadn't been having the world cave in on them for the past few days.

I followed him, limping a little and still wincing at the kink in my neck. Our footsteps echoed off the cement walls and made us sound like a marching band instead of two guys walking.

By the time we got up the four flights of stairs, I pretty much had my old-man walk down. I was barely even faking the wheezing limp.

Coming out of the stairwell, we stepped into the wide hall of what looked like a conference center. Early morning light filtered in through the tall windows and there was a soft hum of conversation in the halls. The cold gasoline smell of the garage still lingering around me melted into the warmer smell of coffee creamer and new carpet.

The man turned to the right and I followed. We passed about five people on our way. Most smiled and nodded, wishing us a good morning.

This didn't really seem like a kidnapper haunt to me.

But maybe kidnapper bosses have a different idea of style. I wouldn't know.

We turned down another hall with no windows. I nearly ran into a younger man, coming out with a file folder tucked under his arm.

He smiled at me. "Good morning, Tom."

I scrambled for something an old man would say. "Y-you too, sonny." He nodded and kept walking.

Did old guys even call people "sonny" anymore?

The guy I was following had gotten further down the hall and I jogged a little to catch up. My face was starting to sweat under the sticky rubber mask and I resisted the urge to scratch it.

I briefly entertained the idea of yelling for help and letting all these people know I was being kidnapped, but another glance at the bulge by the New Yorker's hip pushed it quickly away.

Probably a double purpose in the old man mask, too. Everyone would just think old Tom was getting dementia if I said anything.

We came to the end of the hall and it opened up into a small sort of lobby area. Plush red chairs sat in the corners and a few lamps glowed from the coffee tables in between.

A secretary sat behind a tall counter and I heard keyboard clicking noises. Her blonde head stayed lowered, but she spoke as we entered.

"Do you have an appointment with Mr. Mansley?" she looked up and her gaze rested on me. She smiled. "Oh, I didn't think you were coming this month, Mr. Tom."

I swallowed. No calling *her* "sonny."

"Well… here I am," I made my best attempt at sounding old. So did I make a monthly habit of getting kidnapped and dressing up like an old man to visit my boss? Wolfgang Dankworth's apparent routines only got more baffling by the day.

The secretary nodded. "If you'll just take a seat, I'll page Mr. Mansley that you're here and he should be with you in a second!" She beamed, then went back to tapping on the keyboard with her red painted fingernails.

I glanced behind me and saw that the New Yorker was edging toward the door. He met my eyes and pulled the turquoise notebook out of his coat, putting it into my un-waiting hands.

"Give that to Mansley."

And with his delivery boy duties fulfilled for the moment, he was gone.

I stood there awkwardly for a few seconds, then tucked the notebook under my arm and sat on the edge of one of the red chairs. I resisted the reflex to tug at my hair, since I didn't want to find out what would happen if I unmasked myself in front of the innocent secretary.

I flipped the notebook over in my shaking hands, frowning at the cover. If I was going to be a good little captive, I probably shouldn't be snooping, but right here was the opportunity to answer one of the questions throbbing in my head. Why was *this* deemed a decent ransom? What was so valuable about it?

I cautiously opened to the first page to see a name looped across the paper in green pen.

Liza Allister.

This was her notebook? What would they want with…?

"Mr. Mansley will see you now." The secretary's chipper little voice rang in my ears like an alarm, tolling my guilt of notebook peeking to the whole world.

I jumped violently, sitting up ramrod straight, slamming the notebook shut and accidently dropping it on the floor. "A-alright, thank you, yes ma'am." My response came out a bit louder than I intended and certainly didn't sound like an old man.

The secretary raised an amused eyebrow, but went back to her work instead of screaming a declaration of my imposterhood.

I stood up and bent over to grab up the notebook, almost dropping it again as I did. Sticking it in the dignified hidden jacket pocket I now had sounded better than trying to keep a grip on it with my crazy, shaky hands, so I stuffed it in.

Taking an unsuccessful calming breath, I walked over to the official-looking door at the other end of the room.

"Derrick Mansley ~ Director" read the gold plaque on the door. I knocked more times than I intended.

"Come in," said a voice from inside.

I straightened the collar of the horrible twill jacket and turned the doorknob. The door swung open on well-oiled hinges and I stepped cautiously inside, keeping my hand on the knob. A middle-aged man with salt and pepper hair sat at his desk, writing something on a piece of paper.

He barely glanced up, giving me a slight smile, which I didn't have the composure to return.

"If you could please close the door behind you, Tom?"

"O-of course." I let go and elbowed the door. The smooth hinges slid again and it slammed shut loudly.

Mansley didn't flinch and just kept writing on his paper, the pen gliding perfectly along and leaving its trail of black ink.

My gaze flicked up to a framed quote over his seat. "A hero is someone who has given his or her life to something bigger than oneself."

There was a loud click as he set down his pen. I jumped.

He clasped his hands on his desk and fixed me with an unreadable gaze. I stared back, my heartbeat pounding in my ears.

He tipped his head slightly. "You're very late, Wolfgang."

Chapter 13: Spearmint Breath & Secret Tunnels

From the tone he used for the word "late," it sounded like he'd said "dead.

So this was definitely the displeased boss Mr. New York had been referring to (not that there had ever been much hope this was a meeting about the insurance on my Mustang or something).

I swallowed, drawing myself up in an attempt to gather the gang-leader dignity that was apparently buried somewhere inside me. "Fashionably late."

Mansley frowned, steepling his fingers. "That excuse expired three days ago."

Three days ago. More or less about the time when I had been regaining consciousness at Bad News's shack. Had that only been three days ago?

Well, I'm very *fashionably late. Because I'm* very *fashionable.*

I decided not to push that angle too hard.

"I forgot." It wasn't a lie. I *had* forgotten the meeting (along with everything else).

My hands shook harder, despite my hardest willings that they stay still. I reached to slide my hands in my pockets, but ended up just rubbing my hands awkwardly over the sides of the coat and down to my jeans. What kind of stupid jacket doesn't have pockets?

Mansley raised his eyebrows. I saw his mustache twitch a bit, whether with anger or amusement I couldn't tell. He shook his head and chuckled, standing from his chair.

I managed to stick my fingertips into my jean pockets as he came around the desk. He should have stopped advancing on me about a foot and a half before he did.

I pulled my head back a little so I could at least focus on his face without crossing my eyes.

Mansley's frost-blue eyes narrowed, and he tilted his head. It reminded me of my falcon in a more creepy, in-your-face sort of way.

"Wolfgang, where would you be without me?" His breath puffed a spearmint smell into my face.

Was that a rhetorical question? Back out in the lobby was the only guess that came to mind.

I pressed my lips into a tight line through the rubber of my mask. My gaze felt glued to his.

Mansley waited. "I want you to think about that for a minute."

I did.

Yep. Lobby was looking like the best possibility.

"You'd be in prison for the rest of your life. Your little circus would probably be there with you."

I blinked at him.

"Any attempts to reach the level of things you've been accomplishing would have ended in poorly executed disaster. Without me, you're a clown. An inept Robin Hood with an atrocious name."

Sorry to correct you, but I think that description sums up the past couple of days pretty well. And you're not making anything better.

More mint puffed in my face, making my eyeballs feel cold. His voice lowered to a firm, patient whisper, "So I need you to stay with me on this, okay?"

I swallowed again. "Yes, sir." The words came out automatically, and didn't seem like mine.

"Good," he stepped back and returned to his desk, giving me back a humane amount of space to breathe in.

A lingering smell of spearmint hung in the air around me. I coughed a little. I could feel more sweat under the mask and my cheek twitched with the effort not to scratch it.

There was a small squeak as Mansley sat back down in his chair. He ran a hand over his hair and looked briefly down at his desk before looking back up at me.

"Do you have any idea how much trouble that little stunt at the baseball stadium caused?" His voice was tired and almost fatherly.

Back to this point again. Apparently, blowing up families at baseball stadiums was a bad idea — even among the criminals I hung out with. I scratched at the back of my neck and felt the mask stretch a little. "Um… a lot?"

"A lot that could have been avoided. You almost blew *everything*." He paused for a second, the firm expression slipping, and gave a half chuckle. "No pun intended."

I felt like I should be contributing a bit more to this conversation. I cleared my throat, "Well, we were working on that thing for a while…" *From what I gathered, at least.*

Mansley leaned forward, "I know, but working together requires communication. We'd already sent out the note for the kidnapping and I was going to give you the orders to go kidnap Leif when you came for the meeting. That would have been the better strategic move for you, but you had to bail on me, go for the bomb act instead and make everyone look stupid."

Wait, so I had to have permission from him to do *anything?* How come everyone was coming after me instead of him, if he was my boss?

I wasn't proud of being a villain, but I could at least be my own man without this guy telling me what crimes I could and couldn't commit.

"I'm not your *minion…"*

I shouldn't randomly open my mouth. My thoughts fall out.

But instead of shooting me or throwing me out on my tin ear, Mansley just gave an admitting nod. "True, but I'm here to help you and you should appreciate that."

I closed my mouth and nodded like a broken bobble head. That was a near escape from letting my amnesia slip. And I had a feeling that wouldn't go over well with this guy.

He held my gaze for a bit more, then stood from his chair again and walked over to a small file cabinet in the corner. Papers rustled as his fingers brushed across them. He stopped after a few seconds and reached inside a folder, pulling out a little button box.

It looked sort of like a garage door opener. Or… oh good lord, was that a bomb detonator?

Oh, fantastic. He was going to detonate some bomb and collapse the ceiling on my head for displeasing him. The thought crossed my mind that I was going to die an old man. A fake old man.

But the button clicked under his thumb and nothing happened except a small buzzing noise, then he put it back in the folder.

Mansley walked over to the bookshelf to the left of his desk and ran his hand down the corner where the bookshelf met the wall. He stopped at a spot halfway down and held his index finger there for a second.

There was another buzzing noise, and I jumped.

The bookshelf creaked and swung open like a door, revealing a cement-walled hallway that descended into an enclosed, dark abyss.

Mansley flipped a light switch just inside, lighting up a few bare bulbs and stepped into the hallway. The sound of his shoes clicking on the floor echoed.

I just stood there. I think I was holding my breath for some reason.

His footsteps stopped for a second and turned on his heel to look at me. "Coming, Wolfgang?"

No. Please no.

"D-down there?" I stuttered. Visions of torture chambers filled my mind.

"Yes, of course." Mansley frowned, "Is everything alright?"

Stupid. I probably went down there all the time. And now he was suspicious.

"Yeah, great. Fine. Wonderful." I smiled and rubbed my shaky hands on my jeans before following him. "Just asking. T-to make sure."

Mansley raised an eyebrow, but just shook his head and closed the bookshelf behind us as I stepped into the hallway with him.

Suspicion averted.

Yeah, right.

I was an idiot.

An idiot in an awful, itchy old man mask I was scared to ask if I could take off.

I stuck my hands in my pockets and tried to avoid thinking about it. In fact, I tried to avoid thinking about anything at all. My head ached badly enough as it was. Couldn't I just sit in a thinking-free box for a day or so, to take a break?

Our shoes hit out a unified rhythm on the hard floor and echoed down the hall. I shuffled my feet a bit so we weren't walking in unison anymore.

The light bulbs seemed to be spaced just so no part of the hall would be *technically* dark. We walked from near blackness into painful whiteness about four times before the hall ended.

And it looked like the door didn't have a doorknob.

Fantastic. I'd be trapped in an underground hallway with my creepy, minty-breathed boss forever now.

Mansley simply walked up and put his finger to a small dot where the doorknob should have been. There was a soft click and the door popped open.

Ah, more touch locks.

I relaxed slightly.

I slipped through the door after Mansley and the white light of the hall shifted into a more yellow light. The room was quite unimpressive after the long hall and secret doors I'd had to go through to get to it.

At first glance, it looked almost like someone's garage, with a few more wacky tools involved. There was the same sort of gasoline and metallic smell. Wires and screwdrivers were lying around.

Liza would probably like this place. I wondered if she'd ever been here.

Well, if she were allowed… why send just her notebook and not her in person?

I guess Mansley and I were an exclusive club. With a really big buildup to an unimpressive clubhouse.

Then on second glance, there was an enormous bomb in the corner.

I took an involuntary step back, and my heart rate doubled, but I said nothing. Pretty safe guess that thing was mine.

"Only one last thing for you to do," Mansley's voice came from my left.

I nodded, having no idea what he was talking about. My gaze fell on a bullet shaped dome covered by a tarp. I wondered if it was another bomb.

Mansley looked at me, then at the tarp. "Oh that. The outer housing is totally finished. Got all the bugs worked out of the electronics for that finally. It's one last attachable part on the bomb itself we haven't figured out yet. Should be up and running soon, though." He stuck his hands in his pants pockets, surveying the bomb quietly.

Such a calm conversation.

He glanced over at me again, his brow furrowing in a question. "Did Gregs give you the notebook?"

"Ah… yeah. Here." I awkwardly patted down the pockets of the jacket and slid Liza's notebook out, placing it in his outstretched hand.

"Perfect," Mansley flipped it open, shuffling through the pages.

I stood there next to him with my hands behind my back, getting a distant view of Liza's cursive writing and geometrical sketches. Something in my stomach lurched as he stopped at the page with a detailed drawing of a giant bomb.

Mansley stroked his mustache as his gaze flicked over the paper. A smile tugged at the side of his mouth and he nodded, looking back up at me and flipping the notebook shut again. "I do commend you on choice of cohorts. That girl really is a genius. "

Oh, thanks. I've always prided myself on my good taste in cohorts.

"This…" he held up the notebook before tucking it in his own pocket, "should be everything we need to complete this whole thing. I'd tell you to give her my compliments, but," he laughed, "you know."

No, actually I didn't know. But this gave me a slight idea that the gang was among the people I shouldn't be spilling beans to.

Mansley went back to giving the giant bomb housing a professionally affectionate look, and I attempted to imitate him.

My hands twitched with the urge to rip off the awful mask that still leeched its rubber onto my face.

"Do we have a date?" I asked, keeping my eyes on what was apparently the housing and hoping that this wasn't already a firmly established thing. I could still just… endlessly dance around it and procrastinate if that were the case, and it would just get forgotten. Maybe.

Mansley stroked his mustache down with two fingers and sighed. Spearmint mingled with the gasoline smell. "Still working on that one." He glanced up at me again. "You can take the mask off now, if you want. No cameras around here."

Thank heaven above.

I let out a sigh of relief and started working the mask off. It stuck and pinched in weird places as I pulled up the rubber. Mansley's footsteps moved a bit further away as I had the mask over my eyes.

By the time I'd managed to painfully pull it off over my hair and stick it in my pocket, I saw he was over by the bomb core I'd first spotted, tapping a few buttons on a pop-up screen.

I scrunched up my nose and made a few faces, stretching my face out a bit after all that rubber clinging to it. "So, what's the one thing I have to do?"

Hopefully not sell my soul or something.

I rubbed a hand over my face, getting the sticky sweat off, then ran my fingers through my hair, which was even crazier than usual.

Mansley hit another button and swiped a finger across the little screen on the front of the bomb, then turned to me. "This is your bomb. Your big chance at justice. I want you to program it."

I looked around him at the bomb, "Um… okay." *What if I were to say that I don't want my big chance at justice?*

He nodded, his blue eyes serious with the apparent weight of the moment, then stepped aside, gesturing me forwards.

I walked slowly towards the glowing blue screen.

"CODENAME" it read. There was a flashing cursor in the bar and a projected keyboard on the glass screen below.

My fingers moved of their own accord and the name "Eloisa" blinked onto the screen. The bar lit up green and went to another slide.

"FINGERPRINT" was the next word. A wide, glowing circle took the place of the keyboard. The general shape of a fingertip outlined in the middle.

This Mansley guy really loved his digit-scanners.

I pressed my thumb in the middle of the circle and waited for it to load. It lit up green and went to another.

This screen said "KEY PHRASE" with a microphone icon below it. I looked over at Mansley.

"Am I supposed to say something here?"

He nodded once.

I swallowed, thought for a second, then hit the button. It lit up and I cleared my throat. *Something that's consistent with the villain I'm supposed to be playing here. Something morbid and creepy. Come on, think...*

"Um... die by the sword."

Hoping it didn't pick up on my eloquent "um", I hit the button again. The screen loaded for a second, then popped up with a little box.

Did you say: 'Umpire by the sod'?

I hit the "no" box. Try again.

"Die. By. The. Sword."

Did you say: 'Dobby the sword'?

I ran my hand over my hair, "What the hell?"

Mansley cleared his throat, "It just matters that it got your voice in there. You can confirm it."

I sighed and hit the "yes" box.

Count on artificial intelligence to ruin the dramatic, evil moment.

The screen lit up with one big check mark. "Success! Device programmed!"

All annoyance melted away and a chunk of ice settled in my stomach. How many people had I just condemned to death?

I jumped as a warm hand came to rest on my shoulder. Mansley let out a breath, expelling a cloud of spearmint into the air.

"You've done it."

I nodded, trying to force some enthusiasm and failing.

"After all these years, it'll finally be made right. Justice for all those killed that day. The public will see the truth." He stared at the checkmark on the screen, but seemed to be glimpsing into eternity by his expression.

I felt a shiver run through me and felt for my nonexistent

jacket pockets again.

"Their blood has cried out from the ground too long."
Mansley squeezed my shoulder, "Can you hear it, boy?" A moment
of silence. "Your father and mother. Peter. Eloisa. All the others. All
the innocents."

Every freaking moment of every single day, hissed a voice in
my head, spiking out from the fuzzy darkness of my past so clearly it
made me jump. That almost sounded like… my voice.

It was gone in a blink, leaving only the now familiar
confusion.

I winced and swallowed, staring ahead. Fuzzy memories
needled the edges of my mind and I winced as my head started to
throb again. All the others? My family members weren't the only
ones I was avenging? I felt like I should have known that, but it still
surprised me.

Out of the corner of my vision, I saw Mansley look over at
me. "Their song is coming to an end. And you'll be the one to hit the
final note."

Man, this guy should have been the one to take over on my
rallying speeches. I barely had an idea of what he was talking about,
but still, it straightened my back and stirred a sort of pride and
determination within me that I knew shouldn't be there.

I pushed it out of my mind. *This is a bomb. It's going to kill
more people. I need to stop this.*

It was quiet for another few minutes. Mansley closed his
eyes and I wondered if he was praying. If so, I hoped God liked
Dallas better.

My ears buzzed and the pain in my head expanded. The
memories were pushing right at the door. I shook my head a little,
mentally locking my door and pushing a few pieces of furniture up
against it.

Mansley exhaled another puff of spearmint and squeezed my
shoulder again. "I'll stay in touch about the date." He smiled, "Time
for the Wolf to head back to his den, huh?"

I nodded. I had quite enough to gnaw on back there.

Chapter 14: An Apology & a Phone Call

I never thought that sitting in the car with a bag over my head would be my preferred activity. But after that mask and utterly unnerving meeting... I welcomed the scratchy feeling over my face. I'd even bargained to leave it on so I could keep my hands free. With them shaking as hard as they were, the rope chafing was not going to be fun.

My hands were both stuck deep in the pockets of my leather jacket and clenched in fists. Even with the pressure, they still shivered like scared little puppies (in case there had been any doubt in my mind that my nerves were totally shot, at this point).

I'd been clinging to a hope that if I turned around and didn't go through with any evil plans I'd had, that that would be it. I mean, I was the head of the gang, and if I said we were done murdering... what the gang leader says goes, right?

Wrong, apparently.

I had to have some boss hanging over me that I was forbidden to tell anyone about. I was a subordinate for some villainous philanthropist who could probably just release me to the police-hounds with flick of his pinkie if I didn't do everything according to his omnipotent plan.

So simply "not doing" the atrocious crimes that were planned was even less of an option than it had been before.

And I was completely drawing a blank on what I could do instead. *Why couldn't I have just been an accountant with amnesia or something?*

I poked one of my fingers poked through the bullet hole in my pocket and wiggled it around. I wondered from under the bag if it looked like some sort of dirty worm, sticking out like that.

I was pathetic at trying to distract myself.

The road bumped along underneath us and I shifted sideways in my seat, pulling one of my legs up. It was a bit more comfortable. I closed my eyes and leaned back against the seat. But my mind was too busy spinning in circles and digesting all this new information.

Every time I started to drift off, another horrible implication of what I was doing would come to mind and send a burst of ice water down my spine. Another person that could die. Another opinion that would be formed of me. Another piece of my humanity down the toilet. No rest for the wicked, I guess.

I think I drifted off somewhere along the line, because after what seemed like only half an hour or so, the car was pulling to a stop and I was slumped against the window.

I groaned and fumbled the bag off of my head. My eyes didn't want to open, but I rubbed at them and blinked hard a couple of times until they agreed. Outside the window and across the parking lot was a run down old grocery store. A black pickup and a cherry red hot rod were parked at the side.

No place like home.

The New Yorker raised an eyebrow at me in the rearview mirror. "You getting out or what?

I popped my door open and stepped out, steadying myself

against the side of the car. The engine revved and I almost fell over as I stumbled back. The car drove off so fast I wondered if the guy had even bothered to put it in park when he stopped.

Hot-Potato Dankworth, tossed off to yet another undesirable group.

I sighed and straightened my jacket, then went limping across the parking lot to the Den.

The door was propped open with a crate full of wrenches and wires and a savory, warm smell drifted out. Hunger stabbed in my stomach. I walked inside to the slightly more familiar partial darkness, blinking a couple of times as my eyes adjusted from the sunlight outside. Classic rock music played over the PA system and obscured the noises of talking coming from the back of the store.

I followed the aisle that Cardboard had taken me down before. The talking got a bit clearer and I was able to make out a few comments about cars.

Stepping around the corner, I saw the gang lined up at the barstools by the kitchen counter. Bad News was at the stove with an apron on, flipping grilled cheese sandwiches.

So that's what that smell was. I had to steady myself by holding onto the shelving, since just the sight of food returned my knees to a half-jello state for a few seconds. I took a breath and ran a hand over my hair, hoping to make it a bit more presentable after being in a bag so long, then walked towards the counter. My eyes fixed on the sandwiches.

Bad News looked up at the unsteady scuffing noise of my shoes on the concrete and waved, grinning. "Hey. You hungry?"

Only to the point of tunnel vision, yeah.

I nodded, swallowing. "Starving." My stomach growled, accentuating my point.

The gang's heads snapped up at my voice and all of them turned to stare at me. I didn't make eye contact, continuing towards a barstool so I could sit down.

The sound of bare feet hitting the floor made me jump and the next thing I knew, Liza was in front of me, looking me up and down. I stopped, looking from her to the sandwiches on the counter.

Please, just let me eat…

Liza made a slow circuit around me, stopping to look at the back of my head and suck in her breath again. When she got back around to my face, she raised both her eyebrows.

"Well, you made it out surprisingly well for having just been kidnapped by Amazing Man and then some other bloke just the next day," she remarked.

I broke her gaze and noticed I was getting a scrutinizing look from Chris, too. Cardboard smiled at me from around a mouthful of food. Roy seemed too absorbed in the counter to look up.

"What all happened, anyway?" Liza asked, snapping my attention back onto her. "Bloody mess you got yourself into, losing it at the baseball stadium like that… oh!" She snapped her fingers, "… and did you get my notepad back when you made it out?"

Too many questions. I had enough of just my own. Adding Liza's in while sorting out which ones I could actually answer without getting myself in another mess was bordering on a short circuit in my brain.

I opened and closed my mouth a couple of times. "I-I… the notebook…" Pain sliced through in my head and blurred my vision.

"Hey, now," Liza's tone grew a bit more concerned and she gripped my arm to keep me steady. I blinked, wincing.

"C'mon, bud. Sit down and have a sandwich." News gestured to the unoccupied stool by Chris with his spatula.

I was only too happy to oblige.

News scooped a somewhat charred sandwich up off the griddle and flipped it onto a paper plate. He skidded it across the counter to me as Liza took up her seat on my other side.

It took effort to avoid just shoving the whole sandwich in my mouth just then, but I managed to take at least close-to-civilized-size bites. The food gradually filled the hollow feeling in my stomach and my head cleared.

I swallowed my bite of sandwich and peered over at Cardboard, "Hey, are you doing okay after all that excitement the other night?" Talking made the bruise on my jaw throb a little.

Roy shifted in his seat.

Cardboard nodded cheerfully and took another bite of her pickle.

I nodded back and took another bite of my sandwich. The last bite, apparently. That went down fast. Bad News slid another one onto my plate.

"So," Chris's gravelly voice broke the silence. "They just... let you go? After all that?" The way he was looking at me made it feel like he could see right into my mostly-empty, confused mind.

I focused on my plate and pushed my sandwich to the other side of my plate with the pickle. I didn't feel like I could come up with any sort of convincing lie at the moment, so I just nodded. "Yep."

"Did you... get my notebook?" Liza asked hesitantly.

I bit my tongue and shook my head.

She sighed, putting her face in her hands. "That was *all* the bomb studies. All of the most effective bombs and how to build that newest one we used at the stadium in there. All of my... well, all of *our* work, really." She trailed off, leaving me even more in dread of whatever Mansley had planned for us than before.

"So was that something to do with the monthly meeting things or what?" Bad News's questioning baritone made my eyes pop back open.

I opened and closed my mouth a few times and rubbed at the back of my neck, "Um... yeah. I was a little late for the boss's taste." Now I was really starting to sound gangster. But "boss" was the only word that came to mind, since I'd been ordered to keep any name-specifics secret.

"Oh, so the arms dealer is 'the boss' now?" Chris raised an eyebrow and took a swig of his beer.

Okay, so that wasn't the right term.

"S-sorry, I meant..." I stammered. "I meant the arms dealer. Slip of the tongue."

Roy cleared his throat and spoke before Chris could remind

me how "arms dealer" and "boss" weren't easy to mix up.

"The big project moving forward much?" He kept his voice lower than usual and kept tracing his finger over the counter.

I nodded, a sick feeling rising in the back of my throat. "Oh, definitely. Almost ready to go. We're just… waiting on a date."

"That'll be nice," Liza commented, "We'll finally get a hint about what our big move is going to be." Her mouth turned downwards in a sideways slant. "Hopefully more successful than that last one. That was awful." She twirled a strand of turquoise hair around one finger, "I'm really sorry about that one, Wolfy. I know how much you'd been waiting for that one to work." She sighed again. "And no more working out the bugs if I don't have my notes to work with."

Oh, her notes would get put to use soon enough.

I poked at my sandwich. It didn't look appetizing anymore. How could I eat with an impending mass homicide hanging over me? I put my head in my hands and tried to will away the pounding headache.

"I'm making coffee if you want some," Bad News offered.

I blew out my breath and shook my head, "No… I think I'm just going to try and get some sleep. I've heard it's a decent caffeine substitute." I slid off my stool, my legs less wobbly now, and walked towards the rooms in the back.

The talking among the gang got whispery and questioning as soon as my back was turned. I jammed my hands in my pockets and sped my pace.

I kicked the door to my room the rest of the way open, then swung it shut behind me a bit harder than necessary.

Yellow light from the window leaked into the room, backlighting various shadows of junk. One of the shadows moved and made a little squawking noise. I was too worn out to even be surprised.

"Hey, Lucius." I flopped down onto my bed with a thud and stared at the ceiling. Blood pounded in my temples. Guilt churned my stomach. I wondered why my life had this habit of sucking so badly.

There was a fluttering noise and a bird face blocked my wonderful view of the ceiling. Lucius tipped his head and walked up my chest a little, his talons poking into my skin.

I waved a hand at him. "Shoo." He flapped back to his perch.

I closed my eyes. Images of explosions seemed imprinted on the backs of my eyelids. I opened them again.

How could I undo this? This was the big one. Quite possibly my previous life's goal.

The past-me was a serious jerk.

Could I like accidentally jam a knife in the controls or something, at the last minute? Maybe it had a wire or something that could... no... this bomb wasn't going down that easy.

Get through all those security measures I'd just put in place and disable everything? No hiding the amnesia through that one. Exactly how long could I hide this?

How long would I need to? Would my memories actually stay away forever? Did I even want them back?

I sat up and groaned, rubbing my hands over my face. The headache was in full swing now. Who needed a giant bomb? They could just use my head right about now.

I stood from the mattress, still holding my head, and kicked at the dresser nearby. It let out a bit of the pressure and felt good. I kicked it again, harder. My toe smashed on the corner and I hopped and swore. Lucius squawked at me.

I sat back down on the bed and it bounced a bit. It was so soft.

If only I could just get to sleep...

I lay back down and closed my eyes. More explosions and replays of the baseball stadium smoke burst. I swore under my breath again.

Hey, at least my conscience was in full working order. Now if I could just find a way to shut it up for a few minutes...

I lay there, fighting with myself and trying to get to sleep. I don't know how long I did that, but it was getting really old.

Then a rhythmic tapping sounded at the door. I opened one eye.

"Come in," I grunted, sitting up slowly. Still not slowly enough to keep my head from pounding more.

The door creaked open and a blond, spiky-haired head poked in. Roy slipped through the opening and clicked the latch shut behind him. He scuffed the tips of his red shoes on the carpet as he walked over to me.

I watched him. He watched his feet.

"Come to finish your clock-cleaning job?" I asked.

Roy winced. "About that…" he sighed and looked up at me, "I just wanted to say sorry about that, dude. I mean…" He shifted his gaze up to the ceiling and ran his hand over his hair.

"It was just… ow." He reached his other hand up and untangled the buckle of his paracord bracelet from where it had caught in his hair. After he'd successfully freed his wrist, he stuck his hands in his pockets and looked back down at his shoes.

I narrowed my eyes. What was he getting at?

"I wanted to say I didn't mean to rough you up like that. I mean, I shouldn't have. It was just with Cardboard… I've always sorta… looked out for her. You know that." Roy met my eyes for the first time since he'd come in the room. "I was supposed to keep her safe. I just… let my guard down for a bit and she got taken. And then when she didn't come back…" He bit his lip and looked over to the window.

"I got real mad, Wolf. It just made me really wanna have at the guy who took her. Make him regret it and never do it again, y'know? Take revenge for Cardboard. But… she wouldn't want that, anyway. Even if it just made me madder with how long we've both known you." He looked back at me. "But it wasn't your fault. It got outta hand. I should've watched myself better than that. Watched *her* better than that. And I'm sorry."

Well, what do you know? A spark of morality and good had surfaced in this scum pond of criminal life. I blinked at Roy, unsure what to say. It wasn't the most eloquent of speeches, to be sure, but he'd apologized for something I didn't expect him to. Something I honestly wouldn't have.

A toothpick chewing hotshot making me question my deeper morals. Wow, didn't see that one on the schedule for today.

Roy was still watching me, waiting for some sort of response. I swallowed and nodded, "Yeah, it's fine, bud. You're good."

He let out his breath, nodded and let his usual, cocky smile back onto his face. High on my good graces, he plopped himself down on the bed next to me. Pain knifed through my skull at the sudden movement and I sucked in my breath through gritted teeth.

"I knew you'd understand," Roy sounded relieved.

I was unsure if that was specifically because of my life experience or just because I was a generally understanding guy. I didn't ask.

It was quiet.

I cleared my throat a little. "So, Cardboard's... doing okay after all that stuff though?"

Roy nodded. "Oh yeah. She's a tough little kid."

I nodded back, running a hand through me hair.

Roy leaned back and crossed his legs, propping his hands on the mattress. "Y'know," he flashed me a grin, "sometimes I think that even with all we've had to do... all that's happened and all the..." He gestured and made a small explosion noise. "Even after all that," he nodded, "you're still a pretty good guy, Wolf."

The nicest thing I could remember anyone saying to me. I had trouble believing it, but a smile still pulled at my mouth. "Thanks."

We both stared at the wall for a bit. Lucius flapped over and sat on my shoulder.

Roy tapped his toes together and pursed his lips. "I mean, not good like what most people would define that way. All the... yelling and blowing stuff up. Just that you know what's what. You stand up for stuff and your family and all. You watch out for your gang. That's having it right in *here*." He thumped a fist on his heart and nodded.

I hid a slight wince. Gotta get through all the qualifiers first, but yeah. Still the only compliment I can remember. Except maybe Dallas's "I trust you."

How was Dallas anyway? Did Leif make it back okay?

Because I needed more bunny trails to follow in my mind…

Roy sat there for another few seconds, then punched my shoulder gently. "Good talk. Glad I came by. Now you get that nap, bro." He stood up and stretched out a bit before heading to the door. Just as he reached for the doorknob, he stopped and snapped his fingers.

"Oh, I almost forgot. News found this, finally." He pulled what looked like an old flip phone out of his pocket. Frowning, he turned it over in his palm once, "Said it was behind the freezer or something. Liza charged it this morning. Gotta be more careful with your phone, man."

Roy tossed it to me, scaring Lucius off my shoulder. I fumbled around a bit before getting a grip on it. Roy gave me one final salute before swinging out the door.

I flipped open the phone and squinted at the opening screen. A picture of a mountain glowed back at me, along with black numbers showing the time.

4:36pm

A missed alert flashed at the bottom from three days ago.

DM meeting: 12 o'clock. IMPORTANT.

Well, that would have been nice to know. Thanks for losing the phone, past-me.

I hit the little menu button and clicked around. Recent calls. Settings. Extras. Contacts. I clicked on contacts.

"Allister, Liza" was right at the top. I clicked down more through a few names and businesses that didn't look interesting.

"Brown, Christopher." That would be Chris.

"Fernsby, Charles (Amazing Man)." What do you know? I had my worst enemy's cell phone number.

More clicking.

"Knight, Dallas"

I stopped.

Dallas trusted me. Dallas was actually supposed to be a good guy. Dallas could tell Amazing Man about my evil scheme.

I didn't have to stop my plan. I could just secretly help Dallas stop it.

I clicked on his name and it slid to his contact page. A picture of a scared looking Dallas with a bruise on the side of his face showed right at the top. I winced. I should get a better picture where he didn't look like I was about to shoot him. I scrolled down through the other information and got to the phone number.

Going outside would probably be a good idea. Wouldn't want the gang catching me in my betrayal of… myself.

I stood and went to the door, sticking the phone in my pocket. The doorknob slipped under my hand as I opened the door. I looked around. No one in sight. An exit was to my right and just down the hall.

My footsteps sounded deafening to me, but the quiet talking noises from the bakery continued. I slipped out the door and took in a breath as a cold wind blew through the opening. The sun was shining orange and pink on the clouds over the mountain, and all the shadows were long.

I looked at my own shadow and chuckled a little. I was as tall as News.

Shielding my eyes from the sun, I pulled my phone out of my pocket and punched in Dallas's phone number.

I just hoped he still trusted me. I also hoped he didn't screen his calls through Amazing Man.

It rang a couple of times and I bit my lip, trying to plan what I was going to say. Would I really just tell him everything over the phone? What if one of our phones was bugged or something?

There was a click and a familiar, even-toned voice answered.

"Dallas Knight speaking. How may I help you?"

I just about laughed, "Do you even have caller ID?"

A sharp intake of breath sounded on the other end. "Wolf…? I… hold on a moment, please."

The sounds got muffled for a bit and I heard him saying for someone to excuse him for a second. Footsteps, then the sound of a door opening and closing.

"Are you okay? What's going on?" he asked.

I couldn't quite distinguish the tone, though I hoped it wasn't annoyed.

"I…" I cleared my throat, "Well, I'm back at the Den right now. Bad News found my phone, so that's good."

"Okay," Dallas sounded a bit confused. I wouldn't just call him for the sheer joy of having my phone again, obviously.

I closed my eyes for a second. *Get to the point, knucklehead.*

"So I actually… the whole ransom thing was a bit more than it seemed. There's this project and a meeting I was supposed to go to. That ski-mask dude was just supposed to deliver me there. I found out some stuff while I was there and…" I let out a long breath, "Yeah, it's pretty big."

"Alright, so…" Dallas didn't sound sure of what to say, "… is there… I mean, what is it?"

I squinted over at the sun as it settled behind the mountains and licked my lips. "I'd feel better telling you in person, if that's alright. Think we could maybe… meet for lunch or something tomorrow?"

Dallas was quiet for a few seconds. "Okay. Um… there's a place in Millcreek called 'Branches'. Kind of near the zoo… think that would work?"

"Sounds good. I can find it. What time do you think you could get there?"

"Around… I can make it one-thirty or so?"

"Great. I'll be there." A weight lifted off my shoulders and I took a deep breath.

"See you then."

A click and the call ended.

I flipped the phone shut and stuck it back in my pocket. My fingers brushed on the piece of paper that was still in there.

I wondered what past-me would think of this meeting and

smiled.

In your face, Wolfgang Dankworth.

Chapter 15: Grocery Run

The best way to get a good night's sleep is to clear your conscience right beforehand. I can tell you, it worked brilliantly for me.

When I woke up, it felt like I'd slept a year. My eyes actually opened of their own accord and I didn't feel tied to the bed. My head wasn't pounding and the bumps and bruises didn't ache like they had the day before.

Pale, bluish light shone through the sheer curtains and Lucius sat on his perch near the bed with his beak tucked under his wing and his eyes closed. The quiet buzzed in my ears.

I took in a breath and stretched, kicking off the blanket. This would be nice. A day where I actually *felt* like doing something, for once. I sat up, stretched my arms out and yawned. My gaze fell on the little silver flip phone on the nightstand and I picked it up, pulling the screen open.

7:12 am, it read.

Sleeping within the hours that most civilized humans do gave me a nice feeling. It almost made me feel like a civilized human, myself. I chuckled.

Almost.

A tiny bubble with an envelope popped up on the side of the screen. *Text Message,* it informed me. I clicked on it.

Dallas's name popped up, and underneath it, the words: *"Hey, I'm really sorry, but I don't have the money for lunch. Could we meet at the park nearby? I can bring sandwiches, if you want."*

He was so politely pathetic. I shook my head and punched in a reply.

"Don't worry about it. I'll pick up the tab. See you then."

I stood from the bed, sticking the phone in my jeans pocket and grabbing my jacket. The sleeve still felt stiff from blood. It wasn't too visible against the black, I guess. But still, I decided to get a rag and try to clean it up before I left.

I pulled it on over my shoulders and slipped my arms in the sleeves, then opened the door and slipped out. My eye caught the scratchy "rage" label on the door, and I even chuckled a little. I walked down the short, dark hallway and stopped. Dishes clanked and a smell of vanilla and cigarette smoke filled the air.

At least a couple of my gang were earlier risers than I than I had expected.

I stuck a hand into one of my jacket pockets and walked towards the bakery area.

Roy and Liza sat cross-legged on the floor across from each other. They aggressively slammed down playing cards, quietly swearing at each other every now and then. A half-burned cigarette sat smoldering next to Roy's knee, and a bit of haze was in the air around him.

I leaned against one of the shelves, stopping for a bit to watch the game.

I assumed that the kitchen noises were Bad News. And that the smell was cake.

Hey, I'm not complaining. The cake-for-breakfast diet was

starting to grow on me.

"Spit!" Roy's voice split the silence and echoed off the cement walls and floor. He stuck his hands straight up in the air and laughed triumphantly.

Liza stuck her tongue out at him and started scooping up the cards. "I've half a mind to take you up on that offer… how'd you like to get it right in the eye?"

Roy laughed again, holding up a hand as if to shield himself.

Liza began sorting out the cards. "Rematch. This time we play for that beer bottle in the fridge." She nodded her head towards the kitchen.

Roy clapped his hands together. "Deal."

I walked up behind Roy and gave a piece of his hair a tug. "What's the game?"

He jumped, whacking my hand away. "Ow!" The scowl went away as he saw me, "Oh. Hi."

"G'mornin'" Liza greeted, not looking up from her deft card-sorting, "Want in on a game of Spit?"

"I'm good, thanks."

"Oh," she looked up, blowing a strand of hair out of her face. "And how's your head?"

I didn't risk touching it and ruining my luck, but I nodded. "Doing better. The headache's gone down considerably."

"A good night's sleep does wonders, ay?" Liza smirked. "You should try that more often."

Bad News leaned over the counter, his eyes barely peeking over the edge of his sunglasses. "Breakfast is ready whenever you are, guys."

Liza shoved all the rest of the unsorted cards over to Roy. "Be a gentleman and sort the rest of the cards. Thanks." She hopped up to the counter and grinned down at him. I sat down next to her.

Roy huffed, but finished sorting before joining us at the counter.

"Here you go," News pushed plates of chocolate cake and ice cream across the counter. "If anyone wants to drink milk with this, don't be a pig about it. We've barely got any left."

And just like that, I'd found the perfect excuse to get away.

I poked at my cake and scooped up a small piece, "Yeah, about that... I was thinking about going on a grocery run this afternoon. We're running out of a few things, right?" I nonchalantly stuck the bite in my mouth. *Oh please, let this work...*

"Absolutely," Liza took a bite of her own cake. "Pick up some duct tape while you're out. And another notebook, if you don't mind."

"Will do," I nodded, letting out my breath. She was fine with it, at least. I looked up at News.

He'd stopped, mid-ice-cream-scoop, and was watching me with his lips pursed together thoughtfully. I saw myself reflected in his sunglasses. He couldn't properly search my soul with sunglasses on, right?

Bad News turned away from me and finished scooping the ice cream onto Roy's plate. "I'll come with you."

The sudden cheerful declaration made me choke on my cake. Shaking my head, I tried to get my voice back. "No really... " I coughed, "It's fine. You can stay."

"No," News said pleasantly, scooting Roy his plate. "I can come." There was a rare and threatening undertone to his voice. I suddenly got the feeling that if I didn't bring him, bad luck would ensue for me quite quickly.

I watched his back as he dished up more cake, hoping to infuse him with a desire to stay behind.

He turned back around and gave me an innocent grin. "So, what time are we leaving?"

Blast everything. He knew. I wasn't getting out of this. Could I just kick him out by the side of the road? No... Slipping away wouldn't work either. He'd follow in that monster truck of his and I would join the ranks of roadkill.

Out of the hundreds of ideas cycling through in those few seconds, sneaking away from him in the grocery store sounded the best. He seemed like a guy who could become overly occupied with the food choices.

I swallowed. "How about twelve?"

Hopefully an hour and a half would be enough time to shake this grizzly bear off my tail.

#

I spent the hours leading up to our departure scouring the place for tasks News could do instead of coming along with me. I presented all of them to him casually but alluringly, trying to make repainting my door or remodeling the kitchen sound as attractive as possible.

As oblivious as he was about so much else, he seemed to know exactly what I was trying to do. Every offer was either bluntly refused or ignored. He was coming with me. And hell would freeze over before he would decide that I didn't need his supervision.

So we both went.

I opened the driver's side door and slid into my seat, refusing to look over at the passenger side. The car rocked as Bad News dropped into the shotgun seat. I waited until the movement stopped.

"Buckled?" I asked, my voice cracked with the momentous effort to sound amiable.

"Yup." He moved in his seat a bit more, and there was a faint click.

I jammed the keys in the ignition and my keychain robot bumped against the wheel. Its tiny whisk spun and the worn out voice chip activated again.

"Exterminate!" it screeched.

Tell me about it. I gritted my teeth, feeling like doing just that.

Only the odds seemed just slightly better for News exterminating me.

I wrenched the wheel to the side and we tore out of the parking lot. Wind threw my hair into disarray and Bad News put a hand on his hat. In a few minutes, we were on the freeway.

I took in a deep breath and adjusted my grip on the steering wheel. Just a matter of minutes before he'd unmask me. Call out my ridiculous cover-up of a "grocery run." The anger burning inside me died down, doused by icy fear for my life.

I swallowed and looked over at him.

He just watched the road.

I followed suit. I was the one driving, after all.

Change the subject. Keep any thought of Dallas or my memory loss from entering his mind.

"Sooo…" I drawled, "What flavors of ice cream are you thinking? I have a little cooler in the back we can put them in."

Bad News was looking through my CDs when I glanced at him, his face so straight and serious it seemed carved in stone. He didn't answer.

"'Cuz… I mean… I brought a good bit of money from our stock. We can get like at least three." My voice cracked a little and I winced. This was starting to sound like just what it was: a pathetic kiss-up attempt.

News ignored me, shoved a CD in the player and crossed his tree-trunk arms over his chest with a slight sigh.

I shut up and concentrated on the definition of nouns.

We had made it halfway through verbs when Bad News reached over and turned down the volume slightly.

Oh, no. Here it comes. He's going to ask what I'm actually doing.

I mentally stockpiled my different stories of what this trip was actually for and hoped to high heaven that he believed one of them (although "You got me, I'm going out to get an iced latte" didn't sound like quite the thing that would convince him).

He leaned back and tilted his head to look at me.

I kept looking at the road and the steering wheel. My hands were starting to shake. I held the wheel tighter and saw the bones in my knuckles.

News twisted his mouth to a sideways slant and sighed. "You're gonna go tell Dallas about the big plan, aren't you?"

I froze. Any arguments or excuses I had vaporized immediately.

"I... uh... well... no, I just thought I might... um... go into town and get some things. Maybe if he was there or something I could... run into him... but it would be an accident, I'm sure. I mean... he's my enemy's sidekick, why would I... ?"

It was like all my explanations had been tossed through a blender and I was just spewing random, nonsensical pieces of the worst ones.

Bad News was watching me almost sadly. Like he'd be sorry for a few seconds after snapping my neck and tossing me out of the car.

I clamped my mouth shut and swallowed. I was ruined. He knew. He was going to tell everyone else. I'd be killed by my own gang, the bomb-plan would go forward anyway, and people would still die.

My hands were shaking, even from their clamped position on the steering wheel.

Just kill me now, News. I'm finished.

Bad News leaned back in his seat and pushed his fedora back, "Dude... " he sounded almost like a disappointed father — if disappointed fathers called people "dude." He... actually *didn't* look about to kill me

He sighed again, "You still don't have your memory back, do you?"

I shook my head numbly.

News rubbed at his nose, "You've had a lot of problems over the years. I stuck with you through the whole crisis-thing. You had some ice cream. We made another strike or so. And you always pulled through and were fine."

Yeah, "fine," as in back to killing people.

He spread his hands. "You had it from my own mouth that amnesia was an improvement back a few days ago. But as nice as it was to have you smiling and everything for a bit, this... just isn't you, man. And throwing all your plans away like this is going far enough. I'm supposed to watch out for you, and I can't let this happen. We need to get your memory back."

So smiling wasn't me? Wanting perfectly nice people to not get blown up wasn't me?

I wasn't voicing it out loud, but I disagreed quite firmly with News on this front.

I looked sideways at him. He'd put his sunglasses up on the brim of his hat and looked to be absently tying some complicated knot in his tie while he watched me with concern in his deep brown eyes.

"Seriously, man." News dropped his tie back onto his chest and met my eyes. "This is your life goal, practically. You've been working on this for years. For your own good, I can't let you throw it away because of some little memory-lapse."

I shook my head, pulling one hand off the steering wheel to gesture a little. "News, I just… I need to…"

"Wolfgang, this is your *mission,* man. This is what you want." His thick brows furrowed. "Even if we didn't try to get it back right now, your memory would come back sometime on its own. *After* you mess it all up. And that…" he took a breath and shook his head. "You'd… probably kill yourself."

I scoffed. Right. No one could be that invested in killing someone else. No one was that irredeemable.

But News didn't laugh. He kept watching me, more serious than I'd ever seen him. Almost sad. He raised his eyebrows at my doubtful look. "You seen your wrists?"

"Those things that connect my hands to my arms? Yeah, I've seen them. Use 'em quite often, actually." I held up one hand and wiggled it back and forth demonstratively. My cuff slid down to show a jagged, red scar on the inside of my wrist.

I blinked. How had I not noticed *that* before?

I looked over at my other wrist, pulling the cuff back there and turning my arm. Yep, there too.

The car was very quiet for a minute, the music chirping softly in the background.

I was that miserable of a person? And News thought I needed *those* memories back?

No thank you, sir. I'd prefer cluelessness over... well, over *that*. I needed to stop the bomb. End of story. I didn't need to justify myself to every random elephant who thought he knew what was best for me.

News raised his eyebrows at me.

I pulled my sleeves back down and averted my gaze back down to the disc player, watching the words scroll past the screen. *Adjectives.* That was a weird word.

Bad News hit a button and the disc player turned off.

"We're getting your memory back," he informed me.

I snorted, "Just like that, huh?"

He shrugged, "I have something I'm pretty sure will work. Since nothing else really seemed to."

"Sounds good. I have an opening around two o'clock. Does that work?" I raised an eyebrow at him.

His voice hardened and he seemed to grow even bigger for a second. "You're *not* meeting with Dallas, Wolf."

"Excuse me. Who's the gang leader here?" I half expected to be struck down in a moment of News's divine wrath, right there.

Bad News' eyebrows touched the edge of his fedora as he looked at me. It was quiet for a second. "Exactly how much information do you have?"

I frowned at him, narrowing my eyes. "Enough."

"You said you didn't have a date yet. And you didn't tell us a place."

I scowled at a mountain in the distance, wishing it were a volcano and would erupt right then.

"You don't know that bit yet, huh?"

Quiet for a few seconds, then News gave a permissive shrug, shifting gears back into his mellow mode. "As long as you don't know the vital stuff, I guess it's okay. Just meet with me afterwards."

I muttered something not very nice under my breath. Bad

News nodded and sat back in his seat.

A couple of clicks and the adjective song came back on.

I had a few adjectives of my own for my passenger right now, but I kept them to myself.

News flattened his tie back out on his chest and turned his head to look at me. "I did get ice cream requests before we left, too. Mint chocolate chip, cherry... and cookies and cream, I think."

Oh, back to the ice cream conversation *now.*

Fat lot of good that distraction did me.

News looked back out at the pine trees we were passing. "So, yup. You can drop me off to do the shopping while you have your meeting, if you want."

I dug my fingernails into the steering wheel.

"As long as you don't maroon me." He still didn't look at me, but his voice hit a note that prickled my arms with goosebumps.

For the rest of the drive, I had plenty of silence to contemplate the deeper meaning of the phrase "bad luck."

Chapter 16: Lunch with the Enemy

I hadn't thought that there could be a grocery store that looked seedier than the Den.

But the place Bad News guided me to so he could get groceries definitely topped that. Far off on a back road, covered in so much graffiti that I couldn't see the original paint. Slouchy criminal types were pushing in and out through the doors with old paper bags full of produce and cookies.

"The Black Farmers' Market," News called it.

Probably a bunch of illegally imported produce, spiked orange juice and who knew what else. No, thank you.

I was quite willing to drop him off to do the shopping and get back on course with my original plans.

I was a bit cocky in my declaration of being able to find Dallas's lunch place without directions. Turned out, there were a lot of places to eat near the zoo. And searching for a small, shy person would have taken me a bit longer, even if I had known where this mystical "Branches" place was.

The last place I looked was a hipster-y, eco-friendly place tucked in a little side street under a couple of big trees.

"Branches," read the sign in a weird font that actually looked like branches.

About five cars were parked out front. One was a small green pickup that looked like it ran on the prayers of its owner.

Something told me I'd found Dallas.

I pulled up by the curb on the opposite side of the street and cut the engine, sitting back in my seat for a second and taking a few deep breaths. Judging by the disguises we'd had to wear to the baseball stadium, just walking in there as I was probably wasn't the greatest idea.

News had tossed me a baseball hat before he left. No explanation was provided, but I guessed it was probably for this very purpose. I ran a hand over my hair and pulled the hat on over my cowlick, letting the brim sink low over my eyes.

After a minute of deliberation, I reluctantly took off my jacket too, self-consciously rubbing at my bare wrists.

Well, a couple of old wrist scars weren't as obvious as a leather jacket. Hopefully, I'd be fine.

Shoving the keys in my pocket, I got out and went across the street to the door of the café. A grubby little mat welcomed me and a cowbell above the door clattered as I stepped inside.

I craned my neck around to get a good look at the clock behind the counter. One-fifty already. Crud.

The girl at the counter hesitantly edged into my sightline. "Hello, may I help you?"

I straightened, "Uh, yeah. I'm here for lunch with… someone — a friend," I pitched my voice a bit deeper than usual, hoping my voice wasn't particularly recognizable. I turned and looked over at the seating area. Way off at a corner table, I saw someone in a dark green hoodie looking seriously into a mug, his legs dangling down from the tall chair.

I pointed, turning back to the girl, "I'm with him."

158

"Very good," she handed me a laminated sheet of paper. "There's your menu. I'll be over to take your orders in a bit."

I nodded my thanks and started walking towards the table quietly.

Dallas still hadn't noticed me. He cupped his hands around the top of the mug, trapping the steam for a bit. A frown creased his forehead and he put his hands back down with a half sigh.

I cleared my throat, "Hey."

He jumped a bit and looked up at me.

I raised a hand in greeting, "Sorry I'm late. Got a little lost." I sat myself on the chair across from him.

"No, it's fine." Dallas assured, shifting in his seat. "I don't mind waiting."

It was quiet for a few seconds. I looked around the room at all the nature photography, plants and quotes.

"Pretty nice place," I said, "Come here a lot?"

Dallas shrugged, "Sometimes." He looked back down at his mug. I followed his gaze. I think he had black tea of some sort in there.

He rubbed his hands together. There was a tiny blue flash and it looked like his skin almost flickered.

I blinked. What did he have? I didn't see him holding anything just a couple seconds ago…

Dallas sighed and propped his arm on the table, holding the bridge of his nose. "You wouldn't remember that anyway, would you?" It almost didn't sound like he was talking to me.

I leaned forward, "Remember what now?" Something sparked in my brain and I squinted, remembering the odd conversations with the gang involving Dallas zapping… teleporting. Could that actually…?

"So what can I get for you guys today?" asked the hostess/waitress, suddenly materializing next to our table.

We both jumped. I swallowed back a curse. My heartbeat slammed in my eardrums, but silence hung in the air between the three of us.

The waitress raised an eyebrow, hovering her pen over the notepad.

"Well... I..." I stammered, glancing at Dallas, "I don't know, really. Do you want something, Dallas?"

Dallas peeked down at the menu again for a second, then clasped his hands. "Um... Caesar salad maybe?" he said it quietly, like he might offend her by speaking too loud.

"Alrighty, then." The girl scribbled it down with a smile, picked up Dallas's menu, then turned to me, her ponytail flipping over her shoulder. "And for you, sir?"

I glanced over the menu, reading absolutely nothing. "D-do you guys have burgers?"

"We sure do."

"I'll take that, then." I handed her the menu.

"Alright," she took it from me, "I'll be back in a few minutes, then!" Beaming at us, she clacked away in her high heels.

Silence fell again, except for the hum of voices and occasional clank of dishes. Dallas took a sip out of his mug. It looked too big in his hands.

I leaned back in my seat as my heart rate returned to normal. "So, what were you saying?"

"You were the one that wanted to tell me something first," Dallas pointed out.

"It's fine. Give me more time to prepare and I'll be more coherent. Seriously, what were you saying?"

He sighed and set down his mug, looking into it again. Somehow gathering courage from his tea, he straightened and met my gaze.

"Just... Amazing Man's superpowers... um..." he rubbed at the back of his neck. "So he's not like superman or anything, falling from space and all. He was given his superpowers by a government organization. It was a... a new public safety measure." Dallas stopped for a second and raised his eyebrows. "Is this ringing any bells?"

"No." But I was getting a tiny prick of headache, so an old, broken bell was probably trying to ring.

Dallas looked back at his tea, "It's sort of an injection… thing. Tiny nano-robots that give the powers and can be turned off if he turns evil or anything goes wrong. Only the highest level of security can access the control panel with the switches.

"So that organization also chose him a sidekick from the armed forces applications. To… serve our country in a different way, so to speak. And that sidekick they chose was me. They thought the sidekick also needed superpowers as well, so…" he sighed and ran a hand through his hair. "… they gave them to me."

So Dallas was a superhero now? Correction, super *sidekick?* I furrowed my brow, "How come you didn't use them to escape when I had you captured?"

"There's a bit more," he corrected, "I was given forcefields and teleportation, but…" he stopped for a second, wincing slightly. "Messing those up was how I got captured by you before. I was doing more harm than good with my clumsiness in controlling them. So I asked them to turn my powers off."

He pulled at his sleeves a bit, "I honestly did a lot better without having to worry about them. But… after the whole hostage situation with you… they decided I needed the extra defenses on again. Even if… I'm an even worse sidekick than usual with the complications involved." He sighed, lacing his pale fingers back around the mug.

Snippets of the conversation I'd heard at the Fernsbys' when I was just regaining consciousness resurfaced in my mind. There was something about turning something back on that Dallas didn't want to…

I felt kind of guilty now. After all, I was the one who'd kidnapped him… sort of. I mean, there was me, then Bad News, then the gang… but still. I'd kidnapped him before. And I felt like it was my fault on a deeper level, too. He probably wouldn't have needed to be the sidekick if I weren't the mad-bomber villain that needed to be stopped.

I swallowed. "I'm sorry."

Dallas looked up from his too-long sleeves and locked his green eyes with mine. Almost asking if I was joking. I kept my look serious. He looked back down and the corner of his mouth tugged upwards. I heard a quiet chuckle catch in his throat.

"I mean it, Dall," I insisted.

Dallas's mouth quirked at a funny angle, "Just never thought I'd hear that from you. You were never really one for apologizing."

I bit the inside of my cheek. "I'd hope that I'm a bit different now."

Dallas nodded. Neither of us spoke for a minute or so.

I shifted in my seat again. "So… my thing I was going to tell you.'

"Right," Dallas straightened up a bit more and watched me.

My turn to rub the back of my neck and fumble for words. "Okay… uh… "

This was exactly what that henchman New Yorker had told me *not* to do. Did they have anyone watching me? How close of tabs did my boss think he needed to keep on me?

I glanced over at the people at the table nearest to us and dropped my voice to a whisper.

"Before we went to Logan to get Leif and everything, when I went outside to look for clues, the ski-mask guy that we met with later found me out there and was threatening me about something. Like I'd done something wrong and my 'boss' wasn't gonna be happy." I clenched my hands together in my lap, both so Dallas couldn't see that they were starting to shake and to resist my urge to conspicuously gesture to illustrate my point.

"So, you saw the meeting. The guy put me in the car with a sack over my head and took me to this place with a big parking garage and a lot of halls and offices inside. Apparently, I'd missed some meeting, so I had to go to the boss's office."

Just remembering that office made me antsy. I shook it off and continued.

"He kept going on about how I'd be nothing without him and how putting the bomb at the baseball stadium almost screwed up everything and he'd already set up everything for me to kidnap Leif."

Dallas's brow furrowed. "But you signed the note…"

I nodded, "Yeah, but apparently this guy had like advised me on it or was backing the whole thing. I was getting almost a philanthropist vibe. Like I was doing the stuff and he was funding it or something. Were you aware of anything like that going on?"

Dallas shook his head slowly. "We were always pretty sure you worked under your own power…" He trailed off thoughtfully. "What was the man's name?"

I opened my mouth, mentally going back to the events of the day before, scanning for the desired piece of information. But the mental haze seemed to have advanced, covering more patches of my memory. I closed my mouth and frowned for a second.

Come on, I had to remember this. It was just… right on the tip of my tongue…

I squinted one eye shut and looked up at the ceiling, pulling what I could out of my reluctant brain. "M-Mans… Mansfield?"

That sounded about right. I nodded. "Yeah. Mansfield. You heard of him before?"

Dallas chewed on his lip thoughtfully. "I… don't believe I have. I can ask Mr. Fernsby later, though."

I nodded again, picking my story back up. "Well, Mansfield unlocked this secret passageway thing and we went down and I had a bomb I'd been building down there. He'd needed Liza's notebook to complete the last steps in it, but it was pretty much done." I let out my breath slowly and dropped my voice even more. "And this thing is huge. Like, blow-up-half-a-city huge."

"And here are you gentlemen's orders!" Two plates clanked down on the table and I nearly jumped out of my skin. The waitress smiled down at us. "Will there be anything else?"

I couldn't find my voice just at that moment.

Dallas shook his head. "No, ma'am. Thank you."

"No problem," she spun around and clicked back to the kitchen, calling over her shoulder to "just call if you need anything."

Like maybe a defibrillator.

I closed my eyes and rubbed a hand over my face, trying to get my heart rate to slow a bit. My fingers were trembling. I stuck my other hand in my jeans pocket and let out a shaky breath.

"You were saying?" Dallas prompted in a half-whisper.

"Something that would seriously get me arrested." My whisper cracked.

He pushed his salad to one side and clasped his hands on the table. "You're fine, Wolf. Keep going."

I pushed my hat back on my hair and took a deep breath before starting in again, even quieter than last time.

"So he had me set the bomb up with a security system thing. My fingerprint, a code word and a key phrase. I'm the only one that can set anything else in the system on there without setting off God-knows-what prevention system is worked into that thing. And it's also going to be under this housing that he said is partly electrical, so I think that would be yet another security to get past."

Dallas kept his face neutral, but I could see a deep worry in his eyes. "So, it's a giant bomb? Like the ones that…" he stopped short and swallowed, "Where is it going to be planted?"

I shook my head, "I don't have a date or place yet. It was still being set. I was going to be alerted as soon as it was figured out, since I'm still supposed to be heading it up. But I'm sure it's going to be soon."

Bad News's declaration that it was fine to tell Dallas as long as I didn't have the vital bits hardened something in my chest. My word couldn't be just something I could throw away as easily as he thought I could. I held Dallas's gaze.

"I'll call you as soon as I get the rest of the information, okay? I promise."

I promised.

I didn't know much about myself, but a feeling in my gut told me I wasn't the kind of guy that broke his word easily.

My betrayal of my own plans was cemented.

I leaned back in my seat a little.

Dallas nodded, "Okay. I'll wait for it." Saying he trusted me wasn't necessary. He had since he'd said it the first time.

He chewed his lip for a few seconds, then opened his mouth. "Thank you. I mean, for telling me." He swallowed, "I know how much your plans mean... meant, at least... to you." A sincere smile, small though it was, pulled his mouth up. "Not everyone makes use of their second chance. Not everyone turns around."

Dallas gave a nod. "I'm glad you did."

For the first time, I actually felt like one of the good guys. A redeemable wretch. I smiled back at Dallas. It was involuntary, but I didn't try and stop it.

"Thanks."

The bomb wasn't disarmed. Everything was far from safe. But for a moment, safety felt assured on some higher level.

Everything was going to be alright.

And Dallas and I ate our lunch together. Anyone in the café would've thought we were longtime friends.

Chapter 17: Bad News's Method

I didn't quite fancy a death by bad luck, so I got myself back to The Black Farmers' Market as soon as I finished lunch. I pulled into a parking spot near the door and glanced at the clock. Just after three. He should be out soon.

Another ten minutes ticked by. Still, no giant form had darkened the exit.

Only a few lowlifes wandered in and out of the rattling automatic doors every now and then.

I started looking through my CDs for something to listen to that maybe I'd put in the car myself. I pushed the Schoolhouse Rock aside and underneath found a neatly organized collection of classical music.

How sophisticated of me.

I pulled out the first one and turned it over in my hands. Wolfgang Amadeus Mozart. On the corner of the album cover in neat cursive was the name "Rachel Dankworth" with a tiny heart sticker next to it. Huh.

I popped the disc out, stuck it in the player and sat back to listen. It was actually pretty good. Seemed more my type of thing than elementary school facts set to music.

It was the same sort of feeling I'd had after finding my jacket for the first time. Something familiar. Something that felt like home.

Rachel Dankworth... obviously related. I picked up the case up again. It was faded and old looking, wrinkled at the corners with age. The music on the disc jittered and skipped, showing its age, as well. I skipped it to the next song.

Rachel... I rolled the name over in my mind, groping at the vaguely familiar feeling that was starting to morph into a headache.

Maybe it was my mom? I mean, if she liked Mozart, that might give a bit of an explanation as to my interesting name...

"Hey." Bad News's voice rumbled. I jumped a little and looked up at him. He was holding at least three very full grocery bags on each arm and chewing on something.

"See you decided to show back up." News blew a huge pink gum bubble, then popped it with his teeth. "How'd lunch go?"

"It... um... went pretty well."

He nodded and blew another bubble. "You said you had a cooler in the back, right?"

"Of course... yeah." I opened my door, killing the music mid-crescendo and walked around to the trunk. We loaded the groceries in and around the cooler. Surprisingly, some actual fruits, veggies and meat were included in the stock, though I couldn't imagine what News would use them for. Maybe there was some carrot cake on the menu.

I swung the trunk door shut and we came back around to the front of the car. Bad News opened his door and thumped down in the passenger seat. I slid into the driver's' side, turning the keys. The engine rumbled to life and I steered us out of the parking lot.

I looked over at News, who was busy blowing a bubble as big as my head. Maybe he'd forgotten about the whole getting-my-memory-back thing. Maybe I could just start driving back to the Den and he wouldn't even notice.

I turned the steering wheel slowly to the right.

News's bubble popped loudly and he sucked the gum back into his mouth. "Hey, it's the other way."

I froze. "Wh-what's the other way?"

"Where we're going. Turn left."

I swore at him under my breath and rerouted to the left. "Probably not gonna work anyway," I muttered.

News shrugged. "It might not. It's worth a try, though."

He leaned over the glove compartment and popped out my disc that was so offensively not singing about school facts. In a few more seconds, a lonely song about a bill on Capitol Hill played over the speakers, and all was right with the world.

I kept my lips in a tight line as we drove along and listened to various facts about American history and politics, not daring to object. The buildings along that stretch of the road got further and further apart. Minutes and songs went by.

I turned to News, "How much further?"

He pulled up his sunglasses and squinted around. "Just a few more minutes. Big building on the right, I think. It's closed today, so getting in should be pretty easy."

A big building that was closed today? It sounded like he was taking me to another grocery store. Evil Incorporated, probably. Where I got all my bomb parts and leather jackets and falcons.

Favorite shopping malls always bring back memories...

I rubbed at one of my wrists and looked out at the empty field by the road with the mountains looming close overhead. One little house sat under a clump of pine trees, like it was trying to hide from civilization. Doing a pretty good job of it, too.

I frowned. The population seemed a bit sparse for a shopping center, in my opinion.

Still, Bad News didn't tell me to stop and I didn't see anywhere worth stopping. The road kept zipping past, humming under the tires. Trees closed in over the road for a bit, then it opened up.

News tipped his head to the right, "Here it is."

I eased onto the brake and craned my neck around him to see. A big, well-kept building with a glass dome skylight on top sat in the middle of an empty parking lot. Letters stuck out across the front, reflecting the sunlight.

Utah H.P. Informational Center & Museum

H.P.? What was that? And why did News think I needed information about it?

I pulled right up next to the big entrance steps and idled the engine for a few seconds. Up the grand, stone stairway were huge glass doors, leading to a dark interior

I'd lose faith in the most basic levels of security if those doors weren't locked.

"Okay, yeah… nope." I shook my head. "Still drawing a blank. But really, News, I'm good. Let's head out." My foot shifted toward the gas, but Bad News grabbed my arm.

"Not yet. We have to go in first."

"It's locked. And probably has glass break alarms."

He stuck one of his hands in his coat pocket. "I've got a way."

I wasn't one to argue with News's "ways." Swallowing, I put the car in park and pulled out the keys, jamming them in my pocket.

It was fine. If all I'd seen of my life, all the people I'd met and everything I'd seen hadn't triggered anything, I doubted that some dumb museum about two random letters would.

I didn't have anything to lose.

News humored me; I'd humor him.

We stepped out of the car and our doors slammed behind us. I stuck my hands in my pockets and looked up at the building. I basked in the feeling of not remembering it at all.

"C'mon," News straightened his fedora, gave his tie a tug and started towards the entrance. I followed at more of a jog to keep up with his long strides.

We reached the stairs and our feet beat out an uneven, echoing rhythm on the stone. Bad News got to the top first, since he'd been taking them two at a time. He wasn't even breathing hard, whereas I could have probably blown the doors in with all my huffing and puffing.

News pulled a little gadget out of his pocket that looked kind of like a laser pointer.

Distract the guard dogs... good idea.

He pulled out a suction cup out of his other pocket, stuck it to the glass and started drawing a tall oval around it. A quiet humming noise buzzed through the air as the pointer went around, buzzing and glowing white. As soon as he'd completed the oval, News put his other hand to the glass and gave the suction cup a tug.

The big, uneven chunk of glass slid right out and into his hands. He set it on the ground and pulled the suction cup off with a snapping noise.

I stared. "Where'd you get that?" If I'd known that Bad News had been carrying a laser, I would've been watching my attitude more carefully...

News shoved it back into his coat pocket and straightened up. "Liza made it." He nodded towards the hole in the glass, "You first."

I angled myself and slipped through the opening. The sound of my shoes on the stone floor made me jump. Light from the skylight cast weird shadows around plaques and exhibits. I looked back towards the door.

News had just managed to squeeze through. He stumbled forwards a few steps and held his hat, but managed to right himself as he reached me.

His shadow stretched in front of us like a pathway towards the rest of the museum. I swallowed.

"Okay." Bad News stuck his hands in his pants pockets. What else could he be carrying? His massive hand came out enveloping two long, black flashlights. He pressed a button on one of them and a beam of light shot out ahead of us, illuminating a sign.

Utah Hero Project Informational Center & Museum
So that's what H.P. stood for.

Heroes... Dallas's words about Charles being given his

powers by an organization came to mind. *This must have something to do with Amazing Man, then...*

Bad News handed me one of the flashlights. "Here you go. We'll start there," he nodded to the left. "It makes a loop around, so we'll end up back here."

I nodded and turned on my flashlight. The beam cut through the semi-darkness as I turned in a half-circle towards the left.

I stopped. Charles Fernsby was staring straight at me, a wide grin stretched across his face.

"What the...?" I jumped backwards with a curse and just about dropped my flashlight.

Bad News grabbed my shoulder, keeping me from tripping over my own feet. "Whoa, there. It's just a wax model."

That made... more sense. But with my luck, I wouldn't be surprised if the whole police force had decided to spend their Sunday hanging out here.

I gulped in air and nodded, looking away from the figure's unseeing, glassy gaze. The flashlight beam trembled along with my hand as I raised it again.

A wonderful start.

We started walking and News nudged me towards the first plaque, underneath a framed document. "Read."

I didn't argue. He probably had a lot of reading planned for me this afternoon.

Letting out my breath, I stepped up and steadied my light onto the words. "Want me to read out loud?" I muttered.

"I already know the whole enchilada, man." News shone his light up to the ceiling, casting a white glow around the area. "Just read to yourself."

I shifted my gaze to the words at the top of the plate.

The Hero Project Contract: The document that started it all.

Somehow, I doubted that this was the star attraction here. I kept reading.

In early 2018, a project was brought for consideration before the

board of the Superior Protective Intelligence organization (the SPI).
The project proposed effectively creating 'superheroes' to be added
to the protection of each state, stationing them in each capital city.
Said superheroes would be chosen model citizens, brought in and
given their powers by injections of microscopic enhancement robots
that would give them abilities reminiscent of the well-known icon,
Superman.
After a month of consideration and research by the board, the bill
was accepted and leadership of this new branch was given to senior
SPI agent Derrick Mansley.

Excuse me? I squinted and blinked a few times. That couldn't be right... I was just skimming. Maybe I randomly inserted a name I already knew.

I went back and read it again.

Leadership of this new branch was given to senior SPI agent Derrick Mansley.

That had to be a different guy. Someone with the same name.

I shined my flashlight up at the document and the few framed pictures around it. My gaze fell on one of two men shaking hands and smiling at the camera.

I'd seen one of those smiles before. Those blue eyes. The neatly combed mustache. That hair that had gotten slightly more grey over time.

My heart jackhammered on my ribs and I clutched the flashlight tighter. The head of this project was a traitor. He wasn't with Amazing Man. He was trying to blow him to kingdom come.

Good thing I'd told... wait... had I told Dallas the name? I looked up at the ceiling and mentally replayed the conversation.

Well, I'd brought up the subject at least. But the name? Nope, I hadn't clued him in on Mansley. I'd said Mansfield. I'd sent Dallas off with the wrong name.

I closed my eyes for a second, clenching my teeth and mentally kicking myself.

Idiot.

The one thing that everything could hang on. I needed to call Dallas.

My hand that wasn't holding the flashlight went to my pocket. I pulled my phone out and flipped it open. I saw the screen's glow for only a few seconds before Bad News's giant hand enveloped it and pulled it away.

I whirled and made a blind snatch to get it back. He held it above me and shook his head.

I stammered the beginnings of a few excuses. "But I just need to make one quick… "

"Not until we're all the way through the museum," News shoved the phone into his pocket.

I tried to give him a threatening look. He just popped another bubblegum bubble down at me.

Fine. After the museum, then. I'd make sure that wouldn't take long.

I walked over to the next display more loudly than necessary, briefly glanced at the photos above and then directed my attention to the stupid plaque below.

Charles Fernsby: A hero indeed
Charles, an upstanding citizen of Salt Lake City and a well-known doctor, was an obvious choice for the program. As a husband and father, Charles cares deeply about the safety of our country and has four years of military service to his credit.
"I just pray the spotlight doesn't taint my vision while I'm involved in this project," Charles stated, "so that I'll still be able to do the right thing for everyone, despite public pressures."

And another picture of Charles hugging Angela was below that.

Fantastic. Like I needed more confirmation of what a lovely person I was supposed to blast to bits.

I craned my neck up at Bad News, who stood directly in back of me. "Is this all really necessary?"

"Yuppers." He nudged me towards the next exhibit.

I sighed and read the obligatory paragraph about Dallas. Pretty much all stuff he'd told me at the restaurant. Though I hadn't known he had two siblings.

We moved on.

More bits on both of them getting their powers and training to use them… one of the syringes used to inject Fernsby… a few original costume ideas and a story about how Dallas had politely declined a sidekick outfit…

Actually… some of it was pretty interesting. The project was a little odd, but seemed like a generally good idea, I didn't see why I had to have such a big problem with the whole hero thing.

The rest took up another ten or fifteen minutes. I refused to expose my mild interest to News.

It wasn't ringing any bells. I didn't even have a headache.

I sighed and rubbed a hand over my eyes. "Are we done yet?"

News stuck his tongue in his cheek and swept his flashlight beam around the area. "I think so."

Finally, jeez. I started towards the exit.

"Hey, I meant with this *section*." He corrected, gesturing with his flashlight.

I groaned and muttered under my breath, dragging my feet to catch up to him as we went on towards another exhibit entrance.

Bad News gave me a slap on the back that nearly sent me into the wall. "Buck up. This is where it gets interesting." He wiggled his eyebrows

Bad News shone his flashlight up on the spooky looking archway leading to the next branch. I followed the beam with my eyes. In letters that looked like graffiti, it read:

Every hero needs a villain…

My ears burned. I swallowed and rubbed at the goosebumps under my jacket sleeves.

Something told me I had a lot to do with this section.

Chapter 18: Reading Up

Bad News gave his now-familiar gesture of "you first," and I stepped under the archway. I kept my flashlight pointed down, but shadows of wax models were still visible as dim outlines I couldn't quite make out. I wished they could just stay that way.

A whole museum wing dedicated to my evil deeds and proving I was a villain? I hated the idea, but it roused a sort of morbid fascination that kept me rooted to the spot.

I swallowed, "Where do I start?" I was whispering for some reason.

News pointed to my left as he stepped in after me. "Same roundabout display pattern. Start there."

Right. I straightened up and took a deep breath, then walked over to the first display. Photos above and a plaque below. I aimed my flashlight up above first.

I promptly decided I didn't like seeing pictures of myself.

One almost life-sized photo print hung in the middle, glaring down ominously.

I stood in the middle of a debris-strewn street holding an oversized gun at a precarious angle. My leather jacket and shirt were stained with smoke and blood trickled from my split lip. My mouth was open in an angry yell at something or someone off camera. One hand was raised in a defiant and decidedly impolite gesture to the sky.

A tiny copyright in the corner credited it to some big newspaper and the article: "Modern-day Villains."

What was happening there? Who was I yelling at and why? I had a gun... had I just shot someone? I blinked for the first time since seeing the picture, and swallowed.

It felt almost like something prodded at the back of my head. My headache was starting to kick back in.

That wasn't good. I flinched, rubbing at the back of my head as the confusing darkness in my memories shifted, threatening to take shape.

I looked over at the other pictures lining the sides. One was a classic prison mug shot with me holding up a sign that barely held my mile long name and narrowing my eyes at the camera with a cold, murderous look. The next was a smaller, more distant picture of me with the whole gang, excluding Cardboard. I was yelling something again, holding a pistol out in front of me. The gang was holding various weapons.

In the last one, Amazing Man was walking towards me, his hands were spread in supplication and his face wore a pained expression, while I was held back from attacking him by two burly police officers, red-hot rage twisting my own features.

I hated him *that* much? He was a nice guy. A much nicer guy than me. Why did I think I needed to murder someone who'd saved so many people?

I finally tore my eyes away and looked down at the plaque.

Wolfgang Dankworth: Living by the Sword
If ever a man was born to hang, it was Dankworth. Given the

nickname by the media of "The Wolf," Wolfgang Dankworth has set himself against our revered hero since nearly day one. Finding issue with Amazing Man's intentions and actions during the Twin-Bomb incident, Dankworth has made it his sole mission in life to end Amazing Man and exact his revenge.

He has been inextricably linked to numerous terrorist acts across the United States, mainly centering in Utah and Nevada.

I stared numbly at the metal plate, various words echoing themselves again and again in my mind.

The Wolf... Twin-Bomb incident... Revenge... Terrorism... Dankworth... Revenge... *Dankworth... Revenge...*

Revenge for what, even?

Just stop. Please.

My temples pounded. I closed my eyes for a few seconds and took some even breaths, trying to separate myself from the information I'd just learned.

But I was the one I was reading about. This was me.

I clenched my teeth. *No. No, it's not. I'm different. I'm stopping this jerk for good. He's not me. I'm not just gonna let people die without lifting a finger to stop it.*

Bad News's voice came from next to me, echoing a little. "Did you finish with reading that one?"

I let out my breath and nodded.

"Well... there's more to read, man. Get crackin'." He bumped me towards the next one.

My heartbeat sped up. I could hear pounding in my ears and slamming pain through my head.

This didn't seem like a boring school assignment anymore. Torture would be more like it. Legitimately terrifying torture.

Oh, please help this not bring back my memories...

Was I praying?

News nudged me again. "C'mon."

I stepped forward slowly, keeping my flashlight aimed down. I could do this. Just stay distant and unconnected. It didn't have to bring everything back. Taking a breath, I shone the light upward.

Mugshots and a few other pictures of the gang stared back down at me.

Bad News with blood on his shirt and a gun in his hand, but no expression beyond a mildly apologetic smile.

A shorter-haired Liza holding a large knife and threatening someone who was holding onto his little kid in an Amazing Man suit. Blood drew a thick, red line from her forehead down to her jaw and dripped down onto her arm. Tears shone on her cheeks.

Roy holding up a small bomb over his head like a trophy and grinning, blood trickling from his nose and a bruise above his eye.

Chris being slammed against a cop car and handcuffed, his expression tight and cold. Blood on his hands.

Blood everywhere.

My stomach churned. I swallowed again and forced my eyes down to the words on the plaque.

The Pack: Dankworth's Fellow Wolves
Some joined forces with him right at the beginning, some came in later, but the Pack seemed to materialize out of thin air after the Twin-Bomb incident.
The Pack's first brush with the law happened only days afterwards, breaking Brown and a wounded Dankworth out of prison and disappearing. They resurfaced almost two months later, organized, armed and dead-set on the death of Amazing Man.
While to all appearances they seem an inept, ragtag band of hoodlums, multiple encounters have proven them to be no laughing matter. They have built almost all of their own explosives and weapons themselves and have proven quite a force to be reckoned with for our Hero.

I… got broken out of prison?

Fellow wolves… I blinked a few times and turned to the next display right next to that one.

Scarily accurate wax models stared down at me. Almost like

178

they saw something in me that I didn't. I turned my eyes downward again and forced myself to read through the headache.

Members of the Pack:
Liza Allister — No background information known.
Baden "Bad" News — Former mafia involvement. Former pool-hustler. Hit man. Long petty-crime record.
Roy Tucker — Former stock-car racer and Oklahoma trucker. Gang-organized drug-dealing. Well-known Speed-Freedom activist.
Chris Brown — Outdoorsman and hunter.
(Notify authorities with any other known members or information)

So Cardboard was a secret. I remembered Roy mentioning that the baseball stadium was "her first strike." I wondered how soon she'd be on the wanted list. She couldn't be older than six.

Bad News as mafia... that fit like a glove.

And Chris as a hunter.

I could see all those things about Roy pretty easily, too.

My headache didn't seem to be getting too much worse. Maybe I could muscle my way through this. It couldn't hurt to collect a bit more information to help the charade, back with the gang.

Almost as if on cue, my head throbbed.

"How much more is there?" My voice was still a whisper.

"A good bit." News's non-whisper echoed through the building in a rumble. He bounced on his toes for a second, then rocked back on his heels as he looked back at me. "Any memories...?"

"No," I snapped, whirling to glare at him.

He raised an eyebrow. I'd probably said that too quickly.

Biting my tongue, I turned back around and went towards the other exhibits. I'd just skim. Hopefully, that would be a bit less triggering.

Less information, less chance of the memory returning. But enough that I could act like I was still my old self with the gang until the time came for the bomb. Or *stopping* the bomb.

Most common method of attack seems to be explosives…

… All attacks center on Amazing Man, the SPI and supporters of the superhero project. Strikes are organized in such a way that casualties of those unsupportive or uninvolved in the agency are practically nonexistent…

Members of the Pack have been to prison multiple times, but questioning hasn't revealed anything that isn't already obvious… breakouts common…

… endgame still unclear…

This wasn't working. Or… maybe it was, if we were going by Bad News's definition.

Every beat of my heart shot another stab of pain through my head. I closed my eyes for a bit more and made myself breathe slowly. I rubbed my knuckles over my face. A moan came out involuntarily. I tried to make it sound like a cough instead.

"There's only one thingy left to read," News prompted from next to me.

I opened my eyes and suppressed the urge to yell at him. The last plaque didn't have a display. Just a little platform that read "stats."

That shouldn't be too bad. It was small. It was the last thing.

I let out my breath and stepped up to it, aiming the flashlight beam down at the words. I noticed the numbers were the kind that could easily be slid in or out and exchanged to update the data.

Number of major terror acts: 14

People injured: 67

Fatalities… I stopped and looked at the ceiling for a bit. I wasn't sure if I wanted to know that. How many people had I killed?

Only seven.

I blinked. Only? Wait, I hadn't read that… how… ? I looked down at the sign again.

Fatalities: 7.

A cold rock settled itself in my stomach. Seven people. And I knew. Correction, I *remembered.*

A particularly sharp jab of pain forced a sound from my lips that sounded almost like a whimper. I rubbed a hand over the gash on the back of my head and sucked in my breath through my teeth.

But we were done. I'd finished. And getting through a whole exhibit about myself only remembering the number seven was pretty good.

Unless...

I turned to Bad News, who had a sharpie out and was doodling a smiley face on the back of his hand that was holding the flashlight. "We're done, right?" It was more a plea than a question.

He nodded, capping the marker and sticking it in his pocket. "With this section."

I groaned loudly. "My head feels like it's being stabbed. Can we just come back later or something?"

"Well, if your head hurts that might mean there's some memories coming back," News raised his eyebrows and tipped his head down at me. "And besides, we're already here, so you might as well read. Buck up."

I stayed where I was, scowling.

He grabbed the collar of my coat and pulled me along a few steps. I whacked his hand away, but kept walking.

Blowing an especially loud bubble, News shone his flashlight up and around the entrance of the next branch.

A Disastrous Beginning

The letters were shaped out of what looked like scrap metal. Below the arch sat two metallic bullet-shaped things. Bombs. I squinted at them. They looked kind of familiar...

Stop. No, no, no, don't...

But the image my mind pulled up was the metal housing I'd seen by my giant bomb in the basement. Huh. *I guess I like that model.*

I just about tripped over the first plaque, whacking my shin on it and dropping my flashlight. Strange light flickered across the floor as my flashlight rolled. I swore and held my leg.

What kind of dumb museum person puts a plaque *that* low down?

News bent over and scooped up the flashlight. "Want me to just hold the light for you?"

"No," I growled, grabbing it back from him. I muttered under my breath and began to read the large-lettered, low down plaque.

The Twin Bomb Incident: A Disastrous Beginning

Just three days out of training, Amazing Man was put to the ultimate hero's test.

Two identical bombs were planted by a still unidentified terrorist organization, one near Ogden in the North, one in the southeastern corner of Utah.

Even with his powers of flight and superhuman speed, Amazing Man knew he couldn't get to both of them quickly enough, so he was forced to make a split-second decision.

He managed to get through the housing and disable the bomb in Ogden within ten minutes, but while he was en route to the other bomb, it exploded.

124 people were killed in the incident.

One hundred and twenty four. My throat constricted. All those lives. Gone. I swallowed.

There was really nothing Charles could've done. I mean, despite being a superhero, he was still human. He couldn't save everyone. No one could. Sometimes choices have to be made…

But my thought train suddenly took off in the other direction with all the possibilities of what he could have done.

He's a <u>superhero</u>. That's his job: to save everyone. <u>Everyone</u>.

He could have sent Dallas… Dallas could've teleported him… he could have recruited the rest of the law enforcement… the project could've given him super speed to begin with, for goodness sake. That was way more useful than…

I shook my head and rubbed at my temples. What was wrong

with me?

Keep going. Just get through the museum.

I pulled my flashlight up to a small sign with only the word "Fatalities." It was just in the middle of the floor and there was nothing directly behind it. I frowned.

"Where's the exhibit for that sign?"

News stepped up behind me. "It's the rest of the section." He swiped his flashlight over photos and glass display cases filling the rest of the area.

That was a lot.

I rubbed at my head again, mentally steeled myself and went to the nearest glass case. My flashlight beam was getting a little shaky again. I just focused on the photo.

A late-teenaged boy in a baseball hat and t-shirt, grinned up at the camera as he leaned on a car. Black grease stained his hands and smudged his face. A label underneath the sign read "Eli Calloway — died at age 19. Was working nearby at the time of the explosion."

Nineteen… that was Dallas's age. I didn't want to imagine Dallas dying.

I looked at the glass case under the picture. A wrench. A toolbelt. A book. A piece of paper with a label. *Eli's letter to his fiancé.*

Holy smoke. No sense of privacy at all. I turned to the next display.

A mom and her daughter that were visiting a park. A honeymooning couple. A family on a road trip. A veteran. An older woman who was with her husband at home… and her husband survived.

I was starting to feel quite literally sick.

Then I reached a larger display case in the corner of the room. My flashlight batteries came a little loose and the light flickered, so I stopped to fiddle with them. The dim light faded out for a second. I whacked the flashlight with the palm of my hand.

"Oh, yep. That's the one." News's voice cut the silence. The pop of a bubble followed.

I turned to squint into his flashlight irritably. "What's 'the one'?"

"That one you're next to. Big whammy right there." He paused for a second, seeming to hesitate slightly. "Any memories yet?"

"Shut up." I screwed the end of my flashlight back on and pulled the beam up to the exhibit. My eyes fell on the label first.

Dankworth Family

My heart about jumped out of my chest.

William, Rachel, Eloisa and Peter. Died in their home.

My family. This was my family.

My gaze kept going back and forth from each name to that awful word. Died.

My family died because of that bomb. Because Amazing Man didn't stop the bomb.

I felt like I could choke. My breathing sped up, but I couldn't seem to get enough oxygen. I didn't stop staring at the exhibit. I couldn't stop. It felt like a sort of betrayal to this family I didn't even remember, but still carried their names on a paper in my pocket. I had to know about them.

I swallowed and looked down. My flashlight cast long, trembling shadows among the things in the glass case.

A watch. The glass on the face was smashed and stained with smoke but the worn leather strap still folded comfortably under it. My dad's watch.

What looked like a Lego house, half smashed and blackened by fire. The plastic was partially melted together, fusing the happy colored bricks into an ugly, dark mass. Then a small metal brain-teaser puzzle with a peeling sticker on it that showed the same sort of robot I had on my keychain. Peter's.

A CD. Wolfgang Amadeus Mozart. That same scrawling, soft cursive I'd seen earlier had written out a name in pink pen on the cover. Rachel Dankworth.

My mom.

She had dark hair. She loved peanut butter and pink lipstick. She was an amazing baker and the house always smelled like cookies…

It felt like a knife twisted against the back of my head.

Stop it. Stop looking. Stop reading. You're remembering. You can't remember. Keep the amnesia; stop the bomb.

There was a little journal next to the CD. Purple and soft. The edges were singed and the cover was smoke stained, but I could still make out the careful, flowery letters on the front.

Eloisa Dankworth ~ Poet, dreamer and chocolate addict

That was what was in that book. Poems.

She used to show me those poems. Sometimes they were just about something silly, like chocolate chips. Sometimes they didn't even rhyme. But they always felt right.

I told her she would be famous when she was older.

She would just laugh and hide her face from me. She'd say she didn't care. She just liked writing them.

I blinked. What was that?

That wasn't remembering. I'd always known that. I just hadn't thought of it. It didn't hurt like the other times I tried to remember.

Eloisa was too sweet. Ellie would never hurt anyone.

Don't look up. Don't look at the pictures. Stop and walk away.

I looked up.

A picture of Peter, holding a solved Rubik's Cube and grinning like he would split his face. A grubby t-shirt hung down over one shoulder and his hair stuck up crazily on one side of his head.

A picture of Eloisa standing on a patch of grass and fingering the edge of her yellow dress with a shy smile. Wavy hair fell over her shoulders and a tiny bit of lipstick was on her lips.

I smiled a little. She had always hated makeup.

I looked at the next picture. Mom and Dad. Side by side. Dad making a face and Mom laughing about it.

The dimples in her cheeks. The smile lines by her eyes.

Dad's hair, that I could never tell the color of.

That crazy cowlick that seemed to have left its mark on all of us.

And then the biggest picture.

A family portrait. Everyone in black and white, smiling at the camera. Ellie in a white dress that made her look even more like an angel. Peter was sticking his tongue out at the camera and his collar was flipped up on one side. Mom held a tiny little boy in a tuxedo, holding his arms up in a "hooray" gesture and smiling.

Dad was grinning charmingly at the camera. He had one arm around someone slightly taller than himself.

Someone with a huge cowlick who gave the camera a patronizing smile, despite his slow strangulation by bowtie.

Someone I'd seen before.

In the mirror.

The knife feeling stabbed into the base of my skull and I dropped my flashlight.

The knife had opened an old wound.

I was bleeding. Bleeding memories. Words and images pouring out of the darkness and into my mind so fast my vision spun.

I stumbled backwards, doubling over and holding my head. I felt like I could scream.

It hurt. Holy *smoke,* it hurt.

God, no. Please, no.

Stop.

But I knew now.

I remembered. I remembered everything. And it hurt worse than knives.

Chapter 19: Home For the Weekend

August, 2018

The wind whipped through the car so loudly I almost didn't hear my phone ringing. I pushed my sunglasses up to prop them on my cowlick and picked it up from the dashboard.

Mom. Again.

Having her on the phone was almost worse than having Peter in the backseat. Almost. Mom's impatient genes seemed to have doubled when she passed them on.

"Are you here yet? Huh? How much faster can you go?"

I shook my head and flipped the phone open. "Hello, Mother." I put on a British accent and dragged out the last syllable.

"My dah-ling child," she responded in like fashion and I chuckled under my breath. "It's simply *splendid* to hear your voice."

Like she hadn't just heard it ten minutes ago. And again fifteen minutes before that.

I leaned back in my seat and drummed my fingers on the steering wheel. "Mother dear, what part of 'a few hours until I get there' did I fail to communicate?"

"Oh, none of it, dear boy. I was just informed that our milk supply has been exhausted and you know how disastrous that is. Especially considering the chocolate cake we have planned for tonight…"

I raised my eyebrows, "Oh, have you now?"

"Special occasion of a young man coming over tonight," she informed me in a serious tone. "Quite a charming young man, too. Drinks half his weight in milk, though. Could I bother you to stop and pick some up?"

I laughed, "Okay, I suppose if you put it that way…" I shifted out of the British accent, "You know, Mom, you don't have to make a huge deal every time I come home for the weekend."

"Hmm," Mom hummed thoughtfully for a second, as if I'd just suggested a revolutionary idea. "You're right. I'll just make you sleep on the porch and feed you slop instead."

"You know what I meant. It doesn't have to be a sugar circus."

I could almost hear her shaking her head and giving that thin, sideways smile that always meant 'you're cute, but no.' "It's my favorite day of the week. Throwing a party for my grown-up Wolfy boy. Besides, cake is an important part of the diet, remember?"

I half groaned, half laughed and shook my head. "Yeah, yeah, cake, ice cream and peanuts on top… cover all the food groups. I've heard the speech." I looked over at the signs for the town coming up on the right. "There's a grocery store at the next exit. I'll grab the milk."

"Thanks, hon. Oh…" there was a bit of scuffling around like she'd covered the mic for a second. I waited and her voice came back, "Peter wants to tell you something really quick. I'll see you soon, okay?"

"Alright, see ya." I hit the turn signal and pulled off on the exit towards the grocery store as the scuffling sounds continued.

Peter's voice blasted through the speaker. "Wolf! Guess what?"

I winced and held it a little further from my ear. "Chicken butt."

"Amazing Man is coming to town tomorrow! Like… *our* town. And he's gonna answer questions and shake hands and sign stuff and Mom said I could go! Like I could see him fly and lift stuff in person! And maybe I could show him the Amazing Man Lego set I made up!"

Peter was really the biggest fan in the state of this whole Amazing Man thing. And despite what a media circus this whole thing was, I had to admit, it was pretty neat having an actual superhero around — even if all he was doing so far was posing for pictures.

"Sounds amazing," I answered, turning off towards the store.

"Totally." I knew that tone of voice. Peter was probably bouncing on his toes at the very least. "Do you think you could come with me?"

"Sure. I'll have Amazing Man sign my forehead or something." I pulled into a parking spot and sat back in my seat. "Don't think I'd trust him to lift my car, though."

Peter laughed, "Okay, sweet. Here's Ellie. Bye! See you soon!"

There was a bit of fumbling around, it was quiet for a second, then I heard Eloisa's voice. "Um… hi?"

"Was there a reason he handed the phone to you?" I laughed.

"Other than the fact I was sitting next to him, no."

"Ah." The line went quiet. Ellie was awful on the phone.

"How's your day been going?" I asked, popping my car door open and sliding out into the thick August air.

"Pretty well." She was silent for a second, then coughed a little, her voice getting quieter. "It's kind of… quiet here without you home anymore."

My smile faded a little, remembering how she'd cried when I moved out, but I brought the cheerfulness back into my tone. "What?

Leif and Peter not loud enough for you?"

"I mean… I just miss you." She trailed off, sighing. "Peter doesn't like hearing poems."

It was silent over the line for a bit.

I cleared my throat, breaking the awkward silence, "Hey, I have something for you when I get home. A surprise."

I involuntarily glanced through my car window to see the yellow, solidly bound notebook lying in the passenger seat. She went through notebooks faster than some guys go through cigarettes. She'd love this one, I was sure. Yellow was her favorite color. And I always made a point to bring her a little something whenever I came back. It helped with how hard of a time she was having with my being away.

"Oh really?" I could hear a shy smile in her voice.

"Yep. Something for you to look forward to."

"Other than my brother coming back?"

"What, that annoying guy that comes and eats everything and tickles you every weekend?"

"That's him," she laughed softly.

I pushed off my car, grinning, and started walking towards the store entrance. "Well, that guy needs to go get some groceries now, so he can get back sooner. I'll see you soon."

"Bye," she responded, "Drive safely. I can't wait to see you." I could hear the smile was back on her face.

"See ya soon, Ells." I flipped my phone shut and stuck it back in my pocket, closing my hand around my wallet instead.

Now, to get some milk.

#

I was heading towards the door when the floor jolted. I stumbled a little and almost dropped the grocery bag.

An earthquake?

I righted myself and quickened my steps to the door. The shaking of the floor went down a bit. A quick earthquake, I guess.

And then the noise.

It was like thunder, but bigger. Much bigger. It wasn't natural. Like it was half animal roar. The noise vibrated in my skull and made me wince. I put the hand that wasn't holding the milk up to cover one ear and stepped out the door. My feet stumbled over each other a bit, still off balance from the vibrating ground.

What the…

I got myself a bit further out into the parking lot and spun around, scanning the horizon for any clue as to what that noise had been.

And there it was. A huge, black storm cloud of smoke, billowing up high and fast and blocking out the white clouds.

Other people were rushing out of the store and getting out of their cars, staring and exclaiming. A few were getting on their phones.

What direction was that in? South.

South.

I was going south.

My family was there.

That smoke was coming from home.

My insides turned to ice and I felt the blood drain from my face. All the noises around me, everyone else's exclamations and yelling, faded in my ears. I couldn't even think or focus on anything but one goal.

I had to get to them. Had to see if they were okay.

I got my legs to work and broke into a run towards my car, fumbling my phone out of my pocket and punching in the number with shaking hands. Mom's cellphone. I doubted our landline would be in working order.

Probably just a… I don't know. A big smoke bomb. A house fire in the neighborhood. A weird sort of… new smoke-firework.

My eyes went to that horrible cloud of smoke again and I swallowed. I popped open the door to my car and slid in, throwing the milk onto the seat next to me.

The phone made the ringing noise. It was connecting. Mom

was okay. She was making cake. She would pick up and call me some awful nickname in a British accent again.

It buzzed. *"The number you dialed has been disconnected. Please check the number and try again."*

No. Nonono. I'd dialed wrong. Mom had dropped her phone in the sink or something. She was always dropping stuff. Just bad timing. Of course, Mom would finally break her phone for good at the worst possible moment.

Classic Mom. We'd... get a good laugh about this over the weekend...

I shook my head, forcing a bit of a laugh as I stuck my phone back in my pocket. My breathing had gotten so fast I was getting lightheaded and it took a couple of shaky tries before I got the keys into the ignition. I turned them and the engine roared to life.

I gripped the steering wheel so tightly I thought it might break. My eyes couldn't look anywhere but that growing black cloud. *Calm down. It'll be okay. They'll be fine.*

The radio came on, and I turned it up louder than necessary, frantically switching the stations until I found the one I wanted.

I only heard the name of my hometown and the words "bombing incident" before I went numb.

That was a bomb?

I stared at the smoke on the horizon with my heartbeat pounding in my ears. *They... they can't be... no...*

They had to be okay. I'd get to them.

I floored it out of the parking lot.

#

The freeway became a racetrack. I broke the speed limit by at least twenty miles per hour the whole way there.

It still seemed to take a year. And the fact that there weren't any cops around to pull me over was worrying.

Three more exits. Three more... I kept the mental countdown going in my head. All the scenery I usually enjoyed only served to remind me of how far away I still was. The swirling, apocalyptic black smoke charred the sunset. It looked red and ugly.

I'm almost there. I can find them. I forced my illogically hopeful thoughts to scream above the other ones. The ones that were probably right.

I looked up at the sky as the smoke haze in the air grew thicker. It scorched my throat and left a taste in my mouth as I breathed it in.

God, please help them be okay. Please help none of them be hurt. I prayed the same thing over and over, stopping myself just short of pulling the card of "I'll never ask for anything ever again."

I readjusted my focus to the road in front of me just in time. I slammed on the brakes, narrowly avoiding the bumper of a car in front of me and skidding partway off the road.

Car after car lined up, packing the lanes in shiny, multicolored rows. Police lights flashed over the metal, reflecting into the smoky partial darkness. A roadblock was up ahead. The sounds of alarmed yelling mixed with screams and sirens as I popped my door open.

It sort of sounded like I'd always imagined the end of the world would sound.

I don't know why I grabbed the notebook for Eloisa. And I certainly don't know why I grabbed the milk. But holding both of them, I wove my way around the cars and muscled towards the front, near the blockade.

The milk jug actually ended up coming in pretty handy to hold ahead of me while I pushed through the people, packed as tightly as sardines as they screamed at the police. Any sense of personal space was absolutely smashed. Like the already existing panic wasn't enough… I could barely breathe being crammed in there like that.

But finally, I made it to the front of the crowd, right at the police line.

I could see beyond the officers and cars. Metal chunks and charred bits of who-knows-what were flung across the street. What would normally be the bright, cheery entrance to the town was clouded out with smoke. It billowed out and across the street, showing the police lights' beams spinning in the cloudy air.

I craned my neck, looking as far as I could beyond and into the town. My house… just a couple of minutes' walk from here, I was pretty sure. They'd be there, at the house. They'd be fine. They *had* to be.

I set my jaw and started pushing through to the street beyond the cars. A blue-clad arm clotheslined me, smacking against my chest and pushing me back.

"The area's not safe. Stay back here with everyone else." The policeman sounded like he'd already said it a million times.

I pushed his arm aside, "No, my family's there. I can just go in really quick and…"

"Kid, there's a lot of people saying the same thing. We can't let you through. They have search-and-rescue dogs and a medic team and they're getting out all the survivors they can."

I heard shouting to my left and looked over to see another officer dragging a shorter teen girl with choppy turquoise hair back behind the line of cars. She kicked and yelled curses at him, as well as a few sentences I couldn't understand.

She got an arm free and spun around, swinging at him. Her fist caught him in the side of the face and he staggered back. Another cop stepped forwards with a taser and the girl was dragged off to the side.

They were serious about this.

The officer watching me looked away for a second, towards the commotion with the girl. I ducked under his arm, making a run for the other side. I didn't make it more than two yards before two cops grabbed me, dragging back towards the rest of the group.

"Hold it, milkman," The bigger one shoved me backwards into the crowd. I took a swing at him with the jug, but that only served to throw me off balance.

A helicopter flew in, low overhead, and the people's screaming intensified, as well as the push to get through.

I barely avoided being trampled by the panicked crowd and got myself out to the side on the grassy highway median.

This was ridiculous, really. What were the police going to do? Just hold off the frantic family members forever and not tell them anything about what was going on? They could at least let the capable ones through to help in the search.

I looked down at my hands. They shook, still holding the milk and the notebook. *Things I was going to give my family…*

Am going to give my family. Don't think in the past-tense. They're still over there. I just need to get to them.

I sat down hard, gritting my teeth and scowling at the line of cops. My leg bumped something and I looked over to see that I was sitting next to the turquoise-haired girl who'd gotten herself tazed a few minutes ago. She was curled up in a tight, painful ball as she lay sideways on the grass.

She moved a bit, trying to sit up. Her breath came in half-sobbing gasps and she seemed to be trying to say something I couldn't make out.

I leaned slightly closer and frowned, trying to hear.

"He's over there," her choked words twisted through an accent that sounded close to British. "Eli's over there… I can find him… he's over there…" She shakily pulled herself up into a sitting position, her tangled hair covering her face. Another noise that sounded like a sob came coughed out. After a couple of seconds, she seemed to sense my presence and looked up.

I blinked at her.

She swallowed, pressing her lips together, and turned away, pulling at her black tank top straps.

I swallowed, "You got someone over there too?"

Still refusing to look at me, she bit her lip and nodded.

Of course she did, idiot. Why else would she be crying? My gaze went back to the smoke that had somewhat cleared. The blackness still remained and landmarks that always heralded the way to my home were either unrecognizable or gone. Blown to bits like some Lego town that had gotten kicked down.

I felt like throwing up, but pushed back the feeling.

"They're alive," I said, more to myself than her.

"For now, maybe," she muttered. "But those cops won't let anybody go and bloody *check.*"

I glanced over at her again and she rubbed at her eyes. "You know where to look, over there?" I asked.

The girl nodded again. "I know right where he was working. He…" she swallowed and stopped talking, pulling her knees up to her chest to hide that her chin was trembling.

I glanced behind us at the shadowy stretch of grass and the distant mountains. Smoke darkened the sky even further. I picked at the sleeves of my leather jacket thoughtfully. Almost night, and we were both wearing black…

I looked back to the girl, who'd put her face down on her knees. "We could take the longer way around," I suggested quietly. She looked up and I tipped my head to the darkness behind us.

"You know, just slip around. It's dark enough to hide us, but light enough that we can still see. I don't think they'll spot us if we just keep low in the grass. Their plate's full enough with all… these guys." I gestured to the panicked hordes, still pushing to get through the barricade.

She set her jaw and nodded. "Let's do it."

We stood together, with her still a little unsteady. I tucked the yellow notebook for Ellie into my coat and nodded to the girl, "We'll find them."

Her expression set with determination, so that the tears and smeared makeup looked out of place. "Thanks." She tipped her head, "What was your name again?"

Oh boy. My given title always made me lots of friends.

"Wolfgang. Wolfgang Dankworth." I shook her small, cool hand.

I saw a tiny ghost of a smile flicker on her lips for a second. "Liza Allister," she tucked her hair behind her ear and nodded. "Let's go."

Together, we disappeared into the darkness and headed

towards the smoke.

Chapter 20: Promises

I usually thought of dew as something that made my sneakers damp — not something I'd end up getting all over my face, as I crawled through the grass.

I spat out a bit of a leaf I'd gotten in my mouth and squinted up at my rescue-partner ahead of me.

Liza seemed to be a trained expert at this. She slid through the grass and ahead of me like a turquoise-headed snake, stopping occasionally to let me catch up. I would have told her to wait up, but we'd already agreed not to say anything. So I just shut up, ignored the stiff grass poking my hands and kept going.

Only a few yards after we passed the flashing cop lights, I started hitting little burnt grass patches and bits of shrapnel. My hand hit a piece of jagged glass and I yanked it back, biting my lip to keep from cursing.

Clenching my hand into a fist, I pushed myself up a bit and saw that the field of broken glass was just getting started. I'd prefer to be un-shredded for the rescue attempt, thank you.

"Liza!" I hissed. I pushed slowly up onto my knees.

She popped up, her hair whipping around her pale face. Her eyebrows went up questioningly.

"I… I think we're good to just walk now. Just stay low." I got to my feet with a glance behind us at the cops. They had plenty to do already with the gathering mob, and we were beyond the lights of the cars now.

Liza stood, brushing off her damp jeans, and I walked over next to her. I rubbed at the middle of my back and winced, stretching out my muscles after my unscheduled groundhog practice.

She looked over at me. "Got anything on you?"

I frowned, "Huh?"

"You know… in case we have more run-ins with… them." Liza tipped her head towards the cops.

Sure, I'd just seen her kicking and cursing at the cops, but asking if I was armed to fight and/or kill them seemed a bit more extreme.

"I've got my knife and a gun," I said quietly, "But I'm not planning on using them on any cops."

She shrugged, her mouth set in a serious line and her gaze icy. "You never know." And in a flash of turquoise, she'd started off again silently.

I tugged on the collar of my coat, frowned deeper and followed after her at a slightly slower jog. My feet kept catching on bits of metal and I heard the occasional tinkling crunch of glass under my feet. The smoke was thicker in the air now, and I muffled a cough in my elbow.

Distant shouts and barks of dogs broke the silence every now and again, and intermittent flashlight beams illuminated the gutted, broken remains of buildings. It looked like the police were working towards us from the opposite direction.

Flames still tickled along the edges of a few buildings, but most of the stuff was too charred to provide a decent fuel. The old familiar structures were skeletons, and the windows that used to be lined with flowerpots and pretty shutters were black and empty, like soulless eyes. The sides of the street were littered with all sorts of odd things. I saw a baseball hat, a few books, a computer and a sink. All were blackened by smoke and twisted or burnt.

The old main street of the town.

It looked like a war zone.

I shivered and stopped for a second, breathing in through my nose. The air smelled like smoke and burnt plastic. And death — so much death. I closed my eyes for a second.

Please, God. Please help my family not be included in that count...

Liza had stopped cold in the middle of the street up ahead. I swallowed the sick feeling at the back of my throat and came up next to her.

She stared straight ahead, not blinking. Following her line of sight, I saw what had been an auto parts store collapsed in on itself. Bits of the windows and roofing lay at our feet.

Liza's whole body looked frozen in place. Her face was blank and pale, like a plastic doll.

Except for her eyes. Wide and terrified. Staring at the crumpled wreck that was the building like it physically pained her.

I stood there for a second, then put a hand on her bare shoulder, feeling goosebumps. She jumped at the touch, but didn't look at me.

"That where your guy is?" I asked. My vote of confidence in his safety was fast diminishing, if so.

"Eli's in there," her voice was steady. She stopped and swallowed before continuing. "I'm going to go in and find him. H-he's in there..."

Somehow, I doubted that expedition would go anywhere fast without a light. I patted down my pockets. I thought I had a... there it was. I stuck my hand into my jacket pocket and pulled out a small keychain flashlight.

I hesitated. *The only light I have, and I'm giving it to a stranger? What about my family? I need to find them, too...*

I shook my head. *Just a few minutes… that's all.*

"Here," I held the flashlight out to Liza. "I'll wait out here. Call me if you need help."

"Thank you," her voice was husky and she didn't look at me. She took the light mechanically and broke into a run towards the building. Moments later, the turquoise splotch in the dark disappeared through a mangled hole in the side of the building.

I stood there with my hands in my pockets, waiting. And I wouldn't exactly say it was hopeful waiting, either. Just more of a tense, aching sort of pain.

"Eli?" I barely heard her voice over the distant sirens. It was less steady now. She kept calling and there was no answer. I swallowed, pressing my lips together tightly.

Well, I can give myself a bit of a head start, at least. So where is home in comparison to here? I turned, trying to make out my directions from this new set of broken landmarks.

There was our street, branching right off the main road. So just a bit of a way down that road, and there would be a little cul-de-sac. We were at the end of that. I refused to let my bright mental image of our house be scorched and blackened like the rest of the buildings.

A few searchlights from further away brushed the area for a moment, casting eerie shadows. Apparently, the people at the other end of town were more worthy of rescue.

The familiar range of housetop peaks from our neighborhood was smashed and smoking. That star Dad never took off our roof from Christmas five years ago was not to be seen. That was usually my landmark. Now I couldn't even see the top of the roof it used to sit on.

My hands started shaking in my pockets and I clenched them hard. *Just wait a little bit… just wait until you get your flashlight back…*

An almost inhuman scream split the air and I jumped. I whirled to look over at the pile of rubble Liza was in. No, it wasn't from there… goosebumps prickled on my arms and neck.

It shrilled through the smoky air again. Then words.

"Moooooooommm! Daaaaaaad!"

That was from our street.

Screw flashlights.

I took off at a sprint down the road. My feet skidded on broken glass. I ran around the corner and slammed straight into a bent over lamppost, nearly knocking myself silly. Fireworks exploded in my vision as I stumbled sideways. The side of my face tingled and burned with pain, but I forced myself to keep running.

There were about thirty other things I ran into or tripped over, but I didn't stop to identify them. I had to get back home. *Had* to. There was only so much time.

My eye was nearly swollen shut by the time I'd reached my rough estimation of where our house was. I came to an unsteady stop, my lungs burning. Dots still danced in my vision, and it was too dark to make out much. I only saw the distant searchlights and flames flickering over the rubble.

No sound.

"Ellie?" I yelled. "Peter?" My voice cracked and I gulped in air. "Guys, are you here?" The words didn't sound like mine.

Panicked.

I never panicked.

"Dad?" a broken whisper came from the ground to my right.

Peter.

I ran towards his voice, tripping over something right next to him and almost landing on my face. I pushed myself up onto my hands and knees and crawled the last few feet.

"Peter? Peter, c'mon… talk to me, buddy…" My eyes were slowly adjusting to the pitch darkness around me, and I could see his outline. Grubby blue tee shirt. Crazy poof of hair. So still, though.

God, he has to be alive, please… please…

The poof moved a bit, and Peter's white face nearly shone in the darkness as he looked towards me. "W-wolf?"

He was alive.

"Hey, bud… hey… " I reached him. He was pinned under a

giant piece of wood that was splintered on the ends. Part of our house. It was thicker around than he was.

I brushed his hair back from his forehead and looked him over, trying to find if he was bleeding. My gaze rested on the dark patch under him on the grass. It was growing fast and my fingers came away wet and sticky when I touched it. Peter's blood. I felt like I could choke.

Peter's brow furrowed as he looked up at me. "Where's Mom?"

I swallowed, "I-I don't know. Where did you see her last?"

He had to think on that for a second. "Inside. In the house." His voice caught strangely in his throat.

I looked up at the house. Our house. Home.

It was smashed beyond recognition. The wooden walls had been reduced to toothpicks and the bricks from the front rested in broken heaps. A huge, twisted chunk of metal rested on top, sending the roof off in a V shape around it. The house was flattened.

I felt my breathing double in speed. My mind spun and my vision tunneled on the smoking wreck that used to be home.

But I still had the milk for Mom. I still had the notebook to give Ellie right in my coat. Ellie missed me. Mom said Leif had just figured out how to do a somersault the other day. They couldn't be dead. They just... *couldn't* be.

Maybe they'd gotten out. But they weren't here, so where else could they have gone?

Maybe they weren't home. But Peter was here. And everyone always made a point of being right there to greet me when I came back.

Maybe they'd gone down to the basement and hidden there. I mean, if the house was flattened, then that would be the only safe...

We don't have a basement.

Maybe, maybe, maybe...

None of them fit.

There was no way. No one was alive in there.

Mom. Dad. Eloisa. Leif.

Gone.

I was too late.

Peter coughed and whimpered, "Can you get this thing off me?"

I jumped to my feet and started pulling on the beam, gritting my teeth. Anything physical. Something to distract from the overwhelming pain and helplessness creeping into my mind.

Splinters pulled off into my palms and I savored it. Physical pain was so simple. Why couldn't I have just been here sooner? A quick blast and I would have been gone with them. We could have gone together. Like a family. Like we were supposed to be.

I grunted, pulling on the heavy beam again. The wood shifted and Peter let out a scream like I'd never heard before. I stopped immediately. Peter's soft hiccupping cry stuck like a knife in my gut. I couldn't do that to him anymore.

There was nothing I could do.

He was going to die.

My little brother.

Never pull my hair again. Never make up goofy songs and sing them everywhere. Never hide under my arm when the Doctor Who episodes got too scary. Never build another genius Lego creation. I wouldn't see him grow up and measure himself next to me, trying to be taller.

Stop it. He's not dead yet.

I was down next to Peter again. His eyes were squinted closed and tears leaked out the corners, dripping into his ears in tiny streams. He looked up at me and whimpered a little.

"What happened?" he quavered.

I bit my lip, taking a few seconds before my voice would work, "There was a... a bomb, buddy. It kinda... blew up."

"Did it... did it smash our house? Totally?"

I couldn't work past the lump in my throat, so I just nodded.

"What about... Mom and Dad? E-Ellie? And L-Leif?" his face was even paler now. The puddle under him grew. Warm, sticky, awful blood.

I opened my mouth and closed it again. "Th-they're... they were in the house."

Were.

He frowned and I saw his chin quiver. "But... Amazing Man? Did Amazing Man come? They said... " he stopped and coughed so hard his whole body jerked, then went limp again. His voice was quieter this time. "Amazing Man would save us. He could get anywhere. He promised he'd keep us all safe. Ellie said... "

Snippets of what I'd heard on the radio on the drive here came back into mind and a tiny flame started in my chest.

A parade. There was a parade up north for Amazing Man, so he was too far away, being at that. He couldn't make it to disarm the bomb. To save the lives of a whole town.

Peter coughed again and his lips looked too red.

My grip tightened on his arm. "Peter. Stay with me, buddy. Think you can stand it if I try and move the wood again?"

He turned his head so it lay sideways as his blue eyes met mine. The broken pain I'd seen in them just a few moments before was gone. He smiled and swallowed, looking peaceful.

I shook my head. "No. Come on, Pete. I need you to stick around, okay? Just stay with me for a bit longer? Please?" I choked on the last word. Both my hands were on his shoulders now, like I could hold him here and force him to stay. His muscles were relaxed. Mine shook. "Peter?"

It was just him and me. He had to stick around. He had to make it.

Peter gave a trembling grin and a tiny tear trickled off the end of his nose. "I'll miss you, Wolf."

"No, don't *talk* like that!" I almost felt like cussing at him.

He blinked slowly, "Goodnight."

"Buddy, I can't... you have to... "

His eyes closed and he let out a sigh. The grubby, bloody t-shirt stopped moving up and down.

I felt the little guy I was talking to leave. And I was left, by the ruins of our home, holding a shell of the last thing I cared about.

No.

This couldn't be happening.

Just a couple of hours ago, I had my whole family. We were going to have cake and milk and play some dumb board game. I was going to give Eloisa her new notebook. Dad and I were going to work on some banged up motorbike he'd found. I was going to go with Peter to that Amazing Man event.

This was a nightmare. It had to be.

I swallowed hard, but the lump in my throat didn't leave. It worked its way up and into my mouth, ripping out of my throat in a scream that went on and on until there was nothing left in my lungs.

Gone. They were all gone. There was nothing I could do. No rewind button.

I was alone.

I curled inwards, holding the hurt in my chest like the excruciatingly painful wound that it was, and choking on sobs over Peter's small body. I felt his still-warm blood seep into the knees of my jeans. Hot tears dripped off the edge of my jaw, falling onto my little brother.

I felt ripped into tiny pieces inside. Broken and smashed like everything around me.

God... why? How could you? What did they ever do? Why didn't you save them?

Voices and sirens got closer, but I didn't pay any attention. I didn't want to move. I couldn't leave my family like this. Just more victims, more numbers in the statistics of a tragedy that people across the world would maybe shake their heads at before forgetting it two minutes later.

"... area got the heaviest damage... not much chance of survivors... "

The voices got closer and I registered a few of the words, but didn't go to see who had finally gotten here. Everything hurt too much. I might just sit here and die from all the pain inside.

Then a voice I'd heard on the radio. On TV. In so many videos and promotions.

"I should have been here."

My pain-dulled mind snapped into sudden focus and the tears stopped.

Yes, Charles Fernsby. Yes, you should have been here. You should have been doing your job. But you couldn't miss your parade, could you?

I stopped shaking, all the broken pieces of me fusing together inside with the hot rage in my chest.

There was something I could do after all. Something I *had* to do.

I let go of Peter, kissing his forehead before laying him gently on the ground. Then I stood, my back straight. My hand went to the cold handle at my waistband. My gun. The one I'd said I wasn't using against any cops.

Liza was right. I never would have known.

I strode out onto the street, now illuminated by cop car lights that flashed over the blackened buildings, and faced the group huddled down near the beginning of the street.

I zeroed in on the one with the cape and the perfect hair and started walking. Long strides, but not too fast. Even paces. Calm. I slipped my gun out smoothly as I came closer.

Amazing Man looked around the area, not seeing me. His face was just blank. No sadness. No feeling for the lives he'd just let get blown away like confetti under his bootied little feet.

I hated him. I hated him a hundred times more than I'd ever hated anything.

He was going to pay for every single drop of blood he'd spilled.

One officer looked up. "Hey!" He came forward, getting in my line of fire towards Amazing Man. "A survivor! Sir, did you... "

I shot him. Barely even flinched.

Various exclamations erupted and the whole group shifted to try and defend Amazing Man from justice. Guns were pulled out and aimed right in my direction, but I refused to notice.

The superhero just stared at me and blinked in shock, putting his hands up defensively. His spotless suit and cape looked out of place in all the smoke and destruction. *Just needs a few holes in it. And lots of blood.*

I picked up my pace, still keeping a level aim at Amazing Man, calling him every name I could think of, over and over again. My finger inched towards the trigger, but another bang sounded first.

Pain blasted through my side and spread like a wave over my body. I didn't realize I'd fallen over until I felt the back of my head hit the pavement.

I stared up at the swirling smoke, gasping for breath. The physical pain slowly pulled my mind back from my mission. From my family.

It hurts… it hurts…

No. You deserve the pain. Your family hurt worse. Get back up, idiot. Get Amazing Man. Now.

Blood started seeping from my side and my vision swam. I couldn't get up.

Cops swarmed over me like vultures, blocking out the light and yelling words I couldn't decipher.

I moved my arm to push myself up. "S-son of a… " I tried to sit up and finish the curse, but blackness roared over me, fading the nightmare of my life away into nothingness.

#

I didn't know how long it was before I finally got the strength and presence of mind to open my eyes again.

I was lying flat on my back.

The ceiling was grey above me. I didn't know anyplace with a grey ceiling — certainly not my house.

My house.

All the horrible memories came pouring back in and I winced.

My house was gone.

My family was gone.

I was alone. I'd killed someone.

And I still had to kill someone: that joker who called himself a hero.

I blinked at the ceiling and noticed my side was starting to hurt. I figured that was probably normal for the aftereffects of being shot.

My stomach and chest ached. I started shivering, even though I wasn't cold. I clenched my teeth together to keep them from chattering. My throat felt tight and I swallowed, closing my eyes again.

It had to be a nightmare. Mom would call up and say I was sleeping in too late. Leif would tickle my toes and run squealing down the stairs. I would open my eyes and see the yellow ceiling of my room.

I opened my eyes again.

Still grey. Cold. Empty.

I blinked and my nose started feeling funny. Tears blurred the edges of my vision and I blinked them away.

God...

I cut myself off mentally. I wasn't talking to God.

Never. Never, ever again.

He didn't listen. He didn't care.

I forced my thoughts back to here and now.

If I wasn't at home, where was I?

I moved my arm to prop myself up on my elbow, wincing and ignoring the painful dizziness. I looked over my surroundings, blinking to focus my vision.

White fluorescent lights shone down on the cement walls and floor. A window thing with a microphone was in one wall and a chair sat by it. It looked like one of the windows at theaters, where you buy tickets.

Another cot was up against the wall across from me, and a middle-aged man with a beard sat with his gaze fixed on the ceiling. He wore an orange jumpsuit with a belt around his lean middle, and clunky shoes.

I pulled an indifferent expression onto my face, pushing down my emotions.

My side throbbed, reminding me I should really lie down. I ignored it and sat the rest of the way up, examining my own garb.

Yep. I had a jumpsuit, too. Prison it was.

The orange hurt my eyes, and I looked away, putting my back against the cold wall. I still shivered uncontrollably. My stomach hurt. And my heart hurt. I swallowed, scowling at my hands in my lap.

I saw the man across from me shift his position a little. His gravelly voice broke the silence and made me jump.

"Heard what you did. Shooting at Amazing Man."

I looked up at him, then back down at my hands, forcing the hurt in my chest to solidify again. *Yeah, I'll bet you did.*

He sat up straighter and his voice got lower. "I wish you'd hit 'im."

I snapped my gaze up to meet his. Sincere. Anger and hurt hiding in his light brown eyes. He set his jaw and sat forward, giving a single nod. "I lost my Sarah." His voice broke and he refocused his gaze on the ceiling.

I watched him, noticing the traces of tears on his cheeks. "What's your name?" My voice sounded dragged over a field of cactus.

A second of silence.

"Chris Brown," the older man answered. I opened my mouth to say my own name, but he cut me off, looking back down to meet my eyes. "I know your name, kid. Everyone in here knows your name."

I closed my mouth. Considering this was prison, everyone's knowing my name probably wasn't a desirable thing.

"Mr. Dankworth?"

I jumped again. There was someone at the microphone window when I turned to look. A policeman. The officer made a "come here" gesture.

Chris stood and helped me up from the cot. The room tipped

and I just about face planted, but he somehow managed to get me fully upright and over to the window.

I held onto the chair and closed my eyes until the room held still. I opened my eyes. One of them wouldn't open all the way, still swollen from running into the lamppost. I rubbed at it, feeling some dried blood on my forehead.

The officer cleared his throat, "This is not an official interrogation, Mr. Dankworth. However… " He didn't finish his sentence.

I finished it for him in my head.

You're a nosy cop, so you just had to pay me a visit.

"Did you know… " he trailed off, "that it was Amazing Man you were shooting at? Do you remember it or… ?"

I bristled, "My eyesight is in working condition, sir. As is my memory." My voice was still rough and scratchy, but my words were even and cold.

His brow furrowed in a very non-friendly way. I had a feeling I'd probably lost one of the few cops who maybe sympathized with my cause, but I didn't care. The burning in my chest had started up again, taking over so I barely noticed the throbbing in my side.

"So, it was intentional?"

I clenched my jaw together and didn't answer, but I was saying plenty inside.

Yes. Yes, it was. And there will be plenty more intentional attempts before Utah's superhero sees the last of me.

I held that thought, that hurt, and that burning feeling, and pushed them deep down inside, locking them into the core of my being. A promise to Mom. To Dad. To Ellie. To Peter and Leif.

I'd kill Amazing Man.

The Dankworth family wouldn't be slaughtered without a fight.

There was still one left.

And I'd make everyone else wish Wolfgang Dankworth had died with the rest.

Chapter 21: A Bad Egg

April 2022

Those memories hit me harder than any punch ever had. It was like someone had flipped the lights on in a huge building that I'd been wandering around in with just a match. The light was blinding and painful and showed me more than I wanted to know.

I think I fell over.

I don't remember how I got out of the museum, but I'm pretty sure Bad News carried me.

By the time I was able to do anything besides hold my head and blubber incoherently, we were already quite a ways down the road away from that stupid museum.

I pulled my head up a bit and got a big wallop of fresh air in the face. My churning stomach quieted down for a few seconds, but my headache pounded even worse. It felt like my skull might explode.

News was in the driver's seat, his tie fluttering over his shoulder. I think we were speeding. I vaguely wondered why he didn't have Schoolhouse Rock blasting over the speakers. In fact, that sounded more like Mom's disc. The classical music.

Mom…

My stomach lurched and I curled back up with a moan. Why did everything have to hurt so much?

News glanced over at me for a second, then fixed his eyes back on the road. "Get your memories back?"

No, I just thought that exhibit was so fascinating I fell over.

I swore at him with as much energy as I had, which made for a pretty pathetic explosion.

He nodded and flashed me a sideways grin. "See, what'd I tell you?"

I started to call him a few more names, but opening my mouth suddenly seemed like a bad idea. I swallowed carefully, even though my throat seemed to be trying to swallow backwards. My temples pounded. "News…" my voice was a hoarse whisper.

"Hmm?"

"Pull over, please."

News took one look at my face and immediately braked, pulling the Mustang off onto the shoulder and slamming it into park. "Yup. Go."

I popped the door and barely managed to get myself to the grass before I threw up.

Not the most enjoyable experience, by a long stretch.

News scooped me back in the car after I'd utterly emptied myself out and I lay in the passenger seat like an anemic noodle. Part of me felt like shooting something and swearing the whole way back. Another part wanted to curl up in a ball and cry.

I didn't do either, because I honestly lacked the energy. I felt weak and hollowed out, both emotionally and physically. There was nothing left inside me that I could even try to fight back with. I just sat there distantly thinking about my surroundings and anything shallow.

I could feel that my hair was sticking up in front again.

My jacket was warm.

My car smelled weird.

"Hey," Bad News was rooting around in his pockets, setting random things on the dashboard. Among them I spotted a switchblade, a few pop can tabs and a tiny rubber chicken.

I wondered if there was anything he *didn't* have in his pockets.

"I've got some Pepto Bismol, if you want it." News pulled the bottle up and set it next to me.

I looked at the pink container with disdain.

Like that would help.

I didn't remember seeing any billboards advertising that Pepto fixed broken hearts… broken lives… broken people. I was past help. No tiny plastic cup full of pink stuff could fix me.

My nose felt tingly. I swallowed.

News was still looking at me and I saw one of his eyebrows inching up towards the edge of his hat in a question.

I sighed weakly, "Yeah, sure. Why not?"

He gave me a dose, which tasted as pink as it looked, but I was able to keep it down.

Barely.

I survived the winding road back to town and closed my eyes as we pulled onto the freeway. My headache pounded image after image into my mind that I didn't want to see.

The smoke on the horizon. Peter under that beam, bleeding onto the grass. Ellie crying when I left home. My smashed home.

The corners of my eyes stung. I slouched further into my leather jacket, shivering. The metallic smell of blood had saturated the material, but I didn't care. It was my blood. If any Dankworth deserved to be bleeding, it was yours truly.

Leif's face, scared and dirty in the night, surfaced in my mind. Yet another time I wished for a rewind button.

Dad had been with Leif when the house collapsed, and had shielded him with his body, they said. The search-and-rescue team found a scared little boy, crying and stuttering out his big brother's name. I'd already been shot and carted off to prison by that time.

I didn't know he'd survived. Didn't know I had any family left.

Which made it all the more painful when I, his now criminal older brother, was declared unfit to care for him and Mr. Perfect, the man who'd let the whole rest of his family die, took him in. He took the rest of them from me. Why not Leif, too?

He would be seven now. About.

I was a horrible brother.

The worst brother.

More than three and a half years since the bomb. Man, had it been that long? Four years ago this August. It was April now... April...

I opened my eyes and turned to look at Bad News. "What date is it?"

News pushed up his sunglasses and squinted over at the sun on the horizon, as if he could tell the date from that. "Seventeenth, I think."

The seventeenth.

Eloisa's birthday was five days from now. Friday. She would have been eighteen.

I turned away from News and hid my face in my sleeve. It was all wet by the time I drifted off.

#

"Hey, man." Bad News's hand rattled my shoulder in its socket and I jolted awake. "We're home."

Home.

I uncrumpled myself from the corner of the seat and blinked at the abandoned grocery store in front of us, the short burst of excitement dissipating as I realized what he actually meant by "home."

That wasn't home. Home was gone — forever. I was alone.

My stomach hurt. I rubbed my sleeve over my eyes and unbuckled my seatbelt.

News was already out and was walking around the car, like he was going to get me out and carry me in — like I was some sick little kid or something.

I defiantly popped the door open myself and stood up out of the car just as he reached my side. Pain shot through the base of my skull, sharper than it had been for awhile, and I flinched, putting a shaky hand up to it.

News stood there next to me with his hands clasped behind his back like some gargantuan butler. He quietly raised an eyebrow.

I scowled up at him, "Isn't there some ice cream you need to bring inside or something?" I pulled my hand down from my head a little and blinked at the sticky red stain on my palm. Getting your memories back didn't have *that* much physical effect, did it?

News shrugged, "Yeah, ice cream can wait."

The words "who are you, and what have you done with Baden News?" came to my lips, but my head throbbed again, hard, and I lost my train of thought. I sucked in my breath, putting my hand back up.

"You did kind of fall over before I could catch you, and that tile was pretty hard in there…" News nudged me towards the door as he explained. "Think you might have a concussion?"

"I have bigger problems than a possible concussion," I muttered. "How about a dead family? And a totally screwed up life?" My voice caught in my throat and my stomach lurched again.

Why couldn't my memories have just stayed away?

"You'll be okay," News hit the exact middle pitch between comforting and insensitive. "Also… " his voice dropped to a lower rumble, "remember, no one here knows you lost your memory in the first place."

Well that would be *lovely* to try and explain my state in. Whose dumb idea had it been to not tell anyone about my memory loss? Oh, right.

Mine.

I was just a shining beacon of excellence.

My feet caught on the curb as we stepped up towards the main door, and News caught me. I didn't say thank you because his hand hit my rebelling stomach and I was afraid that if I opened my mouth I'd throw up again.

No shadowy figures were near the door as News pushed it open, so I guessed the gang was in the back. The warm vanilla and cigarette smoke smell washed over us and gave me a tiny feeling of comfort. Something familiar.

I stopped for a second and took a breath.

The Den always smelled like this. Almost since the day News brought us all here and we set up our base of operations. It wasn't that long after the bombing. A week or two, maybe.

And then the memories from before the bombing.

Before everything fell apart. We used to drop by this store when we were in the neighborhood and buy ice cream because they made their own here. Peter always raided the free samples more than was polite. Dad ranted about our economy and small businesses trying to keep up when the place closed down. It had been one of the first stores I'd driven to when I learned how to drive...

"Whoa, there," I felt Bad News's giant hand clamp on the back of my jacket to keep me upright. My knees had buckled under me.

I swallowed and blinked away the images, pulling my mind back to the present and regaining my footing on the slick tile.

Voices and laughs echoed from the back of the store, as usual. Roy's loud voice rose above the others. "Okay, okay... listen to this, though... " he launched off into some tale about speeding and cops and random other elements I couldn't hear or didn't register.

News kept a grip on my arm as we walked — almost like he was afraid I'd fall over again. I pushed at his fingers a bit and he let me go. I jammed my hands in my pockets and half-stumbled down the aisle myself, refusing his help even though I probably would have benefitted from the extra support.

Bad News still hovered close. "I'm just going to grab you a hot water bottle and something to drink if you want, then we can head over to your room, okay?"

"Sounds fantastic. Sure." I tried to step out from under his towering shadow a bit as we rounded the aisle corner and came into view of the others. My plan of walking up inconspicuously was thwarted as my toe caught on a loose tile and I pitched forward.

News grabbed my arm again, and I was saved from a faceplant.

The laughter died away and all eyes that had been previously crinkled in merriment went to me.

I stood, putting my shoulders back and my chin up, willing myself to not be knocked over by the fresh burst of memories. All the faces that had seemed so foreign just this morning triggered dozens of stories and pictures in my mind.

Liza. Her mechanical genius coming to play in my first prison break. The trips to the junkyard in News's truck to get parts for various explosives and other weapons she was making. We had held each other together, more or less — especially during the first stretch after the bombing. She told me about Eli. I told her about my family. We just talked, shivering in the dark outside. She was the only girl besides my mom who'd ever seen me cry.

Roy and Cardboard. They had known my family before the bombing. Roy was my best friend. Always visiting the mechanic shop for me to tune up his car when I'd still lived in town. He'd never been one to hold a grudge or get too worked up, but he was more than eager to get a gang going to oppose Amazing Man. Anything run by the government was worth fighting, in his opinion.

Our crazy getaways with Roy at the wheel and cop lights disappearing in the rearview mirror came to mind. Cardboard, always the laughing little bit in the backseat. She used to love me, but since the bombing, she'd been kind of scared of me and kept her distance. I didn't blame her.

Chris. His battered cowboy hat and almost never smiling face. My prison buddy. The picture of "his Sarah" that he always kept tucked in his pocket. Always refusing to talk about her. His almost fatherly talks that relit that fire in my chest and kept me going.

Bad News. Always the intimidation factor, and always the cook. The living gang-legend Roy had recruited for Chris's and my prison break. My self-appointed bodyguard. The guy who forced me to keep living when I didn't want to. News was the solid, optimistic center pillar of the gang, with his big truck, awful coffee and obsession with childish things.

Three and a half years.

I felt a giant hand gripping the back of my jacket again and blinked, forcing myself upright and feeling rather green. I swallowed, teetering a bit. News gave me a pat on the back.

Roy's head was tipped sideways in a sort of curious concern for a few seconds. He relaxed when I scowled at him.

I pushed News's hand off again and walked unsteadily towards my chair.

"Back, I see," Chris said. *Thank you, Captain Obvious.*

"Yup." News ruffled my hair and disappeared behind the bakery counter.

"Well," Roy observed, almost like he was telling a joke, "*somebody* looks like crap."

I wanted to flatten him, but all I managed was a weak punch to his shoulder and a bit of swearing.

He stepped back, rubbing it, and looked over behind the counter. "What took you guys so long?"

"And what's up with Wolfy?" Liza frowned.

I plopped down in my chair and slouched back, holding my stomach.

"Eh, he had a bad egg for lunch," Bad News pushed his hat up on his head and shoved something that looked like a sock into the microwave. "He's not feeling so good."

Ate a bad egg? I *am* a bad egg. I'd let my family die. I'd killed people, and hurt more people. I had a criminal record taller than News.

Roy leaned on the back of my chair, folding his arms, "Think you're coming down with something? You've been acting a bit off for the past couple of days."

"Shut up," I snapped.

Chris watched me for another second and sat back, his facial expression relaxing.

"Roy, go bring in the groceries." News came back around the counter, holding a can of ginger ale and his warm, stuffed sock. He held up the sock. "Hot water bottle's leaky, so I warmed up a rice bag instead."

Roy rolled his eyes and pushed off my chair, scooting it and whacking my head in the process. I swore at him again.

"Man, who knew a bad egg could put you in such a sour mood?" He loped off down the aisle before I could give him any more grief.

"Okay, I'll start making dinner in a bit. Gonna get Wolf to his room first." News walked over and stood next to me for a second, then held out a hand.

"I can walk," I muttered, pushing myself up.

Cardboard edged over next to me and patted my leg, "Feel better, 'kay?"

"Yeah, sure." I forced a smile down at her. It didn't reach my eyes. There wasn't any happiness to draw from, inside me. Maybe I could push the hurt down and act okay, though, once all my emotional wounds scabbed over. Seemed like the best I could hope for.

That, or finishing it. Finally getting Amazing Man. Taking Leif back. Serving justice.

What was I thinking? I was just horrified at the thought of this yesterday. I'd taken measures to prevent it myself this afternoon, when I'd had lunch with Dallas...

Holy smoke, had that really been just a few hours ago?

Dallas and I were friends. I'd given him a promise. My word. And I always kept my word.

But the usual warmth in my chest, the feeling of friendship, didn't seem to be there. It felt like a dying coal.

Dallas had been there. Dallas could have saved them, too. Or at least, helped save them. He was Amazing Man's sidekick.

He'd let my family die. How could he be my friend?

News's hand on my shoulder jolted me out of my thoughts. I'd zoned out again. But my door was in front of me, so apparently I'd been walking as well.

I rested my hand on the doorknob and twisted. The door popped open, creaking a bit. Fluttering from inside reminded me of Lucius's presence.

The falcon was a fairly new addition to the gang, actually. News had picked him up as a birthday present for me when he was abandoned after a renaissance fair nearby. A secondhand falcon… one of his weirder attempts to cheer me up.

It had been Liza's idea to put him to use, getting him to carry a camera so we could get an overhead view on things before our last few strikes. I guess the outside look — with the amnesia and all — made me see for the first time exactly how evil an image having a pet falcon cast cast.

Bad News tapped my arm and I turned to face him. "Hmm?"

He handed me the warm rice-sock, the ginger ale can and something else small and metal. Warm, like it had been in his pocket. He nodded slowly, looking me up and down.

"Think that's it," he said, tugging his tie. "If you need anything else, just holler."

I nodded, "Thanks."

"Yup," News patted my shoulder and started to walk away, but stopped after a few steps and spun on his heel. His tie swung back and forth. "Oh, I forgot…" he pointed towards my armload of stuff, "There was a missed call on that thing while you were zonked out in the car. You might want to return that."

I looked down at my load. The warm metal thing was my phone. And that was really the only thing that it made sense for him to be talking about. I wouldn't have any missed calls on a soda can or a sock full of rice.

"Okay."

And he was gone down the hall.

I pushed the door open the rest of the way and paused, looking around with different eyes. It seemed a bit cleaner, somehow. Probably because I knew what all the junk was now.

Each broken bit of machinery, each burnt scrap of cloth, each piece of crumpled paper... all of them brought images and events to my mind, threatening to send me back in time and tell me their stories — all the individual shades of pain and memory they held.

I closed my eyes for a second and swallowed. I really didn't need that right now. I wanted to sleep. To throw up. To cry. To lie on the floor and not think for a year.

Lucius tipped his head at me and gave a quiet chirrup in the back of his throat.

"Nice to see you, too," I halfway raised my hand in greeting, then sat down on the edge of my bed. I set the ginger ale on my nightstand and rubbed my hands over my face. I let out my breath shakily.

From the flapping noise, I guessed Lucius had flown a bit closer to me.

"You wouldn't believe today," I mumbled through my fingers. "It's like all the worst days of my life rolled into one. I mean... most people *want* their memories. This is like... some disease I just caught back. I hate it. I just... " I dropped my hands and sighed, "And now I'm telling my tale of woe to a bird. I really am going insane."

I looked over at him.

He walked a bit closer to me, looking sympathetic.

I rubbed a finger over his feathers and decided Lucius was better than people.

My phone buzzed in my lap and I looked down. Lucius fluttered back to his perch as I swung my feet up onto the bed. I flipped open the phone.

1 missed call. 1 voicemail. 1 text message.

I looked at the missed call first.

D.M.

I had an idea who that was. I clicked on the voicemail and put the phone to my ear.

"Hey, Wolfgang," a familiar voice began, crackling a bit with static. I could almost smell the spearmint on his breath. "Just calling to let you know we got the date and place all worked out. The meeting of the superheroes is arranged for noon this Friday at a secret desert location. Got a sort of cloaking device going on there, so I'll have to send you the GPS coordinates. Text... call... something. I've got the setup worked out, so it'll be set to go tomorrow. Thanks."

There was a beep and I took my phone down from my ear. Memories of the bomb in the basement dawned on me, along with a new feeling of almost... pride. That was it. The bomb. The same sort of bomb that killed my family would kill Amazing Man. Divine justice, almost. I was so close to the thing I'd been building towards for years.

I mechanically clicked on the text message. It was from Dallas.

"Thank you for lunch. It went a lot better than I expected, honestly. Keep in touch."

Oh, this again... did everything really have to conflict so badly? I'd promised to tell Dallas. I was going to tell him all the details about the bomb, so that we could stop it.

But... did I really want to stop it?

Am I even asking myself?

My stomach did a flip and I groaned, fumbling my hand around on the nightstand for the ginger ale. Instead, my fingers brushed something soft, flat and leathery. A feeling I remembered so well it almost physically hurt. I pulled back like I'd been bitten and looked.

It was dirty. It was stained with smoke, bits of ash and a spot of blood right at the bottom. But it was the notebook I had been going to give to Eloisa. That happy looking yellow notebook for my sister who just missed having me around. I picked it up and noticed my hands were shaking.

I flipped open the cover, brushing the pages. All the poems she could have written here. All the beautiful words she would have read to me in her shy, whispery voice. All the silly doodles and limericks. Instead the pages were blank. Empty.

The lines on the paper blurred in my vision and I rubbed my sleeve over my stinging eyes. This leather jacket had soaked up more blood and tears from me than any jacket should have to endure from its owner.

I blinked at the last few pages. An uneven, torn edge was all that was left of the last page in the notebook. And I'd seen that edge before.

I put my hand in my pocket and pulled out an old, wrinkled piece of paper, soft from folding and re-folding. A revenge note. My mission statement. A reminder of who I was and what I stood for. I'd kept it there for years now. Always in my right pocket.

I unfolded it and it crinkled as I matched it to the torn edge.

For Mom, it read, *For Dad, for Peter, for Eloisa. That which killed shall be killed. Die by the sword.*

My promise to my family.

I brushed my thumb over that puckered tear-mark and another drop fell off the tip of my nose onto the page beside it.

That which killed shall be killed.

I flipped my phone shut.

I wasn't telling Dallas.

He and Amazing Man had broken the most important promise of all. And now, I was breaking mine.

I was getting justice for the Dankworth family.

I knew who I was, now — and this was my mission.

Chapter 22: The Old Me

It took a few days to recover to the point where I didn't feel like jello-man any more.

Those few days weren't fun.

I cried a lot. I threw up a couple more times. I had nightmares almost every time I closed my eyes. I woke up screaming once.

I talked to Lucius. I talked to myself. I talked to the wall. A familiar emptiness ached inside of me so intensely I couldn't even remember what it had been like without it there.

Bad News was pretty much the only one who even came around to poke his head in. He'd check on me, take Lucius for exercise and make sure I ate something. Usually, it was ice cream. Not a big surprise there. I had his full record in my mind now, and his habit of serving ice cream was as dependable as the sun rising every day.

Though I didn't quite appreciate all the memories those

included, I made myself eat it.

Gradually, the violent flashbacks subsided and I somewhat got my feet under me in the current world. The memories didn't hurt as much. I felt like I'd kind of hardened over. Developed a shell.

I didn't want to wear an emotional mask. It didn't feel like me... or the me I'd found over the time of having my memory gone. But I felt like the human equivalent of an exposed nerve, so I grabbed at anything that protected me from all the pain like a drowning man at anything in the water.

Mansley sent the coordinates for the bomb location, but I didn't actually look at them and take the trouble to figure out where it was until a few days later. It was out in what, to all map appearances, was a barren stretch of desert with a tiny town nearby.

The town was at minimal risk, he said. But the superheroes... their meeting hall was right next to the bomb and so the risk they were at was another matter entirely. He'd gotten the bugs worked out of the housing, so we now had a shield and a cloaking device around it that would make it appear as just one of the many red rocks in the area. They'd have a monster bomb right next to them and never even know it was there.

I was free to go check it out any time, as long as I remembered to set my watch for volcano day. Going on Friday was definitely out of the question, unless I wanted to blow myself to bits.

And I, always one for skimming deadlines, finally got my act together and decided to go on Thursday.

I'd just gotten through the shower and stood at the sink, shaving the overgrown stubble off my jaw. I made sure to just watch where I was shaving. I'd forgotten before just how much I hated seeing my own face in the mirror.

I splashed some water over the razor, tapping it off on the edge of the sink.

So just go back out there. Act like nothing happened. Like I haven't been being an emotionally unstable hermit for half the week.

My phone buzzed in my pocket and I jumped. Was it Mansley? Had something come up?

I pulled my phone out of my leather jacket pocket and looked at the caller ID.

Dallas Knight.

I blinked at the name for a second and pressed my lips together tightly. After a second of hesitation, I hit the button to block his number.

It was a fake friendship, anyway. I didn't need that distraction.

I shoved the phone back in my pocket and came out into the hall. Lucius sat on the floor, picking at crumbs while he waited for me. He looked up and flapped onto my shoulder as I came out.

I brushed a finger over his feathers as I walked. I wondered if he liked Bad News better at this point, since he'd been the only one taking him out for exercise. All I'd done lately was burden him with my problems.

And it wasn't like anyone had any reason to like me in the first place.

I sighed, shook my head and came around the corner into the bakery.

Everyone sat at the counter eating except News, who was beyond it at the stove, cooking.

Just like a million other times. Times that I remembered now.

News looked up at my footsteps and waved his spatula. Liza looked up and smiled, giving me a little salute, and Roy and Cardboard gave me twin grins.

I waved back, but didn't smile.

I'd never smile again. Not only did I not deserve to, it felt physically impossible. My mouth was stuck in an unfeeling line.

I slid onto the stool one away from Cardboard, at the end of the counter. Lucius hopped off my shoulder, his talons clicking as he landed on the slick countertop.

News scooted a plate over to me and I looked down at it.

Eggs. A rare healthy breakfast, apparently.

"Feeling better?" News asked, pushing his hat up on his head a bit.

I nodded and dug into my eggs.

"What did you come down with, anyway?" Liza mused, "No one feels *that* sick after just an egg. Doesn't matter how bad it was."

I didn't answer her question. Too much to explain at this point. My memory loss was irrelevant. A freak accident. An unexpected bump in the road that no one else needed to know about. I'd caused enough trouble with it already.

I swallowed the bite I was chewing with a bit of difficulty and pushed my plate away. The appeal of food still hadn't come back to me yet.

I stood up and Chris turned his head to look over at me, "Any plans for today?"

"Meeting in the back supply room in fifteen minutes," I answered shortly. "I'll be briefing you guys on the plan."

It was nostalgic for half a second… giving orders again. Actually taking the helm of the gang and not just faking my way through leading. But the next moment slid it back into the feeling of routine.

This was my life. This was me.

I let out my breath and started walking towards the back, sticking my hands in my pockets. Best to get my presentation together.

#

It had always vaguely amused me how much our setup in the back resembled a schoolroom.

My whiteboard and I were up front, while the gang slouched in various positions in chairs or leaned against the wall as they listened.

The comparison was a bit dark, seeing how my classes centered on various plots to kill a single man. Still, though. *Revenge 101, Professor Dankworth teaching.*

I'd gotten my scrawled stick illustrations and notes mostly onto the whiteboard at the fifteen-minute mark, when my crew started filing in. I heard chairs scoot around for a few seconds and turned from the whiteboard, quietly counting off.

Everyone but Bad News.

Right on cue, he ducked through the door, wiping his hands on a dishtowel. He flung it over his shoulder and leaned up against the wall, nodding to me. He smiled slightly.

"Okay," I shifted my gaze around the room, meeting everyone's eyes individually. "This is the big one, guys. We're finishing it."

Roy raised his hand from where he sat, cross-legged on the floor. He waved it like a little kid, a mischievous look on his face. "Hey, can I go to the bathroom first?"

"Shut up, Tucker." I went back to the whiteboard.

"Now, this… " I tapped my first drawing with the capped end of my marker, "… is our long-awaited justice serving platter: the same kind of bomb from the twin bomb incident, only this time it's got Charles Fernsby's name on it."

I could see Liza's usually easygoing expression harden like mine, her blue eyes going icy. She sat up straighter, setting her jaw. Chris didn't move, but I saw his dark eyes narrow under the brim of his hat. We three had the biggest score to settle.

I kept going, explaining the technicalities and where it was planted.

"And it's set to go off right in the middle of their superhero council meeting thing, which usually goes longer than expected anyway. I've got the GPS coordinates right there… " I tapped the whiteboard where I'd scribbled them, "and in my phone." I patted my pocket.

"And what are we doing?" Liza asked.

I shook my head. "Nothing. It's all done, pretty much. I already set the security system last week. We had the bomb planted and it's set to go off at the right time. The only thing we could possibly do is set a lookout somewhere beyond the blast zone, but I don't see that that's necessary. The media will cover it well enough."

She nodded, biting her lip and looking down at her hands

folded in her lap. "So we just wait?"

"And watch," I set my marker down on the edge of the whiteboard. "Our easiest strike ever. And may it be our last."

There were serious nods from everyone. And an "amen" from News. He was strangely religious about all this.

I nodded. "Dismissed."

Everyone got up, shoving their way out and starting conversation back up amongst themselves. Something about lunch and teaching Lucius how to loop-the-loop.

I started cleaning off the whiteboard, but heard a bit of shuffling behind me. I turned.

Liza stood behind me, her mouth twisted off to the side and her eyes fixed on the half-erased whiteboard. Silence hung between us for a few seconds and I fiddled with the eraser.

"Funny, isn't it?" she took in a breath and forced a small laugh, "Just that we've gone after this for so long... and the end of it is just... so far away." She rubbed her hands together and looked at them. "I don't know... I always imagined something a bit more... personal. Like a knife. A shot at close range. You know, something you can *feel*. Do with your own hands."

I'd always had the same thing in my mind, but the bomb seemed more personal to me. I'd programmed it. I'd helped build it. I'd touched it.

Liza had helped build it too, to a certain extent. It was her notebook, her research, that had finished it off. But she'd never seen it.

She could, though.

Liza swiped the back of her hand over her eyes and forced another little laugh. "Sorry. I'm being an idiot." She smiled at me — a tight kind of smile. "It's a great plan."

I looked back at the whiteboard. The coordinates were right there in the corner. I had planned on checking out the bomb anyway. I had more than one seat in my car...

She turned to go and I cleared my throat. "Hang on, Liz."

She turned back and I raised an eyebrow at her. "Want to go for a ride?"

Driving with Liza as a passenger was infinitely more comfortable than riding with News. A lot less intimidating. She brought along one of her CDs of a band called "The Proclaimers." It was a cheerful combination of classic rock, guitar and Scottish accents.

I wasn't feeling like cheerful stuff at the moment, but it was still decent music. Liza sang along for a few songs. She had a pretty good voice, actually. I didn't want to ruin her ears, so I didn't sing along.

The population thinned out more and more as we drove and our route got dustier. All other cars disappeared. We were alone on the road, driving in between the red rocks and pine trees.

Liza became quiet in the passenger seat, watching the GPS. The music still played quietly. Our blue blinking dot advanced along the winding green line. The last stretch turned out to be a badly-kept dirt road.

I rolled up the windows and handed Liza my sunglasses as we bumped onto the dusty path. Dust billowed up around us in a cloud as I hit the gas. I swear we looked like some sort of ghost car, appearing from the mists of time as we drove down the road.

I shielded my eyes and coughed on the dirt in the air, glancing down at the tiny GPS screen.

"Almost there," I coughed out, pointing our little green pinpoint out to Liza. She nodded, then sneezed a couple times into her elbow.

I slowed down a bit so we didn't skid as we came around the corner of a big rock outcropping. Right behind it sat a dusty building with a strangely angled roof. One entire side was glass, showing a long meeting table inside, and the rest of the windows were scattered at various heights around the rest of the building. It looked like someone had designed it on a dare while he was drunk.

The road ended in a tiny parking lot next to the building, but our green path wasn't done. Time for a walk, then.

"Looks like we're walking for a bit," I muttered, pulling my car onto the small patch of asphalt and putting it in park.

"That's fine." Liza unbuckled and grabbed the GPS. "A bit of exercise never hurt anyone."

We popped our doors open a few seconds apart and stood up out of the car and into the remainder of our dust cloud. I sneezed a couple of times. Liza pulled her shirt collar up over her nose, looking like some weird ninja with the combo of that and my sunglasses.

I walked over to the shade by the building and she followed. We both consulted the GPS.

"So how much farther?" I shielded the little screen with my hand so the image would show up better.

Liza pushed the sunglasses up so they held back her hair like a headband. "It's not that far. Just right over that way."

I looked up to where she was pointing. It was straight out from the big window wall towards a bunch of big rocks.

One, despite all jagged rock edges and red dust, seemed a bit off. Something about the shadow. I squinted at it for a second before realizing what it was. The shadow was rounded and smooth. It didn't match up with the jagged, pointed edges of the rock.

A cloaking device couldn't fool the sun.

I nodded to Liza, jerking my thumb towards it. "That one's it."

She looked at it for a second and nodded back. "Alright. Let's go."

We hiked up the small incline towards the rocks. The sun warmed the sleeve of my jacket, though the air was cold. I gave my collar a tug.

In just a few minutes, there we were. Standing in the smooth shadow of the jagged rock. Our weapon. The same bomb that began it all would end it all. Just a quick blast... the cloud of smoke... the red dust kicked up like the blood of ghosts... I blinked a few times and shook my head, looking over at Liza.

Her mouth was in a small O shape as she looked it up and down. She took a few steps closer and held out her thin, pale hand to touch it. The rock surface pixilated under her touch and pulled back, making a hole in the illusion. Her hand rested against cool metal.

I came up next to her as she brushed her knuckles over the slick surface.

Liza swallowed and pulled her hand back, sticking it in her pocket and seeming to look for something. The hole she'd made in the projected rock surface flashed back into place.

I looked up and squinted at the sunlight over the edge of the bomb. "Big, isn't it?" In more ways than one…

She didn't answer. Her hand came out of her pocket gripped around a small knife. Flicking it open, she pressed her hand back in the same spot so she could see the metal. Her knife's point touched the metal and she scratched it down, making small, stick letters on the smooth surface.

I watched, already having a guess as to what she was writing. I was right, but seeing the shaky words still made my eyes smart.

"For Eli."

Liza took her knife down and rubbed her pale fingers over the letters. Her lips moved silently for a few seconds and she closed her eyes.

I felt like an intruder, standing there and watching her.

She took a shaky breath and looked back at me, biting her lip for a second. "It's sort of… I mean, Eli and I actually met not too far from here." Her hand trembled slightly as she gestured out towards the road. "I was flat broke and had no gas in my tank. My car finally had it right on that stretch over there and he…" Liza trailed off, swallowing. Her voice was softer than usual. "He was my only friend. The only one who actually gave a fig whether I lived or died…"

I didn't say anything back, but glanced over towards the dusty road, pulling my memory back to the empty highway stretch and placing her story in my mind.

Both of our gazes were drawn magnetically back to the

bomb,

She cleared her throat a little and stepped back, looking at the patch of metal for a second before turning to face me. She handed me her knife. "Something you want to add?" Her voice shook, but she hid it well.

I took it and came close to the same patch she'd carved on. My hand shook, but the letters still took shape.

"Rachel. William. Peter. Eloisa."

Their faces, their smiles and the times we'd had, hovered in my mind as I scratched out the words. I swallowed and stepped back, closing the knife and putting it back into Liza's cool palm.

We both stood there, looking at the names for a few seconds before the hologram flashed silently back into place.

Quiet, except for a few noises of birds, gliding high above.

"Do…" Liza began, her voice quiet. She stopped for a second, biting her lip and looking over at me. "Do they go away, d'you think? The ghosts? The nightmares?"

I didn't answer, looking back up at the peak of the giant, bullet-shaped bomb.

She followed my gaze. "I mean… this puts it all to rest, doesn't it?"

Liza had a way of always raising questions in my mind that I didn't want there. I let out my breath, running a hand through my hair. "What else would?" Killing Amazing Man was the end for me. The ultimate goal. What I lived for. I made a point of trying not to think past it.

She nodded slowly, sticking her hands in her jeans pockets and examining the dirty white toes of her sneakers.

Mansley's words came to my mind … from when I had set the bomb… and I repeated them to myself.

"Their blood has cried out from the ground too long," My voice was hoarse. "Their song is coming to an end and we'll be the ones to hit the final note."

Liza tucked a strand of turquoise hair behind her ear as she looked over at me. "That's good, Wolfy."

"Wasn't mine," I replied. "Just… something I heard."

We stood there for another minute before starting back towards the car. After getting in, I sat there in my seat for a few minutes, not starting the engine. I just watched my little Dalek keychain swing back and forth, hanging from the ignition.

It was a weird feeling. I was trying to access all the familiar anger that propelled me forward in the quest, but it only seemed to be coming at half-power. The lingering hesitance from the time with amnesia was still hanging around. Holding me back.

I could almost feel both of our resolves trembling. We weren't killers. Avenging wasn't the same thing. It had a purpose. Maybe a bit of a reminder… a bit more fuel in our fires…

A thought came into my mind and I furrowed my brows, turning it over. I glanced at my watch. We had time.

I turned to look at Liza. "Have you ever been to the Hero Museum?"

She shook her head.

I turned the keys and got the car into gear. "I've got a field trip for you, then."

Chapter 23: Broken Legos

Disguises, while not originally a part of my plan, quickly became so at the sight of the parking lot. News and I had visited while it was closed before. Now, it was most definitely open and was packed full of people.

The museum was offering free admission because apparently that day had been proclaimed "National Hero Day."

If there was ever a bad day for the media-projected villain to come waltzing in...

But hey, free admission was hard to pass up — hence, some improvised disguises.

Liza found some old 3D glasses and popped the lenses out, then tucked all her extremely noticeable turquoise hair up in a stocking cap.

I usually had at least a bit of stubble, so the fact that I'd just shaved it off this morning could work in my favor. I made more use of the old baseball hat from News, put on my sunglasses and took off my jacket. The last on the list was probably the most important, but it made me feel naked.

I shivered in my t-shirt as we crossed the road to the frothing mass of people at the museum. It was a cold enough day that I could blame it on the temperature. Even though I had a pretty good handle on all the awful memories at this point, my hold started to slip as we stepped under the shadow of the building.

Liza pushed her fake glasses up on her nose and hopped onto the sidewalk. "So what are we getting, here?"

"Motivation." I stepped up on the sidewalk next to her and yanked my hat brim further down over my eyes. We both watched the steady streams of people cycling through the entrance and exit.

Liza wrinkled her nose. "All this circus for that bloody Amazing Man. It's sickening."

I nodded and stuck my hands in my pockets. "C'mon."

We blended in with the crowd and made our way inside like sheep being herded into a pen. Everyone chattered excitedly about superheroes and wore some sort of Amazing Man merchandise. T-shirts… capes… hats… even full-on costumes for some of the kids.

I bet Mr. Perfect is enjoying the worship of his adoring fans, hissed the now-constant voice in the back of my mind. *Maybe they're giving him another parade. Those are his favorite.* I kept my lips in a tight line as we bumped through the entrance and into the main greeting center. Even with sunglasses, it was way better lit than the last time I'd been in here. The crowd was definitely thicker, too. Just enough groupies to sink a battleship.

It gave me the same feeling inside as looking at pictures of those big crowds gathered with all the waving flags in Nazi Germany. They didn't know anything of all the death that their fearless leader doled out. They didn't know the flip side of the whole superhero circus. None of them had lost anyone. All they knew was the grinning face on TV that kept them safe from that awful Wolfgang Dankworth.

The choice between good and bad seems so easy when one side wears a cape and tights and the other wears a leather jacket and a name practically made for a diabolical wretch.

No one ever looked past the surface before picking sides. The family man, or the single guy? Perfect hair or cowlick?

None of them cared.

I bit my tongue and looked around, making sure Liza was still nearby. She had her phone out and was pretending to take pictures. One of her sharp elbows poked into my side.

"Where to?" she asked, keeping her voice in conversational tone.

I made a finger-gun towards the back, "Fatalities section. Back there." I pitched my voice deeper than usual, differing it from my normal tone.

She nodded and we began meandering our way past the other exhibits. I kept my hands in my pockets and my head down, while Liza took the approach of chatty girlfriend and hung on my arm, squeaking about things at random intervals. I was just thankful she usually wasn't this bouncy.

"Ooh, dear!" she tweaked my sleeve as we came through the graffiti arch into the villain section. "Let's look over there. They must have a simply fascinating display on that horrid Mr. Dankworth."

I groaned inwardly. "Not exactly... what we're here for... " If there was anywhere I was going to get caught, right next to my pictures was at the top of the possibility list. I cleared my throat meaningfully, "He's stupid anyway. Nothing worth looking at."

"Oh, come on," Liza rolled her eyes and gave my arm a pull before going over to the display herself.

I reluctantly stood behind her, trying to bore holes in the back of her stocking-capped head with my glare. It wasn't quite clear whether she was legitimately interested in reading about someone she'd already known for years or if she was still playing the eager museum-goer and trying to annoy me.

Liza kept her hands clasped studiously behind her back as she scanned everything. Her head tipped a little as she examined the biggest picture of me. The one where I looked to be flipping off the world in general. The picture that shaped my public image more than anything else. I should've seen that dumb photographer. *I should've reloaded and shot him.*

I gave a gusty sigh, folding my arms. "Done yet?"

Liza didn't answer, but turned with a smile quirking her lips as she jerked her thumb back at the photo. "They caught him in a bit of a temper there, hey?"

I bit my tongue. "Yeah, he has an awful temper. Never know when he might just lose it like that. Let's *go.*" I turned, clenching my teeth to hold back from swearing.

"Oh, I can usually spot the blow-ups coming," Liza chuckled, re-stationing herself at my elbow as we resumed our course towards the next section, with me being a bit more of a steamroller through the crowd this time.

I changed the subject, trying to cool off as we walked. "Did you... I know Eli wrote you letters sometimes. Did you keep them all?"

Liza's smile withered a bit, "Yes," she nodded.

A second of silence.

"Why do you ask?"

Fuzzy memories of the exhibits prior to the one of my family came to mind, like memories of a fight before the knockout punch. I sidestepped a small family and gave my ball cap a tug. "I think there might've been one you didn't get."

Her eyes popped open wide behind the fake glasses and her sharp, uneven fingernails dug into my arm. "Where?"

I pulled my arm away from her pinching grip, missing a step and accidentally bumping into some guy and his little kid. "Whoa, sorry." I regained my footing, adjusted my hat and looked up.

"No problem," the man gave a forgiving but distracted smile from behind his sunglasses and kept walking.

My eyes stayed on the kid in the grubby hoodie behind him.

Leif.

That was my brother. That guy was Charles Fernsby. But why the sunglasses...?

Liza grabbed my sleeve and twisted it so I was looking back at her. Her voice was a hiss. "Wolfgang, *where?*"

I slapped a hand over her mouth as a few looks were directed our way. I gave a forced laugh. "Um... with the Amadeus Mozart, of course. Where else?"

Cue mental cussing and kicking myself. I wished I could sink right through the tile floor and disappear. We shouldn't have come. I couldn't take the risk of getting caught when we were this close.

No one kept eyes on us for very long — probably just putting it down to another one of those weird exchanges you always hear in public.

Liza's eyes glared at me from over my hand. The glasses were knocked sideways on her face and I straightened them as I uncovered her mouth.

I let out my breath and gave Liza a look. "Don't." My voice hit a low, threatening note.

She kept her eyes fixed solidly on my face. "Where's the letter?"

"I... just follow me, okay?" I pulled on my hat brim and started back off towards the entrance to the fatalities section. The crowd thinned, the closer we got. There was practically no one around by the time we got all the way back there. It was appallingly unpopulated, compared to how many people were flocked around every little attraction in the dumb origin story section.

There were only about seven people total wandering around the memories of all the lives taken that day. Lives that would have continued, but for the negligence of their revered hero. Some people nodded as they solemnly read the plaques, a few wiped away tears and the rest just looked like they got lost looking for the bathroom.

I don't know why I was surprised. Respect for the dead wasn't a huge thing among superhero groupies (speaking from years of experience).

Liza came to a stop next to me, her sneakers squeaking on the tile. "In here?"

I nodded. "This... " something caught in my throat and I

coughed. "This is the memorial section for all the people who died in the bombing."

Liza blinked, realization flooding her face.

"Eli's is over there," I pointed to the first exhibit I'd wandered over to the other night. "The memoir they have for him is a letter to… to you."

Liza didn't stick around for any further explanation. She dashed off to the exhibit, leaving me standing at the entry. I watched her freeze in front of the picture for a few seconds before turning her eyes downward to the glass case that I knew held the letter.

I turned away, took a breath and started on the roundabout way to get to the corner exhibit. The Dankworth family memorial.

I'd read over my note a million times. I knew every word and every time my hand shook and the pencil had squiggled.

What I needed was to see their faces again. Remind myself what I was fighting for. Who I was fighting for.

I came around the corner, not looking up at first, mentally steeling myself. Then I looked and ground to a halt.

Apparently I'd miscounted. There were three other people in this section.

The sunglasses-disguised Amazing Man, a custodian and my brother.

"It's just a little spot at this point," the custodian was telling Fernsby as he slung his mop over his shoulder, "But I tell you, there was a pretty obvious blood splotch on the floor after that break-in the other evening. Don't know how it got there, but it dried pretty hard overnight. It was a pain in the neck to get to come up, too."

I'm sorry?

"Funny," Charles tipped his head down at the spot on the floor. His voice sounded different… like he was trying to disguise it. "I wonder if they fought?"

"The camera footage is sketchy, but it looks like they just wandered around with flashlights and then took off without stealing anything. Butterfingers, too. They were dropping their flashlights left and right…" The custodian shrugged. "Anyway, hope you have a nice visit, sir."

"We certainly will, thank you." Fernsby gave him a smile as he walked off. It slid off his face within the next few seconds as he turned to the exhibit. A serious, sad look shadowed his face. He didn't even notice me. I kept my head lowered, pretending to read another exhibit.

I wondered again about the sunglasses and gruff voice he was using. And he wasn't as clean-shaven as he usually was, either.

He was trying to hide. Just like I was. This was practically a holiday made in his honor. He should be prancing through the streets like the peacock he was and signing autographs until his hand hurt. Why didn't he want to be noticed?

Charles sighed and put an arm around Leif's small shoulders. Leif leaned his head against Fernsby's arm. They both stood there for a bit.

I stepped a bit closer, frowning half from jealousy and half from curiosity.

Leif turned his face up, the sprouts of hair from his cowlick falling backwards a bit. "What was she like?"

I stopped and pretended to be absorbed in a plaque while still watching them out of the corner of my eye.

Charles swallowed. "I can't say for certain. I didn't know her." He paused, forcing a small smile onto his face for Leif. "I know she was a poet. A dreamer. A chocolate addict."

Cheater, I thought in disgust. *You read that off her notebook.*

He kept going. "She was shy and sweet. She loved her family more than anything." He ruffled Leif's hair, "She loved playing with you." His voice caught a little and he looked up at the ceiling. When he spoke again, his voice was hoarse. "I know she didn't deserve to die at fourteen."

The break in my heart stretched a bit more and I winced. Those were all things I'd said to him. Accusing him. Shouting the injustice of the lives he'd let end because of a stupid parade. He repeated them because they were all he knew of my sister besides a display in a museum. And he sounded sad that he didn't know more

— that Leif didn't know more.

Leif rubbed his sleeve over his nose and tipped his head up to look at the pictures and little trinkets in the display. He pressed his nose up against the glass and looked at Peter's half-melted Lego house. "I kinda remember once... Peter built me a robot or something and we played a game on the porch."

I remembered that. It was on the weekend. I accidentally kicked Leif's robot and built it back all wrong with the legs and the arms switched up. Peter howled with laughter when he saw it.

"That's not what it's supposed to look like, Wolf!"

I felt a ghost of a smile tug at the corner of my mouth, but quickly bit it back.

Leif didn't continue. I wondered if he even remembered that. He just looked back up at the pictures for a few minutes.

"I remember Ellie wrote me a poem for my birthday one year," he commented. "I remember helping Mom make peanut butter cookies. And Dad tossing me in the air sometimes."

Leif didn't say these things with particular emotion, just a sort of curiosity — a wondering at what his original family was like, beyond his little memory snippets. He rocked back and forth in his dirty sneakers. "I remember Wolfgang hanging me upside down and tickling me when he came home."

He talked like I was with them. Dead. Killed in the blast of the bomb.

Partly true.

Leif turned to Charles, his small brow furrowed up. "Do you think he ever does anything for Eloisa's birthday?"

I jumped a little, turning my head back to the plaque in front of me. Yeah, I was definitely doing something for Eloisa's birthday this year. I was avenging her death. I was settling the score... throwing the fact that she never had another birthday back in the universe's face. But suddenly that didn't seem as noble a flag to wave as it had a few hours ago.

"I'm..." Charles paused a second, resting his gaze on the family portrait hanging above the case. "I'm sure he does. He..."

loved Eloisa very much." His tone was sincere, almost remorseful. "He loved you all very much."

"Why not anymore?" Leif's simple, earnest question made me flinch.

Charles looked down at him for a bit, searching for an answer. "Wolfgang... he..." there was a pause and he looked up at the picture again before turning back to Leif. "His love kind of got... changed. You know like those Lego sets that you can take apart and if it's... say, a lighthouse, you can turn it into a car or a robot?"

Leif nodded.

"The thing is that he... his love got broken. It went into tiny little pieces all over the place and he tried to put it back together, but it got built back differently. It doesn't work the way it used to... it's still broken inside. It's twisted and... wrong now, but he still thinks it's love. It's..." Charles trailed off and sighed, dropping his hands from the gesturing he'd been doing to illustrate and tiredly adjusting his hat. "I don't know. Does that make sense, bud?"

"I guess," Leif stuck his hands in his pockets, turning his attention back to Eloisa's notebook. "But the pieces can go back into the right places sometime, right?"

Charles was quiet for a few seconds. I waited for him to just spit it out and say no. I was already superglued in place. But he nodded slowly. "If they get into the hands of the right builder."

Leif looked satisfied with that answer. He brought one of his hands out of his hoodie pocket and he rubbed it over the glass case. "Can we go now?"

Charles nodded, swallowing. They turned and I quickly looked the opposite direction, adjusting my cap and biting my lip.

There were a few quiet noises of talking and then their footsteps moved on past me. Charles was walking right by his metaphorically messed up Lego set without even knowing it. By the time I dared look up, they were just disappearing out the door.

All the energy and rage buildup to the point of looking at the exhibit felt deflated, but I still shuffled my way over to the case. I looked over all the trinkets. The unfeeling, professional obituary that reduced my family's collective life to a blurb.

The photos. Mom's hair that never got silver. Peter, who never got past my chest in measuring himself against me. Dad's infectious grin I'd never see again beyond flat photographs.

The fire in my chest that I'd almost become addicted to burned inside me, but something niggled. Something felt wrong. I couldn't shake Fernsby's words — that I'd put myself back together all wrong. This wasn't what love looked like.

My hands shook and I unconsciously felt for my leather jacket pockets.

I looked at Eloisa's picture. Her tiny, lipstick-painted smile and bright, hazel eyes looking back at me. What would she say?

Hey, sis. I'm blowing up people for your birthday. Hope you like my present.

She'd be dumbstruck. Horrified. But then… she wasn't here. This wouldn't have had to happen if she had been.

I looked at the portrait and my eyes rested on little Leif, grinning his tiny grin in his little tuxedo. Leif was here. There was still another Dankworth, even if he didn't bear the name and barely remembered me as anything but that scary man that blew things up and came to breakfast with a bandage on his head once.

Not much to go on, but could there possibly be another chance with Leif? Could I get myself put together in the right way and put the past behind me? Forgive? Forget? Ripping my spine out sounded less painful than leaving the rest of the family unremembered. A dusty corner in a museum, that was all they had.

But in the hands of the right builder?

I groaned and pushed my sunglasses up to rub at my face. Another crisis. Just what I needed.

I let my sunglasses fall back in place and decided to head out to the car. Driving seemed to straighten things out in my head sometimes. I'd just get Liza.

A look over in her direction changed my mind. She had her head rested up against the glass and her shoulders shook. Both of us knew how awful I was at comforting people. Liza preferred to work through it alone a lot of the time, too. I'd wait for her in the car.

Ten minutes alone with my thoughts resulted in an intensified crisis and a raging headache. A misty-eyed Liza walked up in the middle of a heart-to-heart between my head and the steering wheel.

"What's up with the head-banging?" she asked, her voice cracking a little.

"Nothing," I muttered, yanking my seatbelt on over my leather jacket, now comfortably back in place. "Just... a hard week. Gets to you sometimes."

I slammed the car into gear and we zipped off.

"Anything... I mean, was the letter... good?" I asked.

Liza shrugged, swallowing. "It wasn't anything terribly deep, you know. He didn't know he was saying goodbye. Just... teasing me for losing my temper once and saying he loved me..."

I nodded, biting my tongue.

Liza was quiet for a bit, aside from a few sniffles. Then she turned to me, "Thanks for taking me. I... just seeing that stuff gives you a bit different perspective on things."

Oh, I knew.

Now to decide what perspective was actually the one I should be sticking to.

Chapter 24: Runaways and Pep-talks

Each minute that ticked by became my new least favorite time of the night.

At that particular moment, two-fourteen was the lucky winner.

I tore my eyes away from the red numbers and looked back up at the ceiling, blinking away the imprints on my vision. My body felt tired, but my mind was more awake than a caffeinated chipmunk. Questions upon questions… crises galore… enough moral dilemmas to sink a battleship… my head felt ready to explode.

I groaned and flopped my pillow over my face. The mental battle only intensified with my eyes closed.

It was like there were two of me… two Wolfgang Dankworths fighting in my mind.

One was the normal me. The one I'd begun to slip back into. The gang leader. The one who knew what he was doing and how he was going to do it. The avenger of his family and sworn enemy of

Amazing Man. Driven. Angry. Violent.

The other... I'd thought him either long gone or the result of a temporary lapse of sanity. He probably wouldn't have existed outside distant memory... if it hadn't been for my amnesia episode. The reluctant defender of Amazing Man. The one that shied away at the thought of killing and called a boy named Dallas his friend. The big brother. The thwarter of the other Wolfgang's plans. Overall, an idiot — but a much better person than the alternative.

I wasn't sure which one was the real me.

But both were as annoying as all hell.

Back and forth they went... or *I* went.

I had to go through with tomorrow. It was my duty... the ultimate obligation to my family and everyone else. It was my promise. My sole purpose on this earth, that I'd stuck to for years now.

The world didn't need to be fooled by these "heroes" any longer. A waste of taxes and security effort — that's what they were. The showy flight and super-strength didn't make up for everything lost... everything that slipped between the cracks because of all the focus on these clowns.

But everything I'd done... all the things I'd realized while my memory was gone.

I'd let this whole revenge thing twist me into something else. Something that wasn't me. I'd become a villain.

I'd put myself back together all wrong. This wasn't what love looked like. I was still broken inside.

But I wasn't irreparable.

Charles Fernsby knew better than anyone all the things that I'd done... and he still thought I could be fixed. He sounded... almost like he could forgive. But could I forgive?

An image from the day I had breakfast with the Fernsbys came to my mind. Charles. No media around. No one watching but his wife, Dallas and me. The expression that showed the incredible burden of guilt he bore. His smooth, charismatic voice cracking as he spoke to me.

"I just want to tell you again while I have the chance that… I'm sorry. I really am very sorry…"

It wasn't a show. He actually regretted what he'd done. He didn't hate me, and was begging for me to forgive him. To turn around. He thought there was hope for me.

And what about Leif? I still had a brother. I still had a sliver of a chance at family, in the shape of a grubby little boy.

I hadn't realized quite how much cleaner my slate was than I'd thought. I'd just gotten out of prison last month, for all they were able to convict me for. If there were any time to start over, it would be now.

I pulled the pillow off my face and glanced over at the clock again. Two-seventeen. Minutes pass like ages when you're reconsidering your life.

I threw my pillow down to the foot of the bed and stood up, raking both hands over my already wild hair. The moon shone down through a patch in the clouds, casting eerie shadows over the abandoned parking lot and through the curtains. I could hear the distant noises of owls and crickets keeping up a steady background rhythm to the night.

I sighed and pulled back the curtains, resting my head on the cold window. Watching the moon and listening to crickets for a few minutes did nothing to help my mental tail chasing, and I stepped back again.

Lucius sat with his wing over his head, sleeping soundly, but he looked up at me as I started pacing the floor. I ignored him, keeping up the futile march while I finger-combed and pulled at my hair.

I'd never been one for pacing, but there I was, getting a pretty good start on wearing a rut. I just needed something physical to do. I concentrated on my socked feet, thudding out a beat on the floor. Back and forth. Back and forth.

Words from Liza came back to haunt me. Her questions from earlier.

"Do they go away, d'you think? The ghosts? The

nightmares? I mean… this puts it all to rest, doesn't it?"

Doesn't it?

Then my own words, tired and resigned, but still questioning. I repeated them out loud.

"What else would?"

I stopped in my pacing and gave my hair another thoughtful tug.

The right builder. Forgiving Amazing Man.

Maybe there was another way than the one I'd been so stubbornly sticking to all these years.

When had blowing things up ever helped anything? Had I ever felt better afterwards? It was like kicking something when I was angry. Nothing but a selfish vent of anger. It just stoked a fire that probably shouldn't even be there in the first place.

I was continuing the cycle. I would kill Jilly and Beckett's dad if I went through with tomorrow. Angela's husband. The only dad Leif really remembered.

It might give me closure, sure. But what would the loss do to them? Break them? Twist them into what I'd become over the years?

I had to let go of this poisonous promise. That's what my family would want. Not more death.

This was my last possible chance to turn it around… pull this thing up and salvage what I could.

Even if I couldn't be with Leif… couldn't be present to see him grow up like a normal brother should… he could at least be proud to claim the Dankworth name, not ashamed since I'd stained it with so much blood.

For him, I'd try. Oh, God, I'd try.

I closed my eyes and bit my lip, hesitating a bit before breaking my three and a half year long silent treatment of "the right builder."

It was probably the least eloquent prayer in history. The religious equivalent of a hobo scuffing off the street into the throne room and awkwardly waving at the king in hope of coaxing a smile.

I was pathetic and I knew it.

But I do think I got that smile.

It felt like a weight lifted off my shoulders. Like I could hold my head up again.

Even if no one else could stand to forgive me, I'd gotten forgiveness from the One who counted.

I opened my eyes and looked around my room at all the mementos, threatening notes and weapons that had piled up over time. I didn't need all of it, really. Because now I was thinking in terms of what all I could fit in a backpack. All I needed was my clothes, a gun, a few knives maybe…

It was two-thirty by the time I flopped back into bed with my backpack packed and my watch set for early.

I was running away from my own gang in the morning.

#

The morning air was a cold contrast to my bed as the chirping alarm on my watch startled me awake. I sat up and blinked at the wall opposite me for a few seconds, trying to remember why I'd set my watch for this ungodly hour.

Oh, right. Running away to be noble and good, for once.

Hey, better late than never.

I fumbled into some clothes, and pulled my cold leather jacket on. As it settled over my shoulders and I zipped it up, the weight of what I was doing began to settle on me. I sat down to tie my shoes. I yanked the laces tight and stood up, bumping my foot on the backpack I'd stuffed full last night. Wouldn't want to forget that.

Lucius looked up at my scuffling, puffing his feathers and giving his best bird-scowl. I swung my backpack over my shoulder and squinted at him for a second before patting my shoulder.

"Yeah, c'mon." He could redeem himself too, I supposed. Tag along, while I was at it.

Lucius flapped over and perched atop my backpack strap.

I started toward the door, but stopped for a couple of seconds to look around. My gaze stopped on my phone, on the nightstand.

Might be nice to have, yeah.

I stepped back and grabbed it, flipping it open. Dead. This thing had horrible battery life. Oh well, I'd charge it up later. I stuffed it along with my charger into my pack. I still had my watch, to keep time.

It was six at the moment and the bomb was set to blow much later in the evening. I had about fourteen hours to get it disarmed. I could probably walk there and still have time. No one else would have to know. And for the ones who did, I'd be long gone by the time they found out.

I shifted my pack and Lucius flapped, whacking the side of my head. I barely noticed, still standing there, thinking.

What would the gang think? Regardless of all evil intentions and criminal inclinations, they were my friends — but I was abandoning the common purpose that held us together.

The thought of writing a note crossed my mind briefly, but I couldn't think what I could write. I might come back sometime and explain. But right now I needed to get away... pull myself out of this... disarm the bomb without all of them convincing me otherwise.

I'd just disappear.

Me and my falcon, my leather jacket, infamous face and black Mustang.

Right.

I sighed and stepped out into the hall before I could do any more second-guessing. The door creaked on its hinges as I swung it shut behind me. No other sounds were in the building. Just a few faint bird noises from outside and distant traffic sounds coming from the town nearby.

I craned my neck around to see the door at the end of the short hallway. No noisy hinges there. Somewhere in the back of my mind, I felt like leaving should be harder. Maybe the second thoughts and sentimental junk would hit me a bit later.

I put my feet down softly on my way to the door. I could barely hear my own footsteps. Just the faint, occasional sound of my sneakers' rubber soles squeaking on the cement. No risk of waking anyone. Lucius gave a quiet chirrup and I shushed him, not looking back. We were so close.

My hand gripped the cold bar on the inside of the door and I gave a push. The door clicked and opened easily, letting in a cold whoosh of fresh morning air. The perfect smell to fit a new beginning. I took in a deep breath and put out my foot to take my first step of a new life.

It came up short.

I was stopped mid-stride by an enormous hand clamping down on the collar of my jacket. My heart dropped straight down to my toes and I felt my face go pale. Lucius squawked and retreated, flapping back inside and down the hall.

"Bit early for a walk, buckaroo." Bad News's voice came from behind me. He pulled me firmly back inside and the door clicked shut in front of my face. "You should really get a quieter watch alarm."

His self-assigned job: protecting me from everything, including myself. Even when I didn't want him to.

I should have guessed he'd try and stop me. Even if I'd woken up without my alarm, his internal mother-hen-radar probably would have gotten him up anyway, and we'd be in the exact same position.

I'd been so close. Only to be caught by my own gorilla.

I'll kick him in the shins and run away. I'll sock him on the jaw and make a run for it.

Yeah, right. Nobody will disarm the bomb if you die, genius.

News cleared his throat and I forced myself to meet his eyes. Or his sunglasses. His arms were folded across his chest and his mouth was in a tight frown.

I gave him my best "oh, come on, we don't really have to do this, do we?" face.

News quite clearly thought we did. He shook his head, "I've humored this long enough."

His words froze my blood. He wasn't going to let me. He

was going to beat me senseless and shove me in a closet until the bomb had already gone off.

Oh, please no…

He grabbed the back of my coat again and hauled me out of the hall and towards the back room. Our classroom. I constantly tripped over my own feet, trying to keep up with the rate at which News was hauling me. He didn't slow down.

"N-News, really…" I stammered, scrambling for something to get him to let me go. "I'm just… going out for a bit. Just a short trip. Somewhere I need to go… I mean, something I need to get… I need to…"

He pulled up on my collar further and I coughed at the limited air supply as we came around the corner.

We came into the back room where all the chairs sat around in a lopsided circle, and News deposited me in my giant wingback chair.

I shut my eyes tightly and gripped the edge of my seat, waiting for death. For my deliverance of bad luck,

Nothing for a good few seconds.

I opened my eyes just before his slap hit. It felt like he could have whacked my jaw right off. I fell back in my seat and fireflies danced in my vision. Things were pretty fuzzy for a good few seconds after that. The giant black and white outline in front of me blurred and went double. I was too rattled to find that terrifying.

He said something I didn't make out. I blinked hard to clear the spots floating around his face.

"Wh-what now?" I stuttered, pushing myself back up in my seat. I rubbed at the right side of my face. It felt numb.

News had taken his sunglasses off and was propping his forehead on the tips of his fingers like a careworn mother. A strange image for the guy who'd just slapped me silly.

Sighing, Bad News slid his hand down his face and looked at me through the cracks in his fingers. "You're running away now?"

"That… was the plan," I replied cautiously.

"And you have all your memories back?"

"Every last one."

He looked at me with a raised eyebrow for a few seconds, then looked up at the ceiling. After a few seconds of either thought or suppressing murderous rage, News turned to the door.

"Don't you dare go anywhere," he warned, ducking out. The door squeaked shut behind him and I was alone.

I sat there, rubbing my face and suppressing my panic. If he planned on beating me up more, I wouldn't last a minute. Maybe I could just plead innocence at the last minute and offer to make the cake for this morning...

I swallowed hard and sat on my hands, hoping to keep them from shaking. It didn't do much good.

The door squeaked back open a few minutes later and I jumped, expecting death or a torture machine to be wheeled in.

In came Liza, followed by Roy, Chris and Cardboard. Bad News was the last one in, looking more serious than I'd ever seen him.

I wasn't meaning to be disrespectful at all to News at this point, but my incredulous look in his direction was involuntary. I had a slight idea what he'd brought them here for and I wasn't at all in favor of it.

News leaned up against the wall and pushed his fedora back on his head, significantly nodding to me. "If you're so dead set on this, they at least deserve the truth. And from you, not me or some dumb note."

Fantastic. Just what I *didn't* want.

The gang seemed more annoyed at the hour of this meeting than worried as to what it was about. They sat around, slouched in their seats. Cardboard was almost back asleep already, leaning on Roy's arm. Liza was the most awake and frowned when she saw my backpack.

"What's with that?" she asked, pointing. The rest of the gang woke up a bit at that, and all eyes went to my backpack, then to me.

News raised an eyebrow and gave his classic "begin your speech" gesture.

I opened my mouth and closed it again noiselessly a couple of times. I wasn't getting out of this one. But where to even start?

Clearing my throat, I fixed my gaze down at my shoes. "Well… um… I'm not sure… " I looked up at Bad News and gave a forced laugh, "What's to tell?"

My bodyguard was not amused. "Start with the bit where you got amnesia."

I'd never seen the gang look so instantly lively at six in the morning. Roy, Liza and Chris all began talking at once, each with their own question. It came together at the last, questioning word.

"Amnesia?"

Chris's eyes narrowed, realization spreading across his face the quickest. He'd been onto me right at the beginning.

News smiled slightly, knowing he'd thoroughly put me in checkmate. I had to tell everything now. Right from the beginning.

I took a breath and rubbed my hands together, swallowing. "Okay. Um…" I bit my lip for a second. "You guys know… that time when you caught up to me after the whole opera thing? When I had Dallas in the backseat?"

General nodding.

I took a deep breath and plunged in. I told everything, right from me waking up with my mind blank, through the baseball stadium bombing and up to the "grocery run" the other day. My lunch with Dallas and museum trip with Bad News. And like the brave orator I was, I kept my eyes fixed solidly on my shoes.

The gang was dead silent through the whole thing.

When I neared the end, I faltered. The bit where everything changed. Yesterday and last night.

I shifted my gaze up to the ceiling, "I came pretty close to doing nothing, I'll have you know. I wasn't planning on telling about it because… it almost didn't matter. But… it does now."

I dared to look down and meet Liza's eyes. She just stared at me, her expression unreadable. I swallowed.

"Our outing yesterday was sort of what put it over the edge. I don't think you saw them, but Amazing Man and my little brother were there. They were in front of me at my family exhibit. I guess they were visiting because my sister's birthday would have been today."

My voice caught a little at that, but I pressed forward, looking back down at my shoes.

"I just... overheard them talking about me. Fernsby was explaining to Leif... why his big brother didn't love him anymore. I put myself back together in the wrong way after the bombing, guys. And I think I helped do the same with you. So that kind of kept me up late last night... thinking." I tugged at my hair a bit and bit my lip.

No wisecracks from Roy joking that "that's never a good sign." Nothing broke the silence.

I stood up and continued with my fidgeting. "I just... this is only continuing the hurt. We're doing the same thing to the Fernsbys that we objected to in the first place. It's selfish and disgraceful. And today is our last chance to end it. That bomb blows and it's over. There's no turning back."

My words faded in the quiet room and I swallowed hard. "It's not every day that people get a second chance... a reset button. I did. And I'm taking it."

A fire that actually felt right lit in my chest and I brought my gaze up, looking between to meet all of their eyes. "Call me an idiot... a wimp... a sentimental moron... anything you want. But I'm going to go disarm that bomb. I'm not going to grind my family name into the mud anymore with all this revenge crap. I'm done. I'm forgiving and going to see what I can salvage of my life. And I'll be damned if anyone tries to talk me out of it this time."

The gang... my friends... just stared at me.

I stood there with my jaw set, not regretting a word. The thought crossed my mind that I'd actually given a decent speech, for once. Well, what do you know? Somewhat fitting, seeing as it would be my last one.

Still, no response came. Their faces were just blank from shock.

I nodded firmly, stood and stooped to grab my backpack. "Goodbye. Feel free to keep up the revenge business if you want, though I heartily don't recommend it." I started towards the door.

There was the sound of tiny sneakers hitting the floor, then a small voice.

"I'm coming."

I turned to see Cardboard, standing straight and proud with her bedhead poof of curls and her face set in determination.

My turn to stare. I blinked and opened my mouth, even though I wasn't sure what I was trying to say. Wasn't this just... my thing? I didn't even think she was really awake for all that stuff I was saying.

Cardboard hopped to my side. "You're right. I don't think blowing people up is right. Ever," she stated, folding her arms and looking back at Roy.

Roy shook himself out of his slack-jawed shock and stood up, a bit slower. He swallowed, giving a single nod as he met my eyes. "I'm coming too. You're my friend, Wolf. I've stuck with you through hell and high water this far, and I'll be in on this too."

He marched over next to Cardboard and me. His confidence faltered for only a second and he gave me a sideways look. "I mean... this is really what you want. If you're sure. Because this is big, man."

I just stood there for a second before nodding stupidly. "I... yeah, I'm sure."

Chris and Liza were still seated and staring. Bad News tilted his head a little, still leaning against the wall as he surveyed the mutinous trio of us standing by the door. For a second, I had a giddy vision if the unspeakable "bad luck" we were all about to suffer.

I swallowed and straightened up, my heartbeat pounding in my ears against the high-strung silence in the room.

It was a crossroads. We all had to choose.

"In that case... we'll be going." I reached for the doorknob again.

Then News pushed off the wall, straightened his tie and

walked over. I jumped back from the doorknob.

News sighed and nodded as he stopped in front of me. "About time for a mission change." A smile played at the side of his mouth and he rumpled my hair, stepping to my other side.

"You've got a lot goin' on under that cowlick of yours. Amen, man. I'm in."

It was hard not to return the smile. This turnaround operation was spreading.

"Th-thank you." I looked over at Liza and Chris. They had their own scores to settle. I couldn't decide for them, however much I wanted to. But still I stood there, just awkwardly tugging at my hair and waiting for… I didn't even know what.

Chris's mouth was open in indignant shock. Liza's was closed in a tight line, but I saw tears in her eyes. There was something there. She was wavering on the borderline.

Liza looked from Chris to me, let out her breath and stood up straighter as she walked over to our side. She stopped in front of me, looking up to meet my eyes. She nodded.

"This isn't what Eli would want. I'm with you, Wolfy." A shaky smile pulled at her mouth and she gave me a short half-hug. "Best speech ever." I grinned, the dimples in my cheeks digging in so deep it almost hurt, and hugged her back.

And Liza joined our lineup by the door.

Only one gang member left. I looked at Chris and my heart sunk a little.

His eyes had hardened back up, more bitter than ever. His jaw was clenched and his lips tight. He shook his head. "You're insane. Three and a half years of this… and you think you'll just go join the salvation army after all of it? You're just leaving? Forgetting your family and everyone else that died?"

I bit my tongue quietly for a second, then nodded. "Yeah. When it's all said and done, I don't think repairing death by causing more death really adds up." I shrugged, stepping over to give his stiff hand a shake. "You have my phone number, Chris. Give me a call."

I gave him a salute and our little troop exited the room.

No one else bothered to pack. Planning on coming back, probably. There were just enough seats in my car to hold everyone. They piled in as I threw my backpack in the trunk. Cardboard settled in with Lucius, my still redeemable bird, in her lap as she sat in the back.

I guessed my phone would be a good thing to have, so I grabbed that and my charger out.

I got myself into the driver's seat and turned the key. The clock blinked on. Six thirty-two. I plugged my phone into the charger before getting my buckle on.

Liza leaned over my seat with a frown. "Hold on. When was the bomb set to go?"

"Eight o'clock." I shifted the car into gear and we started out of the parking lot and into the sunrise. How symbolic.

News clicked his seatbelt in place and pulled at his tie. "AM or PM?"

"PM of cour…" I trailed off, suddenly second-guessing myself. It was PM, right?

My phone blinked to life just then and I braked at the curb, flipping my phone open and getting to Mansley's messages as fast as I could.

There it was.

Bomb set to blow in the middle of their meeting, at 8AM.

I swallowed hard. This was going to be close.

"Okay," I squealed around the corner into the main road, "I'm going to stay a lawbreaker for just a bit more, because this speed limit isn't going to cut it. Everyone, buckle up."

Chapter 25: Out with a Bang

Technically, we made it on time.

Seven forty-five.

But fifteen minutes wasn't the breathing room I'd been hoping for. No time for explaining of any sort. We needed to disarm the bomb or get everyone the heck out of there.

And hope to high heaven that they'd listen to me.

I'm pretty sure we looked like a giant sandstorm with how fast I was driving up the dirt road. My sunglasses were the only reason I could even partially see. Any conversation was given up in favor of hacking and choking on the dust in the air.

The tires screeched on the asphalt as I pulled up into the tiny parking lot. I put the car into park, pulled out the keys and waved the cloud out from in front of me to the best of my ability.

There was the bomb. A rock, to anyone who didn't know better.

The housing was my main concern at this point. I mean,

security passcodes were one thing. A giant, hollow shell of solid steel was another.

I unbuckled and got out, slamming my door shut behind me. "Liza, show them where the bomb is. News, see if that laser you've got will get through the metal. Roy, help out and watch Lucius. Cardboard…"

"Can I come with you?" she hopped out of the car, coming up next to me. "I'll help tell the heroes."

One, I didn't want to take the time to argue. And two, a cute little girl actually had probably a better chance of being believed than I did.

"Sure. Just hurry, okay?" I tossed my sunglasses back in the car and started off on a run towards the building with Cardboard right on my heels. Through the glass siding, I could see the table filled up with people, all bent over and talking. And studiously *not* looking out the window.

I slammed through the swinging door into the warm interior of the building. Cardboard and I nearly threw our necks out with how fast we were looking around to take in all the details of the room. There was an empty desk in front of me and a wide hall to the right. Sounds of soft talking drifted on the air. It stopped as the door swung shut with a "clunk" and a familiar voice spoke.

"Did you hear something?"

"Over here!" Cardboard took off sprinting down the hall and I ran after her. My shoes slid on the floor as I came around the corner and I barely avoided running into my small associate. I quickly righted myself, reflexively straightening my jacket as I did so.

Ten people were staring at me.

Seven superheroes and three sidekicks, all in suits and ties. Dallas and Amazing Man were at the far end of the table. Dallas shot up out of his seat, his eyes open wide.

Cardboard and I both started talking at the same time, her pointing frantically and me gesturing.

"… big… outside…"

"… rock… fifteen minutes…"

My voice and her tiny one came together on the word: "Bomb"

Everyone shot out of their seats at that one.

I took a breath and glanced down at Cardboard. "If you guys could…" My sentence was cut off as the man nearest to me flew out of his seat and pinned me up against the wall with as much effort as it would have taken him to lift a paper doll. One hand came up to hold my throat and one he held back in a fist.

Cardboard clapped her hands over her mouth and squeaked: "No!"

"What's your game this time, Dankworth?" the man hissed. "And where'd you take that kid from?"

This was one of my many concerns in this endeavor. I was about the farthest thing these heroes could get from a "trusted source."

I would have defended myself, but that required air that I didn't have at the moment. Instead, I clawed at his fingers and coughed for him to let me down.

"A bomb outside, huh?" His dark eyes narrowed and he tightened his grip. "I wonder who could have planted that? And you brought along a hostage. How nice."

He made a point. That was… really what it looked like. I could hardly congratulate him on his deduction, though. I grabbed onto his hand with both of mine and pulled it off my windpipe as well as I could.

"We've all… done things … we regret," I rasped at him.

Cardboard tried to swing a punch at the man. "He's trying to *help!* Let 'im go!"

"Mr. Hales, sir, if you'd just let him talk…" Dallas's voice broke in.

The man named Hales muttered something and dropped one hand to pat down my pockets, still hovering midair and effortlessly holding me up by the throat with one hand. He unclipped the knife from my pocket and tossed it to the floor, then released his grip on me.

I took a few moments to choke and cough on the floor, rubbing at my throat. Cardboard came over to pat me on the back and scowl at the heroes. Not quite the reception I was hoping for... but what could I expect?

"What do you want?" A different guy this time. None of them really had a good image of me. I could hardly blame them.

"He was *trying* to keep you guys from blowing up!" exploded Cardboard.

I got back on my feet, feeling slightly lightheaded. "I... the bomb..." I closed my eyes for a second and swallowed. "There's a bomb outside. We need to disarm it. It's the same type as the ones from the Twin Bombing. We've got less than fifteen minutes and I can't get through the housing. Just... if one of you guys could punch through it, I could get through the security and finish deactivating it."

Mostly raised eyebrows and distrusting stares in response.

I looked at the clock on the wall. Seven forty-seven.

"Or if you want to, we can just get the heck out of here, but whatever it is, it needs to happen like... now."

"*Guys*..." Cardboard twisted her hands. "It's gonna blow up..."

Fernsby strode over next to me, followed by Dallas. "Where is it?"

A weight lifted off my chest with the feeling of being trusted. I pointed out the window to the giant rock and saw the outlines of my gang by its base. "That rock. It's got a holographic camouflage on it."

Fernsby nodded and looked back over his shoulder at all the doubtful faces around the table. "Come on, men." Then to me: "Lead the way."

I silently thanked him and started off towards the door.

I didn't quite expect the others to follow, but Amazing Man must have been a bit more of a leader among the group than I thought because we got a regular military march going.

We made it to the bomb in fairly short order and joined the group of three adults, one small girl and a bird. I jogged up next to Bad News, "Any luck with the laser?"

He shook his head, turning to face me. "It deflected. Nearly took my head off." News pulled his fedora off and showed me a little scorched line on the side of the fabric. My stomach knotted.

Dallas huffed up next to me and leaned over with his hands on his knees. "I kind of... thought you'd tell me a bit sooner than this, Wolf." He kept his voice low so no one else could hear. "I did... call you. Did it not go through?"

I ran my tongue over my teeth. "There were some complications. I'll explain in a bit."

Liza looked up from where she was picking at the edge of the bomb housing in the dirt. "No chance of digging this bugger up. It's down deep."

Lucius sat next to her, scratching at the dirt by the bomb and looking confused.

"It's fine," Charles began rolling up his sleeves. He rapped his knuckles against the surface. It pixilated and made a crackling zap noise. He pulled back, shaking his hand and frowning. "What's this made out of, again?"

I shrugged, squinting at the break in the hologram as it flickered back into place. "Steel, I think? It's got some stuff in it that makes the camo work, though. That was probably what zapped you."

Though Liza and I didn't have that problem... maybe it's an extra measure that went up.

"Gotcha." He walked up and wound up to punch through. The rest of us stepped back.

I relaxed a little. He'd just smash through this like it was papier-mâché, and I'd have it disarmed within the minute.

His fist smashed against the bombshell.

"CLANG" The hologram pulled back to show the metal.

Nothing. Not even a dent.

Fernsby's face twisted in pain and he dropped his hand, shaking it out. He sucked in his breath through his teeth, letting it out in a groan as he rubbed his knuckles.

Well. So much for super strength. Was he even trying?

Another one of the heroes, a darker skinned man, stepped up with a frown. "Here, let me try." He didn't even bother rolling up his sleeves. Just a quick pull back and his fist lashed forwards at the metal with incredible speed.

Another clang and a loud zap were simultaneous.

Slight dent this time.

He let a swear word slip out as he hopped around, holding his hand.

I looked at my watch, swallowing down the worry that was speeding my heartbeat. "Guys, seriously. Cardboard could do better. This isn't funny. Make an effort."

"Hold on…" Dallas held up a hand. "There's something wrong." He walked over to Amazing Man and looked over his shoulder. "Check the monitor."

"Why would…?" Fernsby glanced at what looked like a second watch strapped to his arm and trailed off. "Oh my."

Something sunk in my stomach, "What?"

Charles walked over and checked the other guy's monitor thing. "Same over here." He looked over at me, his eyes worried. "Is the cloaking mechanism the only thing built into the metal?"

"I… I'm not sure…"

"The nano robots… the things that give the superpowers…" his voice shook slightly, "they've turned off." Fernsby tapped his monitor. "None of us can get through. Our ability to disappears the minute we touch its surface. That's what the zapping was."

I stared. News pushed his hat back on his head. Liza sat back on her heels and cursed quietly.

Of course Mansley could work that out. He ran the superhero program. He knew what would turn off the bots. This almost seemed like a security measure taken against my backing out. So it would still go through, even if I did tell Amazing Man.

I could've sat everyone down and told them a ton of interesting things just then. But again, we didn't exactly have the time for all the complicated explanations.

"Well, gee. Laser eyes would have sure been nice to have," Roy pointed out. "Why didn't the program give you those?"

"It's a scientific impossibility, Mr. Tucker," Fernsby's voice rose like he'd had this conversation a million other times.

I shook myself out of my thoughts. "Then we need to get out of here. Now. If we can get to the town nearby, that's out of range…"

The man Dallas had called Mr. Hales snorted. "Are you kidding? That town *might* be out of range if the bomb were half this size. But this…" he gestured over the tower of fake-rock and shook his head. "Out of the initial blast zone, sure. But all the rocks and shrapnel… the town is far from safe."

Apparently, there was quite a bit Mansley didn't tell me. Or straight-up lied to me about. I knew he was dedicated to the cause of ending the Hero program, but *this*…

I swore under my breath. My impatience about our deadline was quickly shifting into panic. I felt my hands starting to shake and rubbed them down my jeans.

If we left now and totally floored it down the road, we could probably make it past the town. But then my stupid bomb would hurt the people who had absolutely nothing to do with this. I'd recreate almost exactly what killed my family and ruined my life in the first place.

We could evacuate the town, maybe… if the general public would listen to anyone, Amazing Man would be the best chance. Still not the ideal situation. Who knew how many houses… homes… would be destroyed?

The silence hung in the air for a few more seconds, then News nudged my shoulder. "Well? What do we do?"

Because I'm such a wise, benevolent leader.

I ran a hand up my face and over my hair. My gaze went over to the small parking lot below us. The superheroes had brought their cars. We had enough rides for everyone.

Not many other options at this point.

I let out my breath and checked my watch. That got me an instant burst of adrenaline. Eight minutes to eight. I swallowed and looked up.

"Roy?"

Roy was digging around the edge of the bomb housing with Cardboard and Lucius, despite Liza's protests that it wouldn't do any good. He stood, dusting off his hands on his pants. "Hmm?"

"Ready to lead a race?"

His head snapped up, "Heck, yeah." Cardboard clapped her hands and bounced next to him.

I tossed Roy my car keys. "Let's go, then."

He grinned, grabbed Cardboard's hand and dashed off towards the cars. Lucius happily flapped along behind them.

Everyone looked at me. I met Fernsby's gaze. "If you guys can't get through, we can't disarm it in time. We've only got a few minutes and if we want any chance of getting the people in town and ourselves to safety we've got to floor it out of here."

The other heroes looked at me like I'd grown horns. Or, more accurately, morals. Fernsby looked surprised too, but he took it quicker than the others and nodded. "Let's hurry, then."

The guys who could still fly made it to their cars even before Roy. The rest of us were left to make the run on foot.

Roy had the car pulled right up next to the edge of the road and was revving the engine. A grin split his face. Because who cares about imminent, life-threatening explosions when you've got a Mustang?

I stopped next to the car as Liza and Bad News got in and looked back at Dallas, who'd been bringing up the rear in our little parade. "Coming, Dall?"

He nodded and swallowed, his brow furrowed in worry. He rubbed his hands together nervously. They flickered blue, just like I'd seen at the café.

Dallas's powers.

Forcefields and teleportation.

Teleportation.

I froze. "Hold on…"

Roy shifted in his seat, "You getting in or what?"

I ignored him and ran up to Dallas. "So I know it works with touching objects, but if you're touching a person and you teleport, do they come with you?"

"Um… yeah…" Dallas looked confused for a second, then his expression changed to one of near terror. "Oh, no… Wolfgang, I… I'm awful at teleporting. It never works out right and people get hurt and it'll probably…"

I clapped his shoulder. "You'll do fine, Dallas. Get back to the bomb." I went running back to my car, "Liza, get out. I need you."

She obeyed with a frown, "What happened to getting out of here?"

"They're getting out of here, but I've got something. We're disarming the bomb."

Charles walked up with a frown, "What's going on?"

I turned to him. "We've got a way through the housing. Dallas can teleport Liza and me through. It's a big shell and a small bomb core so there's enough room. I can get through the security and Liz can disable the bomb the fastest. She designed it." I was talking so fast it was a miracle he even was able to make out what I was saying.

"But… the housing would disable…"

"Teleportation doesn't require touching anything!" I gestured wildly and pulled at my hair reflexively as I talked. "You're just one place and then you're somewhere else. We can make this." I stopped and took a breath. As soon as I said that we could, a wave of doubts came crashing in. All the ways we could fail… what would happen if we did…

I swallowed, "You guys still go. Evacuate the town if you can. Just… in case, okay?" My stomach flipped at the thought, but I pushed away the doubts. We could do this.

Fernsby looked at me for a second with that same soul-searching look that Dallas seemed to enjoy using so much, then he tightened his lips and nodded. "I'll be praying."

I nodded back, "Do it with your eyes open, man. You've got some serious driving to do." I spun on my heel and followed Dallas up to the bomb with Liza close behind.

We all skidded our way around the rocks and up the hill. I stopped for a minute to catch my breath once we were back in the giant shadow.

Liza pushed her bright hair out of her face. "Time?" she panted.

I checked my watch. "We've got three minutes."

Dallas stood next to the towering bomb, looking up at its peak and balling his hands into fists. I saw him shivering a little bit, but doubted it was from the cold. It was the same sort of scared-rabbit shivering he was doing when I first told him I wanted to help at the opera. His hands flickered again. He closed his eyes and dropped his chin to his chest for a few seconds.

I came up next to him. "Ready?"

Dallas opened his eyes. "I…" his voice cracked and he swallowed. "Just a minute." He bit his lip and clenched his fists harder. There was a blue flash and a zap noise and he appeared a few feet away next to Liza. He opened his eyes and looked back up at me. "So that's… generally how far I can go. With some accuracy, at least."

I nodded, "It's enough."

We all stood in a line next to the bomb, staring at its fake-rocky surface. Liza reached forward and touched the metal, pushing the illusion aside. I saw scratchy letters carved on the metal surface.

"For Eli, Rachel, William, Peter, Eloisa."

She stepped back, turned and met my eyes. "This is for them too."

I kept my eyes on those names as I took Dallas's hand. His hand was cold. Mine shook. His grip tightened until his knuckles went white. He bowed his head and clenched his teeth in concentration.

It felt kind of tingly for a second, there was a blue flash, and the sunlight disappeared. My stomach flipped and my head spun. I swallowed and stumbled a couple steps backwards. My back hit cold steel. The zipper from my jacket clanked hollowly on the metal.

We were inside the housing.

"Wolf?" Dallas's whisper echoed metallically in the darkness.

"Dallas, stay where you are." I closed my eyes for a couple seconds and leaned my head back, swallowing again and waiting for the nausea to pass. No light. No shades of grey. Just dark.

I patted my jacket pockets for my flashlight. My fingertips touched the rubber button on the end and I pulled it out. I aimed it up and clicked it on. It took a few seconds for my eyes for adjust to the sudden light. Everything in the housing was now visible in the dim whiteness.

There, in the middle of the small circle of space, was the same bomb I'd seen in the basement. The security panel reflected off the front of the small, bullet-shaped container. *Bingo.*

Liza sat on the ground, holding her head. The weird feeling after teleportation obviously wasn't just affecting me. Dallas turned, blinking in the light.

A tiny, unintentional smile was on his face. "I got us in."

I nodded, "My part, now." I looked up at the solid metal walls around us and shuddered. The housing seemed so much bigger from the outside. I felt shoved in someone's pocket, now that we were in.

My hands were shaking and the flashlight beam trembled. I forced myself to take a few deep breaths. My lungs couldn't seem to get the oxygen they needed. Was it just me or was the air sort of stale in here? I checked my watch. A minute and a half. *No time for claustrophobia.*

I walked over to the panel and ran my hand over the surface. It blinked on.

CODENAME

A keyboard popped up. I tapped over the letters. My shaking fingers hit a few wrong keys and the screen flashed red. I swore under my breath and tried again.

Eloisa.

This bomb was almost her birthday present. I swallowed.

The screen blinked green and slid to the next part.

Liza came up next to me, "Is it working?" Her voice sounded strained and I noticed her breathing getting a little labored as well.

I nodded and checked my watch, swearing again. *Well, it's a sealed case... there's limited oxygen. And three of us in here...*

Great, like we didn't have enough of a time crunch before.

FINGERPRINT said the screen. A circle came to the surface, looking like a bubble. I put my thumb on it.

Loading...

I clenched my teeth and watched it scan back and forth, agonizingly slowly.

Match! flashed green letters. It slid to the next screen. The last screen. My heart felt like it would pound right out of my chest.

Dallas's footsteps sounded behind me.

"Dallas, don't touch anything," my voice cracked and I gulped in another breath of the stale air. "We still need you to get us out of here." I looked up briefly. The walls seemed to lean inwards, getting smaller. I forced my eyes back down to the screen, checking my watch again.

Forty-five seconds.

KEY PHRASE

A microphone icon popped up and I tapped it frantically. "Diebythesword!" it came out as one panicked word.

The screen flashed red. *Incorrect. Try again.*

I took a deep breath and forced some composure, despite the lack of time and oxygen. I tapped the icon again. "Die by the sword."

Incorrect. Try again.

I swore and smacked my hand on the side of the panel. Thirty seconds now.

"What's *wrong* with it?" Liza's voice rose to a high, panicked tone, far from her usual calm drawl.

I bit my tongue, shook my head and pressed the button again. "Die. By. The. *Sword.*"

It seemed to consider this offering slightly longer. But once again, it dinged me as "incorrect".

Twenty-two seconds.

I slammed the button yet again. *"Die. By. The. Sword."* I practically yelled it, my voice trembling. I was going to die by something a lot worse than the sword if this thing didn't work.

The hot, empty air pressed in tightly around me as I waited for the machine to register my answer and open up…

Incorrect. Try again.

Fifteen seconds.

I dropped my head against the panel and struggled to breathe. "Oh God, we're going to die in here."

It was what I'd always wanted, wasn't it? The end I saw for myself after the Amazing Man quest? I'd die and rejoin my family.

But I still have family… there's Leif… I need to live for Leif. I still have so much I need to fix… I needed to be something other than an idiot who changed his mind and blew himself up at the last minute.

"A-are you sure it wasn't something else?" Dallas shifted behind me, twisting his hands nervously.

"I'm sure," I snapped. "It was…" My thoughts flashed back to the basement room where I set the bomb. This wasn't the first time I'd had problems with this thing… I sucked in a breath, even though it gave me next to no oxygen.

"Dobby the sword."

Ten seconds.

I hit the button again, my hands shaking more than they ever had. I used the last of my breath in a desperate gamble to finally unlock it. "Dobby the sword!"

I watched it, snapping my fingers nervously as it loaded. *Come on… come on…*

The screen blinked green.

Access granted! There was a pop and the solid bomb casing

opened.

Five seconds.

"Liza!" I pulled the casing aside and looked helplessly over the mess of wires and metal. Three seconds now. "Where's the…"

Liza shoved me back, "Here!" Stretching over the bomb, she closed her hand around a thick loop of yellow wire.

One second.

She gritted her teeth and yanked it loose, stumbling backwards a step.

Zero.

There was a blinding flash of blue, then white exploded over my vision and enveloped everything with a hideous roar. I couldn't feel anything. Two thoughts crossed my mind in that split second.

After all these years of wondering, this was what dying actually felt like.

And, if nothing else, at least we went out with a bang.

The roaring whiteness swallowed me and everything was gone.

Chapter 26: Evicted From Hell

I'm dead.

I'm totally dead.

I can't even feel anything. It's just like... numb and floaty.

But do dead people know when they're dead? How am I thinking?

It's dark. I don't think heaven is dark.

Well, yeah, idiot. You went to hell.

The Wolf going to heaven... what a joke.

Something's beeping. What beeps in the afterlife?

Maybe it's my eternal torment. I'm doomed to a dark existence of hearing disembodied beeping.

That seems a bit mild for me. Maybe I got it leveled down by repenting at the last minute. It could be worse.

But if I died... the bomb went off, then. Liza and Dallas are dead too. Amazing Man's dead. The gang. The other heroes. The rest of that town…

Dead. I killed them.

I'm a murderer. Always have been.

Oh God. I'm sorry. I'm so sorry. I tried. I'm such an idiot. Hell's too good for me.

All Leif's family is gone now. And his adoptive dad too.

I'll be known as a horrible person forever. The man eaten up by vengeance. The big, bad, irredeemable Wolf. He'll hate me.

I was wrong. I couldn't turn around. It's too late.

I failed.

Ruined everything.

Wolfgang Dankworth… the villain.

A tiny bit of feeling pricked a pinhole into the numb, endless darkness.

There was something wet on my face, dripping down on my cheeks. I felt my shoulders shaking.

Weird. I didn't feel anything before. Am I taking on whatever demonic form I get to transform into for eternity?

The beeping sped up slightly. The pinhole in the dead darkness encasing me expanded and pain leaked in, burning in my left leg and right wrist. More pain, of course. Wasn't that what Hell was all about? My shoulders still trembled, but I couldn't seem to move anything else. I realized I was breathing. Sobbing.

How can I be breathing? Do they even allow crying in Hell? Well, if ever people had an excuse…

I took in a deep, shuddering breath, trying to get myself under control and swallowed. My face still felt wet and my breath came in short, painful hiccups.

There was something under me. I was lying down on something soft… like cloth. My fingertips twitched slightly.

Sheets? A bed?

That doesn't make sense… I should be lying on the ground. On pointy rocks… on an eternal fire or something…

There were other sounds aside from the beeping now.

Talking. Cordial, pleasant conversation.

Doesn't sound like demons to me. Was Hell actually too good for me? Did I get evicted? Am I going somewhere even worse?

If only I could go back for a little bit. Just a few minutes… tell them all how sorry I was for being such an obsessed idiot…

More tears trickled down my cheeks. Something that sounded like a whimper broke from my lips.

There was a gasp followed by a squeaking noise of rubber shoe-soles on tile. Then a hand touched one of my still shaking shoulders. A warm, thin hand.

"Mr. Dankworth, can you hear me? Mr. Dankworth?" the voice sounded far away at first and then too loud. It took all my mental energy to even make out what the words meant.

I took in another shaky breath and sobbed out something I couldn't even understand. The hand moved up to touch my face.

"Shh… shh… it's okay." The voice almost sounded like my mom. Could I have made it to heaven after all? I swallowed. *God, I don't deserve that…*

But what if this was my chance? My last opportunity to apologize?

I concentrated my strength on pulling my eyes open. They rolled back and closed again the first couple of times, but I finally got my eyelids to stay up. The sudden whiteness made me flinch and almost close them again.

White walls. White ceiling. White lights. How could there be so much clean white?

The form bending over me was still fuzzy. I couldn't quite make out the face — just short, mousy, brownish-blonde hair and a turquoise jumpsuit-looking thing.

I thought angels wore white, not turquoise. And dresses. Jumpsuits seemed a little… weird.

I swallowed again and licked my lips. They tasted salty. My throat felt sucked dry of any moisture, but I still opened my mouth, trying to force words out.

"M-mom?" My voice cracked.

The angel… or whoever it was… laughed softly. She said something. I couldn't figure out the words, but the voice sounded so much like Mom it had to be her.

I forced myself to choke out what I needed to say. "I'm j-just… M-mom I'm so sorry for… I m-messed everything… up and after you were gone I killed… s-so many people b-because I thought… I thought…"

The blurry form standing over me shook her head, leaning over and holding my shoulder again. Her words came through clearly in my mind this time. "Shh… I'm sorry, Mr. Dankworth. You're talking to the wrong person."

I frowned and blinked a couple of times, trying to clear my vision so I could actually see her face properly. "Th-then who…?"

"I'm Abby."

Her voice was still quiet. Kind. It reminded me of Ellie's voice. Was Ellie here?

I could make out Abby's face now. Freckles covered her face like paint splatters. She was smiling a tiny little smile at me. I tried to remember the last time a stranger smiled at me.

She must not know who I am… but she said my name… so how…?

Thinking was starting to hurt, so I stopped trying.

Abby took her hand down and tilted her head at me. "How are you feeling?"

I blinked at her and tried to determine the answer to that question. How was I feeling? My leg hurt… and so did my wrist. But it was still kind of a numb, fuzzy sort of pain that didn't really bother me. And my head felt funny. I felt like I should be feeling more than I was. But then what was I supposed to expect, being dead?

"I-I'm dead."

The pain of it hit me again. So many people would still be alive if it weren't for me. Dallas and Liza didn't deserve to die. No one deserved to die but me. That bomb was mine. The world was probably better off with me gone.

I closed my eyes and more tears leaked out. Another sob pressed up in my chest. My shoulders started shaking again.

Abby's hand touched my shoulder. "Mr. Dankworth, you're not. Really, it's okay…"

It wasn't okay. How could I *not* be dead? I failed. The bomb had gone off anyway. And I had been inside it.

I shook my head and repeated. "I'm dead." It was a whisper. My voice barely wanted to even work.

Abby put her hand on the side of my face and I opened my eyes again. She shook her head. "You came close, I'll give you that. But you're very much alive."

I didn't register what her words meant. I swallowed and coughed. "Is… is this heaven or hell?" Or purgatory? That might be it. It didn't seem extreme enough here to be one or the other. Just a holding cell until they could cook up the proper level of Hell for me…

"Did you hear me?" Abby spoke her words as clearly as possible, forcing my mind into understanding. "Mr. Dankworth, this is a *hospital*."

Hospital. The scattered puzzle pieces in my mind clicked together slowly.

I'm alive.

I survived the bomb.

Again.

I couldn't dig up the proper swear words to express my feelings on that in the moment.

But how? Why?

And there's no one else in here… what about Liza and Dallas? News? Amazing Man? Roy and Cardboard?

If anyone deserved to survive, it wasn't me.

I tried to push myself up in the bed, but Abby stepped forward, pressing me back down and shaking her head. "You need to hold still for a bit. Just rest."

She really didn't know who I was. No one said "Dankworth" like that. It was almost a curse word to the general public by now.

And I couldn't lie still and rest. No rest for the wicked. What happened to that?

But her small hand on my arm seemed like an iron weight I was too weak to move.

I forced more words out. I needed to know. "The... the others?"

Her facial expression stayed unreadable, almost like she didn't want me to know. "Everything's alright, Mr. Dankworth. Just stay still." Abby kept her hand firmly on my shoulder.

"But the... the bomb. My bomb... the heroes... th-there was..." My breath was back to coming out in hiccups.

"Yes, I know. Shh... you're okay." That tiny smile was flickering across her small, lipstick painted mouth again. What didn't she understand? My own safety was the last thing I was worried about.

"Everyone else. Where... where are they?" My heartbeat quickened and the beeping noise followed suit. I felt lightheaded. *If they're dead, I'll never forgive myself. I shouldn't have survived.*

There were so many people I needed to apologize to. So many people whose lives I'd ruined. And they were all gone. It seemed to be my lot in life. I couldn't seem to make it right when I had the opportunity. I couldn't seem to die.

Abby put her hand to my forehead briefly, keeping me back down on the pillow. "They're fine, don't worry." Her voice sounded almost too soft... too comforting.

I shook my head and my mouth felt dry. The walls of the room wavered in my vision. "D-don't lie to me."

"Just rest, Mr. Dankworth. It's alright." Abby's face was getting blurry again, her freckles melting together. I felt dizzy. Spots clouded my vision, closing in from the edges.

I knew I was passing out again. I tried to fight it. A few hard blinks... a weak attempt to clench my fists that shot pain up my right arm... *Stay awake. Get out of this stupid bed. Find out what happened.*

My eyes slid closed against my will and I forced them open

again. The dim outline of Abby's head bobbed, like she was nodding.

"That's it." Her hand slid away. Her voice sounded like it was coming from the end of a long tunnel. "Get your rest."

No. I don't need rest. I can't rest.

Tell me. Where are Dallas and Liza? Did I kill them?

I couldn't make my mouth form the words. The room tipped, my eyes closed again and I went back into the dark that apparently wasn't Hell.

#

Voices prodded at the edges of my mind. I felt like I should know them, but I couldn't make out what they were saying. One was deep and I could feel it in my chest. The other was softer and even. Neither of them said much.

Were they talking to me? *About* me?

I couldn't open my eyes, but I concentrated on the words they were saying. A few of them began to make sense.

Bomb… lucky… awake yet… waiting…

Lucky? If they were talking about me, that was about the worst word in the English language to use. Anything with even minimal contact with me turned to a smoking ruin.

Dallas and Liza… Charles… the gang… it felt like ice water rushed into my veins. Were they dead? What hadn't Abby told me?

My fault… it's all my fault…

I swallowed hard.

One of the voices spoke again, a slightly put-out rumble. I made out all the words this time. "This'll melt pretty soon, here. He better wake up."

My heart jumped up to my throat.

Bad News. Alive.

I tried to sit up… to say something. My head just rolled to one side and I groaned.

"Hey, that's something…" I heard shoes thumping on the

floor towards me.

He sounded well enough. Hopefully we weren't lone survivors and he'd just managed to drag me out of the carnage and to a hospital.

Well, I'm not going to learn anything if I lie here with my eyes closed and be lazy about it... come on, make an effort...

With momentous effort, I dragged my eyelids open. Light came in the window from a blue sky and backlit a giant, dark form standing beside me. I couldn't make out much, but I could see the brim of a fedora.

Definitely Bad News. *And Bad News is good news.*

His mouth moved into what I thought was a smile. It was a bit hard to tell through the blur.

"And Wolfgang Dankworth rose again on the third day and there was much rejoicing," News said.

I blinked at him, frowning as I slowly ran the words over in my mind. On the third day? Much... rejoicing? "H-huh?"

He shrugged and held a blurry shape towards me. "Have some ice cream."

I blinked at the bowl he was holding in confusion.

"It's mint," he qualified.

"News, give him a few minutes to wake up."

The second voice clicked into place in my memory.

Charles Fernsby.

Amazing Man was here. Alive.

Adrenaline jolted through my veins. I had to get up... had to apologize...

I shot upright and my leg exploded in pain. I clenched my teeth with a moan and the room tilted, forcing me back against the pillow. My head pounded.

"Whoa, whoa. Take it easy." Fernsby stepped forward, holding out his hand as if to catch me if I rolled out of bed or something. "You're not in good shape, buddy. Calm down."

Take it easy? Calm down? When I'd just killed who knew how many people?

I bit my tongue and tipped my head back, closing my eyes. The pain subsided a bit and I reopened one, looking down at my legs. My right one was fine. My left one was encased in white plaster. A quick look at my arms showed that my right wrist had received the same treatment. I felt another bandage on the side of my head.

And of course, I was wearing one of those idiotic hospital dresses.

A few broken bones and a dumb outfit. It could be worse. You could be dead.

But what about the others? News and Fernsby hadn't been the only ones in danger…

"How're you feeling?" Fernsby was standing by my bed as well now, his dashing height dwarfed in News's shadow. His hands were stuck deep in his jacket pockets and his brow creased in concern.

"As well as I deserve," I muttered. "I-I need you to… just… l-listen for a… a bit. P-please…" I pushed up a bit slower this time so I didn't run as high a risk of passing out.

"See?" News proclaimed with a proud grin. "He's doing great."

Charles took another step forward, pulling his hands out again. "Wolfgang, lie back down…"

"P-please, just listen," I dug my fingers into the sheets, gripping tightly and closing my eyes.

"I… Charles, I don't have amnesia anymore. That's why I didn't tell Dallas sooner. M-my memories are all back and I just…" I forced my eyes open again so I could meet his gaze, even if I couldn't entirely focus. "I almost went through without trying to stop it, b-but the other day I… heard you and Leif at the museum and… and…"

Charles looked between me and News, furrowing his brow in a question.

I swallowed hard, trying to keep my voice from cracking as I continued. I raised my hand to run through my hair even though it was the hand in a cast and it hurt to move.

"I'm… I'm sorry, Fernsby. I'm r-really, really sorry." Despite my best efforts, my voice was cracking more than a jackhammered sidewalk. "Y-you were right. I put myself back together all wrong and my family would barely even know me. All these years… I've been murdering and hurting p-people and doing the wrong thing… I've been an idiot and a j-jerk and… I'm just really sorry…"

My vision blurred again and I squinted my eyes closed, trying to push the tears back and slow my breathing a little. This was supposed to be me trying to make it right, not me blubbering like a baby.

"So…" Charles's voice came, slow and quiet. "You remembered? And you still… stopped it? You still saved me and Dallas and all the heroes?"

I opened my eyes, swallowing again, and nodded, then shook my head. "I… yeah, but I was too late and d-didn't save…" I trailed off, actually registering what his words meant.

Charles laughed a little bit, "Yes you did, Wolfgang. The bomb didn't kill anyone. It only short-circuited, like the one at the baseball stadium. No one died."

My breath caught in my throat, but I made my hoarse voice work again. It couldn't be this good. I couldn't have heard right. "L-liza and Dallas…? They're okay?"

"Still alive and kicking last time I checked," Bad News rocked back and forth on his feet.

Mr. Fernsby obviously thought that a rather rough way of putting it and gave News a look before putting it in his own words. "Dallas made it out the best of you three. Only a broken arm and rib. Liza's… alive. Still unconscious, but they said she'll pull through."

So all the heroes had lived.

The gang was all alive.

No one in that town had gotten hurt.

We'd done it. The bomb was stopped.

They're alive… thank you, God… thank you… I let out my

breath in a giant whoosh and my muscles went weak with relief. My eyes stung and I blinked. I was getting to be a regular water show, here.

Bad News quietly leaned over and pulled my elbow out from propping me up, forcing me to lie back down. Probably a good thing, since I wouldn't have stayed up for much longer anyway.

I swallowed, looking back up at News and Fernsby. Now that the most pressing question was off my mind, a million others bubbled to the surface. I wasn't sure where to start.

Most of them started with the same word, so I just said that. "How…?"

The two of them exchanged a glance. News shrugged and Fernsby nodded, patting down his coat. He unzipped it and pulled out a folded newspaper, dropping it into my lap.

I picked it up, fumbling a bit with the cast on my hand. It spread out with a crisp crinkling noise and I blinked at the letters emblazoned across the front.

"THE WOLF SAVES HEROES: Not so 'big and bad' after all?"

Below were two pictures. One of all the heroes and a picture of what looked like a giant, blown-up heap of scrap metal. It took me a minute to recognize the smoke-stained surroundings as the rocks by the heroes' meeting hall.

My gaze shifted down to the words below, and I began to read. My vision and mind were clear enough to do so now, at least.

This last Friday, Wolfgang Dankworth proved that there's good in the most unexpected people. Having a change of heart about a deadly bomb planted outside, Dankworth ran in to warn the heroes of the impending danger. While they drove to safety, he stayed behind with Dallas Knight and a member of his own gang, Liza Allister, to disarm the bomb and save the nearby town.
With the limited amount of time left, they were only able to manage to short circuit the bomb, causing it to self destruct with minimal damage to its surroundings, much like the recent baseball stadium

bomb malfunction.

*"I have to admit, I really never saw something like this coming,"
said New Mexico's Terrific Man in an interview. "I mean, The Wolf?
Of all people... but I guess there's good in everyone. He and his
pack saved all of our lives and I'm indebted to them."*

*And in our own Amazing Man's words: "It's never too late for
anyone. Wolfgang Dankworth is as much a hero today as I am, if not
more. It takes more courage to repent... to turn... than it does to be
going the right way in the first place, and I respect and admire him
for that."*

*Knight, Dankworth and Allister are currently in Utah Valley
Hospital, being treated for injuries, and were unavailable for
interviews.*

I read over it again. It felt like my chest would burst from
happiness.

"Well?" News tugged at his tie, peeking over my shoulder.
"Whatcha think?"

*Wolfgang Dankworth is as much a hero today as I am, if not
more.*

I looked up at Charles Fernsby. He had his hands back in his
pockets and was watching me with a smile. He raised his eyebrows
as I met his gaze. "What I said was true, you know. Heroes don't all
have super strength and flight." He laughed a little. "Sometimes
they've got cowlicks and leather jackets."

I bit my lip, somewhat holding back my grin from
completely splitting my face in half. "Yeah." I gave the newspaper
back to him with a nod. "Th-thank you."

Fernsby nodded back, taking it. "And when you're well
enough, you've got a very enthusiastic little Dankworth who wants
to visit you."

Leif. My little brother wanted to see me. He was proud of
me.

I didn't deserve any of this.

"How's he...? Oh..."

I looked up to see Abby standing at the door. She was smaller than I remembered her from waking up before. Though that might have just been in comparison to Fernsby and News.

She smiled, clasping her hands behind her back. "How are you feeling, Mr. Dankworth?"

I smiled back, "Very much alive, thank you."

Chapter 27: Patience and Patients

Don't get me wrong, I was over the moon about actually having disarmed the bomb, getting myself turned around, saving all the heroes... all that great stuff.

And I'd do it again in a heartbeat. But if I could, I'd try to figure out some way that didn't land me flat on my back in a hospital.

My mental fog burned off after a day or so, and after that the invalid life got old pretty fast. Everyone checking on me and asking how I was doing. Not being able to go anywhere on my busted leg without a wheelchair or crutches. The jittery nurses who seemed to be only barely masking their terror of me with pasted on smiles. The nasty hospital food.

But I bore it. I got my leather jacket and normal clothes back after a bit of negotiating, so that made me feel a bit more like myself. Abby, the nurse I was able to stand the most, seemed to be the one generally assigned to me, so that was nice. She didn't seem as scared of me as the others did.

And then Bad News smuggled in ice cream for me, which helped morale greatly.

No one seemed to be too keen on telling me a ton of details about anything and any questions I asked were either met with vague reassurances or exhortations to just get more rest. Everyone was worried I'd stress myself out and affect my health, I guessed. Which was a big part of the reason I wanted to get mobile on my crutches so fast.

It was about three days after waking up that they said I could get up and visit my co-heroes... Liza and Dallas.

"But if anything starts hurting or you get worn out, *tell someone*," Abby insisted firmly as she helped me upright in bed. "You still really shouldn't be up and you have to be careful."

"Yeah, yeah... I know." I pulled my jacket sleeve down further over my wrist cast. I could handle it. I'd handled plenty without professional medical help before. I just needed to see my friends with my own eyes. There still seemed to be something they didn't want to tell me.

I nodded to Abby, "Could I have my crutches?" When given a choice of wheelchair or crutches, crutches were the more masculine choice by far, in my opinion.

Abby bit her lip and tucked her short hair behind her ear. Reluctance showing on every part of her face, she handed the crutches to me from where they were propped up against the wall.

I took them and smiled at her, hoping to impart a bit of reassurance. "Thanks. And I'll be fine, really."

Abby gave me a thin, slightly doubtful smile back.

My first delirious impression of her as my mom had stayed in my mind as a sort of shadow, following her around. Part of the reason it was easier to deal with her babying me, I guess.

I swung the crutches out in front of me and braced myself to swing up, but someone walked in right then. I looked up and stopped.

Dallas. His arm in a sling, a bandage on one side of his pale face and his mouth in the same old pokerfaced line. He limped slightly, but considering he'd just been through a bomb explosion, he looked remarkably well.

And apparently he'd beat me to the punch on visiting rooms.

I blinked at him for a second before getting my voice back. "Um… hey."

Dallas nodded and his mouth moved into that small, polite smile of his. "Hi. Are you doing alright?"

"Aside from a concussion, broken leg and broken wrist, I'm fantastic." I grunted a bit as I completed my mission of getting upright. My vision went a little fuzzy with the change in position and my head pounded, but I shook it off. "Lots of things don't seem that bad within the perspective of having almost died."

"Good point." Dallas put his good hand in his jeans pocket and looked me up and down. "Are you going somewhere?"

"Down the hall to see Liza, if it's not too much for my frail constitution."

"It's called *recovery*, Mr. Dankworth," Abby corrected, sounding slightly annoyed.

Dallas's half smile faded. "Have you… I mean…" he thought for a second, then shook his head, "Never mind."

Oh great, now even Dallas didn't want to tell me things. "What?"

He shook his head, "Nothing. I'll go with you."

"That would be wonderful, Mr. Knight, thank you." Abby smiled at him. "Both of you be careful now."

"Yeah."

"Yes, ma'am."

And with Dallas limping and me awkwardly clomping along on my crutches, we got out into the hall. Not freedom by any means, but hey, it was better than just sticking to one room.

After a little distance down the hallway with Dallas still not saying anything, I cleared my throat. "So. You… your arm doing okay?"

Dallas blinked and looked down at his arm in its pale blue

sling. "It's alright, I guess." He went back to looking ahead and shuffling forward.

His conversational skills or lack thereof were clearly unharmed.

Silence fell again, except for the thump-scrape of my leg cast and crutches.

A few seconds later, Dallas surprised me by actually speaking up again. "It was nice that I actually was able to get my powers to work for once," he commented, glancing over at me. "That forcefield I got up right as the bomb blew... it actually broke all my power-bots with all the energy I put into it."

I stared at him, "Forcefield?"

He looked back over at me with his brow furrowed slightly. "Yeah, you didn't know that?"

Well, it made our survival make a lot more sense now that I did. Yet another detail that no one thought to inform me of. I shook my head. "Hadn't heard. I... kind of remember a blue flash, though, so it makes sense." Silence for a second. I swallowed. "Hey, thanks."

Dallas half smiled again and nodded. "Thank you too."

Both of us could have said a lot more. But we both felt the extra thanks... the final truce. Besides, I'd had enough mushy moments to last me a while and Dallas wasn't keen on mush in the first place. The quiet was warm and friendly.

A nurse I hadn't seen before walked past, nodding to us and smiling as she clicked down the hall in her heels.

I focused on the numbers on the doors we were passing for a bit before realizing I didn't know which one I was looking for. *Brilliant, Holmes.* More brain-haze than I probably realized was still hanging around.

I looked over at Dallas. "You know where Liza's room is?"

He nodded. "I've... been there already." The hesitation in his voice sent fingers of ice down my spine.

No one wanted to talk about her. Everyone who mentioned her flinched.

They weren't telling me something about Liza.

I stopped and locked my eyes on Dallas's. "Dallas, is she okay? What happened?" All the awful possibilities flashed through my mind and I felt my hands starting to shake.

"She's alive," Dallas assured. He broke my gaze, ran his tongue over his teeth and kept walking.

"Alive doesn't necessarily mean okay." I clenched my teeth and swung my crutches out far in front of me to catch up with him.

He sighed and looked up at the ceiling. "She… um…" his voice dropped lower and he slowed by the door at the corner of the hall. "H-her arm. It wasn't really…" Dallas swallowed and met my eyes again. "Liza lost her arm in the explosion, Wolf."

It felt like someone punched me in the gut. I lost my breath for a minute.

Liza. The mechanical genius. The girl Roy always joked was more dexterous than all of us put together.

One of her arms was gone. Because of my bomb. Because of me.

"I'm sorry," Dallas said quietly, "She was the one that grabbed the wire. She was the closest and I didn't get the forcefield around her completely."

I swallowed hard, feeling a little lightheaded. I forced my mouth to move. "B-but she's… she'll live? Is she… is she doing okay?"

Dallas nodded, but his face stayed sad as he pushed open the door. Soft voices came from inside, too quiet for me to place who was talking. Sliding halfway through the partially open door, Dallas cleared his throat. "Hey… "

The voices stopped and he continued.

"It's just Wolfgang and me, sir. Can we come in?"

"Certainly," one of the voices came up past the half-whisper it was before and I recognized it as Mr. Fernsby's voice. "I didn't know he was up and about yet. Come ahead. I was just heading out to make a call."

Dallas looked back at me and nodded before slipping in the rest of the way.

I hesitated, standing there and steeling myself… stockpiling apologies for Liza… for my friend. How could she live like that? How could I live with seeing her like that?

I closed my eyes for a second, bit my tongue and pushed the door the rest of the way open before swinging in.

Charles was just standing from a chair by Liza's bed. He made his way over to the door and nodded to me as he slipped past into the hall.

Liza lay under the white sheets of the bed, her face pale. Her bright teal hair was in a ponytail over her left shoulder. The arm on that side was still there. But below her right shoulder was just… gone. No arm. Only one hand fidgeted with the blanket over the bed.

I couldn't look at her face. Only that awful lack of limb.

I felt sick to my stomach and my lightheadedness got worse.

Liza's soft snicker of a laugh broke the silence, weaker than usual. "Wolfy, you're paler than I am."

I still couldn't look at her. "I… I'm so sorry, Liz…" I couldn't get my voice past a whisper.

"Sit down and we can talk. It's fine. I've always been a lefty anyways."

Ambidextrous, actually. *She's just trying to make me feel better.*

I managed to get my eyes to her face. She didn't look mad at all. She smirked faintly at me through the pain on her face and held out her hand in a "ta-da" motion. "See, I'm just dandy." Her voice trembled a bit.

Oh, God, that should've been me… why her? I swallowed hard, wavering a bit on my feet.

"Dallas, get the idiot a chair before he keels over." Liza shifted in her bed and nodded to Dallas.

I felt Dallas's hand grip onto my arm and guide me to one of the blue hospital chairs next to Liza's bed. The crutches clacked against each other as I put them to the side. My knees willingly gave out and I sat down hard in the chair.

I bit my tongue. My eyes fixed back onto her empty hospital

gown sleeve and my hands trembled.

"Liza... I just... I'm sorry. I should've... it should've been me. If I'd..." pieces of different apologies came out in a jumbled mess. "... you shouldn't have to..."

"Wolfy." Liza's one quiet word sounded louder than any of mine. I stopped, meeting her blue-eyed gaze with difficulty. Her mouth tipped into a sideways smile and she put her cool hand onto my shaking one. "It's alright. It was worth it."

She tightened her lips and gave my hand a squeeze. "Better a one-armed hero than a whole crook, hey?"

A bit of the weight on my chest lifted, but I still didn't feel quite right. "But it... it was my fault. If it weren't for me..."

"If it weren't for you, I'd have just thrown my life away," Liza interrupted. "I'd do it again in a minute, so shut up and stop looking so bloody remorseful."

I blinked at her, rocked back a bit by that. She raised an eyebrow at me and I couldn't help smiling just a little. I saluted her with my casted hand. "Yes, ma'am."

Liza smiled. Her eyes went down to where her arm would have been again. Her smile shifted and she puckered her lips thoughtfully. She glanced up at me. "You know I'm going to have way too much fun inventing some sort of prosthetic. It'll be way better than just my plain old arm, I can tell you that."

I chuckled and nodded, "Of course."

Some sadness still lingered on her face, unable to be hidden even with her best efforts. But her determination to make the best of it — to accept and move forward — made my guilt ease a little. I'd help her in any way possible. I wasn't exactly the optimist extraordinaire, but for Liza I could at least make an effort.

The door made a soft squeaking noise and I looked up to see Fernsby slipping back in, a frown creasing his forehead. He shoved his phone in his pocket and rubbed a hand over his face.

"Is everything alright, sir?" Dallas asked.

Fernsby shrugged and took a seat. "I hope so. Just... something odd."

"Hey?" Liza tipped her head, shifting her position a bit in the bed.

"I've been trying to give the director a ring for the past couple days, but…" he shrugged again, still frowning. "He just doesn't seem to be picking up." Charles looked up at Dallas. "Mansley's trips back to SPI headquarters don't normally take this long, do they? It's been over a week."

Mansley. Derrick Mansley.

How could he have not been one of the first things I mentioned after waking up? I'd totally forgotten. He was a traitor endangering the lives of who-knows-how-many people, and I took three whole days after coming around to actually remember to warn someone about him.

Classic, idiot.

Better now than never, though.

I cleared my throat and sat up straighter in my seat, wincing as I bumped my leg, "Um… Fernsby?"

He turned his head, "Hmm?"

"I… forgot to say something sooner… but Mansley… he's not really who you think he is." I put together the words slowly, not quite sure how to explain.

Fernsby, Dallas and Liza all looked at me. Fernsby's brow furrowed further and he leaned forward. "How do you mean?"

"Well, he…" I licked my lips, "He's not really all for the superhero program. Pretty much from the start, he's actually been backing me up. Said that he regretted what he'd done in running the program when something like the Twin Bombings could happen…" I still couldn't help but flinch at mentioning that.

"But he couldn't back down off his position, so he had to… to be the behind-the-scenes man. To help me exact justice instead of doing it himself. That bomb… was actually built from his funds. Everything I did was funded by him, practically. Mansley's not… he's not in support of the superhero program at all. Almost as bad as I am… was, I mean. And Dallas, it was his name I messed up when I told you 'Mansfield' at the cafe…"

Dallas's mouth opened slightly in surprise. "Ohhh…"

"Hold on." Charles frowned and pursed his lips. He tipped his head at me, "See… now we've got something else odd… did you know it was Mansley? The whole time?"

I nodded, "From the first time we met, yeah."

Dallas rubbed at the back of his neck and looked over at Fernsby, "That's not what he told us at all."

I started in my seat, "Wait, whoa. You *knew?*"

"In a way," Fernsby said slowly, "See, he told us that he had an inside man as your arms dealer. Through the years, there were many of your plans that would have gone through if it hadn't been for Director Mansley tipping us off."

I opened my mouth, but the words all stayed stuck whirling around in my mind. All those plans… the things I thought I'd laid out perfectly. No one could possibly have known. And then Amazing Man would swoop in at the last moment. I'd never been able to figure it out.

And it was Mansley… the whole time, it was Mansley… but…

My thoughts finally came out, "Why would he do that? He paid for our weapons. He covered our tracks and kept me out of prison, for the most part. He said he wanted the program to be torn apart so he could be free… that he wanted justice…"

"And he funded us too," pointed out Dallas, "Yet he helped you." He paused, biting his lip, "And you said that bomb was built with his help?"

"Practically *by* him." I leaned back and reflexively reached to run my hand over my hair. My cast thumped up against my forehead, but I barely noticed. "So if he was for you guys all along, then why didn't he tell you anything about the single thing that put you in the most danger?"

"And what does he gain," mused Fernsby, steepling his fingers, "by paying both of us to keep going?"

Liza's even, thoughtful voice broke in. "He's playing both sides of the chessboard, lads." Her eyes were squinted thoughtfully up at the ceiling. "How does he keep his job? How to keep himself needed? Simple. All you need is a hero…" she gestured to Charles, "… and a villain." She gestured to me.

Her hand dropped and she puckered her lips. "And Wolfy… you just took away his villain. No wonder he's not answering his phone."

Chapter 28: Giving the Slip

Abby didn't have as much faith in me as I would have liked. She poked her head in a few minutes after our discovery and made the very decided decision that I'd "worked myself up enough."

Well, did she expect me to just sit back sipping tea and calmly discuss the fact that someone I'd looked up to for years was a dirty, double-crossing traitor?

I was coddled away from the others and back to my room against my will. Before I could even hear what they were going to do about Mansley, too.

Thankfully, Charles came by a bit later to fill me in on the abbreviated version of their plan.

"I'm going to see him." Fernsby set his lips in a tight line as he met my eyes. He sat down in the chair next to my bed, clasping his hands between his knees. "I checked with the program. Mansley's back. But he's still not answering his phone and his secretary says he's not taking calls."

"Yeah, gee. I wonder why." I rubbed at my wrist cast and frowned, "Why don't you just call the SPI on him? Tell them he's corrupt. That…"

Charles shook his head, "I'm not passing final judgment before talking to him. I've learned my lesson on that. There could be something going on behind the scenes that we have no idea about."

Even though now I was technically on Fernsby's side, his methods of working things out were still beyond me. It might've just been my view still coming out of the criminal world, but my strong inclination was to schedule Mansley for an appointment of bad luck with a certain Mr. News.

But hey, whatever was involved in bringing him to justice, I wanted in on it. I shifted my position in the hospital cot, readying to get out. My crutches were propped right next to the bed.

I nodded to Fernsby. "I'm coming."

He opened his mouth for a second, then closed it again, raising an eyebrow. Concern tightened his expression.

"What?"

Fernsby bit his lip and looked doubtful, "I don't think you're really in any state to go anywhere, Wolfgang." He put out a hand as if to calm me down. "It's fine, really. I'll deal with it."

Indignation rose in my chest at his words. I was so done with all this hospital babying junk it wasn't even funny.

I tipped my chin out stubbornly. "I've been lazing around here long enough. This is my battle, too. And someone needs to be carrying a gun, in case your three-percent chance that he's an innocent little lamb doesn't pan out."

Charles sighed and rubbed his hands on his jeans. "I'm not that dumb. I'll be stopping back by my house to grab something to arm myself." He stood, putting one hand in his pocket. He walked over and patted my shoulder, nodding. "You've done an amazing amount to help, really. You deserve some rest."

I bit my tongue to keep from swearing at him.

He must have picked up on the murderous expression on my

face. "Listen, you can ask the doctor if you're good to go and if he says okay, then you can call me and I'll come back and pick you up. Alright?"

That was his checkmate move. There was no way they were letting me out of the hospital yet. Nothing I could do would change that fact.

I rubbed my hand over my face and gave Fernsby a look.

His eyebrow twitched upwards again and he shook his head. "I'll see you later, okay?"

"I guess."

And with a farewell wave, he was gone.

I sat there stewing for a few minutes, then Abby poked in.

"Lunchtime," she announced.

I held back a groan and thumped my head back on the pillow.

She smiled her tiny, amused smile and slipped the rest of the way in with the food tray propped on her arm. She walked over and set it on my lap. "You'll recover faster if you actually eat, I can tell you that."

I gave the smooshed sandwich and soggy tater-tots a pained look. Bad News had spoiled me. Sure, about eighty percent of the time he made cake and ice cream, but he was an infinitely better cook than whoever was back there doling out all these prepackaged nightmares.

I flicked at the unnaturally white bread atop my sandwich and wrinkled my nose.

Abby propped a hand on her hip and tucked her honey-colored hair behind her ear. "Also, you have a couple more visitors waiting outside to see you."

My head snapped up, "Who?"

"Mr. News and Mr. Tucker."

"I'll see them now, sure." I set my lunch tray to the side as I spoke, hoping I didn't sound too eager.

Abby frowned, "While you're eating?"

"Yeah, I'm fine," I assured her, shifting my voice to hopefully sound nonchalant. "Send them ahead."

She shrugged and walked back out into the hall.

Just a few minutes after the tiny pixie exited, a fedora-wearing giant ducked through the doorway, followed by a spiky-haired hotshot. Bad News had a familiar looking lump in his coat.

I saluted them. "Hey, guys."

"Heyo." Roy sat on the foot of my bed with a bounce and grinned at me, his toothpick poking out from between his teeth.

News peered back out into the hall for a second before walking over to me. He pulled the smuggled container out of his coat and tossed it into my lap along with a spoon. "Got some blackberry this time."

I couldn't help grinning as I popped the lid off the mini ice cream cup "Thanks."

"No problem, bucko. Gotta make sure you have some good food." News seated himself in one of the hospital chairs and it creaked dangerously. He put his hands behind his head and leaned back. "So, how goes it here?"

"And could I have these tater tots?" Roy poked at my lunch.

I answered Roy first. "Be my guest, please." Then to News, "If I keep my perspective straight, it's better than prison, so," I shrugged, "I can't really complain." My spoon cut into the smooth top of the ice cream and I stuck the bite in my mouth, letting the cold sweetness dissolve on my tongue. God bless ice cream smugglers.

News nodded and leaned backwards in the chair, pushing his hat back on his head. "I talked to Liza a bit and she said something about that Mansley dude... what was up with that?"

Any hint of a smile melted off my face. I swallowed the bite in my mouth before answering. "Yeah, he's... a jerk. Just putting Fernsby's and my pieces together, he's been playing everyone in this game for his own gain and... yeah, he's really a..."

"Son of a gun," News finished, one of his eyebrows going up. About as much surprise as I could expect from News — on anything.

Roy stuck his toothpick in his pocket, then popped one of the tater tots in his mouth and chewed on it doubtfully for a few seconds.

"You guys gonna turn 'im in?" His chewing stopped and he went over to the garbage can to spit the tater tot out.

I stabbed my spoon into the ice cream again. "Fernsby is. *I* apparently need my rest, so I'm just going to stay here while he heads over to have a showdown with Mansley by himself."

"That stinks." News commented, watching as I drilled my spoon deeper into the container. "You helped, too. He shouldn't get all the fun."

Roy blew a raspberry over the garbage, shaking his head. "And I don't see why you still need to be cooped up here. I mean, your leg is in a cast, isn't it? You've got crutches. There's not a whole ton else they can do."

They had voiced my thoughts exactly. I bit my tongue and shrugged. "Well, the doctors make the rules around here and Fernsby's just driving back to his house to get a gun before taking off. I'm stuck." I bit a tiny bit more ice cream off the end of my spoon. "I mean, what else am I going to do? Break out?"

All three of us froze as the words left my lips.

I was talking to the guys who'd planned more prison breaks than birthday parties.

Bad News's mouth twitched into a crooked smile. "We might be able to arrange something."

#

I admit, when you think about it in comparison to prison, hospitals are a piece of cake to escape from. Crutches did make me a bit obvious, but I'd been told I could exercise anyway, so I had an excuse.

News had gone downstairs a few minutes ahead of Roy and me with the explanation that he needed to "get a few things ready." He would see us in the lobby.

Roy insisted that I needed some sort of disguise, so I wore his sunglasses. I doubt it did any good, aside from partially hiding my probably guilty-looking face.

"There's the elevator," Roy hissed, grinning. "All a piece of cake from here. We've just got the waiting room to get through."

It was my personal opinion that the waiting room was the prime location for getting caught. My being in the hall wasn't suspicious because I was allowed to be there. If I weren't, we would have already been caught three times. But I hated to dampen his optimism, so I kept my mouth shut and whacked the elevator button.

We stood there for a few seconds and I fidgeted with my crutch handles. Nervousness twisted in my gut.

A bell noise dinged and the doors slid open. Roy stepped in, spinning on the toe of his sneaker and nodding to me. I followed him into the small, antiseptic-smelling container. Something tightened in my chest as I stepped in, making it hard to breathe.

"Heading into the final lap," Roy announced gleefully as I hit the button for the ground floor.

The doors slid closed and I swallowed, feeling my heartbeat accelerate. What was wrong with me? I was in an elevator. Not a T-Rex's mouth.

My eyes stayed fixed on the metal of the doors. Shiny… closing me in and sucking out the oxygen… just like the shell around the bomb…

My hands were shaking hard and I closed my eyes. I forced myself to breathe against the pressure squeezing in my chest.

This is ridiculous. I'm being stupid. I don't have claustrophobia this bad. I never have.

Despite my reasoning, I remained unable to get a good breath.

Obviously, going into a small space and nearly getting blown to bits had intensified things a bit.

I'm taking the stairs next time. I don't care if I'm on crutches. I swallowed hard, gripping my crutch handles.

Roy had never been particularly good at noticing if something was wrong, so he simply stood next to me, bouncing on the toes of his red sneakers and counting off the floors as we went down.

"Floor two…" he dragged out the last word slowly, holding it until the elevator chimed again. "And ground floor! Home stretch!"

The doors glided open and I sucked in a deep breath like I'd just been held underwater. I swung out as quickly as I could and just stood there for a few seconds, gulping in air and trying to stop shaking.

"Got the car right outside the door," Bad News seemed to materialize next to me. I jumped at his words. He pulled at his tie and nodded out to the main waiting room area. "And Cardboard's sitting in there."

Roy came up next to us, twiddling the toothpick in his fingers. A grin still stretched across his face. "Man, this is the easiest place we've ever had to break you out of. Not even any guards." His voice echoed down the shiny, fluorescent-lit hall.

News whacked the backside of Roy's head with his huge hand, "Shut your pie-hole, Einstein. We're not out yet." He glanced over at me and frowned. "You doin' okay? You look kind of pale."

My heartbeat and breathing were just beginning to slow down, but I still felt shaky. I nodded, swallowing. "I'm f-fine. Let's go." There weren't any more elevators on the way, thankfully. And I needed to get to Fernsby before he took off. I swung my crutches out in front of me and made my crippled way toward the waiting room.

Bad News walked beside me, accepting my statement without question. "So pretty much, we just need to get through the waiting area without being noticed…"

"I'll head out first," Roy piped. He skidded around us and dashed out of sight around the corner. The automatic door was sliding shut as we rounded the corner after him and I saw him through the glass jumping into the driver's seat of his car. He landed and gave us a thumbs-up.

Escape vehicle in place.

The lady behind the desk at least seemed distracted with some paperwork and didn't notice us. Sunlight from outside came in through the windows, adding some natural light to the sterile environment.

All the chairs were empty except for one that held a tiny girl with frizzy hair and an orange hoodie, swinging her bare feet. A large, blanket-covered mound sat next to her on the floor. Cardboard looked up at the sound of my approach and waved enthusiastically. "Hey, Wolfgang!"

I flinched. The lady at the desk looked up at my conspicuous name and glanced over in our direction. She frowned at me and tilted her head in concern.

"You don't look well... do you need to sit down?"

Yes. In my getaway car. I swallowed.

Then footsteps and another voice from behind us. "Mr. Dankworth, where do you think you're going?"

I turned slowly to see my warden in turquoise scrubs marching towards us.

Abby.

I was screwed.

A shrill whistle cut through the air. Abby and I both jumped, turning towards the source. Bad News took his fingers out of his mouth and bounded over next to Cardboard.

"Folks," he boomed out in the most attention-demanding voice he could muster. "Today, you're in for a treat. Music, by Bad Cardboard. And guest." He reached down to the blanket and tore it off the thing it was covering with a dramatic flourish. Cardboard hopped down and clicked something on the front of the object.

A birdcage.

"What in..." the lady behind the counter was on her feet in an instant. "Sir, what do you think you're...?"

Lucius shot out of his now uncovered and open cage with a squawk and the woman screamed.

"*Nooooow, I have a friend named Rufus Xavier Sasparilla,*" News belted out in his roaring baritone, "*And I could say to you that Rufus found a kangaroo that followed Rufus home...*" Cardboard picked up on the cue and joined in the wild song, bouncing around on other chairs in the area. Lucius flapped around the room, targeting random flower vases and knocking them over.

Abby stood, frozen in shock, with her mouth hanging open.

I didn't blame her. I wasn't far off from that myself.

Bad News didn't stop in his top-volume Schoolhouse Rock recitation, but gestured widely towards the door and gave me a shove in that direction that almost sent me off my crutches.

I snapped out of my dumb amazement. This was their distraction. The diversion so I could get away. Standing here gaping like a fish was wasting it.

I got a move on, swinging my crutches out far in front of me and making for the door as fast as I could. The glass sides slid apart and I heard the rumbling of Roy's car engine. I barely caught myself as the rubber tips of the crutches snagged on the edge of the door.

My shoes hit on pavement. I was outside.

"Hey!" Abby's voice was cut off as the doors slid shut.

I pulled the passenger side door open and got in, throwing my crutches in the back. "Go!"

Roy didn't need a second prompting.

His hot rod left rubber tire marks in the parking lot as we squealed out.

#

I told Fernsby that I had gotten an early release.

It was technically true. I'd just gotten it dishonestly.

He looked skeptical, and I didn't blame him. After our daring escape and a hair-raising, Roy-style car ride, I'll admit I was a little shaky and more than a little lightheaded. And my paleness probably hadn't improved since News's remark on it earlier, but I had a bit of a bargaining chip in the form of my "old Mr. Tom" mask that Roy had found back at the den. Fernsby was intrigued by that new aspect of my and Mansley's meetings and didn't take too much coaxing to let me come after that.

We made pretty good time and soon a tall, college looking building loomed in front of us with the words "Superior Protective Intelligence — Hero Program Center" emblazoned across the front.

The disgust I felt as we drove up was for a very different reason than it had been on all of my other visits. The heroes were pretty good guys. I knew that now. But the organization behind them... it was like looking at a shiny apple that I knew had a giant, nasty worm eating away at the core.

Charles parked in one of the special spots painted with a Superman symbol. One of the few "reserved for superheroes" spots.

I put on my mask, and we went in.

The hallways were a lot more crowded than they had been the last time I'd visited. Everyone cleared out of Fernsby's way, though. Whispers of the name "Amazing Man" buzzed in the air.

Old Mr. Tom hardly got the same reaction. I said hello to a couple of interns who recognized me — or, more accurately, recognized the mask — but mainly, I just followed in Fernsby's wake of awe through the busy hallway.

Mansley's secretary was on the phone when we entered.

"No, ma'am. Yes, I'm sorry, Director Mansley's not taking calls today. Would you like me to give him a message for you?" A slight pause. "Alright, I'll tell him. Thank you for calling." She set down the phone and glanced over at us as she went to get a pen. "I'll be with you in a moment."

Then she did a double take, her brown eyes opening wide. "Mr. Fernsby, sir!"

Fernsby nodded and smiled at her, "Hello. I'd like to see Director Mansley personally, if it's not too much trouble."

"Why, yes... yes of course..." the girl flustered, tucking her somewhat tangled hair back behind her ears. "I mean, he said he didn't want to see anyone, but I-I'm pretty sure that for Amazing Man he could make an exception... I assume it's urgent?"

I seemed to be totally invisible to her.

Charles nodded again, "Thank you. And yes, it's quite urgent."

She gestured towards the door. "Go ahead, sir. He's been alone in there since early this morning. I haven't seen him, but..."
As Fernsby passed, her gaze finally flicked over in my direction and

she furrowed her brow in concern. "Why, Mr. Tom! What did you do to your leg?"

I blanked, since I obviously couldn't say I'd just survived a bomb by the skin of my teeth. Roy had broken his leg once, so I just blurted out his explanation. "I… um… was bouncing on a trampoline and landed wrong."

I'd always been horrible at playing the role of an old man. The girl's face clearly showed that she was questioning Old Tom's sanity.

I shuffled after Fernsby before she could call some assisted living home to come cart me away to where there were no trampolines for me to hurt myself on.

He'd left the door open, so I slipped in after him, shutting it behind me.

The office was empty. And not just a no-one's-in sort of empty. More like a no-one's-planning-on-coming-back sort of empty. All the neat stacks of papers were cleared off the desk. The paperweights and desk lamp were gone. The pictures were off the walls. The books were off the shelf.

Fernsby stood in the middle of the room, taking everything in. He stuck his tongue in his cheek and shook his head, disappointment clear. "He saw us coming. We missed him."

I was quiet for a second. "Maybe not." I swung over to the familiar old blue file cabinet in the corner and pulled open the middle drawer. It wasn't as full of papers as it had been, but there were still a few file folders. I stuck my un-casted hand in each of them, feeling along the bottom. My fingers hit the edge of a small plastic box.

"Bingo." I pulled the box out and held down the red button. There was a familiar buzzing noise and I smiled.

Charles frowned. "What was that?" He seemed a little unnerved at the familiar sight of me with what looked like a detonator box.

"A lock." I thumped my way over to the bookshelf. The mask was getting itchy, so I pulled it off before bending down to run my finger along the edge of the wood against the wall. I felt a scratch in the paint about halfway down and pressed my fingertip on it.

"Bzzzt"

Hinges squeaked and the secret door swung open.

Charles blinked and stared.

I nodded, "Yeah, I know." With a deep breath, I ducked into the hidden passageway and flipped the light switch, gesturing for him to follow. "Down here was where we had the bomb construction going on and all. I don't think anyone else even knows about it."

Fernsby swallowed his shock and followed me, "Probably a safe bet." He gave a short, humorless laugh. "Also a definite indicator that his commitment to this scam is higher than I originally thought." His hand brushed the gun bulge on his hip. He reached to shut the bookshelf door.

Panic tightened my chest as he started to pull it closed and I gripped onto his arm reflexively. *"Don't."*

Charles looked over at me in confusion.

I tried to come up with a more reasonable explanation than "I'm already having a hard time breathing in this tiny, enclosed hallway and if you shut the door I'm probably going to throw up."

I swallowed. "It… it locks behind you. If the other door is bolted, we'll have no way to get back out."

Fernsby nodded in understanding and let go of the door.

We made our way down the long hallway as it descended deeper and deeper into the building. My chest got tighter as we descended, but I argued with myself enough to keep from making my lack of breathing too obvious. Still, my crutches rattled from my shaking hands.

Finally, the door at the end came into view. A tiny beam of yellow light fell in a strip over the wall and floor, coming from the slight opening between the door and its frame.

I swallowed and managed to breathe a bit easier as I pushed the door open the rest of the way and stepped into the tall-ceilinged room.

I'd remembered it as almost a garage before — lots of tools, papers and random things lying around — but I barely recognized this place. Totally scoured from anything that had been here before. Scarily clean.

Fernsby stepped in behind me and looked around.

I shook my head, my eyes resting on the corner where the bomb had stood. "He's clearing out. Removing any evidence," I muttered.

Charles stepped out further into the room, starting towards a white door in the corner, beyond the empty shelving. I followed.

"He could still be here," he said to me, his voice low. He slipped his gun out and held it by his side as he turned the doorknob. It opened into an office looking area with a walnut desk, a leather chair and a small fireplace grate. It looked like a perfect picture from a magazine. No papers sitting around. The file cabinet drawers were all open.

He'd gutted this place, too.

Fernsby zeroed in on another door across the room. He moved over quietly and opened it, holding his pistol at the ready. It opened into a dark stairway that led upward. An escape route.

Fernsby looked back at me... well, at my crutches. He frowned, clearly not getting a very safe-looking mental image of me going up those stairs.

"It's fine. I'll stay here." I assured him. "He might still be hanging around, so I'll... stand guard."

Hit him over the head with my crutches or something if he shows his ugly, mustachioed face.

Charles nodded and dashed off up the stairs and into the darkness up the stairwell.

I tilted my head and watched him for as long as I could, then looked over the room again. Quite extravagant for only a part-time office. Maybe this was his reading room, too. Maybe he worked out all his super complicated, double sided plans down here and needed a more comfortable chair.

A fireplace still seems over the top, though. Really. I glanced over at it and realized that it was still smoldering. My breath caught in my throat.

If he were taking off… destroying evidence…

I hobbled my way over there, set my crutches to the side and went down to look closer at the smoking, mostly-burnt papers. There were a few documents that I couldn't make out anything on but the heading, addressed to Mansley. And then a couple of blueprints. Mostly too splotchy and burnt for me to make out much…

Then my eye caught a familiar shape on one of the blueprints pushed to the back. The giant, bullet-shaped bomb housing, diagramed out from every angle.

I grabbed it by one corner and pulled it out onto the floor in front of me to look at it. *The plans for my bomb… I don't remember seeing these…* I frowned and looked at a few of the notes in the corners. My gaze froze on the date.

June, 2018.

Two months before the Twin Bombs.

But they said it was an unknown terrorist organization. That's what all the news reports said. They'd never been able to track them. The bombs were a mystery. They had just… happened.

I had blamed Amazing Man for not stopping it… for not doing his job. Everyone had blamed Amazing Man. Even Charles Fernsby.

But if Mansley had the plans… if Mansley built the bombs…

I rubbed a hand over my face and cursed quietly, feeling dizzy with shock.

This whole time.

That… that son of a…

I was still staring at it when Fernsby came staggering back down the stairs, huffing and puffing like the big bad wolf with asthma. I looked up at him, trying to formulate the questions in my mind.

He shook his head, leaning up against the wall. "He's… gone. We missed him. He took off. Took everything."

"Not… everything," I swallowed, finding it hard to get my

voice to work.

Charles looked up at me and leaned forwards. "Wh-what? What did you find?"

I held up the singed, half-blueprint. It wavered in my shaking hand. "I found the Twin Bomb culprit."

Chapter 29: Of Justice, Mercy & Moose

If we're talking explosions, the news about Mansley on the media was up there with the best of them.

And that's coming from me. I've seen a lot of explosions.

His public image basically dropped off the Empire State Building and plummeted to a fiery death at the earth's core. Which he quite deserved, all things considered.

We came back with the evidence. Fernsby headed off to the police to start the ball rolling on getting the program shut down. I was squawked over, shoved back into the hospital, and given the honor of being their first patient to be slapped by a nurse. And I thought that would be it. I'd get a newspaper with my breakfast the next morning saying that a piece of pond scum named Derrick Mansley had been thrown in the clink.

But there was more investigation.

Much, much more.

As it turned out, Mansley wasn't just playing both sides of the chessboard. He'd gone out and carved his own chess pieces to play with.

When the superhero program started out, it had stayed around purely for the novelty of it. The public loved it and all, but it was diverting a lot of funds into something that wasn't really necessary. Superheroes were great for all their show and flash, but the normal police force was doing just fine, thank you very much.

And for a while, the program lost steam.

It wasn't needed. They'd shut it off, send the candidates back to their lives and send Mansley back to his old job with a quarter of the pay.

Mansley saw what his game was missing — what needed to happen for him to keep his job — so he decided to go custom-make himself a villain. Throw out a bomb, frame the hero for the massive loss of life… someone would emerge ready to commit the rest of their years to avenging their loved one.

Sure enough, out from the wreckage came just the man for the job.

Me.

Complete with leather jacket, evil name and a serious temper problem.

And so began the hero-and-villain smackdown that Mansley had wanted. He egged us both on. He gave us both the weapons we needed and sat back to watch, enjoy, and roll in his mounds of money.

All had worked out wonderfully for him until his precious bad-guy had gone and gotten amnesia. Kind of yanked the rug out from under his perfect plans, there.

Each newspaper found some new awful aspect to focus on… how much tax money he'd gotten into this project… how many people had suffered… the levels of deception involved… but the one thing no one seemed to be able to figure out was just where he'd disappeared to.

Mansley could have teleported to Mars, for all anyone knew.

He'd just vanished. The SPI hadn't appointed him to such a high position for being an idiot. He was one of their best agents. Trained to disappear in a blink, if need be. And that was exactly what he'd done.

The investigations and searches kept going full steam ahead. But time went on. It wasn't looking good for finding him. He was just... gone.

And I was somewhat surprised with myself, but I didn't care as much as I thought I would. Sure, I would have loved to punch Mansley in the nose... cuss him out... all that good stuff. But the rage burning in my chest that I'd felt with Amazing Man and wanting to get him... it just wasn't there. This was more an annoyance. An itch. But it didn't define me.

It annoyed me no end, what a clean getaway he'd made. Just the lack of justice in this whole thing. Again, I tried not to think about it. And tried to keep my prayers a bit more gracious than: "Really, God. Any time, with that fiery wrath."

But I had to keep my priorities straight.

There were more important things to worry about than that despicable skunk cowering in hiding somewhere out there.

For instance, making sure I kept myself from getting thrown into prison right alongside him.

Or, more accurately, keeping my mouth shut so Fernsby's lawyer buddy could do his thing. Hardly an open-court thing, this was more of a poorly attended, drawn-out debate in an upper-level SPI meeting room.

I pulled on my tie uncomfortably, shifting my leg cast around to a bit more of a comfortable position as I sat.

"... so after all that's happened, plus the fact that Dankworth has served quite a bit of time," the lawyer, Silversmith, spread his hands. "I say it's time to let bygones be bygones. Mansley was the real head of operations. The Wolf and his Pack are no longer criminal threats. I think pardoning them would be the best move for everyone."

Fernsby shifted in his seat and looked over at me.

I raised my eyebrows briefly, still keeping my mouth shut. Silversmith was a lot more persuasive on this front than I could ever hope to be, and I wasn't about to fudge everything up.

"Not all the gang members have served their time, however," countered the prosecutor, Jefferson, tapping his pencil on the table. "There are still a few blotches on the record no one has addressed. The damage of property at the museum and the baseball stadium…"

"Hardly worth a prison sentence."

"Aaaand the incident with Agent Friday at the opera." Jefferson steepled his fingers. "Not all Pack members were present for the key redemption of saving the heroes, either. Mr. Brown's location is unknown and he still has quite a few unanswered-for crimes."

Silversmith faltered a little. "My client has no memory of the opera incident."

The one unwanted memory that had actually stayed away. I actually still couldn't remember a single thing from the entire day in which I'd gone to the opera. I rubbed at the back of my head.

"The circumstantial evidence still weighs pretty heavily against him. And are we really gonna let the whole gang get away scot-free after everything?" Jefferson spread his hands and gestured to me like the mute exhibit I was in this whole affair. "This is an almost four year string of terrorism and acts of violence. Will there be no consequences? What will the media say if the SPI just lets this go?"

Excuse me, I think all the injuries and hospital time counted as pretty good "consequences". Liza's not even here because she's still recovering… I opened my mouth, then closed it again, biting my tongue.

"I find that they have a fair amount weighing in their favor as well," Silversmith clasped his hands behind his back, his tone getting a little harder. "Mansley was using them as tools for his own ends. They've proven themselves to have turned." He stopped for a second and tightened his lips before giving an admitting nod. "There… isn't much we can do by way of Mr. Brown, but I'd say the rest of the gang deserves their freedom. The agency is dropping charges."

I let out a breath slowly, feeling some of the tension inside me loosen. The knot still stayed tied in my stomach. I should have gotten Chris to come along.

Not like he would have listened, though… he holds his grudges even tighter than I do. And that's coming from… well, me. Look how much it took for me to turn around.

Jefferson pursed his lips thoughtfully and rubbed his knuckles on his stubbly jaw. He looked up at the ceiling, then back down at Silversmith. "I still say… the agency needs the last word, James. Something to show we're not just swayed by every heart-wrenching redemption story into dropping everything without batting an eye. Keep the warrant out for Brown. And I believe some fines would be…"

"They'll be paid in full," Charles Fernsby met Jefferson's eyes as he turned. He nodded. "All fines will be paid, sir. By me."

Jefferson watched Fernsby for another second, almost like he wasn't sure if this was a joke. He looked over at Silversmith, then nodded slowly. "Then… I guess Dankworth and his Pack are free to go."

Silversmith smiled.

From the mouth of the SPI — I was free to go.

I wasn't a wanted criminal anymore.

Holy smoke… been awhile since that was the case… I ran my fingers through my hair and just stared, fighting the urge to burst out laughing, while my defense lawyer and the prosecutor shook hands. Just how far fetched a possibility this would have been, just a month ago… the total and sudden shift boggled the mind.

I'd always sort of rolled my eyes at the whole "nothing is impossible with God" spiel from Dallas and Fernsby. But… yeah, I'd considered myself a pretty impossible case.

Me — alive, in the clear and on the straight and narrow again?

Hey, God. Just… so you know… you're awesome.

I snapped out of my prayer as Charles put a hand on my

shoulder.

"Hey, ready to go?" He grabbed my crutches from where they leaned against the wall. Everyone else was already filing out of the room.

"Um... yeah." I braced myself on the chair and pushed up, taking my crutches and positioning them back under my arms.

Fernsby held his hand out to make sure I was steady before we both started for the door. He looked over at me with a relieved smile on his face. "That went well."

I nodded, smiling back. "Fantastic. I... um..." I gestured a little and cleared my throat, trying to keep things from getting sappy. "That was really... I mean, thank you for everything. Giving me a hand with all the legal stuff and the fines."

Charles smiled wider, holding the door open. "It's my pleasure, believe me."

I swung through and out into the hall, turning towards the stairs. I'd actually gotten pretty good on the crutches in the past week. Especially at the task of going down stairs. I'd tried an elevator exactly one more time since finding I had a problem with them, just to satisfy the curiosity of Bad News regarding claustrophobia.

Never again, thank you.

Fernsby and I got ourselves down to the ground floor and out into the well-lit lobby.

Dallas and Leif sat in chairs by the door, waiting. As soon as we came out, Dallas shot to his feet and Leif shot over to us.

"You're not in jail!" crowed Leif, giving my leg a hug. Well, someone had mastered the art of blind optimism. I couldn't help but grin.

Dallas moved over slower, his face tense with worry. He tapped his fingers on his wrist cast. "How did it go?"

"Great," Charles grinned, patting my back. "He's free to go, along with the rest of the pack. The agency's dropping all charges."

Dallas's expression shifted to sheer relief and joy. Pretty much the only unguarded facial expression I'd ever seen on him.

I laughed. "Come on. I'm pretty sure I know someone who's got some celebratory ice cream for the occasion."

We happy few got outside onto the sidewalk and started towards where Dallas and Fernsby had parked their cars. Leif stayed by my side, keeping a small grubby hand resting over mine on the crutch handle. He couldn't seem to get enough of the whole "older brother" novelty. Since they'd allowed him in, he'd been competing with News for the prize of most frequent hospital visitor.

I toyed briefly with the concept of actually attempting some sort of family again. Having Leif with me.

Leif caught me looking at him and grinned.

I grinned back, ignoring the small knot re-forming in my stomach. There was only so much I could do for him, and I certainly wasn't the family that he needed to grow up in. One older brother couldn't do everything, no matter how hard I tried. *Can I really take him away from all this? He already has a family…*

Dallas's voice broke into my thoughts. "Leif likes you so far, at least," he said reassuringly.

"'Cuz he's my *actual* brother," Leif broke in, not liking to be talked over the top of. He shuffled his feet on the sidewalk in a weird little skip-step. "And I like saying his name. Wolfgang." He accentuated every sound in a way that reminded me why I hated that name.

"Dankworth. Wolfgang Dankworth." Leif tipped his head backwards to look at Dallas. "Is my last name Dankworth too?"

Dallas looked over at me before shrugging, "Technically, yeah."

"Cool," Leif grinned and did another skip-step, hopping over to splash in a puddle while he was at it. "Leif Dankworth. Leif Dankworth." He repeated it like a tongue twister.

Well, he liked it at least. That was a start. But the novelty of a new last name would wear off… I swallowed and bit my tongue. I couldn't take him. He had a family here. It would just be me being selfish again.

My phone buzzed against my hip and made me jump. *Nerves*

of steel... I stopped walking and pulled it out, flipping it open to see who was calling.

"Brown, Christopher"

I stared at the screen in confusion. Chris? I'd thought he was long gone. He'd washed his hands of me. He hadn't made contact... hadn't even showed his face since we disarmed the bomb. What would he...?

The phone buzzed again. Well, easy way to find out... pick up.

The one gang member who hasn't been pardoned...

"What is it?" Charles stopped as well, and looked at me in concern.

"Just... go ahead to the cars. I'll catch up." I adjusted my crutches and hobbled a little ways away as I hit the button to pick up.

There were a few seconds of quiet and I thought I heard breathing. I frowned.

"Hello?"

"Kid?" Chris's voice came over the line. It trembled. He sounded almost scared. I'd never heard his voice like that.

I felt my heart rate accelerate. "Yeah, I'm here."

How dedicated was the SPI to finding Chris? Had they already tracked him down, where he was in hiding?

He swore quietly, but it didn't sound like he was directing it at me.

"What happened?" I gripped the phone tighter, "Where are you?"

"I just..." he began. "There was..." he took in a breath and cursed some more before continuing. "I'm driving back into Utah now. I was up at my shack in Idaho for the last week... just... hunting. And there was this moose. Huge moose. A monster. Never seen a bigger rack in my life. I was kind of on his trail for a few days and... I..." his voice trailed off a little for a second.

I could feel my hands starting to shake a little. "Are you okay?" He sounded physically fine, aside from being shaken up. What could have freaked him out this badly?

Still using curse words as commas, he continued. "I'd lost some sleep... I wasn't on top of my game, and this morning I went out and... I had the moose right in my sights. Any regular day, and I would've nailed the sucker right there." Chris let out his breath slowly, "But I... I missed. I missed him and scared him off and... oh, God..."

I bit my tongue and waited tensely for him to continue.

"There was... there was someone else in the woods. I didn't see him, I swear. And my shot didn't hit him... but that moose... he... he was in his way. The moose zeroed in on him. The guy didn't even see until the last second. He tried to run, but... the moose... it trampled him."

I was no outdoorsman, but I'd heard plenty about moose from Chris. They might look big and bumbling, but they were anything but clumsy and cute charging straight at you with two giant battering rams.

The trembling in his voice got worse, though he was obviously trying to hide it. "H-he's pretty messed up. I didn't mean to... but it's my fault. I..." he stopped talking for a second and I could almost see him closing his eyes and clenching his jaw. Trying to calm himself down.

He started again, his voice hoarse. "I'm taking him to the hospital in Logan, but I don't think there's much they can do." His voice cracked. "Wolfgang, it's my fault. He's going to die."

I didn't know what to say. I swallowed hard and opened my mouth, "D-do you want me to come?"

Chris didn't answer, but I heard his stiff breathing over the line. "I just... I don't know," he said finally. "I don't know what to do. I've never..."

"I'm coming," I interrupted him. "See you in a bit."

"If... if you want," I'd never heard that helpless note in his voice before. "See you."

I flipped the phone shut, turned around and started back down the sidewalk. Dallas still waited for me, while Charles and Leif had continued on and were just getting into the Fernsbys' car.

"Who was that?"

"Chris," I answered. "He was hunting and had a bit of an accident. How fast can we get to Logan?"

Dallas blinked, "Well... I... we can take my truck and it shouldn't be too long, but..."

"Right," I swung my crutches out and made my way towards Dallas's truck. "Let's go. Just... don't tell the SPI, okay?"

"O-okay," Dallas followed me.

Two things I really didn't see happening today: the infamous "Wolf Pack" getting pardoned, and Chris resurfacing with a moose-attack victim.

Not really what I had seen on the schedule.

Just goes to show how a day can go unexpectedly.

#

Chris had always been a bit of a pacer. Liza was always joking that we could hook him up to a generator and not have to pay electricity bills ever again.

He could probably power the whole hospital, at the rate he was going in the hall. Back and forth, over and over. Twisting his hands and scowling at the floor. Not the usual "couldn't care less" scowl, either. More like a "caring too much and not liking it" scowl.

I hadn't seen that since I'd first met him in prison.

It was a little hard to approach quietly with a broken leg, and he looked up as soon as I came around the corner from my long battle with the stairwell. He wasn't kidding when he said he'd lost some sleep. His face was pale and there were dark circles under his eyes. His cheeks looked hollow under his usually well-trimmed beard.

If I had grown a shell over the years, Chris had to have grown a double shell around his already prickly surface. But it was cracked now. He looked guilty, upset... and maybe even a little scared.

I nodded to him as I swung over. He nodded back, sinking

into one of the hallway chairs and running a hand over his face.

Silence.

He glanced over at me again, his gaze going to the white button-up I still had on under my leather jacket, even though I'd taken off the tie.

"Who let you into a dress shirt?" he muttered, not sounding like he actually wanted to know. Just needing to grump at something.

I shrugged. "How's... the guy doing?" I asked, setting my crutches aside and taking a seat next to him.

Chris cussed in response, his facial expression darkening.

We were both quiet for a second and he let out a shaky breath. "Looks like he went through a meat grinder, I swear."

I winced, tightening my lips. "Where were you? What was the guy doing out there?"

"I don't even know." Chris twisted his hands more. "I was at my old hunting shack up in the woods. Most abandoned place in the world. Never seen anyone else up there in my life besides the elk and moose and deer... what that idiot was doing up there was beyond me..." He rubbed a hand over his eyes.

A nurse with graying hair in purple scrubs stepped out of the nearby room holding a clipboard. Her brow wrinkled with concern, but she gave us a kind smile. "He's... conscious. Partly." She took a breath and her smile faded into a sad, resigned look. "I don't think he's going to make it, Mr. Brown. Did you happen to know his name?"

Chris groaned and put his head in his hands, tipping his cowboy hat off center. "No," he mumbled.

The woman put a hand on his shoulder and was quiet. "You can go in and see him if you want. He's not going to last much longer, I'm afraid."

"It's my fault," Chris swallowed and put his hands down, staring straight ahead of himself. His face was paler than ever. "If I'd been more careful..."

"It was an *accident,*" I corrected. "It was out of your hands.

Just… his time to go."

"Don't start that crap on me, kid," Chris muttered. He got to his feet, took a deep breath and nodded. "I'll see him." His voice was gruff.

I got to my feet with some difficulty, since Chris still didn't seem to fully register the fact that I was on crutches and I had to do it myself.

The nurse nodded once to Chris and then looked at me doubtfully. "Is he a friend?" She looked like she thought it more likely that I was a patient.

Chris hesitated for a second, then gave a nod. "Yes." He met my eyes for a second, then looked away, took a deep breath and walked into the room. The nurse stood aside, holding the door. I thanked her quietly and followed Chris in.

My gaze fell on the room's occupant and I suddenly felt sick.

Holy smoke, Chris wasn't kidding with the meat grinder comment. Moose quickly moved about five levels up on my scale of dangerous animals.

A bandaged, bloodied figure lay on the bed in the middle of the room. An oxygen mask was over his face, his eyes were closed and an IV tube ran down his arm. His breaths rattled and rasped in the air, sounding like they took an immense amount of effort. Disheveled salt-and-pepper hair stuck out over the top of the bandage around his head.

Goosebumps prickled my arms. I could barely even see what the guy used to look like underneath the moose mauling. *What he ever did to deserve that…*

Chris stood beside the bed, looking haggard. He kept his eyes fixed on the face of the man and his mouth stayed in a tight line. I moved over next to him, fighting back the bile in the back of my throat. It was painful to even look at the figure in the bed, but I couldn't tear my eyes away.

The man rasped out something and tried to move. Chris closed his eyes with a grimace. Something froze inside me. I squinted at the man's bloody face, getting a funny feeling that I'd seen him somewhere before.

But where? This guy had been in the Idaho wilderness... out in the woods, probably camping or hiking or something... the chances that this was someone I knew...

And then he opened his eyes, looking straight at me. Penetrating, frost blue eyes.

I sucked in my breath sharply and caught a tiny hint of something I hadn't noticed before past the blood and antiseptic smell. It was barely noticeable, but I smelled spearmint.

I nearly choked. My eyes went wide and I felt the blood drain from my face. The room spun for a second.

It's him. Good Lord, it's him...

Chris ignored my strangled noises and put a hand on the man's arm. "I'm sorry," he whispered. The man didn't look at him, still staring at me.

"Chr-Chris?" my voice shook and I still didn't take my eyes off the blue-eyed gaze fixed on my face. "I... I know this guy."

Chris's head snapped back around to look at me. "What?"

I swallowed hard before speaking, "He's... this is Derrick Mansley."

"The director of the superhero program?" Chris looked confused.

How could Chris not know? Mansley's face... all that he'd done... it was all over the news. *You'd have to be living under a rock to...* I stopped, mid-thought. *Or you could be up at a cabin in the wilderness for the past week.*

I nodded slowly, "Well, yes — among other things."

Mansley stiffened in his bed and his breathing got more labored. He closed his eyes again, moaning weakly.

"See..." I bit my lip, "He's actually... he's the 'arms dealer' I've been meeting with. The one that supplied us with everything. He's the one that tipped Amazing Man off to those plans that shouldn't have gone sideways. He's... " I faltered, "also the guy that... that planted the twin bombs."

Chris just stared at me. He looked down at Mansley, shock

and disbelief mixing on his face. "This guy? Mansley did…?" His voice rose and then broke off.

"Fernsby and I went to try and catch him, but he'd already taken off. He's one of the SPI's best agents. He had more than enough training to just vanish. No one could find him and it looked like he'd just made a clean getaway." I looked down at the pathetic form in the hospital bed. "Apparently… looks can be deceiving."

Mansley had covered his tracks. He'd planned for any outcome. For three and a half years, he'd played his game perfectly, never even being suspected. He had made absolutely sure that no one would be able to catch him.

And in the end, he had been trampled down by a runaway moose.

If the fear of God hadn't worked its way into me yet, I certainly had it now. Along with a redefinition of divine justice.

We can plan, we can scheme, we can be the best there is… but if nothing else, our retribution can even come in the form of a wigged-out moose.

I cursed reverently under my breath.

Chris didn't take his eyes off Mansley. "So he…" He stopped and swallowed, "he was the one that killed my Sarah? This guy?"

I nodded, "Along with my family and Liza's Eli."

His brow wrinkled and he pushed back his hat. For once, Chris Brown didn't know what to think. Just a few minutes ago, he'd been absolutely wracked with guilt about taking an innocent life. But now that it wasn't innocent anymore… was he supposed to be happy? Vindicated?

He just looked lost and torn. Confused.

"It wasn't Amazing Man, then…" he muttered. "We've been after the wrong guy this whole time." He took a breath and looked up at the ceiling to cuss quietly.

"Guess justice happens on its own sometimes," I commented, fingering my crutch handles and watching the blanket over Mansley's chest rise and fall unevenly. His rattling breathing filled the silence.

To want to kill the guy who had done it — all these years.

And this was how it ended.

It was... oddly peaceful. Quiet. Eerie.

Chris and I both watched him for another minute.

Rise and fall... rise and fall... the breaths got shallower and shallower, then Mansley let out a kind of coughing sigh and the room was quiet.

He was gone.

I shook my head, "Live by the sword. Die by the... moose."

Chapter 30: Family

August, 2022

"Anyway," I heard Liza take a deep breath and let it out, blowing into the phone speaker. "Long, technical ramble aside, I think this next prosthetic I'm working on should be the right one. So hopefully, within the month..."

"You'll be armed and ready?" I shifted my hand on the steering wheel of my car and grinned. The warm wind whipped around my face and through my hair as I turned down a bend in the road.

Liza's snicker came over the line. "Ohh, that was bad, Wolfy..."

"What?" I pretended to sound insulted, "True, isn't it?"

"Well, one would hope," she responded. I heard a few things clanking around on the other end.

I straightened out the wheel again and put gentle pressure on the gas pedal. "The Den holding up okay as your base of operations?" I asked. "Anything you need?"

"It's working quite well, actually. Nice having all my tools where I'm used to keeping them." She let out a sigh. "But even with me, there's only so long I can stay cooped up inside tinkering with things. I'm turning into a bloody mole in here."

I nodded slowly, moving my phone to my other hand. "Sunlight, then."

"Yeah, sunlight would be nice. Don't think that's anything I can call for Baden to bring me a truckload of, though."

"Well, there's plenty of it out here," I assured her, looking at the pinkish sky above me. "Clear up your busy tinkering schedule and we can go hiking next weekend. Get you into the fresh air and out of the danger of turning into a mole."

She laughed a little, "Sounds good. I'll try not to talk your ear off with all the technical hullaballoo and actually make some human conversation."

"Ah, I'm used to it by now. It's very intellectually stimulating." I squinted at the hood of a car poking out further down the road. "Hey, I'm gonna have to let you go. Cop coming up and I need both hands on the wheel."

"Wolfgang Dankworth," Liza put on a dramatic newscaster voice, "caught talking on the phone whilst driving. Oh, will his evil deeds never cease from mankind?"

"Oh, shut up," I laughed. "Talk to you later."

"Cheerio."

I hit the "end call" button and dropped my phone into the glove compartment just as I passed by the cop. My Mustang and I merited barely a glance.

I let out my breath and leaned back in my seat, running a hand over my hair. A familiar gnarled tree passed on the right, checking off another in the list of landmarks before I got to the house.

The yellow gift bag sat in the passenger seat, trembling a

little in the wind, but staying in place with the weight of the things inside. I grinned and turned my eyes back to the road. *The kids'll love them.*

My stomach growled, almost like it was trying to remind me that spending my precious little money on Legos was *not* making it very happy. But I ignored it. I liked ramen and grilled cheese. I got extra rations from News (give you one guess as to what those were). And I was about to get a full weekend of good food, anyway.

A tiny buzzing noise came from the glove compartment and I glanced down.

"Fernsby residence"

What could they be calling about? Maybe they needed me to pick something up. Or maybe this was a certain junior member getting impatient.

I checked for cops, pulled the phone up and hit a button. "Hello?"

"Where aaare yoouuu?" Leif's voice groaned.

Yep. Impatient check-in with the tardy big brother.

"I'm coooomiiing," I groaned back.

"You're taking foreverrrr…"

"Well, I'm almost theeeerrre. Chill ooouut."

Leif snorted, trying to hold back a laugh, and I grinned. I slowed up and steered the car around another corner.

"I'm close, bud. Had a bit of a… thing at work that took a bit longer to clean up than I thought, so I had a late start. Give me…" I looked at the clock on my radio, "…four minutes. At the most."

"M'kay."

There were a few voices behind Leif's and a bit of scuffling.

"Is that Uncle Wolfy? Can I talk to 'im?" came an excited squeak of a voice. Jilly's, I guessed. Or Beckett being way too excited.

Then Angela's distant voice. "What are you…? *Leif,* I told you…" She heaved a gusty sigh, there was a "hey!" from Leif, and Angela's voice came through clearer.

"Hi. Sorry about that. I told him to wait patiently. But…"

Another sigh. You had to admire how much she put up with. I mean, I like kids, but watching three under the age of ten for more than a couple of days would drive me insane.

I just laughed. "Runs in the family." The Fernsbys' road came up on my left and I spun the wheel to pull onto it. "Listen, I'm really close. See you guys in a sec, okay?"

"Alright, bye."

The phone was re-stationed in the glove compartment and I kept my attention on driving. Mailboxes and beginnings of other driveways slid past as I drove. Grey mountains stood off in the distance and trees were thick in between the houses, making it look less populated than it actually was.

With the downfall of the superhero program, Charles's central location in the state capital was less of a requirement. I'll tell you, he was quite eager to relocate to a house in a quieter location. It helped quite a bit to keep the reporters away. And it helped that there were fewer neighbors to point and stare at the sight of The Wolf going into Amazing Man's house.

A few more winding turns down the narrow road, and I saw the driveway I was looking for. A sign was stuck in the dirt and pine needles, that read "Fernsbys," carved ornately into the wood. Then a smaller one right next to it, made out of sun-bleached cardboard and a garden stake.

"+ 1 Dankwurth"

He had really taken to that name, I tell you. Even if he couldn't spell it.

Dad would've been proud. Mom and Ellie too…

I was learning not to flinch at their names anymore. The happy memories and the knowledge I was doing what they would have wanted eclipsed the ever-present emptiness inside, filling it with the warmth of happy memories instead.

I wouldn't ever forget.

But, counterintuitive to what I'd thought over the past years, instead of trying to avenge their death, just rebuilding a normal life made them feel closer than they had in years.

I smiled a little and turned onto the gravel drive. My car wheels crunched on the rocks as I puttered up towards the house. One last bend and I was there.

The log cabin-looking house glowed yellow from its windows in the purple-y partial darkness. The front door was swung partway open and I heard sounds of laughter and clanking dishes seeping out.

As always, I felt my muscles relax as I put my car into park next to the Fernsbys' green minivan. It didn't matter what was happening in the rest of the world. Here was always a place that felt... well, I don't want to say peaceful. They certainly had their moments. But... just secure and welcoming. Like home.

I unbuckled and clicked my door open, swinging my legs out. I stood and tucked my keys into my pocket. A muffled "exterminate!" chirped from my pocket as my Dalek keychain bumped against my hip.

The yellow bag still sat in the passenger seat, so I leaned over and snagged it out. As I turned to go in, two figures appeared at the door. The small one with the hair as insane as my own shot out like a bullet towards me.

"Wolf!"

I barely had time to brace myself before Leif came barreling into my middle, nearly knocking the wind out of me. He wrapped his arms around, holding onto the slick leather of my jacket.

I coughed, regaining my balance a bit better, and ruffled his hair. "G-good to see you too, buddy."

He tipped his head up to grin at me before swinging around to my side and half pushing me towards the door. "C'mon! Dinner's all ready."

The other figure still stood on the porch, his hands in his pockets and a partial smile across his face. I waved with my hand that wasn't on Leif's shoulder.

"Hey, Dall."

Dallas waved back, staying at his post.

Leif poked me in the ribs, "Hey, Mom said you had a

surprise for dessert. What is it?"

"Well," I started up the steps to the door. "I can tell you two things. It's surprising. And we're having it for dessert."

"Woooolf…" Leif flopped against me, half groaning, half laughing.

I ignored his protests and stopped by Dallas before going in. We shook hands and I grinned at him. "Nice to see you here. Stopping by for dinner?"

He shrugged. "Just helping Mr. Fernsby out a bit with a few things around here that needed to be done." We started inside and Dallas nodded to me, "You okay? After that… thing… earlier? There's a bit of a…" he motioned next to his face, squinting at me, "There's a cut on your cheek."

I reddened a little, "You get all my work history, don't you?"

"Well, when your employer is my father, it's kind of hard not to," he tried to hide a smile. "There's always a learning curve in the handyman job. And on the bright side, you know what *not* to do with water heaters now."

"Got that right," I lowered my voice, "and let's not… bring that up, shall we?"

It seemed to be my lot in my new job. Either the people gave me so much space it was like they thought Dracula was fixing their sink… or I accidentally blew something up. Sometimes both. Needless to say, I was still getting into the swing of actually working like a normal person again.

The warm, savory smell inside the house hit me full in the face as we walked in and I breathed it in deeply.

"Uncle Wolfy's here!" Beckett yelled out, bounding down the stairs. A few seconds later, he and Jilly had joined Leif in crowding around me. Jilly hung on my pants and I had to grip my belt to keep her from pulling them down.

Beckett pulled on my sleeve. "What's the surprise dessert?"

"Oh, so it's the surprise dessert you're excited about, not me?" I put a hand over my heart and pretended to look hurt.

"Kids, say hello nicely," prompted Angela, stepping into the entryway. A small smile played across her lips as she glanced up at me.

"Hi, Uncle Wolfy," Beckett said, clasping his hands behind his back like a proper English gentleman for about ten seconds.

"Hello nicely," piped Leif.

Jilly was less inclined to follow her mom's orders. She tucked her stuffed pig under her arm and tugged on my coat sleeve. "What's in the bag?"

I held the yellow bag just out of her reach. "Stuff. You'll see soon enough, peanut." I shook my head at the groans and "whyyy"s that followed and looked up at Angela. "So, what's for dinner?"

"Tater tot casserole," she replied. "And it's nice to see you, Wolfgang." The second bit was added louder, as an obvious example to her kids.

"Nice to see you too, Angela," I responded loudly with an exaggerated nod.

A hand clapped down on my shoulder and I turned to see Charles grinning at me. He nodded, "It's a good thing you showed up, Wolf. The kids would have gone and eaten me if I'd told them to wait any longer."

I shook his offered hand and glanced over at Angela, "On that note, let's go eat before we're eaten."

Jilly and Beckett went running off into the dining room ahead of the rest of us. I followed at a less breakneck pace with the others, despite Leif's pulling on my arm to try and get me to go faster.

Charles tipped his head and frowned a little, seeing the cut on my cheek. "What happened to your face?"

I knew exactly what he was talking about, but dodged the topic in favor of not activating Angela's mother-hen mode.

"Dashing good looks happened to my face." I gave him my most cheesy, winning grin.

Dallas coughed and I elbowed him.

Charles raised an eyebrow, but didn't say anything.

We all took our seats around the table and I stashed my yellow bag under my seat. Jilly had won the rock-paper-scissors tournament and gotten the seat next to me (other than the one that Leif always got).

Angela brought the food to the table and set it in the middle before sitting down next to Charles.

"Let's say grace," Charles looked around the table at everyone, then bowed his head.

Two small hands, one from either side, grabbed hold of mine. Jilly's was soft and smooth against my rough skin. Leif's was sticky… as always. I held onto each of them, my hands enveloping theirs. I bowed my head slightly, but didn't close my eyes, just looking around the table at everyone.

Just the fact that I was… part of a family again…

Sometimes I wondered if it was possible to just explode from happiness. It felt quite likely at times.

Leif peeked one eye open at me and puckered his mouth in a frown.

"Dear Lord, thank You for the wonderful meal and the wonderful woman who made it. Thank You for the good day and that Wolfgang made it here safely. Help us to have a good and restful weekend and honor You with it. Amen." Charles opened his eyes and brought his head up.

"Wolf didn't close his eyes," accused Leif.

I raised an eyebrow at him. "And how would you know that?"

"Well I just *peeked* to see for a little bit…" He trailed off and ducked his head as Angela laughed.

Dinner went as dinners usually did at the Fernsby house.

Someone always spilled something within the first five minutes. It was Dallas that time, surprisingly. Though he probably set the record for the most remorse and fastest cleanup.

Leif had his usual bargaining session about how many veggies he had to eat. Jilly paused the meal to sing us a song, accompanied in silent duet by Pinky the pig. Beckett ate enough for two kids his size.

Overall, it was very loud and very happy. And very different from my usual dinners.

When everyone was done eating and all the dishes were more or less cleared off the table, I pulled out the mysterious yellow bag. The three kids immediately lapsed into respectful silence.

I waved the bag back and forth in front of me dramatically for a few seconds before setting it down and reaching in. "Aaand… catch, guys." I pulled out three little Lego sets and tossed one to each kid in order.

Jilly got a little farmyard set (it had a pig and I couldn't resist), Beckett got a fireman and Leif got one with a Dalek and the tenth Doctor.

Gasps and squeals erupted from the three of them and I grinned. Leif busted into his right there, of course, and in under a minute, he had the Doctor assembled. He set him in front of me.

"Get out your Dalek and we can fight," he poked me, adjusting the Doctor's position.

I pulled out my keys and set my dinged-up old keychain next to his new Lego figure. "There." I bumped it into his Doctor, who fell over with a tiny clatter. "I win. Now…" I sat up straighter. "That wasn't all. We still have our surprise dessert."

Reverent silence fell again.

I shrugged. "If you guys are interested, of course. We could just stay here…"

"No, no! Tell us!" Beckett bounced in his seat.

"Weeellll…"

Charles started up a drumroll with his fingers on the table, grinning at me.

I cleared my throat dramatically. "We're driving back into town… and then we're going to Lucky Scoop."

"Ice cream!" peeped Jilly, hugging me. "Thank you!"

Leif pushed his chair back, scooping up his Legos, "I get to ride with you, okay?"

"The Dankworth-reserved seat is all yours," I grinned back, standing with him.

The cowbell above the door clattered as I pushed inside the vanilla-scented interior of Lucky Scoop with Leif at my heels. The interior design bespoke a bar at first glance, what with the bar counter and hanging lights. But no bottles sat behind on the shelves — just sprinkles and ice cream sauces. And the only wall decorations were a few framed Calvin and Hobbes strips.

My shoes squeaked on the black and white tile. I walked up towards the red barstools, giving a smile and wave to the familiar figure just exiting the back room.

He waved back and saluted me with his ice cream scoop, a grin pulling his mouth sideways. "Hey, howdy hey."

"Hey, howdy hey, yourself, News." I took a seat at one of the stools and propped an arm on the counter as he got back to his station behind the counter.

Bad News tugged on his apron strings and nodded at Leif, then looked back at me. "Come for dinner?"

Leif stared at me, looking like he'd just gotten a glimpse into paradise. "You come here for *dinner?*"

I coughed, "Occasionally… very occasionally. And no, News, I didn't. Dessert for the Fernsby and Dankworth clan, actually."

"Gotcha. Pretty quiet in here tonight. You guys've got the place to yourselves." News grinned, pushing his hat back. He craned his head back a little, looking into an open "employees only" door. "Roy! Cardboard! We got company!"

The cowbell above the door clanged again and the four Fernsbys and Dallas walked in.

I turned with a wave, "C'mon up, guys. Tell Mr. News what you want."

News gave a nod as Jilly and Beckett scrambled up onto the red stools. "So, this'll be on your tab, I'm guessing."

I nodded back, patting my leather jacket pocket with the

bullet hole in it and feeling my wallet. "Yep. I got it covered."

Footsteps came forward from the back, and I heard Roy's voice. "Hey, man!" He strode out with Cardboard close behind, a grin splitting his face. "How's it going?" He leaned over the counter to me and I high-fived his outstretched hand.

I noted with amusement the aprons they both wore. News had obviously cracked down a bit more on the cleanliness factor in here.

"Well, pretty good," I grinned back. "Job's nice to have, and all."

"Yeah, tell me about it," Roy grinned. "Nice that you're dusting off the old everyday-mechanic skills."

Cardboard's curly head poked over the edge of the counter so I saw only half of her face and the tips of her fingers. "Did you teach Lucius to loop-the-loop yet?"

"Still working on that one, peanut." I boinged one of her curls. "I'll be sure to bring him in and show you as soon as he gets it, though."

Her brown eyes flicked over to Jilly and went half-moon-shaped as she smiled. "Hey, Jilly."

"Hi," Jilly said shyly around the piece of her hair she was nibbling on the end of. She kicked her feet. "Can I have your special?"

"Mm hmm," Cardboard nodded. "I'll go back and make one." She bounced off towards the back. I'd tried her "special" out once and just about keeled over from pinkness overload. I guess little girls have an immunity to that, though.

"I want chocolate, please," Beckett told News, wiggling in his seat and craning his neck to meet the giant's eyes.

Leif got a Bad News Sundae, which was basically all the flavors in the world scooped together with root beer and sprinkles on top. I'm still pretty sure Leif is the only one that eats it, aside from Bad News himself.

Charles and Angela got some sorbet to share and Dallas had vanilla. I had a coffee shake. I was his only customer on the coffee

338

front, anyway. No one else could stomach the stuff, even if it was mixed with ice cream.

As soon as everyone got their things, News brushed out from behind the counter to the front window, flipping over the sign so it showed the "sorry, we're closed" side.

I frowned, "You don't need to close up just because…"

"Only fifteen minutes early," News assured me, going back to his station to make himself his own Bad News Sundae. "Besides, we need our dessert too." He elbowed Roy.

In just a couple of minutes, the last three barstools in the U shape were filled up and we all sat, eating our ice cream. Everyone's mouths were busy with their treats and I was able to make out the faint strains of "I'm just a Bill" over the speakers.

I leaned on the counter and turned to get a better view of News, "Haven't had any customer complaints about the Schoolhouse Rock yet?"

He shook his head, "Nope. It's educational. They can learn something while they're here."

Dallas furrowed his brow skeptically. "Most people already know this stuff…"

"I like it," Leif defended around another bite of his sundae.

I shook my head, taking a drink of my shake. "To each his own."

Bad News propped his sunglasses up on the brim of his hat. "You know, I was thinking of something the other day. Another business partner we could take on." He tucked his spoon behind his ear and leaned forwards, clasping his hands on the counter.

"Chris is doing really well with the hunting stuff up in Canada. More moose meat than he knows what to do with. So, what would you think if we were like… the *Lucky Scoop and Moose Meatery*?" He spread out his hands as if displaying it on a sign.

Charles and Dallas exchanged a look.

I raised an eyebrow. "I don't think…"

"Oh come on," News rolled his eyes like I'd just put down the idea of the century. "We can do moose burgers and shakes or something. I mean, what else are we going to do? Just let Chris eat all that meat himself?"

"Much more jerky and he'll break his jaw," Roy put in.

"Well, it's your business, guys." I laughed.

News grabbed his spoon from behind his ear again and went back to his ice cream. "Then expect some moose burgers in the near future."

Dallas glanced at News, then at me, then back to his ice cream.

Whatever. Honestly, News could sell anything when he brought out his charm and people got past his size.

I leaned back again, running a hand through my hair. My fingers hit the thick scar on the base of my skull and I rubbed at it thoughtfully. It barely hurt anymore. What I would have done without that, though... what my life could have been like right about now if it hadn't been for that ugly gash on the back of my head...

Prison. Or worse. I felt the scars on my wrists as I brought my hand back down.

God had to get used to my mental hobo-in-the-throneroom visits. I was thanking Him for a lot, nowadays.

Leif put his head against my arm, smashing his cowlick down halfway. I felt a tiny poke against my side and looked down to see him poking the bullet hole in my pocket with his Lego Doctor. He looked up and beamed at me.

"I'm glad I'm a Dankworth."

I ruffled his hair. "Me too, buddy."

Funny how stuff works out like that sometimes. People all have their own stories of how they got where they are. Wild chances that totally changed the courses of their lives. Crazy coincidences... or divine mistakes, whatever you want to call them.

For me?

I got amnesia.

And it was the best thing that could have happened.

Acknowledgements

Yeah, I know. Like no one ever reads these things. I said to myself when I became a writer that I'd "never do one of those boring lists of names at the back because those are stupid".

But then again, I never really expected to have so many names to list. And there are some serious rockstars behind the creation of this book that need to see their name in the book.

First off, thank you to my awesome family. To my grandparents and aunts and uncles for cheering me on. To Judah for taking my book seriously and taking with me about it and laughing at all the right spots. To Boaz for bugging me to write even when I didn't want to and hounding me down every time I wrote a new chapter. To Addy for sitting up late with me and coming up with a bunch of ridiculous random quirks for my characters. To Mom for losing precious sleep to read and edit and get excited with me. To Dad for being the sole genius behind Derrick Mansley's demise, and for bragging on me to like… everyone. To Levi, Gideon and Cyrus for listening to my stories and making awesome Lego guys themed after my characters. And to Maggie and Ezra for being adorable little weirdos. I love you guys. Don't die, it might turn me evil.

To all my blog people for reading and commenting and everything. Emma, Kate, Squid, Erin, Courtney, Alyssa, Victoria, Kinsey, Ruby, Julia… I'm probably forgetting a lot, but all of you guys are awesome and I loved seeing your comments and talking with you every week.

And a huge group-hug thank you to the One Year Adventure Novel community.

To the Survival 3.0 crew: Cassie for being Wolfgang's second mom and helping me so much with critiques and weird, late night rambles. Megan, again for being a critique queen and having some awesome tips and brainstorming ideas. Delaney, for being the fangirl extraordinaire that she is, for adopting Wolfgang and getting excited and generally being her fangirly self. Samantha, for screaming at me a lot and being Dallas's mother and being a very bad influence for painful writing. (Of course I also owe a lot to Atlas, Kaz, Kendra and Sofie as well. So you guys get those bonus thanks.)

And now on to the OYAN readers. It's literally like half the forum so I can't list you all, but at least off the top of my head, some of the reader list can get in here. Krystal, Jaina, Jake, Johnny, Sandy, Kathryn, Jane, Abby (two of them. I love you both), Leah, Nina, Jacob, Elaina, Anastasia, Emma, Laura, Keara, Claire, Ethan, Garret, Dara, Bethany, Lilly, Autumn, Elijah (and lil bro Samson), Katrina, Maria, another Samantha, Reece, Ashley, Shaina, Ellie… and a ton of you guys who I don't know your actual names. But you're all amazing and I couldn't have done this without you guys.

The fact that Blank Mastermind still lives in the "short stories" section of the forum is a testament to the fact that I would have never even gone past the first chapter without all of you behind me.

It's been a rollercoaster, you guys, and I wouldn't trade it for anything.

And last but definitely not least, YOU. Whoever you are, reading this book. You're amazing and I appreciate you a lot and you're kind of blowing my mind right now by the fact that you're reading my book.

Thank you all more than I can say, and stay awesome. <3

About the author

Rosey Mucklestone is the oldest of nine crazy kids and the daughter of two awesome parents. She lives with her family and two dogs in Missouri, spending her time writing, reading, baking and waitressing. Topics she's passionate about include: the ocean, the Bible, mountains, fandoms, stories and characters in general. She's never gotten amnesia and doesn't plan on it, but life is full of surprises, so who knows?
You can stalk her blog at: www.writefury.com

FIC MUCKLESTONE
Mucklestone, Rosey
Blank mastermind

04/10/19

CPSIA information can be obtained
at www.ICGtesting.com
Printed in the USA
LVHW021148100219
607031LV00003B/569